# SILVERMAN'S SHADOW

## J. H. D. SETRIGHT

First published in great britain as a softback original in 2019

Copyright © J. H. D. Setright

Typeset in Dante MT Std

Editing, design, typesetting and publishing by UK Book Publishing

www.ukbookpublishing.com

ISBN: 978-1-913179-35-9

For my incredible wife Charlotte and my loving family.

*"Ordinary riches can be stolen; real riches cannot."*
**– Oscar Wilde**

*"Money never made a man happy yet, nor will it. The more a man has, the more he wants. Instead of filling a vacuum, it makes one."*

**– Benjamin Franklin**


*"An investment in knowledge pays the best interest."*

**– Benjamin Franklin**

# Prologue

Silverman's Shadow was written to be the first in a series of films featuring Wolf and Kelly's escapades. Please find below, for your enjoyment, a sneak peak at the start of Silverman's Shadow the movie, starting with a scene not included in the book.

## SILVERMAN'S SHADOW SCREENPLAY — SNEAK PREVIEW

**Written by**
**J. H. D. Setright**

INT. CONFERENCE ROOM, LINSTRAAD GROUP, GROSVENOR STREET, MAYFAIR, LONDON – DAY

Two-shot of CAPTAIN MICHAEL KELLY and PROFESSOR CHRISTOF WOLF sitting together in Tutum Capital's meeting room. They are facing an unseen man, looking perplexed and anticipant.

CAPTAIN MICHAEL KELLY (V.O.)
If you had told me six weeks ago that the Forbes 100 Rich List was a joke. And that the real rich list was made up of trillionaire crime lords, I wouldn't have been surprised.

But now I actually know that. It's a big fucking eye opener, you know? I'd never even heard of this Shadow character, and it turns out he's worth more than Gates and Buffet combined!

EXT. CARLOS PLACE, MAYFAIR, 2014 – DAY

Establishing shot of polished, suited TUTUM EMPLOYEE, on his lunch break, headed for a Mayfair cafe.

> CAPTAIN MICHAEL KELLY (V.O.)
> Anyway, so this whole thing really got cooking a few years back, when one of these crook trillionaires got himself robbed, and this Shadow guy's walked away with close to ten billion dollars.

MUSIC: BLACK SABBATH, PARANOID

Wide-angle shot of SHADOW's SUV pulling up and men inside kidnaping TUTUM EMPLOYEE into the SUV.

INT. SHADOW'S SUV ON CARLOS PLACE, MAYFAIR, 2014 – DAY

Master shot of seven masked and armed men occupying SHADOW's SUV. They take TUTUM EMPLOYEE's key fob for the building.

They cover his face with a chloroform drenched cloth and he falls unconscious. SUV is driven on and turns down Grosvenor Street to the entrance of Tutum Capital.

EXT. TUTUM CAPITAL, GROSVENOR STREET, MAYFAIR, 2014 – DAY

High-angle shot of six masked armed men piling out of SHADOW's SUV, leaving ROBBER SEVEN at the wheel.

They enter Tutum Capital, a beautiful Victorian building. ROBBER SIX waits on the door.

INT. TUTUM CAPITAL RECEPTION, GROSVENOR STREET, MAYFAIR, 2014 – DAY

Master shot of ROBBER ONE using TUTUM EMPLOYEE's fob to enter the building's reception. ROBBER FIVE peels off from the group. He holds a gun to TUTUM CAPITAL RECEPTIONIST's head and puts one hand over her mouth. ROBBER ONE, ROBBER TWO, ROBBER THREE and ROBBER FOUR run off upstairs.

INT. TUTUM CAPITAL, THIRD FLOOR, MANAGING DIRECTOR'S OFFICE, 2014 – DAY

Master shot of ROBBER ONE, ROBBER TWO, ROBBER THREE and ROBBER FOUR dashing into the office of TUTUM CAPITAL MANAGING DIRECTOR. Three suited bankers occupy the room. One of them is TUTUM CAPITAL MANAGING DIRECTOR.

> ROBBER ONE
> On the wall! All of you! Now!

Wide-angle shot of the three men shuffling towards the wall, held at gun point. ROBBER TWO addresses them in a calmer more senior tone.

> ROBBER TWO
> Today you are preparing a transfer, are you not?
> Gentlemen, that transfer will be going to our accounts.
> Which one of you is the Managing Director?

Medium shot of the three men looking at one another. The JUNIOR ASSOCIATE speaks up.

> JUNIOR ASSOCIATE
> I am.

Master shot as two of the robbers keep their guns on the others, while JUNIOR ASSOCIATE is pointed over to a desk. Sat at the desk is ROBBER FOUR, typing into a PC. ROBBER TWO walks over and stands next to the desk along with JUNIOR ASSOCIATE. ROBBER FOUR looks up from his computer.

> ROBBER TWO
> Password?

Over-the-shoulder shot (ROBBER TWO) of JUNIOR ASSOCIATE, who looks at the screen and shakes his head. ROBBER TWO holds his gun to JUNIOR ASSOCIATE's head.

> ROBBER TWO (CONT'D)
> Password please?

JUNIOR ASSOCIATE goes white and looks ill. ROBBER TWO cocks his pistol. JUNIOR ASSOCIATE begins to whimper and shake his head.

> ROBBER TWO (CONT'D)
> Fine, have it your way.

Master shot as ROBBER TWO shoots JUNIOR ASSOCIATE.

> ROBBER TWO (CONT'D)
> Anyone else care to try? Or should I just kill you both
> now?

Close-up of TUTUM CAPITAL MANAGING DIRECTOR, who shakes his head and proceeds forward. Two-shot of him and ROBBER 4 as he types in the relevant password. ROBBER FOUR takes over and continues typing.

> ROBBER TWO (CONT'D)
> There, that wasn't too hard?

Close-up of TUTUM CAPITAL MANAGING DIRECTOR, who looks with desperate contempt at ROBBER TWO. Close-up of ROBBER FOUR, who looks up from his typing again at ROBBER TWO.

> ROBBER TWO (CONT'D)
> Again!

Master shot as ROBBER TWO holds his gun up at TUTUM CAPITAL MANAGING DIRECTOR, who again types in the password and ROBBER FOUR takes over. After more furious typing ROBBER FOUR looks up.

> ROBBER TWO (CONT'D)
> Ah! I am sorry about this! If you wouldn't mind? Just once more I think!

TUTUM CAPITAL MANAGING DIRECTOR plugs in the final password needed and ROBBER FOUR hits enter. All four ROBBERS proceed to leave. Close-up of ROBBER TWO, who turns as he is about to shut the door behind him.

> ROBBER TWO (CONT'D)
> Much obliged, gentlemen! Much obliged!

EXT. TUTUM CAPITAL, GROSVENOR STREET, MAYFAIR, 2014 – DAY

Low-angle shot as ROBBERS stroll out of Tutum Capital with weapons holstered. As they re-enter SHADOW'S SUV they pull out TUTUM EMPLOYEE and dump him, unconscious, outside. The SUV pulls off.

MUSIC: GLORIA IN EXCELSIS DEO, VIVALDI MAIN TITLE SEQUENCE

EXT. DORCHESTER HOTEL, PARK LANE, LONDON – DAY

Establishing shot of WOLF, seen appearing from the Dorchester Hotel and entering a chauffeur driven, MERCEDES (S-CLASS).

EXT. THE MALL, WESTMINSTER, LONDON – DAY

Sweeping aerial shot, as WOLF's MERCEDES (S-CLASS) is followed down The Mall, past Buckingham Palace and down to Horse Gardens Road.

EXT. ENTRANCE TO THE BRITISH FOREIGN OFFICE, WESTMINSTER, LONDON – DAY

Establishing-shot, WOLF is seen alighting at the entrance to The Foreign Office. He is seen trotting across and up the stone stairway to the main building.

INT. MAIN ENTRANCE HALL, BRITISH FOREIGN OFFICE – DAY

Master shot shows a hubbub of journalists and officials gathering in the grand entrance hall, which has been cordoned off for a United Nations award ceremony. WOLF is seen walking to his labelled seat in the front row. Close-up of WOLF and one empty chair labelled CAPTAIN MICHAEL KELLY next to him.

Wide shot of LORD TATENDA, the minister for the United Nations, who is due to be giving out the awards and is standing and waiting for PROFESSOR KELLY behind a microphone mounted on a lectern at the centre of the hall. TATENDA is about to begin when he sees KELLY pacing quickly down the centre gangway and towards his chair. Once KELLY, having been watched by everyone, is finally seated, we see a close-up of TATENDA as he commences his award speech.

> LORD NATHANIAL TATENDA
> Good morning ladies and gentlemen. We are here today
> to pay tribute to Professor Christof Wolf and Captain
> Michael Kelly.

LORD NATHANIAL TATENDA (CONT'D)
Both of whose efforts have brought known terrorists to
justice and saved thousands of lives. The United Nations
and Commonwealth owes you both a great debt for your
services.

Wide angle shows the crowd's applause.

LORD NATHANIAL TATENDA (CONT'D)
Professor Wolf, Captain Kelly, your work with global
intelligence services has been instrumental to UN
operations for decades.
Her Majesty has seen fit to appoint you both with the
United Nations Special Service Medal in recognition of
your exceptional and devoted service!

The atrium erupts with applause and KELLY and WOLF make their
way up to the podium. TATENDA's entourage produce two A4-
sized ornamental boxes, containing their medals and accompanying
documentation. TATENDA smoothly shakes WOLF and KELLY's
hand and distributes the medals. Applause continues as we see two-
shot of WOLF and KELLY smiling.

INT. MAIN ENTRANCE HALL, BRITISH FOREIGN OFFICE –
DAY

Master shot sees the press and crowd behind WOLF and KELLY
having all but dispersed after the ceremony. Wolf begins to slip back
into his coat and scarves as he and KELLY are approached by three
official looking men. The leader of this trio (DOUGLAS), waves
them back to their seats. DOUGLAS is stick thin, pale as a ghoul and
speaks with a thick Glaswegian accent. DOUGLAS is seen shouting
at WOLF and KELLY and cajoles them to their feet and they are
hurried out by DOUGLAS and his men.

EXT. BRITISH FOREIGN OFFICE, WESTMINSTER, LONDON –
DAY

Aerial shot as WOLF and KELLY are bundled into the middle SUV of a battery of three. They pull off and back around to The Mall, towards Mayfair.

EXT. UPPER BROOK STREET, MAYFAIR, LONDON – DAY

Aerial to establishing shot of WOLF and KELLY's SUV as it pulls up outside a magnificent authentic Victorian townhouse and they are yanked out by DOUGLAS. They are ushered into the property.

INT. LORD CORK'S HOUSE, UPPER BROOK STREET, LONDON – DAY

MUSIC: LASCIA CH'IO PIANGA (SOPRANO), HANDEL

Dolly-zoom shot of WOLF and KELLY being led through the entrance hall and onto the ground floor meeting room at the end of the corridor.

INT. MEETING ROOM LORD CORK'S HOUSE, UPPER BROOK STREET – DAY

Master shot of the inside the meeting room. WOLF and KELLY are greeted by a panel of six men. In the middle of these men is LORD CORK. LORD CORK is an established elite in his sixties. He is a super-wealthy, global socio-economic and political puppeteer of puppeteers. He speaks with a powerful received pronunciation.

    LORD TOBIAS CORK
    Do sit down, gentlemen.

All the men who were standing take their seats at either end of the table arrangement. CORK barks at an invisible servant.

    LORD TOBIAS CORK (CONT'D)
    Some tea please!

Medium shot as CORK sits back down, he adjusts his immaculate, dark navy, pinstripe, three-piece and gives WOLF and KELLY a wide smile.

LORD TOBIAS CORK (CONT'D)
I expect you would like some tea? Please.

Two-shot of KELLY and WOLF as MAID ONE and MAID TWO, in full Victorian regalia, pop up with two assorted trays of tea pots. The pair whisper their preferences to MAID ONE, MAID TWO pours with perfect precision and they disappear, ninja-like, into thin air.

LORD TOBIAS CORK (CONT'D)
Firstly, may I say how sorry we are, that you were both dragged here from your ceremony so... unceremoniously. My name is Tobias Cork and you have been called here as a matter of national and global security. I am here in this room, representing the Prime Minister of the United Kingdom. The men to my left and right represent various factions from around the world, who have come together to a united end.

LORD TOBIAS CORK (CONT'D)
In short, gentlemen, we require your help.

Master shot as KELLY stands.

CAPTAIN MICHAEL KELLY
Okay, buddy, so, first off! Who the fuck are you? Tobias Cork? You represent the Prime Minister? Well I don't fuckin' see him! You've got a very nice house and some nice fucking tea! But Daddio, I don't believe a word you're fucking saying!

Two-shot as WOLF whispers to KELLY.

PROFESSOR CHRISTOF WOLF
Captain Kelly, please. This man is Lord Tobias Cork
and I happen to know, that not only is this man a close
personal friend of the Prime Minister. He is also a friend
to the entire British Royal family and a billionaire in his
own right. It is therefore entirely plausible, that Lord
Cork is representing the Prime Minister to whatever end
he is alluding to.

This interjection calms KELLY. However, persisting, he turns to the
panel.

CAPTAIN MICHAEL KELLY
Okay so, say you are for real? You wouldn't mind if I ask
for his fucking name and station!

Master-shot as LORD CORK attempts an interruption.

LORD TOBIAS CORK
Really this is quite outrageous! William, you don't have
to bow to this...

GRANGER the smooth Californian FBI agent to CORK's left
interrupts.

WILLIAM GRANGER
It's okay, Toby, I don't mind... I'm William George
Granger.

CAPTAIN MICHAEL KELLY
Oh! Okay! Oh! So your name was what? William George
Granger! Will Granger! Okay! Let's see about that!

Medium shot of KELLY, who begins to furiously dial into his
smartphone and makes a call.

WOLF whispers to KELLY.

PROFESSOR CHRISTOF WOLF
Captain Kelly, I think he is telling the truth, I think we
should hear what they have to...

CAPTAIN MICHAEL KELLY
Hey! Fuck off!

KELLY turns away as someone answers his call.

CAPTAIN MICHAEL KELLY (CONT'D)
Hey Amy! Hi yeah! It's me, Mike! Yeah! No! no, no look!
England's fine, shit! Listen! Amy! Amy! Hey! I need you
to run a background check on a Mr William George
Granger, look for public officials, police officers, CEOs,
diplomats, politicians.

KELLY pauses allowing AMY to search, shooting daggers at the
panel.

CAPTAIN MICHAEL KELLY (CONT'D)
Have you got anything yet? Okay great! Just send
through what you have to my phone right now! Great!

Master shot as KELLY slams the phone on the table triumphantly
and they wait for the information to come through.

KELLY's phone buzzes and he snatches it up and begins anxiously
searching through to find GRANGER. Close-up of KELLY as he is
successful and his face drops a little seeing GRANGER is a senior FBI
director.

CAPTAIN MICHAEL KELLY (CONT'D)
Oh! Okay! So maybe you are who you say you are, but I
still don't trust a fucking word you say!

LORD TOBIAS CORK
Perhaps, gentlemen, now I think we have correctly
established we are not deluding you! It is fair to impart
that we have not been entirely forthright in our actions
thus far.

Medium shot of CORK, who glances at KELLY for him not to
interrupt again.

LORD TOBIAS CORK (CONT'D)
To put things more plainly, Captain Kelly, Professor Wolf.
We require your unique skills, for a sinister and complex
problem, that if left unchecked, could put the balance of
the free world into question! The nature of this problem,
our meeting here today and all subsequent endeavours, it
shall be known, are completely and unequivocally off the
record. To that end, on the table in front of you are two
documents, each leather bound and sealed. If you would
be so kind as to open, read, sign and witness each other's
documents, we can suggest to you both the terms of your
mission.

Two-shot as WOLF and KELLY begin to read their documents.
WOLF finishes first and pulls out his Mont Blanc pen to sign and
does. KELLY finishes a little after.

CAPTAIN MICHAEL KELLY
Okay so, I'm not signing this. I'm not signing this!

KELLY consults his document.

CAPTAIN MICHAEL KELLY (CONT'D)
This says that if I share anything said in this room, you're
going to prosecute me under UK and international law!
And that these powers of prosecution include and are not
limited to, extradition, bankruptcy and imprisonment!

Wide shot of KELLY looking up at CORK from his NDA.

CAPTAIN MICHAEL KELLY (CONT'D)
Fucking imprisonment! No! No! I'm not signing your
little, non-disclosure agreement! Fuck you! I don't give a
shit if you are the Lord of England!

LORD TOBIAS CORK
Mr Kelly! It should not be at all suspicious, that we are
requesting you sign this NDA!
It should not be a question, but an honour to sign this
document and be called upon for such a confidential and
high-profile mission.

Medium shot of CORK, who switches to more sinister tone.

LORD TOBIAS CORK (CONT'D)
You were not always a Captain in the New York City
police department, were you, Mr Kelly? You were a Chief
Warrant Officer in the United States military, were you
not? Now, I know for a fact that one does not climb to
that office, without a serious compassion for duty and a
fierce propensity for patriotism. Mr Kelly, you are going
to sign that document, not just out of duty, patriotism
and sheer curiosity. You are going to sign because I am
going to paint for you, an image of two scenarios.
One scenario is of a decorated war hero and a fantastic
field agent, outperforming his peers in his service and
being rewarded in kind. Neither the FBI, CIA or US
Military would begrudge a senior position, field or
otherwise, to someone as dynamic, if a little direct, as
you, Captain.

# Chapter 1

## HARVEY WALSH

Professor Christof Wolf was no stranger to British weather. Having been born and raised in the Austrian Alps, he was quite accustomed to freezing winters. However, this conditioning had not quite prepared him, in initial visits, for the type of cold harboured in the UK. The professor's native Austrian air, though sub-zero, was pure, dry and somehow invigorating. Conversely, the damp and cutting winds that rushed down Park Lane to greet Wolf, at the entrance to the Dorchester Hotel, consumed his body like a school of frozen piranhas.

The professor had learned from previous visits not to take the British weather reports at face value, always needing to remind himself of the impending arctic-windswept ecosystem. Like many other non-Brits, Wolf was astounded by the natives' consistent and chronic denial of the seemingly obvious elemental parameters. He felt the British seemed not only content, but proud it would seem, to underdress by mandate. Insistently optimistic, he deduced Brits must dress according to the temperature reports, while paying no heed whatsoever to the wind or rain. This was incredibly frustrating for the professor, who endured with disbelief, frequent dirty looks from underdressed Londoners. He often contemplated why on earth they would put themselves through this. He certainly felt that their reasoning could not be based on ignorance. In his extended travels of the globe, Wolf had never encountered a nation, who analysed and discussed the weather as much as the British. Even in his own family's mountain

1

village, Wolf recalled, where the weather is a massive factor in everyday existence, it was never as often the ignition or feature of conversation quite as frequently as in the UK.

Professor Wolf's car was in the process of a three-point turn, as he entered the vehicle. Having had just about enough of the aggressive January bluster, he sought the immediate sanctuary of the car's heated leather seats. Relishing being unencumbered by effects, he removed his Fedora and secondary scarf, while jostling into a comfortable position. Immersed further into his pre-heated refuge, the body warmth which clung to the inside of his thick soft overcoat made him shudder, as if sinking into a hot bath. He looked outside at the windswept city rolling by and felt warmer still, cut-off from the elements and cocooned in 21st century luxury. Hyde Park Corner, Victoria and Buckingham Palace, all whisked by, as the superior German suspension cradled him like a babe in arms down The Mall and on to the entrance of the Foreign Office. With a don and a flick and a jostle and a kick, the professor re-dressed, hiked himself from the car and re-entered the cold. Clamping down his hat, he half walked half trotted towards the towering threshold of the Foreign Office.

The main entrance hall's atrium had been hastily modified and restricted for the purposes of the morning's endeavours. The vast ceiling height, covered only by glass, served to incentivise the professor to keep his overcoat on, as the wafting chill within was almost as harsh as the open air. Wolf was relieved to see heaters set up near the seating area and even more delighted to find his labelled seat directly opposite one. Approaching his allotment, the professor formulaically removed his hat, scarves and coat to reveal an immaculate, dark-navy suit. He folded his coat and scarves precisely and gingerly put them underneath his chair, placing his hat carefully on top. With a quick scouting glance around the room, he reclined and crossed his legs. Settling, Wolf folded his arms and waited as the room quickly filled up. The righthand side of the podium was clearly for press officers and photographers. A film crew had set up in front of the podium, while to the podium's left sat a curious collection of random officials and individuals, whom the professor could not help feeling were simply present to fill the room. The podium was erected atop the centre stone staircase, closest to the rear of the atrium. As Professor Wolf was due to be receiving an award, his seat was in the first row of only two chairs. Next to him was an empty place, labelled Captain Michael Kelly. The ceremony was due to commence at nine-thirty, with the presentation being around nine-forty-five. Professor Wolf took a glimpse at his watch, to see that it was nine-twenty-seven and he began to fret as to the whereabouts of the missing captain.

Wolf's award was to be the United Nations Special Service Medal. Although the Professor did not hold this in particularly high regard, a part of him felt honoured to accept it. However, Captain Kelly's truancy was now casting doubt in the professor. He felt nerves and insecurity well up in his chest, as he saw Lord Nathanial Tatenda ascend twitchily towards the podium. Questions began to form in the professor's mind. Had Captain Kelly not been bothered to turn up? Was he, unlike him, still a man at the top of his game? Had Kelly deemed it beneath him to travel to accept the award in person? Had he been forced not to attend by an urgent case?

Lord Tatenda was now bearing down on the lectern, looking down at his watch. Clearly aware of Captain Kelly's absence, he smothered his mic piece and leant back, talking from the side of his mouth, to the officials and assistants clustered behind him. Content to proceed without Kelly, Lord Tatenda dropped his sleeve back over his watch and looked up at his audience to begin. However, with a shrug he stopped himself and turned back to his entourage. Professor Wolf bent round in his seat and squinted towards the main entrance. Captain Kelly's audible muttering of profanities was only slightly masked by the slamming treads of his boots pacing down the centre gangway that led to the podium. The noise of his footsteps seemed to be disproportionate to Kelly's slight and stocky stature. By the time the young captain had found his way to the professor's side, his face was red and his brow moist. Panting and still swearing, he launched himself into his chair, causing its legs to creak and slide on the hard-stone floor. Ignoring the room's attention, the captain wriggled out of his coat, to expose his rather informal attire, consisting of blue jeans and a woollen jumper.

As a school master surveys their assembly, Lord Tatenda banked his gaze across the magnificent atrium at the Foreign Office. As Tatenda bent forward and hugged the lectern, the press woke up. Flickers and snaps from cameras and the jostling of journalists filled the cavernous foyer. Lord Tatenda waited for the commotion to settle, before beginning his presentation. The son of a successful Zimbabwean merchant banker, Tatenda had been privately educated to the highest level in the UK.

Having himself had inordinate success as an investment banker and fund manager, he had become involved in politics and gained a peerage. As the Minister for The United Nations, it was his station to assist in the duties of the Foreign Secretary in the capacity of the Commonwealth and United Nations. In this instance, Tatenda was to distribute two medals for special services rendered to Professor Christof Wolf and Captain Michael Kelly. This would have been an excuse for an easy day for his Lordship, who would not have begrudged any time delay. However, today Lord Tatenda had arranged a dental appointment and wished for proceedings to be as speedy as possible. He did not, therefore, mince his unrehearsed words.

"Good morning, ladies, gentlemen and members of the press. We are here today to, briefly, pay tribute to Professor Christof Wolf and Captain Michael Kelly. Both of whose efforts have brought known terrorists to justice and saved thousands of lives. Even these medals, which her Majesty graciously bestows upon you, do not properly repay the debt the United Nations and Commonwealth owes to you for your services.

"Professor Wolf, your work with global intelligence services and insight has been instrumental to UN operations for decades. Captain Kelly, your efforts in the field as an officer and a marine, as well as your service to UN special forces, have been equalled by very few."

A brief applause erupted from the left-hand side of the room, that depleted as it rippled through to the press on the right. Lord Tatenda paused impatiently and exhaled with authority, to silence the room before continuing.

"It is in this vein of deep gratitude and appreciation, that we appoint Professor Wolf and Captain Kelly with the United Nations Special Service Medal, in recognition of services rendered. Would Captain Kelly please approach the podium now, to accept his award."

As he said this, the atrium awoke with applause again and Kelly made his way up to the podium. Lord Tatenda stepped back to his entourage, who produced an A4 sized ornamental box containing Kelly's medal and accompanying documentation. His handshake and exchange of medal package was smooth and well-practised. Though a moment of awkwardness did arise, as Kelly moved to leave the podium, he was ushered back behind it, by one of his lordship's aides. Amid the continuing clamour, Tatenda bellowed out to the professor to also proceed forward.

"And now if we could ask Professor Christof Wolf to approach the podium as well!"

The clapping swelled slightly as the professor rose to meet and shake the Minister's hand, receive his own medal and join Kelly behind the podium. The pair of medallists stood mirrored next to each other behind Lord Tatenda for a few seconds, swivelling their smiles across the audience. After as brief a time as decorum would allow, Lord Tatenda concluded.

"My thanks for your appreciation, ladies and gentlemen, and a big thanks to these two fine examples again! For their incredible efforts and service to this country, The United Nations and the world."

Satisfaction was more evident across the face of Tatenda than the medallists at this point. Tatenda had wanted to get away early, and proceedings had been kept to a minimum. However, any smirk of achievement was now washed away by the initiative of his aide, ignorant to his minister's motives. To Tatenda's horror, his aide approached the lectern's mic and nervously cleared his throat.

"I think w-we would all like to hear a few words from the Professor and Captain Kelly. So, if you don't mind…"

The aide stumbled to the end of his sentence and finished his instructions with body language, motioning Professor Wolf to the stand. Wolf had not intended to impart anything and had not prepared a speech. As a man of control and order an unexpected challenge like this was an annoyance. He glared at Lord Tatenda and his Lordship's aide as he approached the microphone. Wolf spoke slowly and deliberately to minimise the amount he would need to say.

"Good morning and thank you. I am, of course, honoured to receive this award and commendation for services rendered to The United Nations. I can only hope that I can continue to serve justice to the highest possible standard. As I enter my twilight I shall certainly consider this, a poignant reminder of my life's work to do just that!"

The professor could have continued; however, he made momentary eye contact with Tatenda, who masked rolling his eyes with a turning smile. Upon seeing this Wolf cleared his throat and, bowing slightly, withdrew from the lectern. As he walked back Wolf made eye contact with Kelly, who like Tatenda, rolled his eyes at him as they crossed each other. Captain Kelly jaunted to the stand and addressed the audience with a relaxed disinterest. His accent was an Irish-New York cocktail, that made him sound even more offhand. To the professor, he sounded more like a child feigning gratefulness for a grandparent's Christmas present.

"Yeah, so, thanks for this award. Err, it's real nice, I'm definitely going to keep it somewhere nice. Thank you to the Queen, of course. Thank you to The United Nations and err, yeah! Thanks a lot."

Kelly held the medal's box up, as if it were some kind of sporting cup. He admired his medal, before nodding at the audience, awaiting further applause and retiring back to the professor's side. No one further approached the lectern and another of the Lord's aides shepherded the captain and professor back to their chairs.

Before very long the press and crowd behind the medallists had all but dispersed. However, as Wolf began to slip back into his coat and scarves, he and the captain were approached by three men. The leader of this trio waved them back to their seats and began to address them. He was stick thin, pale as a ghoul and spoke with a thick Glaswegian accent.

"Right so you've got your medals, have you? Happy, are we? Great! Well, it's time for us to go somewhere now and I've got a three o'clock at the House of Lords. So, you know, if you wouldn't mind hurrying a wee bit."

This mysterious official looking Scotsman paused for a split second, however, not satisfied with the level of fervour in the captain and professor's movement, he sharply raised his voice to a bark.

"That means let's go! Come on, old man! Up you get! Oh Mike. Did you come all the way from New York? Aww that's nice. Well I don't actually care! I just want you in the wee car outside, alright, princess. Come on, Cinderella, your fucking carriage awaits. Prime minister's business! He's got someone who wants to see you both! Alright! You can wipe those stupid 'oh what's going on here' looks off your faces! You can ask your questions later! Alright!"

This man continued to mutter obscenities to himself, as he marched the pair into a six-seater SUV, waiting for them outside. Such was the professor's fascination with this undisclosed pick-up, he now barely registered the howling storm outside. The man who had coerced them into the back of his SUV was now in the front passenger seat, shouting into his mobile. The partition prevented the professor and captain from hearing the details of his conversation. However, from the battery of cars in front and behind them they could tell this man was someone of significant authority. The SUV took the group back pretty much the way Professor Wolf had come from his hotel on Park Lane. However, before reaching Hyde Park Corner the driver dipped into a side turning in South Mayfair. They drove through the clinically sandblasted streets to a private house. The driver pulled up, double parked and the skinny Scot peeled out of the cockpit and yanked back the passenger side sliding door. He, with wiry and unexpected strength, hustled the professor and captain out of the vehicle and through the opening door of a beautiful Victorian Townhouse.

The professor was impressed by the sense-inspiring interior of this mysterious Mayfair property. The original wood panelling was perfectly maintained. The grand entrance was beautifully arranged with a striking staircase leading to the first floor. The ceilings and doors were notably tall, and the massive walls were donned with huge traditional period paintings, mainly portraits. Kelly and Wolf were led into a long gaping room at the end of the entrance hall. In the centre of the room was a cell of long tables all joined together. The back of the room was bordered by enormous French windows and beyond, nestled a modest but well-crafted garden and terrace. Even in the dark and bleakness of January, this room still seemed bright and lifted the professor's spirits. As the medallists entered, six men, seated at the far end of the conjoined tables, rose to greet them. The man at the head of the table extended his arm and beckoned Wolf and Kelly to sit on the two chairs positioned nearest the door at the opposing end of the table. The beckoning man was Lord Tobias Cork, the owner of the property's freehold.

Lord Cork was from an established family, his father had been a Lord and his father before him. Notwithstanding his life being cloaked in nepotism and inheritance, his raw ambition, academic intelligence and street savvy were unquestionable. What's more, through active asset management Lord Cork had somehow managed to grow and consolidate his family's wealth to a standard above his forefathers. A modern inherited billionaire, he did all he could to mask his fantastic affluence and raging arrogance. Now in his early sixties, Lord Cork was keen to further strengthen his family's holdings in preparation for the succession of his son, Andrew Cork. His Lordship involved himself in all affairs of state as well holding active long positions in most global markets. He also made it his business to be one step ahead, in terms of international information. It had been his life's mission to rub shoulders with the incredibly few people who wield genuine global influence. Now an older man, he had not only assimilated into this upper-upper echelon of society, but was a serious player within it. There was no election rigged, no terrorist attack sanctioned, no financial boom or bust, without Lord Cork's knowledge or direct involvement. He regarded himself as a tacit governor of the free world, a puppeteer of puppeteers.

"Do sit down, gentlemen."

Lord Cork's deep and powerful received pronunciation rolled in crescendo over the long table towards Wolf and Kelly. His Lordship turned briefly to his five colleagues to sit down and then barked to an invisible servant.

"Some tea please!"

As he sat back down, Lord Cork adjusted his immaculate, dark navy, pinstripe, three-piece and gave the medallists a wide, gleaming smile.

"I expect you'd like some tea? Please."

He almost gave them no choice, for as he pleaded, two maids in full Victorian regalia popped up with two assorted trays of teapots. The pair whispered their preferences to the maids, who poured with perfect precision and disappeared, ninja-like, into thin air. The tea was very aromatic and clearly of superior blend. Kelly and Wolf were plainly impressed and looked at each other with sincerity for the first time since their paths had been inextricably linked. However, their attention was quickly diverted back to his Lordship.

"Firstly, may I say how sorry we are, that you were both dragged here from your ceremony so...unceremoniously."

He smiled for a split second, musing at his own turn of phrase.

"My name is Tobias Cork and you have been called here as a matter of national and global security. I am here in this room, representing the Prime Minister of the United Kingdom. The men to my left and right represent various factions from around the world, who have come together to a united end. In short, gentlemen, we require your help."

Captain Kelly was not a man to keep quiet and had been holding back in sheer curiosity since being barrelled into the SUV at the Foreign Office. This speech by Lord Cork could have continued but Kelly, visibly disturbed and distrusting of his Lordship, could not help himself.

"Okay buddy, so, first off! Who the fuck are you? Tobias Cork? You represent the Prime Minister? Well I don't fuckin' see him! You've got some very nice tea and a nice fucking house! But Daddio, why don't I believe a fuckin' word you're saying!"

Kelly had really riled himself up and was now out of his seat and making violently towards the door. However, he was fished back by the surprising strength of the professor's sweeping grip. As the professor gently pulled Kelly back to his seat he casually whispered, "Captain Kelly, please. This man is Lord Tobias Cork and I happen to know, that not only is this man a close personal friend of the Prime Minister, he is also a friend to the entire British Royal family and a billionaire in his own right. It is therefore entirely plausible, that Lord Cork is representing the Prime Minister to whatever end he is alluding to."

Professor Wolf had been used to his lecture tours of late and found himself adopting a rather patronising tone, as if correcting an errant question from a student. Nonetheless, this interjection seemed to calm Kelly and almost allowed for Cork to continue, before Kelly piped up once more.

"Okay so, say you are for real? You wouldn't mind if I ask for his fuckin' name and station!"

As he harangued the panel opposite him with this fresh challenge, he pointed to and singled out a rather stern and sinister looking member of Lord Cork's team. Lord Cork attempted an interruption.

"Really this is quite outrageous! William, you don't have to bow to this..."

Before Lord Cork could finish, Director William Granger (FBI) held his hand up at his Lordship to cease.

"It's okay, Toby, I don't mind..."

He paused, stared aggressively at Captain Kelly and announced securely, in a thick, smooth Californian accent, "I'm William George Granger..."

Kelly did not give Granger a chance to go any further.

"Oh! Okay! Oh! So, your name's what? William George Granger! Will Granger! Okay! Let's see about that!"

Kelly had really worked himself up once more and began to furiously dial into his smartphone. As he drew the headset to his ear, the professor calmly whispered again to him.

"Captain Kelly, I think he is telling the truth, I think we should hear what they have to..."

Kelly did not reciprocate the professor's gentle candour and interrupted. "Hey! Fuck off!"

Kelly turned away from Professor Wolf as he heard the international dial tone break, and somebody answer at the other end. The Captain continued purposefully so all present could hear.

"Hey Amy! Hi yeah! It's me, Mike! Yeah! No! no, no look! England's fine, shit! Listen! Amy! Amy! Hey! I need you to run a background check on a Mr William George Granger, look for public officials, police officers, CEOs, diplomats, politicians."

Kelly paused, shooting daggers at the panel, while Amy had a chance to act at the other end, before he continued.

"Have you got anything yet? Okay great! Just send through what you've got to my phone in the next thirty seconds okay! Great!"

Kelly ended the call and slammed his phone down on the table triumphantly. The men at the other end of the table looked to each other in astonishment. None of them had expected a reaction quite like this. An embarrassing and silent few moments dragged past, as some men sipped their teas, while they waited for Amy's response. Sure enough, after an excruciating thirty seconds, Kelly's phone buzzed and vibrated such that it resonated throughout the room. Kelly quickly snapped it up and frantically scrolled through the profiles and photos of William George Granger. The entire room, except for the Captain it would seem, already knew the result of this test. The professor almost felt sorry for the captain when Kelly clearly matched Granger's photo to that of a senior FBI director. Kelly, however, was not deterred by the embarrassment of having been proved wrong and continued to barrage the panel in front of him.

"Oh! Okay! So maybe you are who you say you are, but I still don't trust a fuckin' word you say!"

Kelly would have gone further; however, a stern, fighting glance from his Lordship was enough to silence him and as the Lord rose from his seat, Kelly returned to his chair.

"Perhaps, gentlemen, now I think we have correctly established that we are all who we say we are! It is fair to impart that we have not been entirely forthright in our actions thus far."

At this juncture Lord Cork looked at Kelly as if to suggest he not interrupt again. Kelly looked back as though he had not fully comprehended his Lordship's previous statement.

"To put things more plainly, Captain Kelly, Professor Wolf. We require your unique skills for a sinister and complex problem that, if left unchecked, could put the balance of the free world into question. The nature of this problem, our meeting here today and all subsequent endeavours, it shall be known, are completely and unequivocally off the record. Everything is to be kept in the closest secrecy and confidence. To that end, on the table in front of you are two documents, each leather bound and sealed. If you would be so kind as to open, read, sign and witness each other's documents, we can suggest to you both the terms of your mission."

His lordship slipped back into his chair and allowed for the professor and the captain to follow his instruction. Wolf and Kelly did oblige, reached for their respective documents and began to read. The professor was a very fast reader and within moments had reached into his pocket. He withdrew a beautiful Mont Blanc fountain pen and signed the document. Kelly, on the other hand, ignored Wolf. Instead he continued to frown and curse under his breath, while making his way through the legal literature. After a short time, Captain Kelly lifted his head to Lord Cork, having finished his studies.

"Okay so, I'm not signing this. I'm not signing this! This says that if I share anything said in this room, you're going to prosecute me under UK and international law! And that these powers of prosecution include and are not limited to, extradition, bankruptcy and imprisonment! Fucking imprisonment! No! No! I'm not signing your little, non-disclosure agreement! Fuck you! I don't give a shit if you are the Lord of England!"

All parties remained seated while Kelly's foulmouthed analysis resonated. Lord Cork fixed his gaze on Kelly and raised an eyebrow, with an air of almost threatening confidence, before conjuring a more authoritative tone and addressing him directly.

"Mr Kelly, the information, identity and very nature of this interchange is of the highest order of national security to the governments of the free world, not to mention the United Kingdom and the United States of America. It should not, therefore, be at all suspicious that we are requesting you sign this NDA. Admittedly, if breached, the terms are harsh but rightly so. Mr Kelly, it should not be a question but an honour to sign this document and be called upon by your country for such a confidential and high-profile mission."

Lord Cork switched to a calmer and more sinister tone, before continuing.

"You were not always a Captain in the New York City police department, were you, Mr Kelly? You were a Chief Warrant Officer in the United States military, were you not? Now, I know for a fact that one does not climb to that office, without a serious compassion for duty and a fierce propensity for patriotism. Mr Kelly, you are going to sign that document and Professor Wolf is going to witness it. You are going to sign it, not just out of duty, patriotism and sheer curiosity. You are going to sign it because I am going to paint for you, an image of two scenarios.

"One scenario is of a decorated war hero and a fantastic field agent, outperforming his peers in his service and being rewarded in kind. Neither the FBI, CIA or US Military would begrudge a senior position, field or otherwise, to someone as dynamic, if a little direct, as you, Captain."

As he made this last utterance, he glanced at the CIA and FBI officials on the panel, who nodded in accordance at Kelly. It dawned on Kelly that his Lordship was offering up an incentive to accept this mystery mission. Kelly, still further intrigued, was far from sold and continued to furrow his brow and pout as Lord Cork resumed.

"Another, more regrettable picture, would be of a man demoted in the ranks for consistent misconduct. A man at the end of his pathetic road, having to endure the final injustice of being completely striped of all manner of responsibility. Being forced to retire forever. Totally cut off from any military, law enforcement or security-based endeavour whatsoever. Cursed to walk the earth, for the remainder of his existence, with nothing more than the memories and remorse of his poor decisions made.

"Mr Kelly, I ask you. Can you see into the future? Can you envisage yourself in one of these situations? Mr Kelly, regardless, you need to know, that when God asks for your hand, you better give it to him!"

Kelly looked as if he was about to explode and felt, perhaps duly, that he was now being directly threatened. At this point, Professor Wolf felt he should interject once more to attempt to calm Kelly and the escalating situation. These were powerful men and Wolf feared them, if Kelly did not. The professor was very concerned that Kelly did not create a situation that would cause inevitable backlash on him.

"Captain Kelly, I know you think his Lordship is threatening you. But even if he is and what you say is true, this is just a piece of paper stating we cannot discuss what is said in this room. I have signed it and I don't care because, not only is an NDA commonplace in instances such as these, even if I were to discuss proceedings, violation of an NDA is very difficult to prove and even harder to prosecute; but, more than that! I truly feel that the subjects to be discussed, if we do ever get around to signing! Will not be such that we will have any volition whatsoever, to share anything with anyone, except those present here today."

Kelly looked at Wolf and did seem much calmer, having listened to the soothing Austrian inform him, almost attorney like, on the realities of his situation. He whispered very quietly to Wolf.

"So, you're a professor, right? You're smart? You know this stuff?"

Kelly penetrated the Austrian's retina like a laser beam, with his mother's brilliant-green Irish eyes and the professor felt his trust flow through him. Satisfied that Wolf had told the truth, he snatched a brief look up at the panel, before grabbing one of the pair of pens on the table and signing his document. Wolf and Kelly then sheepishly swapped parchments and witnessed each other's NDAs. Even once he had submitted to Cork's agreement, Kelly still maintained his unwavering air of questioning disrespect.

"Okay so I've fuckin' signed it! So, answer me now! Why me! Why us! What makes me and this old guy so goddamn special! If this is fuckin' bullshit! Or you're going send us to die or something! Is this about what happened in Baghdad? Are you guys tying up loose ends here! What the fuck is going on! Answer me!"

Kelly had now worked himself up to a piping red rage and was standing and pointing at Lord Cork in fear and desperation, having committed his signature. Kelly knew now, that not only had he been threatened by powers who could apparently make or break him, he had signed their document of secrecy and allegiance. He knew he could possibly still avoid conscription to his lordship's mission, but the door was rapidly closing on any opportunity to do so. Lord Cork, however, having had enough, stood up and bellowed.

"Captain, sit down!"

Captain Kelly froze in his onslaught and his face lost all expression. The tone and general authority exuding from Lord Cork was too much for Kelly's indoctrinated military training, which caused him to drop his shoulders and relinquish, as instructed.

"If you will allow me, Captain? I will now be able to enlighten you both, as to the details of this most serious matter."

Cork paused and paced over to the three-metre-high French windows, looking onto the rear terrace. He continued in a somewhat rehearsed fashion.

"Once you have both accepted this mission you will receive full documentation and a full team of operatives. You will use this room as a base for your operations and all information will be kept and stored here. Once I elaborate on the basics of this mission you will both, as you have so poignantly demonstrated, Captain Kelly, have queries and questions. I ask you please, for the sake of all our valuable time, permit me to finish and be satisfied that you both are aware of all the relevant information before either of you interrupts again."

He paused briefly once more, to ensure his audience concurred, before turning back to the window and explaining further.

"This is a mission that shall have no name, no official record and no official recognition by any institution or individual. In this mission, to all intents and purposes, you will not exist. This is a necessity, as the opposition in this mission have a reach that extends into all major global institutions. It is of paramount importance, therefore, that no one know of your purpose or existence.

"To give you a rough background: For the past seven years, without the knowledge of any police department or intelligence service, one man has acquired the control of a, conservatively estimated, thirty percent share in all global criminal enterprise. Prostitution rings, human trafficking, smuggling, narcotics, arms-dealing, kidnapping, protection & extortion are being globalised by this one man to devastating effect. The genius of this one man, is that his identity is completely unknown.

"For the past three years the FBI, CIA, MI5 and a host of other national and international intelligence agencies, have attempted to track and gain knowledge on this man. All of their endeavours, without exception, have resulted in failure and death. Our governments have wasted time, resources and lives in the pursuit of this man to no avail! We have therefore decided to unite the world's intelligence agencies, to fight fire with fire. We decided together to engage a small, entirely secret and dedicated team of agents, to covertly track and gain significant intel on this man. Through our system and process of selection, the pair of you have been handpicked from a database of thousands! Based on your skills, capabilities and experience, you, Professor and you, Captain, have what is deemed necessary to spearhead this mission.

"It is without further explanation or ado, that I proposition you both as such. Gentlemen, your mission, should you choose to accept it, is to source the identity and location of this man, code name – Harvey Walsh. Though you will not have the support of the FBI, CIA, British intelligence or any other agency, you will be guaranteed to find no impediment in your operations to this endeavour, from any of these institutions. In other words, you will have free reign in your actions; however, the consequences of your actions will be unsupported and should remain untraceable. I say again! You will stay, off the radar.

"It is time, now that you have all the relevant information, to make a choice. When making this choice, gentlemen, I urge you to consider, that while stations can be acquired and monetary rewards great, so too can fellowships be revoked and careers dissolved. It should be certain in your minds that to be selected for this mission is a privilege of great magnitude. A privilege, which comes with an equal magnitude of risk and responsibility. Our recruitment process has seen fit, that not only do you two have the talents to succeed in this mission, but the conviction and valour to accept it. The fate of the free world is, to a certain extent, in your hands now, Professor Wolf. And Captain Kelly, while you clearly begrudge authority, I can guarantee, however, you cut it, this will be the single greatest and most rewarding undertaking of your life. I would ask you now, gentlemen, to signify your understanding of this by standing."

Both men paused and cautiously glanced at one another before gradually getting to their feet. Chins proudly raised and in part convinced of Lord Cork's persuasion, they stood to attention awaiting further instruction.

"You will now return to your homes for one week to make arrangements and put your affairs in order, before moving to London indefinitely. You will each be afforded lodging in a neighbouring safehouse upon your return. You will obviously speak to no one of these events and when you return to this location in a week's time, you will be confirming your permanent allegiance to this cause and will be asked to sign a further document, ensuring the legality of your appointment. In return for your round the clock service, you will be remunerated with ample financial compensation. When your mission is complete you will be endowed with a commendation or reference of your choosing, for any position at any institution in the world. And be prepared, gentlemen, because your investigation will not cease, until Harvey Walsh is identified and found."

Kelly and Professor Wolf paused slightly to register their brief, before turning to leave. They were both relieved that, although sworn to secrecy, they still had been given the option never to return, even if this meant risking their future careers. However, Kelly could not resist one more fleeting jibe as he marched his way behind the professor on their way out of the meeting.

"So, the UN thing was bullshit then! The medals! They were just to get us here without anyone getting wise?"

Lord Cork turned from the window to stare at Kelly, who himself had turned back from his course towards the door.

"Your medals stand, gentlemen. But yes, their appointment and your appointment here today are not entirely exclusive. You do understand, Mr Kelly, that we cannot have loose ends and we must mask our actions in every capacity. And please, it should go without saying, that you should not undertake any further research or inquiry into this matter until you have returned to this secure location. We would hate for your mission to be over before it starts."

Bemused, bewildered and consumed with curiosity, Kelly and Wolf turned and respectively made passage for New York City and Vienna.

# Chapter 2

## PROFESSOR CHRISTOF WOLF

Professor Wolf's penthouse apartment nestled on a prestigious tributary of the Schulerstraße, in central Vienna. His beautiful, turn of the century building housed only eight flats, six of which occupied its own floor. The professor's ceiling height was not as favourable as the lower floor flats. However, the view from his expansive roof terrace more than made up for this. Having landed at the close of the afternoon, Wolf had plugged himself into his iPod, detaching himself from his journey. Wolf had been rekindling his love of nineteen-eighties funk and was listening to a playlist of classics, allowing the jostling rhythm to charm his spirit and sustain a relaxed and optimistic mindset. His cab pulled up outside his apartment building and he alighted. Nostalgia filled his nostrils and lungs, as he breathed in his home air for the first time since arriving back. The fresher, cleaner but colder air seemed warmer and more clement than the harsh damp of London.

Grinning, the professor approached the door of his stucco-fronted main entrance. He was comforted in the knowledge that the door would be opened for him and that the familiar heated concierge reception would hit him, like a comfy slap from a giant pillow. As he spotted the penthouse's owner approaching, the concierge was able to open the entrance doors from a trigger behind his desk and was trained to do so. Shoulders and hips swinging in time to his music, Wolf waltzed into the reception. With a stutter-step and flick-like dance move, Wolf removed his hat, smiled at the concierge and continued towards the elevators beyond. Still dancing to himself, the professor spun as he popped the button to call the lift. Raising his shoulders and nodding his head in time to the music, he watched, as the digital display registered the elevator descending through to the ground floor. He entered the mirror lined enclosure and selected the fifth floor. Once the doors closed, he began to gyrate his body with more inflection and, aware that the concierge could see him, began to work a pointing motion at the elevator's camera into his dance moves. Having reached the building's summit, the lift's doors slid open and he strutted out onto his landing. Spinning his key on its ring around his finger he, with exact coordination, halted its rotation and slid it into the front door. He entered his tastefully modernised lateral apartment and immediately synced his music to his Sonos sound system. The eighties funk now gently pumped through his home, allowing the professor to remove his earphones and disrobe.

Having anticipated his arrival to the minute, the flat had been cleaned fastidiously by his cleaners, almost immediately beforehand. Afflicted with a high level of obsessive compulsive disorder, Wolf could not abide any mess or clutter. His home was arranged just as he liked it. Any variation to this status quo was deeply disturbing to the controlling and ordered mind of its owner. From his haircut and clean shave, to his pressed, tailored and unblemished clothes, Wolf strived for geometric efficiency and minimalist perfection. The professor despised the unnecessary and struggled daily to house the essential, without compromising his sterile, uninhibited environment. As a result, his apartment was completely disinfected and void of effects. The clinically arranged fine artwork, sculptures and minimalist furniture was the only thing separating his flat from a cellular grouping of white boxes. Particularly since his wife had been taken from him, he found himself unable to relax until at least his house and possessions were in reasonable order. This obsessive behaviour had been limited by the presence of his two daughters, whose rooms now lay immaculately maintained, just as they left them. However, having returned briefly following university studies, both his daughters had long since flown the nest to make homes of their own.

Having habitually and compulsively inspected every inch of his home, Wolf retired to his master bedroom's dressing room. He neatly and quickly disrobed completely, folding his discarded garments into an elegant wooden washing box. He expertly laid out a matching outfit onto a pouf, positioned in the middle of the room, before exiting to his en-suite bathroom. The professor blasted himself with the all-consuming wash of his oversized chrome showerhead. Satisfied that he had cleaned and rinsed every part of his skin's surface, he dried himself and re-entered the dressing room. He garbed his bottom half and returned to the bathroom, which had now de-steamed enough for the mirror to facilitate a legible reflection. Having applied various products, brushed his teeth, combed his hair and shaved, he admired his rather lean and well-kept form in the mirror and, content with his appearance, he returned to the dressing room to complete his routine. Stealing a look at his watch, he noticed that time had elapsed. He had only moments before his seven-thirty appointment was due.

Not wishing to spend any night alone, the professor had a string of friends and contacts who would regularly visit and stay with him. He would constantly battle with his obsessive-compulsive cleaning in the presence of his guests, who would be bound to precise and regimented rules. However, for Wolf the anxiety of increased filth and cleaning was a welcome trade-off for the company it came with. The professor was a lonely and social man. He found himself in the unenviable predicament of while on the one hand being unable to let go of the feelings and memories of his wife, but on the other being an empathetic man who craved consistent affection. To that end Wolf had barely settled, before he heard the familiar buzz of the concierge desk. He swept over to the intercom system and witnessed his intended visitor on the camera facing the concierge. Without bothering to speak into the intercom, he buzzed his visitor up, dimmed the lights a little and made quickly for the kitchen.

Wolf's kitchen was extensive and faced onto an open-plan dining area. A large, steel-topped island ran parallel to the main worktop and was fitted with four swivelling stools, ideal for intimate entertaining and cooking. Wolf selected two wine glasses and a half-decent red wine. He poured two small portions and set the bottle down to breathe. Listening for the door-bell, Wolf walked to the front door. Just as he reached the entrance hall the door sounded and he pulled it back to reveal his young and beautiful caller.

Several decades his junior, Veronique was a twenty-something year old, Belgian PHD student, studying at the University of Vienna. Having been used by her pimp boyfriend throughout her teens, Veronique had saved money and fled to Austria to study. Following a degree, she had conscripted to the Austrian federal police. Unfulfilled working as a traditional police officer, she had sought postgraduate study as a means to an end. She wished to graduate to more academic detective work and private investigation. Despite having waged a long-term relationship with a fellow German postgrad, she had found the professor fascinating. His superior mind, wealth of incredible knowledge and vast experience had rendered the professor a distant fantasy and out of Veronique's league. She had been proved wrong, however, as they began to exchange discussions both in and out of lectures and seminars. Veronique's youth and beauty had been physically irresistible to Professor Wolf and in turn, his security, power and empathy served only to compound this young student's infatuation.

For a casual affair their relationship seemed perfectly and naturally organic. They shared similar ideas and both knew a long-term situation was unrealistic. However, both shared a primal attraction for one another, despite their age gap, and the carnal thrill of a student-teacher liaison was the cherry on top. Furthermore, while the professor relished the sensual flamboyance and fervour of youth that radiated from Veronique, conversely Veronique, who from her past was more than accustomed to the immature perversions of younger men, was refreshed and enamoured by her professor's simple, gentle, yet powerful sexuality.

Veronique's face, though youthful, leaked the expressions of an older woman's experiences. Her hair was tied up in a neat, high-set, pony tail which accentuated her long angular features. She was slight and well-proportioned in stature. Her dark hair was highlighted with golden streaks. She dressed and made herself up with a practised balance between catering to men's attractions without denoting an air of obvious promiscuity. The couple spoke in English, their universal language, and indeed the language of their lectures and seminars.

"Good evening, Fräulein."

Veronique's heels clicked as she crossed Wolf's threshold and she broke her consciously passive pout, to beam up at the professor. She leant in and kissed the air next to Wolf's right cheek. Feeling his soft, freshly shaved face, the pit of her stomach welled with anticipation and excitement at the prospect of the evening's romance ahead. She floated, cat-like, past the professor and made her way familiarly to the kitchen. Wolf traced her footsteps back to the kitchen island on which the red wine lay waiting. The eighties funk still reigned over the couple as Veronique flicked her pony tail to the side and slipped out of her sleek black raincoat. Shaking out of her coat, she exposed her figure-hugging black dress. Carefully and deliberately she bent over and procured a stool from under the island and crossed her legs over the top of it, folding her coat on the adjacent stool. Now well-positioned, she reached for her red wine, took a sip and looked longingly at Wolf and his flawless kitchen.

"So, Chris, how was London? Did you get your medal?"

Without verbally responding the professor scurried off to his study, where he had stashed his memorabilia. On his way back with the ornamental box, containing his UN award, he already found himself contemplating the divulgence of operation Harvey Walsh. As he strode back to show off his appointment from London he felt sure Veronique, however enticing, would surely not be worth confiding in. Though he also felt certain she would be able to handle and keep the truth of his London trip a secret, he did not really want to burden her or himself with this extra knowledge. He did, however, find himself feeling that it would be nice to share his secret with someone, other than the belligerent Captain Kelly. He also knew that Veronique was an exceptional sleuth and would be able to tell if something was bothering him, or if something deeper was harboured in his discussion and reaction to his UN medal receipt. As he re-entered the kitchen to confront Veronique with his plunder, he did his best to bury and mask anything in his body language or communication that would give away the truth about his activities in London.

"Here we are, Veronique. Look at what Daddy's got."

Saying this, he set the box down on the kitchen island directly in front of Veronique. She loved the paternal reference and again felt a swell of excitement in the pit of her stomach. She looked up at Wolf and bit her lips together while blinking slowly and flirtatiously. She then fixed her eyes on the box before her and opened it. She caressed the medal with her slightly windswept, but well-manicured hands.

"It's beautiful, Professor. I love it. May I?"

She glanced back at the professor who watched her pony tail flick once more as she turned. Veronique did not wait for a response and placed the medal over her head, letting it hang down over her neck. She turned to face the professor, who was still standing slightly behind her stool, sipping his wine. She puckered her lips at him, raised her shoulders and smiled, modelling his award.

"I think that's the best place for it."

As the professor uttered this, he smiled and linked eyes with Veronique's. The couple, in the depths of fresh romance, could not help themselves any more. The tension and anticipation between the two had reached its peak. Veronique, consumed with bodily exhilaration and adrenalin, shakily slipped down from her perch, pushing Wolf gently back in his stance as she did so. Positioning her body as voluptuously as possible, she stood with her legs parted to attention. Still staring silently at Wolf, she seamlessly and subtly loosened the zip on her dress as far as it would comfortably go. She then ran the straps of her dress off her shoulders, allowing it to fall to the floor. She stepped out of the ruffled pile she had made, stuck her hips to the side and pulled her hair loose from its ponytail. As her hair flowed down and her body flexed, the professor's eyes widened and his animal instincts took precedent.

"How about now?"

Veronique smiled and giggled as she enquired. She dropped her shoulders in submission and slowly walked the few strides into the professor's embrace. They continued their sensitive and electric intimacy without leaving the kitchen. By the time they had finished, the wine had had more than enough time to breathe; however, any ambition to cook had evaporated.

The time was past nine o'clock, as Wolf emerged from the shower for the second time that evening. Veronique had not re-dressed. Instead she was sitting on her kitchen stool, swaying quietly to the music and sipping her third small glass of wine. As Wolf entered the kitchen, she trotted past him and towards the master en-suite. Wolf called out after her, as she ran.

"Would you like some Chinese food, if I order some?"

"Yes!" she called back fleetingly to him, shutting his bedroom door behind her.

The couple had just enough time to settle when the concierge rang with their order. The Professor collected the pre-paid package of Chinese food and served it up, hospitably and delicately for himself and Veronique. They were both fairly famished and initially made no attempt at communication. The medal, which Veronique had only removed post fornication, still lay idly and visibly on the kitchen island. Veronique spied it from the corner of her eye as she ate. Having slurped a fresh mouthful of chow mein purposefully into her mouth, she motioned to Wolf and pointed at it laughing.

"Chris, it was so hot wearing your medal just now."

Wolf managed to muffle a laugh back at Veronique and as he ate she continued.

"You're such a badass!"

The professor shook his head and mumbled back, "No, I'm not. Oh What? Because of the medal, Fräulein? It was really nothing."

However, despite the professor's disagreement, Veronique defended her assertion.

"Yes you are. They don't just give these out, Chris. I'd love to know the real reason they gave it to you. Uh?"

"What do you mean the real reason?"

Wolf was startled and worried by this pertinent enquiry. Worse still, Veronique had visibly picked up on her professor's shifty defensiveness. Wolf had let his guard pretty much all the way down and Veronique had, subconsciously or otherwise, breached his normally infallible defence mechanisms. Veronique flicked her pony tail back, looked up at the professor and set down her chopsticks, before calmly delving further on the offensive.

"I didn't mean anything, Chris. I just meant, you must know why you got this award. I was just asking, that's all?"

She spoke with a moderate, passive but somehow stern tone. This threw Wolf off further, who felt she already knew something was amiss. He would now have to do his utmost, to somehow casually mask the truth.

"It was nothing really, V. They chose myself and another man, for a culmination of services rendered. Not for one specific case. It was pretty boring and quick, to be honest."

Veronique, unfazed by her lover's casual deflections, knew from this reaction he was hiding something.

"Oh, so you must have had some time in London, no? What did you get up to?"

In the professor's opinion this was an ingenious question. She was a trained lie detector and she was deliberately setting him up to be untruthful or at the least withholding. The professor shrugged as casually as possible and began to be expressive with his hands, as if lightly recounting his travels. He vied desperately not to hesitate or stutter through his fabrications.

"Well actually not much, by the time I got back from the Foreign Office, there was barely time for a quick lunch before I was back in the car to the airport. Plus, the traditional English weather was more than enough to stop me venturing further."

Wolf laughed at himself and could not help but break Veronique's piercing eye contact and retreat to his takeaway. Veronique did not let up.

"Where did you have lunch?"

Once again, she consciously placed Wolf in a position where, to her mind, she was convinced he had to lie. Conditioned to recognise any flicker of unnatural movement in voice or body, she watched her target with even more intensity than she had during their intimacy. The professor struggled through his current mouthful, nodding and making chewing noises. He then slipped a response from the side of his mouth, while still munching and avoiding eye contact.

"In the Hotel, the Dorchester."

The professor tried to continue eating casually, as if undeterred and affected by this cross-examination. Still, Veronique fired on.

"What did you get?"

Now she was really getting to him. Wolf crammed down yet another mouthful of Chinese and sat up. He finished his mouthful while attempting to carefully convey an expression of remembrance not creativity.

"To be honest..."

However, Wolf was barely able to get his first sentence out before Veronique interrupted, smiling and maintaining a playful insolence. She was entirely dissatisfied with the direction the conversation was taking.

"To be honest, Professor, I don't think you're telling the truth. I called the Dorchester to check you would be here tonight. And I called just after lunch – they said you'd not been back since the morning?"

Veronique paused, seeing the professor squirm before her. However, she did not give him a chance to retort and resumed ostentatiously.

"Do you know how many boyfriends I've had cheat on me, Professor? Do you know how many times I've been hustled and used by men? Men just like you, Professor?"

She answered her own rhetorical belligerence, after another brief pause, once she realised she had clearly latched onto something juicy.

"Enough times, Professor, to know when someone is lying to me. What was it, Chris? Were you seeing another woman? I mean, I don't mind really. I suppose I have a boyfriend, so it would only be fair. Although, I do think it a bit strange you would choose to see two different women, in two different countries, on the same day. Ha! See! I told you! You're such a badass!"

The professor was taken aback by this jaded assumption, although somewhat flattered. He now, admitting his initial concealment a failure, chose to retort with a cleverer tack.

"Veronique, I have to say, I am flattered by your assertion, but I was not seeing another woman at that time! You are, however, absolutely correct – and very cleverly spotted! I did not have lunch at the Dorchester and, furthermore, I doubt that you even called the hotel! But there you are. You don't have to trick me, Fräulein, I am telling you the truth! And the truth is, I am not actually allowed to discuss what went on at the ceremony, nor anything thereafter."

Wolf's straightened and now totally honest face, somehow instigated an eruption of laughter from Veronique, and subsequently Wolf. Veronique, although somewhat convinced, was not entirely satisfied and once their laughter dispersed, she probed again.

"You know, Chris, I really wouldn't mind if it was another woman, it would be unfair of me if I did."

The professor felt that it was easy for her to say that, now she was half convinced he was telling the truth. He responded to consolidate his entirely factual explanation.

"Veronique, you are right. I would certainly not choose to be with two different women, in two different countries, in a single day – as you say. That would be exhausting and quite impossible for a man like me."

Veronique interrupted giggling. "Don't put yourself down, Professor!"

Wolf continued over her, humorously, "No, no! It would be quite impossible. Besides, while you may not, I realise how fortunate I am to have any kind of intimate contact with a person such as yourself, Fräulein. Objectively, I find it to be unlikely in the extreme, that I would attain even a single similar relationship to that which we share."

Veronique, maintained her youthful mocking.

"It could have been a hooker! Professor! Uh?"

They both were consumed by laughter again for a time, before the professor broke the silence with a change of subject.

"Veronique, will you stay with me tonight?"

"Yes, of course…"

She replied with a casual but sensual switch of tone. Wolf let his body, and hers, do the talking for the evening's remainder. Wolf avoided further discussion of his UN appointment.

# Chapter 3

## CAPTAIN MICHAEL KELLY

T he smell of coffee and cologne wafted and mixed throughout the stale wooden desks lining Captain Kelly's floor, at his Brooklyn precinct of the NYPD. It was first thing in the morning and Kelly, harbouring his secret mission, wandered tentatively through the lines of desks to his office. His path, however, was instantly and repeatedly hindered by the jeering, banter and embraces of the men populating his route. By the time he reached his office, he had heard every medal joke conceivable and was glistening red with embarrassment. However, as he turned to close the door, in what was meant to have been relief, he was confronted by Sheriff Barker. Barker had been patiently awaiting Kelly, having taken a seat behind the captain's desk. Kelly closed the door on himself, before turning to Colonel Barker and standing to attention.

"Sir!" Kelly barked, in customary respect of rank, particularly as this was not a Sheriff he knew well.

"At ease, Captain!"

Barker sighed back at him, leaning back in his chair and gesturing for Kelly to take a seat. Kelly duly sat down on a chair pulled up, normally for visitors, and awaited Barker's ominous words. Barker was a New Yorker through and through. He considered himself to be of an older and harder generation. He had been a battle-hardened field officer, before gradually being promoted. However, though his intelligence and work ethic would have propelled him to higher ranks, the colonel's temper and disrespect for authority had held him back. In this respect, he could empathise with Captain Kelly.

"Ah Michael! You really fucked up this time. I mean you've obviously fucked up before, but I think this is it, Mike. Yep! You're going to the Commissioner's office. I don't know what you've fuckin' said or done to deserve this, but it must have been something bad! Because I got the call from the Commissioner's office, even before you left London. You've got go there immediately. And don't ask me any questions because I don't know and, Kelly, I don't want to fucking know! Okay! Now fuck off! Get out of here!"

Kelly tried to plead with the Sheriff.

"Okay, sir, but..."

Kelly was instantly shot down by Barker.

"Go! Kelly, get the fuck out of here!"

Kelly promptly left in the direction of the police parking lot, to pick up a car and make for the Commissioner's office downtown.

Having been previously directed through the Commissioner's bustling police office, Kelly approached the Commissioner's receptionist. He swallowed hard with dread and anticipation, at his unexpected summoning.

"I think I'm here to see err, the Commissioner? My name is Michael Kelly."

Kelly enquired like a child sent to the headmaster's office. The receptionist glanced up habitually from his computer and responded, with a monotone disinterest.

"Oh yeah, you can just head right in."

The receptionist pointed towards what was evidently the Commissioner's office. Kelly, wishing he would have at least been asked to sit in the waiting room for a few moments, bravely pushed the door open and entered the fray. For the second time in a day, Kelly was surprised upon entering the room. Instead of the imposing and rotund figure of Commissioner Fonetti, a tiny, slither of a man had risen to greet him from behind the Commissioner's desk.

"Please, Captain, take a seat."

The skinny man quickly re-seated himself, before Kelly could properly size his slight stature and continued.

"My name is Commander Newman and this morning, Captain Kelly, we have something to discuss by order of the Commissioner and the New York City Police Department."

Newman sat up and really straightened his back as far as it would go, before sighing slightly and staring down the captain.

"This is obviously a very serious matter, Captain Kelly, and an act of possible terrorism."

The commander was sustained, and indeed revelled, in the perplexed and endangered expression that Kelly now displayed. Commander Newman continued, still more threateningly.

"If you are not entirely truthful in your statements from this point on, Captain Kelly, you will certainly face charges and trial. Captain Kelly, I'm going to need to know now, without exception, everything that happened at your little ceremony in London."

The captain's eyes bulged out of their sockets in horror. Questions shot across Kelly's psyche in a dazed shock, as he absorbed the Commander's accusations. How had the NYPD managed to come to this conclusion? How could they have known what happened after the ceremony? If he told Newman the truth, he would certainly face breaching Lord Cork's agreement. However, while this was something he felt unable to do, the other alternative of carefully masking the truth could have even harsher repercussions.

Kelly defensively stalled and stuttered back at Commander Newman, "What? Well, I-I don't get it? What am I supposed to have done? This is crazy! I, I'm not a terrorist!"

Commander Newman was uninterested in Kelly's emotions and choked-up questioning. He was solely interested in the captain's account and nothing more. This was clearly his brief and all he cared about.

"Captain Kelly, we have reason to believe that you may have been involved in terrorist activities while in London and may be continuing those activities, right now! So please, Captain Kelly, spare no detail and don't waste my time!"

Newman sat back in his chair having put pressure on Kelly to open-up. Kelly did his best to seem as respectful, intimidated and truthful as possible, while fabricating his version of events.

"Well, sir, I-I flew to England and landed. I got to the hotel and tried to get some sleep. I couldn't sleep, and I-I woke up late. So, I got to the ceremony late, just as it was starting. I took my award, left and went back to my hotel..."

Newman had heard a particular hesitation in Kelly's speech, as he recounted leaving the ceremony. Newman leapt on this infraction like a hunting dog on a lay fox.

"And you went straight back to your hotel and got the plane, right?"

Newman made an antagonistic noise, mimicking a gameshow host's buzzer, signifying his discontent with Kelly's story.

"Eh! Eh! Wrong! Captain Kelly! Need I remind you again, what will happen, if you lie to me right now! So, for your sake, I'm going to spare you this once. But, Kelly! If you lie to me now, it will be very, very bad for you. Now, tell me! What did you do after the ceremony?"

Kelly was trapped on one side, between the snarling, biting Scylla1, that was Commander Newman and the NYPD. While on the other side, he faced the swirling, cavernous, blackhole of Charybdis2 that was Lord Cork and everyone else. He subconsciously elected to take his chances with Scylla and maintained his masquerade of bewildered, stuttering innocence.

"I, I don't get it, Commander? W-What am I meant to have done? I'm really struggling here, sir..."

Kelly did not get far in his staggered babbling, before the impatient and probing Newman interrupted once more.

"For Christ's sake, Kelly, we know you met with some unknowns in London! We know something was discussed! And events have transpired since, such that we now know! That whatever it was you discussed, was directly related! To terrorist activity! So, Captain Kelly, I'll ask you again! What happened in London, after the ceremony! Who did you leave with?"

Kelly, faced with damnation whatever he communicated, attempted to be as truthful as possible. He concluded that the NYPD must have been in London and had seen him exit with Lord Cork's henchmen.

"Okay, so I left the ceremony with some UN officials. They gave me and this other guy, the four-one-one on our awards in their car. Then they dropped me somewhere in town. I got a cab, came back to my hotel and flew home."

---

1. *Scylla – Homeric legendry dog-headed monster*
2. *Charybdis – Homeric legendry whirlpool monster*

Newman was furious that he had neglected to mention his interaction with the UN officials post-ceremony. He was also determined that Kelly was withholding further information.

"Oh! So, you forgot to mention that you did actually meet with someone. Actually, a whole group of people! And they gave you the four-one-one? What does that mean? Please elaborate on your conversation with this group of individuals now, before you really piss me off!"

Kelly had given the commander an inch and Newman was gunning for a mile with this inquiry. Kelly had succumbed to confessing what Newman already knew. However, now the commander was asking for more. Kelly had to think quickly and come up with something to satisfy his interrogator.

"They just told us about the award and why we'd been chosen. You know, what an honour it was and yada yada! Nothing about terrorist plots! And besides, Commander Newman, I thought the UN were the good guys..."

Finally frustrated with Kelly's fumbled explanations and clearly not getting what he needed, Newman became spiteful and menacing.

"Kelly, you are a moron. A wreck-loose. I've seen your file. Quite frankly, Captain Kelly, you're a disgrace. A decorated hero, no! No way! I've analysed the travesties and catastrophes that litter your record. They don't just outweigh your achievements, they obliterate them! There's no way in hell, that you were selected for a UN commendation of service by merit!

"I have been informed by authorities and forces far above even my own station, that your selection to receive that medal was a ruse. A ruse designed to conceal a terrorist plot of some kind, possibly to infiltrate the UN and commit terrorist acts against the free-world and United States of America! Now, Captain Kelly, are you saying that you're telling the truth! Answer me!"

Newman had now risen to his feet and was poised, knuckles down, on the desk, bearing down on the shrivelled captain. Kelly, recognising his mental limits, gave up any attempt to fabricate further and simply shut down his responses to simple denials. He quietly and timidly stuck to his original story.

"No, Commander. I just don't know what you mean."

Despite this subsequent denial, Newman kept on at Kelly.

"So, you are denying any involvement in terrorist activity? You are denying you got into that car in London, drove to a house where you met, discussed and conspired against the United Nations and the United States of America?"

Kelly's eyes watered as he valiantly maintained their fix on Newman's. He was supremely rattled and now felt sure that he had been tailed for the duration of his London trip. However, somehow Kelly managed to confidently reject his commander's present allegations.

"I don't know what to tell you, sir? No, nothing like that happened."

Visibly enraged, Newman had had enough.

"Alright, Kelly! You're clearly not in a mood to cooperate. So, you can get out, you're indefinitely suspended, without pay! We will look into the investigation and be in touch over the next three to six months. If you feel like talking, you've got two weeks before you're officially under the total control of our jurisdiction. But don't worry, we'll write to you in a few days with your copies of the various warrants that we have pending. Until then you'll not be allowed to leave the state! That's all, Captain Kelly. And unless you'd like to cooperate further? You can get out!"

Kelly looked stunned and discernibly upset, to the delight of Commander Newman. He got up, turned heavily, and left in a slump. He retreated into the elevator and was still spinning, even as he emerged back into the freezing morning air. He shouted to himself like a madman in the street for a few moments, before finding his way back to his police car. Clambering into the cabin, he sniffed the air and strained, taking a moment to rouse himself from his state of shock. Having composed himself somewhat, he drove carefully back to his precinct. Not wishing to re-enter the building, for pride and emotion's sake, Kelly surreptitiously parked outside his workplace and took a cab home.

Kelly, having returned to his tiny two bedroom flat, in a downtown apartment building in south Brooklyn, proceeded to stay there. Only occasionally venturing out to the local liquor store, Kelly barricaded himself inside, in a state of debunked hibernation. Since he could remember, the police force, and military before that, had been Kelly's source of friends, family and entire existence. Having been put under investigation and suspended, he found himself void of human contact. He felt neutered, disconnected and deeply depressed at being immersed in this helpless situation.

There was little he could do, but wait for events to unfold, until the Commissioner's office had sent their warrants and began further interrogation. He knew his every move must be under surveillance. His phone, computer, car and apartment building, he was certain, were all being monitored around the clock. By the third day of this isolation, he had ceased bathing. This created a foul cocktail of musty body odour, rotting takeaway, stale beer and open vodka bottles.

Defiantly and adventurously, however, despite all this plight, Captain Kelly still followed his gut and stayed loyal to Lord Cork, Professor Wolf and Mission Harvey Walsh. He knew his appointment was something special. He also felt sure that his involvement in a terrorist plot and for that matter Lord Cork's, was complete fantasy on the part of the NYPD. Neither of his commanding officers, Colonel Barker or Commander Newman, had allowed him a genuine word in edgeways, and yet they had definitely missed a trick somewhere. Yes, they saw him leave with henchmen. Yes, they may have seen him enter Lord Cork's house. They may have followed him everywhere throughout the entirety of his trip. However, Kelly felt sure they were not in the room with Lord Cork and the other FBI, CIA and accompanying officials. The captain was also certain that Cork's property was held in a company name, because had the NYPD known it belonged to Lord Cork, they would surely know that any activities therein would not be of a terrorist nature.

Kelly had always been an independent thinker and while it had kept him alive on his various battlefields, it had also consistently got him into trouble. However, in this instance trouble had already found him and it was now a question of survival. Lord Cork, subconsciously or otherwise, struck more fear into the heart of Kelly than the NYPD did. Furthermore, the NYPD were definitely misinformed. On top of this, Professor Wolf, who for some reason Kelly trusted, had had no problem whatsoever with Cork's credibility. In fact, Wolf had endorsed it. However, it was on this third day of self-inflicted solitary confinement, that Kelly was stirred from his wallowing.

On his regular morning trip down to the building's communal area to check his pigeonhole for mail, Kelly had expected to see a familiar emptiness within. On the previous two days' inspection, he had been wary of the NYPD's warrant letters. This had culminated such that each time Kelly opened the mail box his heart raced and his cheeks flushed with anxiety.

Kelly had not felt this bad checking the post, since being bombarded with college rejection letters in high school. This time, however, his shaken soul homed in on an official looking letter, leaning innocuously against the side of his mailbox. Kelly wished to quickly extinguish the fire this letter had lit in his consciousness. He quickly grabbed it and slammed the mailbox shut. As he ascended the stairs back to his asylum, Kelly, still in his crusty pyjamas and dressing gown, tore open his letter. It read as follows:

Dear Captain Kelly,

**We are writing to you with the full jurisdiction and authority of the New York Police Department (NYPD) to inform you, in writing and without prejudice, of the matter disclosed herein.**

The NYPD is aware and accepts full responsibility for the accusations, regulations and sanctions imposed on yourself, Captain Michael Kelly, in relation to the appointment of your United Nations Special Services Medal.

Henceforth and as a direct result of these accusations, regulations and sanctions imposed, we the NYPD, unreservedly and wholly apologise. We wholeheartedly and unequivocally nullify, take back and reverse all accusations, regulations and sanctions imposed on yourself, Captain Michael Kelly, in relation to your appointment of the United Nations Special Services Medal.

In addition to this official and written apology, the NYPD would like to extend the following, stated hereafter, in final settlement of this matter, for the remuneration and deformation endured by yourself, Captain Michael Kelly, by the related activities of the NYPD. For the settlement stated above, the NYPD will guarantee: twelve months' paid leave, twelve months' salary in advance (in cash payment) and promotion on return, to the rank of Major.

By signing and returning this document, you, Captain Michael Kelly, will be agreeing to the terms and conditions described above, completely and in perpetuity and you will thereafter agree to not bring any legal proceedings whatsoever, against the NYPD, with regard to any events, actions or sentiments, in relation to your appointment of the United Nations Special Services Medal.

Once again, the NYPD regrets and deplores the wrongs that have been done to yourself, Captain Michael Kelly, with respect to your appointment of the United Nations Special Services Medal. With this settlement, the NYPD aspires to, in some part, compensate yourself, Captain Michael Kelly, for any current and sustained negative effects, you may, or have yet to encounter, as a result of said wrongdoings.

Yours sincerely,

*Commissioner Fonetti*

*I hereby confirm that I am Captain Michael Kelly of the New York Police Department and that I am of sound mind and able reasoning. I hereby confirm that I have read, understood and agree, in full, to the terms and conditions of the agreement detailed above. I can confirm that I am signing this agreement in good faith and agree to abide by the terms and conditions therein.*

**Captain Michael Kelly (Print Name)**

————————————————————————

**Date**

————————————————————————

**Signature: Captain Michael Kelly**

————————————————————————

# Chapter 4

## THE CALL

In the five days since Professor Wolf's meeting with Lord Cork he busied himself, not just with Veronique, but with settling his various upcoming and regular affairs and appointments. Wolf was readying himself for what he was convinced would finally be his career-defining case. Hopelessly bored with his lecture touring, consultancy and fleeting romances, Wolf had felt more and more trapped by his age with every year that passed. He sensed maturity's rapid venom increasingly catching him and was more than relieved to have been handed this fascinating assignment. Wolf wanted to believe every word Cork had said; however, his deeply ingrained scepticism still reverberated through his subconscious. The question Kelly had so abruptly posed to Cork had stuck at the back of the professor's mind ever since their meeting. Why them? The professor's ego wanted to think that his selection had been from a well-oiled algorithm and rigorous profiling. In reality, Wolf felt washed up. Granted, Professor Wolf had a sterling record of prolific and high-profile cases under his belt, but this had been over a career spanning decades. In truth, his last case, of any notability, had been more than ten years ago.

Therefore, on the fifth morning since his meeting in London, when his apartment phone rang, Wolf was in two minds. His optimistic ego, on one side, knew this was opportunity calling. While, on the other side, his seasoned cynicism was acutely cautious, to the motives and agendas harboured at the other end of the line. The professor let the phone ring, as he eased himself gingerly towards the receiver, lifted it off the cradle and put it to his ear.

"Guten Morgen?"

Wolf knew he should have opened in English; however, remembering his pledge of discretion to Lord Cork, he answered in German. The voice at the other end was unmistakably that of Lord Cork's lanky Scottish henchman.

"Professor Wolf, this is a secure line! But look! I've only got a few seconds! So, shut up and listen! Be at the traffic lights on the corner of Park Lane and Upper Brook Street at eleven a.m. in two days' time, alright? And don't stay at a hotel! Come directly! Unless you've had a change of heart that is! Now, don't ask questions! Just be there!"

The Scotsman rang-off abruptly and the line went dead. This was it as far as Wolf was concerned. This was his chance at ultimate glory. Even if this was some devilish ploy or conspiracy, it still represented a captivating challenge too tempting for Wolf to pass up. This was precisely what Wolf was looking for and why he now whirled himself around, accelerating his plans to make for London for the foreseeable future.

Having, as best he could, set his affairs in order, the professor now sat in the back of a taxi on London's Heathrow corridor. Wolf, a man of impeccable prudence, had more than enough time to spare upon arriving at Heathrow. He was, therefore, not at all stressed to encounter significant traffic on his approach to Central London. Wolf, not trusting anything, had instructed the driver to take him to the Dorchester Hotel. However, upon entering the vehicle, he had redirected the driver to Upper Brook Street. Having expected to arrive early, the traffic en route had meant that when the professor's cab pulled up at his destination, it was already ten-fifty-eight. Wolf hastily dragged himself and his suitcases from his taxi and made for the corner of Park Lane, not more than twenty paces ahead.

Professor Wolf instantly spied his mark. A tall, dark and distinctly official-looking man stood, his arms folded with cold, staring down Park Lane. He was dressed in a dark suit and wore no overcoat. He was not smoking, and his body language demonstrated that he was clearly waiting for something. As the professor approached this man at the corner of his destination, the man turned sensing Wolf's proximity. This man was evidently a little taken back by Wolf having gotten so close without detection. He smiled at Wolf, calmly welcoming him.

"Oh! Professor. I didn't see you there. I hope you had a good trip?"

As he said this, the official extended one of his huge hands to Wolf for shaking. Wolf, slightly taken aback himself by the sheer size of his new acquaintance, silently dropped his suitcase and obliged. The tall man quickly and effortlessly hoicked up Wolf's suitcase and extended his other arm for the second.

"Please, Professor, let me carry your cases, you must be tired after your trip."

Not wishing to argue and still in an impressed silence, the professor handed this huge man his other suitcase and the pair made their way together down Upper Brook Street. After a few minutes walking into Mayfair, the professor and his chaperone reached the familiar house in which Wolf had first met Lord Cork. His chaperone was promptly buzzed-in and ushered Wolf through the entranceway of the striking Victorian townhouse. The chaperone gently set the professor's luggage down and instead of heading for their meeting room as before, Wolf was led up the gorgeous wide-set staircase to the first floor. Atop the stairs was a corridor with four closed doors, two at its west side and two at its east. The stairs entered the corridor at the east side and the professor was guided into the room immediately facing the flight of steps. The room was smaller than the meeting room but, as an office for two people, it was grand by any standards. Lavished in, brilliantly maintained, authentic period décor; two large, leather-topped, bankers' desks faced each other on the north and south ends of the square room. The ceiling heights were impressive, at over three and a half metres, and the cornicing was tasteful yet flamboyant.

Sat slumped at the desk facing the door was Captain Kelly who, not surprised to see Wolf, did not get up. The professor looked briefly back at the closing door, watching the mysterious tall man leave, before tentatively and politely reuniting with Kelly.

"Good morning, Captain. You must forgive me. It had been my intention to be here early as well. But the English roads were not kind to me. Still, I suppose we had better get used to it and the weather too, yah? Is it me or does the weather seem to get worse every time I come here? Ah! But there I go! Immediately talking like a native about the weather."

Wolf paused as Kelly swivelled to-and-fro on his exquisite, leather-backed, Victorian desk-chair. Kelly was obviously showing signs of frustrated insecurity. He, like Wolf, was a control freak and hated to be kept in the dark. It was this obsession for fact and truth, that had made the pair such prolific law enforcement officials. Kelly, not making any effort to fill the void of the professor's pause, gave Wolf no choice but to continue his chatty small talk.

"I trust you had a pleasant journey? Obviously you did because you got here early. I hope you haven't been here long?"

Captain Kelly fixed his eyes on Wolf as his body still swivelled back and forth. He paused a little to muster a jet-lagged mutter.

"Yeah it was fine. I got in about an hour ago. I've just been waiting. I'm really lagging."

Wolf gave Kelly an empathetic expression of sympathy at his condition and tried to put him at ease.

"Yes, Captain Kelly, I have to confess myself I am feeling the effects of traveling too. And I only came in from Vienna. It was a little unreasonable, yah? Not to permit us to stay in a hotel prior to this morning's appointment! I can also empathise, that I too am feeling somewhat confused and suspicious of this entire affair by the way! Without question, they have asked us to risk a lot for, not so that much in return. To be honest, this Harvey Walsh affair has really turned my life completely up-side-down."

Kelly did seem calmed, although the professor could not tell if he was just fatigued. Kelly responded briefly and without effort.

"Yeah. I've given up trying to understand anymore."

The professor was spared any further interaction with a distinctly despondent Captain Kelly, as the door re-opened and Lord Cork entered. Evidently not planning to stay, he was still holding his Fedora and had not removed his fine, thickly-woven, black overcoat. Cork's turquoise cashmere scarf had fallen either side of his shoulders and he did not bother to take a seat. Spying Kelly at his future desk, and Wolf perched on the side of it, he addressed them both bluntly.

"Good morning, Captain Kelly, Professor Wolf. I trust your journey was a safe one and you are both ready and prepared for what awaits. From henceforth, this will be your office. Next door is my office, when I am here, which I hope should not be too often. Downstairs, you will find the meeting room has been set up as your coms and intelligence cluster. You have a team of ten operatives directly under you. Each of those operatives will have their own sub-teams that they will instruct according to your orders. You will report to a man, I believe you have already both met.

Harry Douglas, my executive director, will be your main point of contact for reporting. Anything you relay to him, will come straight back to myself."

Lord Cork registered his subjects' obedience and continued with a sharp confidence.

"Now, as before, there is a simple non-disclosure agreement on each of the desks in front of you, leather bound and sealed. These agreements simply swear you to confidentiality and also lay out the terms of your engagement, which will be as follows. You will each receive a fee of twenty-five thousand pounds per calendar month. This is an indefinite contract, that ends in one of two ways. The first instance would be a breach of contract. This would be a breach of secrecy, a failure to comply with orders to the detriment of the mission, or a voluntary withdrawal by one or both of you. The other way this contract ends is via completion. Your contract will be complete once you have sourced the true identity and confirmed the location of the person known as Harvey Walsh. Upon completion of this contract, you will each be entitled to claim a five-hundred-thousand-pound bonus, as well as positive reference to an institution of your choice. As was agreed.

"Well, gentlemen, I have an appointment in Kensington at twelve o'clock, that I am already late for. So, if you would be so kind as to quickly read, sign and witness each other's contracts. I will leave you in the very capable hands of Mr Douglas, who I will call in momentarily."

Kelly and Wolf made for each other's contracts, opened them and began reading. As before, Wolf had finished and signed his documentation well before Kelly had, begrudgingly and hesitantly, filled out his paperwork. The three maintained silence, as Cork inspected the respective documents. Having made sure they were in order, he smiled at Wolf and Kelly and summed up.

"Well, Captain Kelly, Professor Wolf! Welcome to Operation Harvey Walsh. You will now be fully brought up to speed on proceedings by Mr Douglas."

Cork strode over to a phone on Wolf's desk, nearest the door, lifted the receiver and dialled Douglas's office.

"Hello Harry, I think we're ready for you now."

Not awaiting response, Lord Cork slammed the phone back down and went for the door. As he opened the door to leave, he turned and bid farewell to his new recruits.

"Thank you, gentlemen! I have arranged for your luggage to be sent directly to your lodgings at a safehouse close by. Mr Douglas will provide you with the keys and address. I shall return, at some point, to check up on you. Until then, Captain Kelly, Professor Wolf, I suppose I'd better wish you good luck and happy hunting."

Not a minute after Cork left, in a whirlwind of vicious tenacity, Harry Douglas burst through the wood-panelled door. His mad staring eyes leered at Kelly and Wolf as he almost floated, like a Celtic wizard, into the room.

"Right, good morning, ladies, so you've both heard what his Lordship's had to say. This is Operation Harvey Walsh, right! It is totally secret, right! There can be no slip ups, right! There can be no fuck ups!"

Douglas glared at the two men he commanded, as if to seek some kind of reaction. Dissatisfied and disappointed with the bewildered but somehow comfortable vibe he was getting from Wolf and Kelly, Douglas continued more aggressively.

"What a minute, hold on. You don't know, do you? You both haven't worked it out, have you?"

Douglas paused again, still hoping to have ignited a response. However, neither the captain nor the professor reacted quickly enough for Douglas.

"Look at you both sitting there, like wee fat cats in your upper-class chairs and your massive, ridiculous, rain forest endangering desks!

"No, no! I get it! You've just signed your big contracts for all that money. And Oh! That bonus clause, referring you to any institution in the world, not bad, right! But you boys, you still don't get it! Your every move will be under my watchful eye and my scrutiny. I will be all over you like a suit from the pound shop! Gentlemen, you sneeze, I'm feeling it! And let me fill you in on another thing! It is very, very likely, that you will fuck up! So, please, tell me now! What are your weaknesses? Go on, I'm interested! I need to know! Tell daddy your secrets? Come on! Might as well get it out now, guys! Because, let's face it! I will find them! They will emerge! And I will be there, ladies! Jaws fucking open, when you fail!"

Douglas paused one more time, harshly glaring at Kelly and Wolf, before further cracking the whip of his authority once more.

"Oh, you guys still don't get it, do you? You guys aren't the first Nancies to get fucked at this Prom night! Oh, did you think you were? Aw! That is sweet. Did you think it was our first time as well? Well I've got news for you! We're not fucking virgins! No, we're not! Girlies, we're the school fucking jock, we've taken more virginities than horny Viking! That's right, kids! You're not the first! And I dare say, you won't be the last, specially wanked-off, lambs to the slaughter, that his Lordship's signed up! You guys are the dregs of the selection pool! We have had some pretty impressive guys come through here! And fail horrendously, mind. But you guys, nah! You guys? I haven't even really read your files, but I can already tell you ain't cutting the mustard! You see, you're into the big leagues now, ladies. And don't think you're the hot shot rookie, straight out of high school neither! You're more like those guys who, by some unfathomable twist of fate, find themselves scraping into the squad. Your only chance of staying alive, let alone succeeding, is to listen to exactly what I say! And do exactly what I tell you! And just try your best, my wee little minions! Not to fuck up!"

Douglas broke off from his berating and registered, with peaceful satisfaction, the vacant dismay in Wolf and Kelly. Douglas, having subdued and broken his subjects, resumed with a lighter and more matter-of-fact tone.

"Right so, come on, guys, if you think I'm bad you just wait. You wait until you get out there and have to sift through the shit of criminal world's underbelly. The guys out there! They're the ones who you should be upset about. I might be harsh but I'm only here to protect you!

"Alright, guys, enough of the intros. In your apartments you'll find a full brief, with all the cases and intel relating to Harvey Walsh. Downstairs is my office, when I'm here, which won't be that often. Because quite frankly I've got better things to do than babysit a clapped-out professor and Captain Catastrophe! Next to my office is a team of guys, some of whom you've already met. You will be responsible for them! They will follow your orders! And it is your sole purpose, to ensure that those orders, are my orders! Got that, Sunshines!

"I'm going to fuck off now. And I will leave you this morning to get acquainted, with the positively cosmopolitan cocktail of sharks, rats and vipers that make up your team! Now I would say don't let them get out of line. But in your cases, I've actually already spoken to them all. And all of them will be watching you both like a fucking hawk to make sure neither of you does anything fucking stupid, okay..."

Douglas let up once more from his speech and glared, with a calm and sinister menace, at Wolf and Kelly. He straightened his lean frame, turned and made athletically for the door. Before leaving, he violently swung the door open such that it flung on its hinges. Douglas trapped the door in its rotation with a talon like grip, showing tremendous dexterity and strength. He then gave the couple one more parting exclamation before slamming the door behind him.

"Remember! You're representing a lot of very powerful people and institutions here! Do not fucking embarrass me..."

Not a moment had passed for Kelly and Wolf to absorb and contemplate this spew of coarsely put instruction, before a fresh entrance creaked at their door. A woman, who Wolf instantly recognised and was more than amazed to see, strutted in. She smiled at Wolf before turning to Kelly and addressing them both.

"Good morning, gentlemen, I'm Maya. I'm your chief intelligence officer. I'll be your lead, in charge of all field intelligence and operations. If you like, guys, I'll take you down to the ops room and introduce you to the team?"

Wolf had cycled through a wide range of emotions in the few moments since Maya entered. He had, as soon as laying eyes on her, figured out her identity and function. He felt one-upped, out-smarted and emasculated. However, an older and wiser man, Wolf was able to put his ego aside and maintain his adoration for the younger woman.

"Genius, Fräulein! Bravo! I applaud your performance. There was not a trace of doubt in my mind, I was totally convinced. I am enthralled by the lengths this organisation will go to, to vet its employees! Maya, is it? Oh, that's a much prettier name than Veronique."

Kelly looked confused, tired and on the verge of an outburst. Seeing this, Maya did not wish to have Kelly's temper kick things off to a bad start and moved quickly to address the pair.

"Yes, Professor Wolf, both of you were vetted and tested in ways you cannot imagine and will not know. It was my facility, as Veronique, to make sure you could keep our secret. Confidentiality is key! And our profiling found that, with your wife's passing and your children leaving home, you would be particularly susceptible to the charms of an insecure, younger woman. The fact that, even when you knew I thought you were lying, you still never told the truth about our mission, not even a little, was impressive."

She registered that Wolf's knowledge had been satisfied and brought up to speed. Maya then turned her attention to Captain Kelly.

"And you, Captain Kelly, and please do not interrupt me! We had the FBI call your Commissioner. It was us who told them about a terrorist plot and it was us who arranged for your meeting with Commander Newman. And you, even when faced with exclusion and suspension, you still stayed loyal. And when you did remain true, it was us who arranged for you to be sent a generous settlement."

Kelly looked at Maya distrustfully and still registered confusion, as to the nature of her relationship with Wolf. However, still wishing to maintain control of the situation, Maya did not allow Kelly to interrupt.

"Yes, you were both tested. We needed to be sure of complete loyalty. We needed to do things to ensure our confidence, that would challenge the very weakest parts of your personality. I apologise if you feel tricked or cheated, but this is not my decision. My decision is to do what's best for the mission and I hope you both can understand that. Now, you are both to come and quickly meet the rest of the team. Then you must go to your apartments and prepare to start your research tomorrow. You must get some rest, you will need it. Now please, follow me."

Maya and her new bosses descended the stairs to the ground floor hallway and through into the ex-meeting room, now central communications and operations hub. This vast period room had been filled with modern desks and work stations. The entire space was littered with monitors and mounted flat-screens. Dashing back and forth and generally milling, were the various members of Team Harvey Walsh. A larger, grander work station, with a huge panel of television screens was set up at the top of the room. As the trio entered the room, Maya led Wolf and Kelly towards this more substantial work station closest to the door. The groupings of people inside the room clearly registered the presence of the two newcomers and three of their number filtered towards the core work station to greet Wolf and Kelly. Maya noticed them approaching and took her cue to introduce the key members of Team Harvey Walsh.

"Okay, guys, so, this is your Intel Point, Daniel Oppenheim. He was a detective for ten years before working for MI5. He is an excellent profiler and will be responsible for building as much information as possible on Harvey Walsh. He will be making sure we are one step ahead and don't get our operations guys in trouble. Essentially, he spots the things that others miss."

Mr Oppenheim was a slightly porky man with an exceptionally blasé disposition. His camp, disinterested tone was sarcastic and stunted the flow of conversation and though clearly highly intelligent, Wolf wondered if Oppenheim was perhaps slightly autistic, as he seemed consistently emotionless and impartial. As Maya introduced Oppenheim, his bulging eyes rolled visibly between her, the wall and the two newbies.

"Yeah, that's me I suppose. Not much to me really, is there? You're Captain Kelly. And you're Professor Wolf. Yeah, pleased to meet you. Yeah. Could we have done this tomorrow, though, you know, when they have actually been briefed on Harvey Walsh?"

Oppenheim shrugged, almost annoyed at the situation and turned away chuckling slightly to himself. He had evidently thought this introduction pointless and wished to detract from his involvement. He glared at Maya before looking to the rather enormous man on his left and, using body language alone, passed him the baton of introduction.

The man to Oppenheim's left was Omar Lopez, the Operations Point for Team Harvey Walsh. He was almost six-foot five, built like a lean heavyweight boxer and wore an expression of one who had experienced more than their fair share of violence. He was dark, good-looking and tanned. Upon Oppenheim's gesturing, this giant of a man sniffed and intensely switched his burning eyes to Wolf and Kelly.

"The name's Lopez, Omar Lopez. I was US marines for fifteen years. I will smell the enemy, so you don't have to. I've got my team, John, Pierre and Patrick. And if you let us alone and allow us to do our thing. We're pretty fucking good at what we do! Oh yeah, and I will not send any of my men out to die, so don't even think about it..."

As he introduced his team, he had pointed to the group of dangerous looking men huddled round a smaller desk arrangement at the opposite end of the room. Satisfied that they had fulfilled their respective protocols, Oppenheim and Lopez, not wishing to impart anything further, turned impolitely and returned to their work areas without farewell. Maya, wanting to keep up the momentum, quickly introduced the final Point member of Team Harvey Walsh. This was the IT Chief Co-ordinator, Josh Hakimi.

"Okay, so this is Josh. He is head of all IT, cyber intelligence and operations."

Hakimi was tall, slim and wore his hair in a large, slightly unkept, afro-like frizz. An Iranian-English mix, with African heritage, Hakimi was highly mathematically and spatially inclined. Like the majority of vastly bright IT workers, he demonstrated a continuous subconscious contempt for all those who are unable to write code in multiple languages. However, he was somewhat less cynical than his colleagues and harboured a rather sweet and genuine social affection for others.

"Hello! I like your outfit, Professor, very dapper! I really enjoyed reading both your profiles! Michael, your service record is incredible! I don't think I've ever met anyone who's killed more people in action! Maybe Omar?"

Hakimi drifted off a little, as he posed himself this question. Kelly, not wishing to recollect, nor discuss, exactly how many people he had slain on the battlefield was evidently insulted. An awkward silence followed, before once again Maya had to use her peer-leading social skills to intervene.

"Right so, guys, you've pretty much met everyone now, at least all your leads and points. I think this would be a good time for you both to head back to your apartments. Now, if you wouldn't mind following me?"

Maya smiled at Wolf and Kelly, before leading them back out into the hallway and through to the front door. She quickly popped upstairs, to fetch Wolf and Kelly's apartment details and keys. On her swift return she handed them two envelopes and prepared to send them off.

"Okay, guys, so in these packages, you will find the address of your apartments and the keys. Also a safe-phone and bank card. This phone is all you have to link you back to us if something happens. It has been mapped to have all calls scrambled and its location proxied. On the phones you'll find a list of all the team's contact numbers. But you won't be able to add contacts yourself or change any settings. If you need to do this later, Josh will do it for you. Keep these phones on you, charged, at all times. Do not lose them! If you lose them it's really bad, trust me – I lost my phone once and Harry, he almost fired me.

"In your apartments you will find briefing papers on Harvey Walsh and you will both be expected to have read most of the material come tomorrow. You will also find your bank cards, which again have been custom made and designed to have all account and withdrawal activity masked and proxied. Just like the phones, guys! Do not use any other card, keep it on you always and do not lose it! I personally advise you to walk together and get acquainted, it's a short walk to Marylebone from here and it's not raining yet. Please be back here for eight-thirty, tomorrow."

Maya slunk back inside and left the couple to tear open their packages and find their address. Kelly, realising they were to be housed in the same building and not knowing London, relaxed and turned on his new smartphone, leaving Wolf to announce the address.

"Right, Herr Kelly, here we are. We are going to – George Street, Marylebone. Does that thing have navigation?"

Wolf pointed at Kelly's now-activated smartphone.

"Let me see. Yeah it does. Where was it? George Street Marylebone?"

Wolf nodded and waited, shivering slightly in a gust of icy wind, as Kelly typed the address into the satnav search bar.

"Okay here we go. It's this way," announced Kelly, as he pointed them in the right direction and they set off together. A little time elapsed, while they each took in their surroundings and the events that had just transpired. They were both anticipative about the information awaiting them on Harvey Walsh. Kelly was already thinking he would need to have Wolf read and summarise any material verbally. Bright as he was, Kelly's crippling dyslexia had always hampered his success in any non-practical endeavours. Keen to get to know his new partner, Wolf began to chat with Kelly.

"So, I don't know about you, Captain Kelly, but I don't know whether to be confused beyond belief or excited like I'm a young detective again! Charged with a seemingly insurmountable challenge?"

Kelly interjected. "Yeah I guess. And jeez, Professor, call me Mike."

The professor continued in reciprocation. "Ah yes, of course. And please, Mike, err, call me Christof. So, what's your story? I understand you are a decorated war veteran? You must have had some pretty fascinating experiences?"

Kelly, self-effacing when it came to his chequered military history, scowled at Wolf slightly as he answered.

"Nah, nothing like that, Chris. I'm a bum. A nobody. But I am a bullshit detector! And I'm no fucking pussy neither. I don't like lies and this world's full of them. And I still don't trust a fucking thing we're doing here. You seem to be very calm, considering we were basically pressganged into this. And not just by anyone. These are serious guys, with serious connections. They've already shown me they can fucking make or break my life in a fucking instant. They made a few calls to the commissioner, she said! That's fucking funny, who makes a few fucking calls to ruin a guy's life? What the fuck? And the worst part! Yeah, they're a conglomerate of intelligence organisations, from the world's most powerful nations! But who is Lord Cork? Some rich guy? Why is he leading this? What's his fucking angle? Rich guys like him don't do shit unless they're getting a fucking taste! Know what I mean?"

Kelly looked to meet Wolf's sympathetic face, as they walked on, and he continued.

"There has to be something more to this. They can't just hire two assholes like us! Fucking blackmail us! Pay us! Spend money, time and resources on us and expect us to believe it's because we're fucking all-stars! Bullshit! Nah! Wolfy, this whole thing stinks. I'm just going along with it, because they got me by the balls and probably you too by the way! And they ain't letting go any time soon! We got no choice, Chrissy! We're prisoners! And we don't even know it! I mean, come on! If we violate our contract, it'll be worse than jail. Shit! Maybe I should have just gone to jail! Shit…"

Kelly's super direct quest for truth and his suspicion of power and authority, though perhaps founded, was unsupported in this case, at least in Wolf's mind. As such, he continued to try and calm Kelly with further sympathy.

"Michael, Michael, I agree with you! I said, did I not, just now? That I was confused beyond the point of belief."

Kelly snapped back at Wolf, interrupting. "No! You said you didn't know whether you were confused or excited! Don't try and fucking manipulate me, Professor! I got a great memory for things I hear and I'm in no mood…"

Wolf widened and rolled his eyes at Kelly in a sarcastic but playful way and continued to attempt to calm him.

"Come on, Mike, you know what I meant! I'm confused, just as you are. Even if I don't show it! But, Michael, you have to admit, we cannot pass judgement on this operation until we have at least read the brief that awaits us. Also, I think that it is precisely because they have invested so much in us, that it is even less likely that we are being engaged under false or shady pretences. And, Michael, I am also sure you are being too modest about your achievements. Please forgive me, Captain, but you are from New York?"

Kelly began to open-up a little, as for some reason, he had remained trusting of the Professor since their meeting.

"Yeah pretty much. My parents are Irish, but I lived in New York for my childhood. I got into drugs and gangs as a kid and my folks made me either join the armed forces, get a job or leave. I couldn't get a job and my parents kicked me out. Then, as soon as I was eighteen, I enlisted and got drafted into the US Marine corps. Classic, right? It was great, as a kid. I got sent in to fight all over the world. Wolfy, I loved it you know? I'd never been anywhere. The sights, the chicks, the cool people! But, they say that I've got a real problem with authority. Always have had. Even since I was real young. Even with my mom and dad. Anyway so, pretty much anything good I did. You know? Any lives I saved or anything, was always overshadowed by some asshole raining on my parade. Manipulating me, telling what to do, always making me look bad! As I got older, I was more able to control it. But then it was like, it would build up! And then when I did finally snap and break myself on some colonel or general, it would be so much worse! Eventually, I got a really bad rep, with most of my superior officers. I got myself blackballed. They started sending me in to die. They wanted to get rid of me. But, you know! I fucking stuck around! When they got tired of trying to waste me, they tried to send me away. They wanted me to manage a fucking junior's boot camp! When they told me, I freaked out so bad I, err, I pulled my gun on the general. You know, right there and then in his office. Stupidest thing I ever did! I wasn't going to fire! Obviously! I was just pissed! They fucking knew that!"

A brief awkward silence fragmented Kelly's tale as he glanced at Wolf, who avoided meeting his eye.

"Anyway, that was all they needed. They got rid of me right fucking there! Fucking court-martial and an instant disbandment from all forces. That was a big kick in the nuts, Professor, I got to tell you! And I'll never really get over it. It's probably why I've gone along with this and not jail. But from that day on my life was never the same. I got a job in the NYPD and just been living day to day ever since. Years have flipped off the calendar!

You know I think I'm getting really soft, Professor! I feel so sloppy, so old. So, fucking broken…"

Kelly was a far harsher and harder man than Wolf and he had clearly depressed him with his regalement. Feeling this, Kelly quickly shifted to a more jovial tone and continued.

"But hey, Professor, enough about my shitty life! I thought I was old and fucked, jeez! How must your old-ass feel!"

Kelly bashed the professor on the shoulder spiritedly as he said this, not wishing for Wolf to take him too seriously.

"Ah, yes, Michael, youth is not my strong suit. And yes, since I retired from being a full-time intelligence officer, I have been lecturing my boredom away at various universities throughout Europe. So, we are both agreed, Mein Herr. We are both trapped, confused and disbelieving, while at the same time intrigued at the glimmer of redemption and a return to the days of glory. Mine are a little further back, but still it's the same. We must be sure to keep this in mind, when trying to pick out any holes or inconsistencies in our Harvey Walsh brief. I expect we'll be reading well into the night, depending on how much material they have gathered."

Kelly was immediately weary of having to undertake too much reading.

"They can't have that much information, surely? They don't even know who he is. That would be suspicious to me in itself! Like they're flooding us with information or something, you know? To confuse us or something. I'm not fucking staying up all night, Professor! You might love to just put your little reading light on and read the fucking night away, but I'm dyslexic, Professor! I can't fucking read! I don't fucking read! You saw me with the fucking contracts! Wolfy! You're going to have to read, real quick. Because when you're done reading, you're going to be explaining, you feel me?"

Wolf was briefly cast back to his student days, when not too dissimilar requests had been demanded of him. He rolled his eyes and smiled at Kelly, consenting.

"Yah, yah, that is fine, I actually enjoy reading. At least this way we'll be able to discuss the case together."

Wolf nodded in further confirmation as Kelly responded. "Yeah, well. Good. Thanks, cause I can't fucking read!"

The pair continued to chat intermittently until they reached the entrance to their apartment building. The concierge, familiarly to Wolf, buzzed the door, which promptly swung open revealing a neat little lobby and reception. The concierge greeted them from behind his desk. Suited and booted, he was an ancient looking man of Far Eastern descent.

"Mr Kelly, Mr Wolf! I'm Bernie, your concierge. Please come in, your numbers are twenty-eight and twenty-nine. The two on the top floor. The lift is just around the corner, through there."

Bernie pointed past his reception desk and through to the end of a marble-lined hallway. The couple smiled and proceeded in the direction of the lifts. As they passed Bernie, he coughed, making Kelly look back at him. Meeting Kelly's eyes, Bernie pulled back his porter's uniform overcoat to reveal a black, MP-5 sub-machine gun, its butt tucked securely away in a specially woven pocket. He flashed his white teeth with a wide smile at Kelly and whispered, "Don't worry, boss, you sleep easy."

Kelly, ironically slightly terrified by the old concierge, followed Wolf into the lift and up to the top floor. The building was, like most in that area of London, Victorian in styling. However, this modernised apartment block had been recently refurbished and was more like a boutique hotel inside. Wolf and Kelly's apartments occupied the entire top floor and were well furnished, clean and modern. When the lift doors opened, Kelly and Wolf separated and entered their respective lodgings.

Wolf was more than satisfied with his new abode. He, being used to the sound proofed, high quality, modernised buildings in central Vienna, had been worried about enduring a creaky old Victorian flat. However, his apartment had been triple-glazed, modernised throughout and while the reception and bedrooms were all in-keeping with a modern-Victorian chic, the bathrooms and kitchen were twenty-first century.

Having deposited his hat, coat and scarves in the cloakroom at the entrance, Wolf found his way to the master bedroom. He saw his suitcases, neatly positioned, next to his superking-sized bed. He was also relieved to see an en-suite bathroom in the corner of the room. He promptly used its facilities and rinsed his face. Having refreshed himself somewhat, Wolf examined the rest of the flat. He had a substantial kitchen and reception, along with two double bedrooms, two bathrooms, a guest lavatory and a study. Located in his study were the files and briefs on Mission Harvey Walsh. They were stacked in several cardboard boxes, either side of the desk in the centre of the room. Wolf gauged that it would most likely take all night to read and absorb all the material in front of him. Even then, he thought, he would still be unable to analyse anything significantly. He would simply need to take in as much of the material available as possible in the time available.

Wolf began to prepare himself for a long night of study. He dashed to his suitcases and withdrew a sealed washbag. Inside lay Wolf's coffee and cafetiere. He made for the kitchen and proceeded to make fresh coffee. However, before the professor had finished boiling his water, he heard a knock at the door. Wolf quickly rinsed his hands, drying them with a dishtowel, on his way to the front door. It was Kelly.

"Have you seen how much shit there is? How can they expect us to read all this by tomorrow! See! I fucking told you! These guys are trying to swarm us with information! They're fucking trying to confuse us, Chrissy!"

Wolf resumed his, now almost habitual, duty of calming Kelly's rabid temper.

"Please, Michael, come inside! Let's go through this together. We can only do as much as we can. Besides, I think we only need to get the gist of things until tomorrow. Besides, I always find I am normally in a state of total confusion pretty much until I crack a case, when all becomes clear. I know how you feel, but we're in this together. Come, have some coffee with me and we'll cram through this brief together."

Relieved, Kelly followed Wolf towards the kitchen and the professor made an extra cup of black coffee for his partner. Kelly took the beverage and sipped it lightly.

"Shit, thanks, professor. It needs sugar, but that's nice coffee."

The professor, flattered and glad of Kelly's more temperate mood, beamed back at him.

"Danke schoen, danke schoen, Herr Kelly. I always make sure and take some with me when I travel. Particularly to the UK, where you know tasty nutrition of any description is hard to come by! Come now, I'll take the pot into the study and we'll get started."

With that Kelly, somewhat reluctantly, tailed the professor into his study. The pair opened the boxes and sifted through the papers within, attempting to coordinate and organise their brief into manageable sections.

Wolf and Kelly spent the afternoon collating and analysing the various transcripts, profiles and police records of anything and everything that had been associated with the suspected activities of Harvey Walsh. It was a sea of information. The number of intelligence transcripts, both online, video and sound recorded, was astounding. Conversation upon conversation had been recorded and documented, in the hope of catching anything that would link the team to their target. Kelly was helping to organise the material on Walsh, while Wolf would read through large stints of papers before relaying the important points to Kelly. However, about two and a half hours into their research, Kelly had gradually fallen asleep in the study's large armchair. When Kelly awoke it was dark outside and Wolf, having made quite a dent in the material, suggested they break for dinner.

"Ah, Michael, I didn't want to disturb you. How are you feeling? Have you eaten today? I think it would be good for us to go out for a break and maybe get some dinner?"

Kelly was tired and famished, having only slept a few hours and not eaten since his plane ride. He nodded at Wolf and dragged himself up from his armchair.

"Yeah, Wolfy, I'm famished. Let's find something to eat and get out of this fucking paper storm for a while."

With that, Kelly returned to his apartment briefly and the two reconvened at the lift's entrance. They descended together and bid good evening to the concierge, as they entered London's freezing night air. Wandering in search of a suitable establishment, they came across a lively looking gastro-pub in a tributary of Wigmore Street. They wriggled through the jostling bar area and made their orders, Kelly a bottle of beer and Wolf a pint of ale. They both, having quickly read the dinner menu as their drinks were served, ordered the pub's fancy version of traditional English fish and chips, before heading over to a more secluded table. Once they had made themselves comfortable and taken a few long draughts from their drinks, the duo's minds were back on the case.

"So, Michael, it would appear, now that I have managed to fill in the gaps a little, that Cork may not have been deluding us. It would appear, that this situation, case, whatever you wish to call it, is unimaginable, unprecedented and impossible to fake. I can clearly see from the transcripts in particular that this is the real thing! It's quite impressive really. This man, Harvey Walsh, is clearly a genius. From what I can see, he is like the English's great folk hero, Robin Hood! Except of course while Robin Hood chose to re-appropriate his spoils among the poor and deserving (supposedly), this man simply seeks his own aggrandisement, power and criminal wealth. This man is systematically taking over global organised crime. Through ingenious and anonymous means. He has undoubtedly and with great success, plotted and diagrammed the sectors and operations of all prominent criminal organisations around the world. He is now in the process of forcibly acquiring the knowledge and assets, to control and dominate the entire informal sector.

"It is not surprising, therefore, that most of the transcripts are the conversations of various criminal leaders around the world. But there are none, I repeat none, on Harvey Walsh himself and virtually all of these transcripts, fortunately for you and I, Captain Kelly, say the same thing. They are all condemning this Harvey Walsh! And communicating their dismay at the anonymous and clinical way in which he is penetrating and destroying their businesses. Harvey Walsh has regimentally, with pre-meditated and calculating design, begun to control every criminal enterprise in the Western world. From prostitution and human trafficking, to insider trading. I fear, Michael, that even with the financial and institutional backing of Lord Cork and his associates! This is quite possibly a task for which we are categorically mismatched. If we are to succeed in this mission, we will need to operate under the radar and work together to the best of our abilities. Because, Herr Captain, another obvious distinction I found from the transcripts and information, is that anyone who has crossed Harvey Walsh, hence perhaps the reason for his namelessness, has been killed! Understand, Michael, that from what I have been reading, we were in grave danger, as soon as we signed Cork's agreement. Just knowing about Harvey Walsh could get us killed."

Sensing that this last sentiment had seriously disturbed Kelly, Wolf quickly went on in a more positive fashion.

"However, I think our next move, before we get too panicked and lose our cool, should be to know what we know, but wait until we have seen what the team has to say tomorrow morning. However, I think it best that we consult directly with Lord Cork as soon as possible, to further discuss the way in which this mission is going. Because, I think you'll agree, Mike, going after a man like Harvey Walsh, is not something you can do with a dozen-strong team, cooped up in a London safehouse. I think we should request more men, more protection and, I don't know what the expense budget is for this operation, but it should be generous."

Kelly still had a familiar look of bemusement and was disheartened to the point of disinterest.

"Look, Chrissy, this situation is all fucked up. Neither of us should be here. We're trapped, Wolfy. And there ain't a goddam thing we can do about it. Like I said. They've got us by the balls! We're just going to have to take each day as it comes. Thanks for reading all that stuff, though, I'd never have been able to get through it on my own! Even if I wasn't fucking exhausted! But I agree with you, I think the only thing we can do, is see if Cork's guys have got some kind of plan. And if they don't, you're right! We got to fucking talk to Lord Cork and get some more answers, real ones. Because if they think that after three years finding nothing on this guy, you and I are going to come up with the goods just like that! It's fucking bullshit!"

Kelly now realised he was working himself up again and consciously tried to stop himself with a change of conversation, as he sensed that Wolf might be growing tired of his constant moodiness.

"But you know what, Wolfy? I don't want to hear any more about this fucking case anyway. We should try and make the best of this while we can, huh? I can see our food coming over. The weather's not great, but it's warm in here! I bet these British girls are hot. And we've got no competition! Because I've seen the British guys here and they're total pussies!"

As he said this, he made eyes at the young, girl-next-door looking barmaid presenting their food and continued to Wolf.

"Hey and that reminds me! What was with you and that chick at Cork's house anyway? She's fucking hot, I got to tell you. You and her, met before?"

Kelly's playful suggestion was bang on the money and Wolf hastened, with slight embarrassment, to explain the tale of Maya's deceptive alter ego, Veronique.

"Well, Captain Kelly, you know I never like to discuss these things in the open. Any intimacy shared between a man and a woman should, at least in some part, be kept discreet. However, as my trust was violated without compassion, it would seem, I suppose, that I should have no qualms in telling you that Miss Maya came into my life as a young and beautiful PHD student. I remember seeing her in the front row of my lectures and seminars a few times, before she began to approach me and ask questions. Her questions were quite intuitive, but looking back, I should have known. I was just besotted by her charm, her youth and her openness to an old man like me. It seems obvious now that she would make the first move, but yes, Michael, your suspicions are correct. Over a period of months, leading up to our appointment, Maya posed as a student, Veronique! To vet me and make sure I could be trusted. When I found out today, I have to say it was a total shock."

Kelly sympathised and laughed empathetically at Wolf, before chuckling a response.

"Wow! Chrissy! She totally played you, huh? Wow! That's amazing. So, you actually had sex with her! Fuck! Wow! I mean, Jesus. Why the fuck didn't I get that kind of treatment! That's amazing! I bet she was incredible. Or maybe not, maybe she was playing a part. I bet Maya's incredible, but was Veronique? Do you think she would have done that? Varied her sexual performance based on…"

Kelly realised that he was becoming a little personal and insulting and backtracked in his rhetoric.

"I mean, that's fucked up though, isn't it? And you never suspected anything?"

Wolf looked up from his dinner, mid-mouthful, and nodded as Kelly continued.

"Wow! That's amazing. That's pretty fucking good though! I'm kind of glad we got someone ruthless enough to do that working for us, you know? Hopefully she can reproduce that kind of deception on Harvey Walsh! I'm sorry though, bro! That must have been weird? I hope you didn't have like, fucking feelings for her or anything, did you?"

Kelly paused, to allow Wolf to finish his mouthful and respond.

"Nein, Michael, nein. I certainly did not love Veronique. It was not my love for her which shocked and hurt me. It was the fact that she managed to have me so fooled, so quickly, so easily. And more than that, now I look back at it, it was so obvious. I just think that a younger version of myself wouldn't have fallen for this. That's probably why they didn't try this on you. You'd be too smart for it! You know she just made me feel like an old fool and that's pretty much my worst fear! It's the reason I took this case! I am so paranoid about getting soft and losing touch as I get older."

Wolf now paused, to allow Kelly to finish off his current mouthful of fish.

"Well, from what I can see, Professor, you're a really smart guy! If this is you having lost touch, I'd like to have seen you in your prime! Sorry! I mean, I'm sure you haven't lost your fucking touch! I'm sure you're just as smart as you always were. I mean you read really well! And you talk fucking well too! Better than me! And English is my fucking first language! I really do think you're a pretty smart guy, Professor! Besides, err, how old are you exactly? Like eighty?"

Kelly laughed to himself, at his amicable jibe and Wolf responded in kind.

"No, Michael, I'm not eighty. I'm one-hundred and eighty. And sometimes I feel older!"

The couple continued to chat and drink, exchanging stories of cases and escapades past, until the evening drew into night and the pub thinned out. Having settled their bill with their new cards, they, merrily warmed by booze, pottered back to their new apartment building. However, as they passed the concierge, Bernie gave them a distinctly dirty look, unimpressed by the new recruits' inebriation. Undeterred and a little before midnight, the two found their way to the top of the lift, said their goodnights and retired in preparation for the morrow's promise of tribulation.

# Chapter 5

## AVRAM ABRAHAM SILVERMAN

Only mildly hungover, however, still acclimatising to their new surroundings, Wolf and Kelly made their way on foot, to their office in Mayfair from South Marylebone. Having been reluctantly invigorated by the bracing weather conditions en route, Wolf and Kelly arrived promptly and refreshed to their new office. They were greeted at the door by Maya, who accompanied them into their first-floor workplace. Once quickly settled, Maya started straight at them.

"So, guys! You should now be up to speed on Operation Harvey Walsh?"

She looked at the two, on either side of the room seated at their desks, and awaited response. Wolf saved Captain Kelly and answered for them both.

"Yes, Fräulein. We have had a chance to get up to speed on Harvey Walsh. We were hoping to speak with Lord Cork and also be brought up to speed on any current plans in motion that we are undertaking to find and identify the subject."

Maya looked distraught, disappointed and reactionary, as she responded.

"Actually, Professor, I was hoping you would be the ones coming up with the plans. And no one speaks to Lord Cork without Harry's say so..."

She paused and let her displeasure sink in before continuing.

"Okay, so you guys have nothing. Nothing! Really? You have no ideas whatsoever to do with Harvey Walsh. You must have something? What am I going to tell the guys downstairs? They're waiting for orders. What am I going to tell Harry? He's wanting to know your initial strategy and game plan?"

Wolf and Kelly looked insecure and shocked at this news. Kelly shuffled up in his seat and interrupted. "Wait, Douglas wants to know our plan? Oh! That's rich!"

The Professor was less flippant about Douglas's looming presence and enquired gently of Maya, "When is he coming?"

Maya rolled her eyes and stated the truth. "In about ten minutes."

Kelly reacted poorly to this bulletin. "What! Oh fuck! Shit, Professor! What are we going to tell him?"

The professor tried to remain calm and focus on the information he had been given on the case. He responded to calm his partner, yet again.

"Relax, Mike, it's all going to be fine. I will just ask Mr Harry Douglas some questions and hope that he relays at least some of it back to Lord Cork. I will also say that from what I can see, from the limited material we have been given, he is right! Captain Kelly and I are destined to fail! This man Harvey Walsh is a menace! And a menace far beyond any of us. We will surely need more resources and a larger team."

Maya still registered a lack of enthusiasm and was plainly unimpressed.

"Guys, do you really think Harry's going to like that attitude? What do you think he's going to say? Fuck, you're going to make him angry! Just say that you need a little time to work on it, but please, guys! You've got to give him something! Come on, Chris! Give me something or I'll get it too! I'm supposed to have prepared you both! Jesus!"

Wolf, immediately feeling guilty at his standoffishness and highhandedness, remitted further.

"Please, Fräulein. We do not want that! Michael and I have come up with a starting point! Of course we have! We have been analysing and discussing this case all night! We have found that this man, Harvey Walsh, penetrates all factions of criminal undertaking. Therefore, we thought it prudent to analyse the global criminal underworld as a whole, to try and diagram and understand any consistencies we could find. After all, Fräulein, how does one search for something that does not exist? You have to narrow down the parameters for search until you isolate your subject's activities to find a trail! We have, so far, only narrowed down Harvey Walsh to the criminal underworld. However, within the criminal underworld there is one thing that is rife throughout! A common denominator, if you will! And it is this, common denominator that is the essence of our nascence and indeed the basis of our starting point in this case.

"What I am talking about, Maya, is money laundering! Money laundering is at the centre of any and every criminal enterprise throughout the world! Nay, it is a necessity! This will be our starting point and will form the basis of our plan! We use our IT and Intelligence teams to penetrate money laundering systems globally like never before! Thus tracking and categorising major money laundering factions. Once we have this intelligence we will be able to spot any anonymous, strange and larger holdings or transactions. Eventually, we will find the money that Harvey Walsh must have accrued."

Wolf, pleased with his confident and pertinent speech, gazed triumphantly at Maya, who was still apparently less than impressed.

"Okay, well I guess that sounds a bit better than: 'we need more stuff'! But seriously! You guys must do better next time! Harry's going to eat you alive! So, simply, Professor Wolf, exactly how do you want to go about using money laundering to catch Walsh?"

Wolf cleared his throat and responded resoundingly.

"Simply, Fräulein, we find out who the biggest money laundering institutions in the world are, the real ones. And then we find out who they are working for. Anyone who remains truly anonymous and has sizeable holdings could very well be our target."

Maya cleared her own throat and nodded in vague approval. She then promptly turned and headed towards the door to leave. She glanced back before departing to bid them a frosty au revoir.

"Okay, I guess that's fine, guys. I'll be back up in a minute, probably before Harry gets here."

With that, Maya took her leave and left Wolf and Kelly to nervously anticipate the arrival of Lord Cork's executive enforcer. As she left, a welcome interlude emerged, as two Victorian maids entered with tea and toast. The pair busied themselves setting out refreshments on the desks, as Wolf and Kelly sat back comfortably. Though the maids had barely finished before shouting could be heard from downstairs. Looking to at each other as they heard this clamour, the maids made a rapid exit.

Wolf and Kelly were not alone for long, as a crescendo of uproar and fast-running footsteps approached their office from the stairs. As Wolf and Kelly heard the man, who was obviously Douglas, arrive outside their door everything went quiet. The door was opened gently, and Douglas allowed it, very deliberately, to swing open completely before he ventured in. Douglas walked in slowly and purposefully. He was somehow even more sinister and ghostly when calm and silent, than when in a bowling rage. He carefully and terrifyingly addressed his subjects.

"Okay, guys. Let me get this straight. Maya tells me you think we need more men and more money, to take on Harvey Walsh? And you want to talk to Lord Cork and ask some questions? Well fire away, because this is as close to Lord Cork as you're getting! But before you do, two things! Firstly, do you have any idea how much money, time and coordinated institutional effort has been invested into you two bozos! More than I'd care to think! That's how much! More than you would believe! Do you think those cards, phones and the equipment you've been given comes cheap! Do you think it's cheap to set up totally anonymous travel and communication for you both! For your own protection I might add! It costs us fucking loads and loads of money, fuckwits! So, no! You're not getting any more money or men!

"Don't you boys get it! Did you not listen to Lord Cork? Oh, I'm sorry this one's clearly simple!"

Douglas waved a tired, gesturing arm at Kelly as he turned his attention to Wolf.

"But you, Professor, I expected more! The whole fucking point of Operation Harvey Walsh is that it's supposed to be under the fucking radar. If we go and hire a load of guys and flash the budget everywhere! For your fucking nan to see! I'm mean that's what we were doing before and failing! The whole fucking point of this is fighting fire with fire! We need to stay small, covert and unregistered! Do you know how hard it's been to mask all of your funding so far? Fucking virtually impossible! That's how fucking hard, sonny Jim! God, you guys are fucking pissing me off! And you haven't even started! And that brings me on to my next point! Fucktards!

"Secondly! Maya said you said you've been up all night? Really working all hours! Cracking through the material! Justifying your grossly undeserved salaries! Wrong, you fucking cunts! You were out at a fucking wee bar in town last night! You fucking lying twats! Arseholes!

Don't you ever! Ever! Fucking lie to me again, understand! I will rip your fucking cocks off, stuff them up your arses and make you wish you'd never been born! And what's your big contribution after your and Captain Catastrophe's little piss up? Fucking money laundering is the key! As if we hadn't already thought of that! And I'm going to shut your stupid little fucking moronic plan down right here, right now! Tell me! What's the key to all successful money laundering? What is it! Answer me, you fucking cunts! Oh! I get it! Of Course! You don't fucking know! Because you don't fucking know anything! Do you! You're about as useful as glass in cocaine! I'll tell you what, guys, I'm going to tell you. Just to fucking put you out of your misery! The secret to money laundering, you fucking morons! Is that it's fucking secret! What fucking money laundering operation, makes itself available to the likes of us! None! Of course! You fucking arseholes! The whole fucking concept of money laundering is to hide activity from guys like us! How were you planning on getting this information!

"I love it! You guys have actually managed to find the one thing we just really didn't fucking want! More fucking anonymity! God, I already hate you guys! You two are going to be the death of me I can already tell!"

Wolf and Kelly were absolutely spellbound. This fanatical Scotsman could talk for the world and seemed to be able to simultaneously hold several arguments in his head whilst still, very quickly, being able to process new information. This man, though foul-mouthed in the extreme, would have made a fantastic advocate and was virtually unstoppable in his rhetoric.

"Look, I tell you what, guys. I can see you're totally overawed by this whole experience and maybe it's all just a bit much for you. I tell you what, I'm just going to fuck right off and see what Lord Cork's got to say about this fucking travesty of a commencement. I mean particularly you, Captain Twat! You put up such a fucking fuss and made such a song and dance about your fucking big break! We all knew, including your fucking pathetic little self by the way, that you were going to jump at this! Start acting like a soldier, you fucking useless piece of trash! And you, Professor, get off your fucking high horse! You're last year's old news, old man! Both of you need to buck your fucking ideas up! Go the fuck downstairs, listen, absorb! And try and fucking learn something from the team! Who've been working on this project, some of them, for fucking years by the way! Read! Your fucking material! Don't go out to fucking bars and get fucking pissed! This is not some fucking country stroll, ladies! This is proper secret mission, right! We're after a very fucking dangerous man! And the way you're going! You're going to get one of us fucking killed! You need to be fucking calculating! Fucking sharp! Fucking on your game! Not like a couple of floundering toddlers not fit for purpose!"

Wolf and Kelly remained in a stunned silence, gawping at Douglas.

"Alright, look, boys. I'm going now, and I'll be back later. But for fuck's sake! You're both probably going to be in a lot of trouble as soon as Lord Cork hears about this. But in the meantime, get your fucking acts together! Because right now you are a fucking embarrassment and that's just what I fucking told you, just fucking yesterday! I did not want to fucking see! I fucking knew it! You're both fucking arseholes!"

With that final utterance, Douglas stormed out and left the two to fearfully await his return. Wolf and Kelly remained seated behind their desks, as they silently recovered from Douglas's onslaught. After a short time, they quietly ventured downstairs to their team, in the hope of sympathy and counsel. Upon entering their main coms room, they spied Maya fixed on the large work station at the top of the room. They approached her and occupied the two vacant chairs to her left and right. Kelly spoke first to Maya as they sat.

"So, what the fuck was that, Maya? I don't think Harry's very happy with us. I think we're fucked! Lord Cork's going to pull us from the case!"

Kelly felt sure that Douglas was presently arranging for their dismissal. Maya, however, was used to Douglas's way and was more optimistic.

"Come on, Mike, it's not that bad! Besides, you guys got what you wanted, right? Harry is talking to Lord Cork. And is, no doubt, relaying what you said. Lord Cork is a smart guy. I'm sure he can distil Harry's negative edge. I wouldn't be too surprised if you got your wish. The guys here actually think it's quite smart, the whole money laundering thing. I mean yes, it is very hard to trace. But if you do, then you get a positive trail on his money. That could be a massive factor in monitoring his movements and maybe eventually finding him. Come on, guys, uh! Let's get Daniel and Josh over here."

Maya motioned to attract the attention of the IT and Intelligence Points and beckoned them over to her core workstation. Oppenheim and Hakimi both wore expressions of amusement in the knowledge that Douglas had just unleased himself on Kelly and Wolf. As they both approached the seated trio and stood over them gleefully, Oppenheim interjected.

"I see you've got acquainted with Harry? He's fun, ain't he? You, err. You chaps had a little idea, did you? Ha!"

He giggled loudly and abrasively to himself before resuming.

"Had a little idea of your own? I can just see it now! What! Maya, you should have been there to see it! I bet they were really confident before Dougie went in there! Ha!"

He giggled again harshly to himself and continued.

"He is really bad, isn't he? I mean. Let's be fair here, he can be terrifying. But you'd met him before? How could you not work out just from meeting him? I mean, you know. Don't fuck with this guy! Hello? Why didn't you guys do a bit more homework? Why did you go out drinking? Come on! I mean, that wasn't smart, guys, was it? That's all I've got to say. Except that I think that your money laundering idea is quite stupid. Yeah, quite stupid certainly. But also, in a way, quite brilliant as well. I just like to say that. Yeah..."

Hakimi, still smiling patiently and listening to Oppenheim, now chose this moment to express his admiration for Wolf and Kelly.

"Well, guys. I think that you guys are just great! I think it's great how you stood up to Harry and Cork! I think it's a great idea to go down the money laundering route. I can easily map and trace transactions from any account in the world as long as I have the right intelligence! Why not trace Harvey Walsh! Anyway, I think it's all great! And I think it's definitely something we should look into. I just hope Douglas doesn't napalm it before it's had a chance."

Maya, liking the vibe she was getting, wanting to soften the blow and isolate the situation should a dismissal have been imminent, suggested they enter Douglas's office.

"Okay, guys, I can see that we all think the money laundering angle is plausible. Why don't we get some privacy and brainstorm next door in Harry's room a little? We can do this until we hear further instructions or Harry comes back."

The group followed Maya out of the coms room and into Douglas's office. Harry's office was very similar in design, layout and décor to Wolf and Kelly's. It was located next to another of Lord Cork's, mostly vacant, offices; however, this office was not vacant. Inside was Douglas, who had not left the building since haranguing Wolf and Kelly. Douglas, on the phone, looked up from his desk, seeing the group storm in. He covered the mouthpiece of the telephone, on the other end of which was Lord Cork.

"Golden! Fucking! Rule! Snow White and The Four Retarded Dwarfs! Assumption is the mother of all fuck ups! I never left the building, fuckwits! Fuck off! Actually, don't fuck off! Get in here! I want to speak to you!"

Douglas aggressively hastened them in and the group clustered into Douglas's office in silence, allowing him to continue his telephone conversation.

"Yeah, okay, mate, well if you say so! No, yeah? I'll introduce them. I will. I will brief them and get them down there. Look, well if not Mr Fucking Big Bollocks, who is? Right, yeah! Fuck you too, your Lordship! Yeah okay, speak soon, speak soon! Ciao…"

Douglas hung up the phone and surveyed his subordinates with a deathly gaze. Satisfied with their bemused silence, he enlightened them on his interaction with Lord Cork.

"So, look it turns out that Lord Cork. By some miraculous and unfathomable mystery! Actually likes your idea. Not your fucking crazy suggestion to speak with him direct or get more of anything! But you whole money laundering malarkey. Yah, he actually wants to run with that! So, if you don't mind, I need to tell you guys exactly what to do. Alright, boys and girls."

He looked in search of obedient concurrence from his team and satisfied, continued.

"Right! So, you fucking twats might not know this. I'm talking to you, poor man's Stephen Hawking! And you, an even more retarded Chief Wiggum! Almost a year ago, a finance guy got fucked by a guy, who everyone in the criminal underworld thinks is Harvey Walsh. They know this guy as 'The Shadow', right! Now, this finance guy has offered up a reward. His fund got raided in broad daylight and a huge amount of money stolen. A nine-figure sum, gentlemen! Not fucking chump change! Now, this money was transferred anonymously, through offshore transfers. This finance guy! He has put out a reward of five hundred million for anyone who can successfully identify or locate the person who stole his money! We are one hundred percent sure that this 'Shadow' character is Harvey Walsh. We have been tracking the movements and interactions of this finance guy since this incident. His name is Avram Silverman and we've documented his various meetings with a veritable plethora of candidates putting themselves forward with theories on this 'Shadow' person! You'd both know all this, by the way, if you'd read your reports! And not been out last night like a couple of fucking frat boys!

"Anyway, the point is a few of these bounty hunters have actually succeeded in getting a sniff at Harvey Walsh. And they've still given us no real information and they've all been cold bloodedly murdered, of course, but you know. The point is this guy Silverman is quite possibly, in Lord Cork's mind, a veritable gold mine of information. This mine must be excavated, gentlemen. And that is where you come in.

"You are going to use the information we give you, to pose as bounty hunters. We will set up a meeting for you, either later today or tomorrow, and you'll forge a relationship with Silverman. Become his pal, get Kelly to suck him off, I don't care, right! Just get him to think you're on his side! And tell him you've gathered information on The Shadow! But whatever the fuck you do! Do not! Fucking give the game away! If he, even for a moment! Thinks that you're not a couple of gun slinging brokeback mountain bounty hunters! Then you're to get out of there immediately! We cannot have our cover blown! Particularly not by a couple of fucking namby-pamby fuck-twats like you two! Right, Captain Catastrophe, Professor Zimmer Frame! Crack on upstairs to your wee office! Fucking wait there and try not to fuck up! While me and the other adults talk and try and put some meat on this skeleton of a plan I've been given! Yeah! Go on! Fuck off!"

Douglas shouted Wolf and Kelly out of the room and resumed talking to the others, while the two team leaders left for their office to anticipate the nature of their first field mission. The pair waited in silent and nervous contemplation for about fifteen minutes, before they heard the familiar rumbling of footsteps outside their office. Douglas spun in, followed closely by a trotting Maya. The two had obviously come up with further details and Douglas began to impart his instructions.

"Right, so Mum and Dad have had a little chat and we think it's best for you two to go down and meet old Silverman first thing tomorrow morning. We're already arranging the meeting now, so that's already done. Now, you'll both be posing as bounty hunters as agreed! Do you think you ladies can do that? It won't be too hard for a couple of wee fairies like you? Well it better not be! You'd better fucking pull this off! Look at me,

I'm already getting pissed off! Your very presence is fucking me off right now! Do you know that! I was perfectly calm downstairs! Do you know that! Anyway, you're going to say that you've got an anonymous backer and that you basically are who you are! A couple of twats, Professor Wolf and Captain arsehole Kelly, hired by some crazy old rich guy, who by the way, you will say you've never met!"

Douglas thrust a parchment at Wolf before continuing.

"You will take this with you to his office, it's only down the road by the way! It's an agreement for him to sign. This will just be an agreement confirming the terms of his reward offer. This will be your in.

"You will now go away! And actually fucking read all the material you've been given! Then you will be prepared with information, not only on this guy, but on all the other bounty hunters who've been killed and all the other known information on Harvey Walsh! Then you might actually stand a chance of impressing this guy! As opposed to just turning up like the couple of fucking clueless twats you are right now! Fucking embarrassment!

"You will then! Once you have charmed him into thinking you're not total arseholes! Try and ask him about money laundering. Get him to open up a bit. Get this fuckface to spill his fucking guts to you on money laundering. Make him think that by telling you everything he knows about money laundering and its big players! He'll be helping you get closer to his precious fucking Shadow! Get as much info as you can, and your phones will be recording it all! Okay! Got that, morons!"

Douglas stepped back, putting his hands on his hips defiantly. He resumed, not awaiting a response.

"Right now, go on and fuck off home! You're fucking useless until you've read and understood all that brief anyway! Go on fuck off! Get out of my fucking sight! I can't bear to look at either of you right now! I'm so terrified you're going to fuck this up tomorrow! It's so simple! A fucking trained monkey could do this job! But I just know something's going to happen, you'll both find a way! That's the only thing I am fucking sure of! You'll find some way of fucking me!

"You see the truth is, Lord Cork actually likes your fucking money laundering idea! He's actually had the fucking confidence to throw you in to meet a guy! Who you should know! Is probably one of the most clued up guys on money laundering in the world! In fact, I wouldn't be surprised if he is directly involved in a bit of the old money laundering himself! So be fucking careful what you say! And make sure you do as much research as humanly possible on this fucking guy Silverman! Okay! Look! I am fucking begging you, guys! Please! Just please! Just try as hard as you can! Not to be your fucking selves! Just try and be someone who doesn't fuck up and disobey direct and simple fucking orders! Got that, fuck holes!"

Douglas glared at the pair, squinted in disgust at them both and turned to leave. He wafted, phantom-like out of their office, while Maya remained. She waited for Douglas to depart before reiterating his instructions to Wolf and Kelly.

"Okay, you guys, you heard Harry. It's time to go back to your apartments. And for God sake, it's like déjà vu or something! This time, read your material, know it! And be back here for nine o'clock sharp tomorrow. You'll pick up your bounty agreement and head over to Silverman's office. And try to relax! It really looks like you got away with what could have been a really bad start! Even though Harry's an asshole, Lord Cork's gone with your idea and this field mission seems pretty simple. You just have to be yourselves, except you're bounty hunters and instead of Harvey Walsh and Lord Cork, it's the Shadow and an anonymous rich guy you've never met. Now come on, guys! You better go now. You'll need all the time you can get! And don't worry, a bit later today we'll email your phones an encrypted and more detailed brief of the further details."

With that she left the two men in peace and returned to her core work station downstairs. Wolf and Kelly gradually, and still in slight shock, put their coats on and prepared to start out. They walked back through the crisp morning cold to their apartment building and settled down to read and absorb the remaining material on Harvey Walsh.

The following morning, Wolf and Kelly had arrived early and far more informed. They had been issued with their agreement and reminded once again of their instructions. They had arranged to meet with Silverman at his Mayfair office for ten-thirty. By the time the pair had settled and been fully briefed, it was time for them to walk down to Silverman's. Silverman's office was less than a mile away and the pair walked slowly through the streets of Mayfair, until they reached the edge of Grosvenor Square and neared the entrance to Silverman's impressive Victorian office building. Tutum Capital was the name, in fine ironmongery, across the entrance columns of Silverman's terraced Victorian townhouse. This was

Silverman's main investment club, which he had founded and built-up over years. The pair entered, trying not to be intimidated by the wonderfully maintained original Victorian wood panelling and brass piping. The décor was elegant and authentic, unlike many other ultra-modern and slightly scruffy looking similar establishments in the area. Located at the left of the entrance hall was a minute but tidy reception desk, behind which sat a steely receptionist. She addressed the two as soon as they entered.

"Good morning, gentlemen. How can I help you?"

Her tone was friendly but enquiring and the Professor answered officially.

"Good morning. We are here to see Avram Silverman. We have an appointment at ten-thirty. Christof Wolf and Michael Kelly?"

The receptionist relaxed a little and glanced quickly down at her appointments list, to confirm what she already knew. She smiled up at them and instructed them politely, "Okay, guys. Mr Silverman's office is on the first floor. There's a bench outside at the end of the hallway, you can't miss it. Wait on the bench and he'll call you in when he's ready. Let me know if you need anything else at all. Can I get you guys anything while you wait? Some water, tea, coffee?"

Wolf and Kelly, having already had ample refreshment back at their base, declined and made for the elegant, brass-lined, wooden stairway leading to the first floor. Atop the stairway, Wolf and Kelly looked to the end of the hallway. Sure enough, a long, leather-topped, antique wooden bench nestled between two decorative plant pots. The pair marched to the bench and took their seats, as instructed.

Moments later the double doors, to the left of the bench at the end of the hall, opened a crack and a head popped out. The head was scarred, experienced and sinister; though, somehow also kind, good looking and inquisitive. The face had dark, deep brown eyes and darker brows. His dark locks flopped down slightly over his face as his head pushed through the doors. He blew his locks up and over his eyes as he instructed the professor and captain.

"Morning, gents. Hope you didn't mind the wait. The general will see you now. Please come in. Would you like some tea, coffee, water perhaps?"

As he made these offerings he swung the doors open further to reveal his slight but athletic frame and expensive British-tailored suit. This man was full of contrasts in his appearance. As while his suit and its trimmings were perfectly presented, his face, hair and general aura was slightly slovenly and unkempt. Wolf and Kelly declined the offerings of refreshments once more and made their way further into Silverman's office.

The office, in keeping with the rest of the building, was beautifully arranged and proportioned, exactly as it would have been in its original creation. With a few essential modern touches, Silverman's office was a grand representation of an older and timeless Victorian design. Silverman himself was a stout, solid and stocky man. His hair was a very dark chestnut brown and combed back in a neat side-parting. He had a slight wispy stubble, even features and a pair of kind but piercing eyes. His eyes changed from the light amber colour on his outer pupil to a murkier brown towards its depths. He was dressed in a finely tailored, dark navy-blue suit. He was seated behind his grand desk facing the door, directly in front of a set of beautiful sash windows overlooking a green corner of Grosvenor Square. He spoke to Wolf and Kelly as they entered in a deep, nasal, north-London accent.

"So! Please come in! Come in! Yeah! Make yourselves at home! Yeah! So err, now we got that out of the way, why don't you start by telling me what the fuck it is you're doing here today? I mean it's just that, I think my offer is fucking simple, don't you, Jamie?"

Silverman looked to his colleague of contrasting appearance, who had let Wolf and Kelly in, but did not wait for a response.

"No, it's okay, Jamie. You don't need to answer that. These boys know it's simple! Don't you? You have come here today because you either don't trust me! Or you want something from me! Or! Probably most fucking likely by the way! Both! Now isn't that fucking right, gentlemen! Professor Christof Wolf! Captain Michael Kelly!"

Professor Wolf tried cleverly, to defer his motives back to his anonymous backer.

"Well, Mr Silverman. We are just acting under the instruction of our anonymous backer. We have been trailing this Shadow for a long time now and when we get close, our backer just wants to be sure of payment. That is all. Perhaps we can…"

Silverman did not allow Wolf to finish.

"Now wait a fucking minute there, Professor! I'm going to fucking shut that down right away, mate! You are your boss, mate! When you fucking take your salary and fucking sign your contract, mate! You accept the responsibilities that come with it! Don't fucking come in here and try and lie and deceive and manipulate your way around me! You're fucking insulting my intelligence is what you're doing! Look at Jamie here. When Jamie's at work, he knows he's representing me! So, he would never dream of saying to someone, for example, 'oh sorry, I know I'm being an arsehole but it's my boss!' because that would make me and him look like arseholes! Wouldn't it! So just fucking be honest with me, before I have Jamie fucking dump you and leave you at one of our refuse sites. Just admit right now you don't trust me! And then tell me what you fucking want!"

Wolf and Kelly looked at each other in an adrenaline fuelled calm and the professor responded, thinking quickly.

"Well, Mr Silverman. You are absolutely correct and I agree and apologise. My associate and I are here today to request that you confirm your offer, by signing our agreement which simply mimics your terms of remuneration and stipulates our immediate payment. We were also hoping to ask you a little bit more about how your money was stolen. We are tracing money laundering circles and believe we have found a link such that if we knew a little bit more about how your money was procured, it could lead us to a trail of the Shadow's activities."

Tailing off a little at the angry expression on Silverman's face, Wolf came to a halt and waited for Silverman to respond.

"Firstly, I don't know what the fuck you're talking about! Who the fuck is The Shadow? What the fuck is that? You're fucking looney, mate! Why mention that! Secondly, mate, even if I did know what you were talking about, I definitely won't be signing anything, mate! Go on then, let me see your little fucking contract!"

Kelly produced the agreement and passed it over the desk to Silverman. Silverman opened it up with one hand and rapidly skimmed through it. He then playfully raised his eyebrows to Wolf and Kelly before slamming it down on the desk and signing it. Having done this, he retorted, "Alright, there you go! I've fucking signed it! But I tell you, mate! It doesn't, still doesn't mean a fucking thing! What is your backer going to do if I don't pay him? What's he going to do? Send down his biggest and baddest? Send down you two? Maybe he'll take me to court? Either way, mate. It's all a joke yeah! Because even if he wins his judgement in court, yeah! Or his heavies come down here! All my fucking money's offshore anyway. No one can get to it, yeah! Un-fucking-traceable!"

Silverman paused momentarily, rotating in his chair and staring out of the window towards Grosvenor Square.

"To answer your other question. When my client's and my money was stolen, we were raided, and my men held at gun point. A guy holds a revolver to my colleague's head and makes him transfer these funds to an anonymous account, see! Yeah! Then they fucking shot my colleagues and fucked off! So, don't fucking come in here! And fucking challenge my fucking honour! Or ask fucking stupid questions! If you're so informed on the fucking situation, you should know this anyway! What are you, a fucking lemon! Jamie, do you know? I think these guys are fucking mugs! Do you know that! Alright so fucking talk to me now. I've signed your little fucking agreement! And by the way, you can trust that I will pay your fucking greedy little master! If he can do what needs to be done that is!"

The professor answered Silverman carefully and respectfully.

"Mr Silverman, thank you so much for understanding, and confirming your intentions to honour our agreement. We really did not want to get off on the wrong foot."

Silverman interrupted. "Well you sort of have done, mate! Don't give me sugar, mate! I fucking hate sugar! If you're giving me sugar, you're trying to manipulate me! Now you got my fucking signature! Now just fucking tell me what else you want!"

Wolf continued trying not to incur a further interruption.

"Well we would like to know as much as you can tell us about money laundering. As we believe that this is the key to the situation."

Wolf had been carefully trying not to directly allude to the Shadow again, as Silverman obviously wished to remain as discreet as possible with respect to his own involvement.

"You come in here! You insult me! You lie to me! You make me sign your agreement! And now you're telling me I've put myself through all of that! And you're banging on about money laundering! Of course, money laundering is at the fucking centre of everything! Doughnut! Don't say it like you've fucking invented fire, mate! Money laundering is at the centre of every criminal enterprise. From the bottom to the top, gentlemen. Money laundering is ever present. But you can't think that you can come in here and tell me to give you a list of investors who I think might be money laundering! And you can't tell me that anything I know about money laundering will make you any better off! Because, I would have thought it was obvious to men like you, if I knew something about money laundering, that could help my situation, I would have already fucking dealt with it!"

Silverman paused and exhaled before continuing in a calmer, more sympathetic fashion.

"Sorry, look, I know you boys mean well, I can see that. Even if you are a bit fucking shifty! We're on the same team I suppose. So, I will tell you this. If you do want to use money laundering to find your bloke, you'll need to penetrate the largest criminal organisations in the world. You'll need to analyse their movements, from the ground up. You'll need to examine everything, throughout all their operations. You'll have to travel the globe, my friends. You'll need to interview and speak to the gangsters. Some of whom have had their empires threatened, and in some cases, totally pull apart. Only then will you get close to figuring out a trail. And, gentlemen, I warn you. All the people who have taken this path before you, have let it consume them. Be mindful, boys. The closer they got, the greedier they got! The more risks they took! And always to a bad end! And still, old Abbsey is no closer to finding his man! So, Professor Wolf, Captain Kelly! I would suggest a good starting point would be to find out who runs the western world's major criminal institutions and try and find out what they know! Feel free to come back to me any time, you've got my number. But if you do come back and you want to leave with your life, I suggest you come back with something better than what you've come in here with today! Now if you don't mind, gentlemen!"

Silverman looked away from Wolf and Kelly, fixated on his computer and ignored the pair as they were escorted out by Jamie Segal, his associate. Segal passed Kelly his business card and smiled at him as they left the office. The office doors closed on Kelly as he noticed that Segal's card had writing on the back. The message said:

*"Be alone at Mount Street Gardens, W1. Eleven p.m. sharp."*

Wolf and Kelly returned to their base with their business card and its ominous message. They were welcomed by Maya; however, as they made their way to their office they could hear Douglas shouting from within. Douglas had been listening in on Wolf and Kelly's entire meeting and was less than impressed. Upon seeing Wolf and Kelly edge into their office, he immediately angled his abuse towards them.

"Oh! Here we are! The great return of the two stars to their wee dressing room, backstage! But I've got news for you, my leading ladies, the director's not very fucking happy, kids! Fuck me that was weak! You were like a couple of fucking school kids in there! You let him fucking boss you! He wiped his arse with your fucking agreement! He fucking hates you! He's fucking bullied you into submission! And now I can guaran-fucking-tee! That you are now both on his fucking radar! Which wouldn't be so bad, if you hadn't've made such a drastically shit impression! It's fucking lucky he hasn't made you already!

"Right, from now on these two fucktards need to be constantly accompanied! That's right! You are a two-man disaster-thon! You need to be constantly monitored to make sure this kind of thing, never happens again! So, on your next mission, I might just leave old Professor Bus Pass back at the fort, you're clearly not fit for battle! At least your wee girlfriend keeps her fucking mouth shut. You're so fucking arrogant, do you know that, Professor! You rub people up the wrong way! This guy Silverman's a real shark, he sees an intelligent academic like you and is immediately distrusting! And then, instead of at least trying to dumb yourself down or detract from this massive overbearing egotistical educational sophism! You make it worse! By speaking like you're at one of your stupid fucking lecture tours all the time! Stop speaking to people like they're fucking twats! It's going to get us all killed!

"So that's it! From now on Maya's going to be going with you both at all times! And for the next few outings, you'll be staying behind, Professor! You got that! So, don't think because you think you're more widely read or experienced than me, I'm not thinking and functioning on a level so far beyond your comprehension! It would hurt your wee brain just thinking about it! Fucking bookworm fuck!"

Kelly, having now fully recovered his jetlag, was firing on all cylinders and had been charged with adrenalin, following the morning's field mission. He had had enough of Douglas's personal and unnecessary insults and silenced him aggressively.

"Alright, sir, that's enough, okay! We get it! Go easy on Wolfy! You weren't fucking there, sir! You didn't see how it was! You didn't see what Silverman was like. You can't fucking talk to us like this! It was one fucking

meeting! We got him to sign the fucking contract and didn't break cover!
He answered our questions! Quite fucking openly! Considering he didn't
want to incriminate himself by talking about anything to do with Harvey
fucking Walsh anyway! And we got a secret fucking message from his
fucking guy! Telling us to meet at a secret fucking location tonight! So
now who's the fucking idiot! Who's an asshole now!"

Kelly produced the business card, with the message on the back, so the
whole room could see. Douglas was staring at Kelly as if about to jump
him. He squinted in hatred and envisagement, imagining how he would
destroy Kelly. Not able to endure any further, Douglas interrupted Kelly's
offensive. He was calmer, colder and unquestionably more sinister.

"Wait! Let me see that."

Douglas walked over to Kelly and snatched the card from him. He
examined it and read the message on the reverse of the card, before pausing
and turning back to Kelly and Wolf.

"Right, so, when were you planning on telling me about this?"

He paused again and menacingly glared at Kelly and Wolf, while
flicking and fiddling with the business card manically in his hands.
Meanwhile, he continued his verbal assault.

"Oh no, it's fine. We'll just keep things from old Harry all the time.
Yeah! That's fine, right! Keeping things from me, guys! Is keeping things
from Lord Cork! Your boss, my boss and someone who can make your
lives very fucking unpleasant! Do you understand me! When you receive
something like this message I'm fucking holding right now! You fucking
come back waving flags and screaming it from the hill-tops! You don't
fucking slink in here! Like a couple of fucking concealing cunts! And keep
this! Or any other fucking information whatsoever by the way! From me!
Or anyone else at this office! Do you not get it! We are a fucking tiny team!
The whole fucking reason! As I've told you a fucking million times now!
Is that it's fucking covert, ladies! Fucking covert! Fucking secret! So that
means we can share all! Fucking all! The information we get! That's how
we're going to catch Harvey Walsh Captain Fuckface! By immediately and
quickly sharing the information we get! As and when we get it! You fucking
saps! So just fucking don't do that again! Alright, ladies!

"Anyway, let's see! So, this guy James Segal gave you his card and it
says to meet him tonight at eleven? Right, well, you two better not fuck
this up like you did this morning! This is great, ladies! I am actually quite

fucking pleased with this! This actually means that Silverman might be letting you in here. He's a smart, fucking obsessively secure kind of guy! He clearly wants to meet you twats on a wee midnight date for a bit of fucking dogging! And by fucking Jove, ladies! You are going to fucking oblige!"

Douglas now addressed the rest of the room, consisting of point operatives Hakimi, Oppenheim, Maya and Lopez.

"Right so you heard, guys, you saw! Let's get everything ready for a second meet tonight at Mount Street Gardens! Come on, it's perfect! It's only up the road! Wolf and Kelly will try and extract as much information as they can by being nice little ladies! Unassuming ladies! Not fucking cocky! Not fucking offensive or standoffish! Fucking just like, normal! Fucking calm! Fucking smart! Fucking professional! Alright! Right, come on, guys! Let's leave these two sorry fucks to get their fucking simple heads around actually coming through on this little bit of luck! Chins up, lads! This might just have saved you."

With that, Douglas led the troop out of Wolf and Kelly's office and down the stairs to the meeting room. As he left, he barked a further few words of caution to Kelly and Wolf.

"You're informed! You're trained! You can't rely on luck forever, ladies! Tonight, we're going to do our bit! You just make sure you do yours!"

# Chapter 6

## JAMIE SEGAL

**M**ount Street Gardens was the perfect place for a secret meeting in Mayfair. It was totally cocooned on all sides by beautiful, redbrick, Victorian mansion blocks. It also had plenty of little passages and pathways in and out. It was solitary but public, and was littered with clean, unpopulated benches. Wolf and Kelly had approached the gardens from the north side, which had two access points from side alleys off Mayfair's Mount Street. This chilling, gothic, yet somehow idyllic area was well lit and the pair immediately spotted their target sitting alone smoking a cigarette a little way to their left. Segal was quietly and unassumingly sitting cross-legged among a row of benches facing the church, at the north east corner of the gardens. Wolf and Kelly ventured closer and took a seat on Segal's bench. Segal waited for the pair to get comfortable before engaging them. He spoke with a slightly polished, but unmistakably southeast London twang. His mannerisms were odd and pronounced, while his entire aura was that of an individual who had punished their mind and body with sex, intoxicants and violence.

"Good evening, gentlemen, good evening. I'm sorry I've had to drag you out from your beds on this awful and positively freezing London night! It's just we can't have any loose ends, gentlemen! If you catch my drift? You do understand that most of the men who have gone after The Shadow, or those who have even been involved with him, in any close capacity, have all been killed. So, it is not just for our protection but for your own, that we must be discreet in the utmost when discussing anything at all to do with The Shadow.

"Now, gentlemen, I must tell you that Abs has sent me to meet with you here, alone and in secret, to promise that he will pay your bounty, once you locate and identify The Shadow. And furthermore, he will help you as best he can in your quest to find said Shadow."

Remembering what Douglas had instructed and that he was listening intently to their conversation, Kelly and Wolf remained silent and allowed for Segal to continue.

"Abs will start, by helping you with a little bit of information and my private contact details. Here you are, you can have that. Take it. Go on."

Segal passed Wolf another business card, this time with a mobile number on the back. Wolf inspected the card briefly before pocketing it, as Segal resumed what was to be a long and informative speech.

"That's my private mobile. Call me when you need to, gentlemen, but don't incriminate yourselves when you do. You never know who's listening. Can't be too careful. Always try and keep it face to face and in the great outdoors to be sure, gentlemen. Alright, so Abs also wanted me to impart to you fine bounty hunting gentlemen that your next step should be to find out all you can about a little lady, well she is actually a Lady! Called her Ladyship, Lady Victoria Garrington.

"If you'll allow me to explain, elaborate and divulge, gentlemen. I will tell you, that to have the slightest chance of trailing The Shadow, you know! Because Abs told you this morning! You will have to get your heads around how organised crime really works. So, in case you were in the dark about this subject and I'm sure you're not. But just in case you were! Let me fill you in a little on the basic principles.

"Okay so, you can basically split criminal enterprise up into three sectors. And within these sectors you've got sub-sectors. Some of these sub-sectors or factions will interweave and swap between the three sectors but, there are three core sectors. So, gentlemen!

"Firstly, you've got sector one. That's whores. Within the whore sector, you've got the two core sub-sectors, or factions, of prostitution and human trafficking. Now the whore sector is present all over the globe and is the oldest of all organised criminal enterprise. Today, the main controlling influence is in Eastern Europe. For assorted reasons, geopolitical and otherwise, that area is perfectly placed for trafficking and prostitution from all continents. Maybe it's because it's sort of in the middle. I don't know. But it's irrelevant, darlings. Why question what already is, that can't help you I say!

"Anyway, the next sector is white-collar. The white-collar sector is made up of three core sub-sectors, or factions, similar to the whore sector. These factions are insider trading, gaming, match-rigging, and cybercrime. Again, similar to whores. This, more modernised form of criminal enterprise, has been engrained all over the world. However, currently the controlling influence on this sector is chiefly located in the United States and Russia. Again, don't ask me why, it's just worked out that way. Maybe they just have the financial and cyber infrastructure on their doorstep over there? Who knows?

"So, the final sector, gentlemen, is the naughtiest of all the three sectors and that is the conflict sector. The conflict sector is actually the largest of all the three sectors. And the conflict sector, accordingly, is made up of not two, not three, but five sub-sectors, if you will. These factions are, contrary to whores and white-collar, more geographically diverse. First of the five, you've got your drugs and narcotics trade. No prizes for guessing what dominates that trade. Yes, that's right, gents. The drugs business is largely influenced by the production and distribution of cocaine. Hence, the power and influence resides mainly in Peru and Panama, where the production and distribution of cocaine is currently at its highest. Then, secondly, you've got arms dealing. This, again don't ask me why, although prevalent throughout the world, seems to be controlled by a few individuals who run their businesses out of South-Eastern Africa. Then for some reason, the third and fourth factions of the conflict sector, are both headed up in Switzerland. You've got theft. The thieves! Good old-fashioned robbers! Then you've got smuggling, fourth. Maybe it's the anonymous bank accounts? Again, gentlemen, who knows? It just is what it is! The fifth faction of the conflict sector, gentlemen! And I hope I am not confusing you here! Is protection. And the power in protection comes with money that enforces it and that is held, for the most part, in London. London offers the financial protection that funds rackets around the globe.

"It is this last point that makes your money laundering scheme quite plausible, gentlemen. For as I have just told you, and as you probably already know, most criminal kingpins worth their stripes will have most, if not all, their ill-gotten gains, invested safely in London banks, property and funds! If not directly, gentlemen, then indirectly! Now while innocent, law abiding businessmen, such as Mr Silverman and myself, are given money to invest and comply completely with the law in every capacity, we are doing nothing wrong and have a duty to our clients of confidentiality and non-disclosure. However, we are also reasonable men, who have a little bit more than common sense, when it comes to an individual's finances. We are also reasonable men, in the capacity of finding and bringing to justice, those who have robbed and betrayed us. We even more reasonable men than that my friends, in helping and assisting those whose motives mirror our own.

"So, to that end, gentlemen! We can tell you who the major crime-lords are. We can tell you how much they've got and pretty much where it's bloody come from. Most of them are our clients! With whom we have total trust. They are totally open with us about the nature of their businesses. They damn well have to be! They're asking us for bloody advice on how to safely hide their spoils! In that respect, gentlemen, we are perfectly positioned to assist you. And it is in that vein of mutual motive and respect, that I impart the following about our friend Lady Garrington."

Segal in full flow, now reached into his pocket for another cigarette, which he smoothly kindled and began to smoke as he went on.

"Lady Garrington is as aggressive, brazen and harsh a criminal as you ever will find! Execute a man in a heartbeat she will! Cold-blooded killer she is, gentlemen, make no mistake! Victoria is very beautiful, nay stunning! She's a bit older now, but in her youth! There was no model, no other woman, as could match her looks and charms! She captivated the hearts of men in her twenties and eventually married a cocaine kingpin from Brazil. With Vicky at his side this man was invincible. Her highly educated English class and ruthless intelligence were no match for the South American narcotics trade. After ten years, though, her partner grew lazy and I believe a little podgy. Either way, she began to tire of her husband. Eventually he became totally emasculated and she began to have affairs with his colleagues and staff. Another few years went past. Victoria and her lovers plotted and executed a plan to supplant her husband and take his business. However, little known to her lovers and her husband, she had also been doing secret and private dealings with another more powerful cartel in Peru. She arranged to partner them in production, while she would arrange distribution for a virtual fifty percent share in the global cocaine trade. She arranged, not a week after her lovers had buried her husband, for the Peruvians to, in turn, supplant and dispatch with her lovers! Thusly, she assumed the command of cocaine distribution across the majority of The Americas.

"Since her rise to such formidable and lofty power she has endeavoured, partly on our wise instruction I might add, to make herself as publicly respected as possible. Hence her marrying of Lord Garrington. A kind and wealthy peer of a powerful family. He's a total arsehole if you ask me! But after all, it always pays to have someone like that as your husband, if you're trying to protect an international billion-dollar drugs empire. However, the point is, she's been losing her market share to this Shadow character! Her gangs, her routes, her trucks and her dealers are all being compromised. She's having money stolen left, right and centre. As if that wasn't bad enough, she suspects her husband knows something about The Shadow from the government's new involvement in his activities over the past three years or so. She's even been trying to use her husband to get inside government knowledge on The Shadow.

"It is Abs' and my belief, gentlemen, that you should, as I said just now, find out as much as possible about this woman, Victoria Garrington. She will be more informed than anyone else on The Shadow and his whereabouts. She should be your starting point."

Segal had now finished and thrown away his cigarette. He was plainly cold and wanted to cut proceedings to be as brief as possible. He rose shakily from his huddled seat on the bench and bid farewell to Wolf and Kelly.

"Right, gentlemen, I bid you goodnight. My apologies again for pulling you out in the cold! Good Luck!"

Eccentrically, Segal kept muttering to them as he walked away, allowing his soft voice to melt inaudibly into the night. Wolf and Kelly waited silently until Segal had peeled into a side passage and out of sight, before hastily making their way back to the office. They had found their way back onto Mount Street when the Professor's phone rang, and he answered. It was Douglas.

"You see, Professor! You see what happens when you keep your little wee mouth shut! That was great! Just great! A great meeting! And guess what! Your new friend Jamie's bang on! You are both going after this Victoria Garrington first thing tomorrow. And I'm especially pleased about that! Do you know why? Because Lady Victoria Garrington, while she's got houses all over the world, apparently, she's sailing in Mexico at the moment. So, you can both fuck off and get out of my hair for a bit! And remember just keep shutting up and then you won't be fucking up!"

Douglas hung up the phone and Wolf and Kelly returned, as instructed, to their apartment for the night, frozen and confused.

# Chapter 7

## LADY VICTORIA GARRINGTON

**H**aving touched down at Cancun International, Wolf, Kelly and Maya were immediately exhilarated and lured from any fatigue by the sun-drenched shores of Mexico. Taking the costal route, they were driven by Lopez down to their destination, a small village near Playa del Carmen. The pleasant, if somewhat commercialised, Maya Riviera flowed by as the quartet made their way south. Keeping a safe distance behind, was the rest of Lopez's operations team. John Beacher, Pierre DeVeron and Patrick Jenner had been ordered to protect and tail their leaders throughout their overseas field mission.

Lady Garrington had been sailing in the Caribbean and Gulf of Mexico for the past three months. She did this to while away the European winter. As a drug-Queen with a controlling stake in the distribution of cocaine across the Americas, she found it best to sail when not in the sanctuary of developed Europe. Her logic was that a constant, shark-like, devotion to motion would make it far easier to evade her numerous enemies. Garrington had moored a vessel of hers outside one of her luxury holiday resorts. Complete with an entourage of viciously competent heavies, she had spent the last week or so admiring the coral and indulging in fresh local cuisine. As she had been relatively stationary for a time, Oppenheim and Hakimi had been able to triangulate her position and form a rough game plan. Under the same guise as was used with Silverman, Maya had arranged for Wolf and Kelly to meet with Lady Garrington, masquerading as bounty hunters in pursuit of The Shadow. They would get as much information as possible on Garrington herself, as well as whatever she knew on Harvey Walsh.

Lady Garrington's resort consisted of a network of serviced villas, spanning a strip of beach front and roughly half a square-mile of land behind it. The resort's beachfront had two jetties for water sports and mooring. The beach itself was sparsely populated by beach loungers and a few high-brow tourists. Near a captivating section of coral, which ran very close to the beach, was the largest and finest villa in the resort. This was Lady Garrington's private residence. Further detached from the other buildings, Garrington's beach-house was, to say the least, well equipped. Set back from its private beach, the villa's high lined hedgerow encased a modest swimming pool. A stone pathway led past the pool area to the main house. Painted all white and set on three levels, this virtual mansion exceeded six thousand square feet. It was endowed with a media room, a three-car garage, a sauna and steam room, a small gym, as well as a lavish glass elevator.

Garrington had been spending her days waking up late. She would sunbathe and take a quick swim, before heading down to her beach restaurant. She had a private area set up at the back of her restaurant, where her men could monitor all access points. Here, around lunchtime, she would eat breakfast. She would then typically head back to her lodgings to rest and consume a number of intoxicants, before venturing back out in the late afternoon. Handbag stuffed with further recreational and prescription drugs, she would later strut out around six in the evening. Garrington would walk through the beachside paths and explore the local bars and clubs. She tended to go for older, married tourists and younger, more vigorous locals. Either way her Ladyship would habitually take at least one lover back from her evening escapades. She would normally take them back to her annexe. This was a detached coach house she had plumbed-in and converted into a private play room. Having had her fill of the night's offerings she would usually slink off to her master suite, leaving her guests to find their own way or be shown out, by her ever present and watchful henchmen.

Although Garrington knew she would be receiving company that day, she had not gone to any great lengths to prepare herself. She had only really made sure not to stay out past two and to be asleep by sunrise. Otherwise her routine had remained unbroken. Hence, as Wolf and Kelly now drew very close, Lady Garrington was still sunbathing in between sleep and consciousness. Her arm was cast over her eyes, blocking them from the beating sun, as she lay sun-kissed and melting into the grass. Her deep, dark-brown locks lay spread to the left of her head and her naturally large and puckered lips flapped with her heavy and lethargic breaths. Her eyes, though covered by her glistening olive arm, were a fabulous chocolatey-amber colour. She had a generous hour-glass figure and while her stomach lapsed with relaxation, her paunch did not hang over her bikini bottoms. Lady Garrington was roused from her lazy slumber, however, by the sound of radios buzzing and her henchmen's bustling activity. Knowing this was her appointment with Wolf and Kelly, she loosely and gracefully flipped herself up and made for the pool. She dove in and swam a few quick lengths, before retiring to her master suite to dry off and prep for her visitors.

Roughly two miles prior to reaching Garrington's resort, Maya had hopped out of the car and been picked up by the ops team. Wolf, Kelly and Lopez were to continue alone, under the premise that Lopez was their driver and would wait outside. Wolf and Kelly would go in together and hope to both get out alive and informed. Having dropped Maya, the trio were at the resort's entrance in moments. The entrance itself was innocent enough with no real barrier to entry, other than a set of impressive open gates. However, as the group entered they spotted that the driveway led to a small security tower surrounded by guards. Lopez tentatively feathered the throttle down the drive and towards the security tower. As the three approached, the guards organised themselves, stubbing out cigarettes and marching inside. Lopez gradually pulled the car to a halt outside the tower and waited. A taller, more menacing security officer, dressed all in black, approached their car and tapped on Lopez's window. Lopez obliged, let the window down a little and attempted a friendly interchange.

"Yeah, you know why they're here, right?"

Lopez pointed to Wolf and Kelly behind him in the back of the car.

"That's Professor Wolf. And that's Michael Kelly. We're here to see Lady Garrington? Hablo ingles? Where can I park, guy?"

The tall man in black heard Lopez but did not offer reply. Instead, this sinister looking man walked away from the car and down a path leading towards the centre of the resort. Lopez and his colleagues in the back were confused and insecure to the point of calling for backup. However, another less intimidating security guard approached the car while on his radio. He leant down and spoke to Lopez in a thick, but welcoming, Spanish accent.

"Hi guys! Can you guys get out of the car please?"

Wolf, Kelly and Lopez exited the vehicle, as ordered, and awaited further instructions. The guard, having got them out of their car, also promptly retired away and yet another, more senior looking guard, emerged from the security tower. He addressed the trio directly.

"Bueno. Hola guys. I hope you had nice trip? Lady Garrington will see you shortly. But first, amigos, I must make sure of a few things, before my friends with rifles aimed at your heads right now will, you know, amigo! Pull the trigger..."

This man was older and more experienced than the other guards and spoke good English. He had clearly been instructed to debrief and security check her Ladyship's guests. He continued to ask them a selection of rhetorical questions.

"Now, guys, I am going to ask you a few questions. There should be no answer to these questions, only action, if you understand my meaning. Firstly, I am going to assume that you have no weapons and that there are no weapons in the car?"

Lopez quickly rolled his eyes and smiled at the guard, before pulling out and placing down his numerous concealed weapons. Satisfied that his point had been fulfilled, the guard resumed his questioning.

"Secondly, gentlemen, I am going to assume that you have no surveillance or malware equipment with you?"

The three looked at each other and shook their heads.

"Okay great. So thirdly, you guys won't mind if I ask you all to turn your phones off and leave them in the car?"

This time all three men rolled their eyes and smiled, as they removed their phones and threw them on the back seat of the car. The guard continued.

"Bueno, amigos! Now you have been officially neutralised, sí! So now fourthly. I am going to inform you both, that while you are on The Lady's land, you will always have a rifle aimed squarely at your head! So seriously, guys, no funny business. Now, Professor Wolf, Señor Kelly, if you would follow me. We need to search you both, before you meet with Mistress.

Mr Lopez, if you wouldn't mind waiting in here with my security team, while your friends conduct their meeting?"

The guard beckoned Wolf and Kelly to follow him and pointed Lopez into the security tower. Wolf and Kelly trailed the guard down the main pathway, through to the centre of the resort and towards the beach. As the pair began to catch glimpses of the beach, through the thickets and shrubbery in between the villas and pathways, the guard stopped in front of a vacant looking villa and ushered Wolf and Kelly inside. Once inside, the pair were strip-searched at gunpoint without compassion or ceremony. Having now been totally convinced of the pair's neutrality, the guard led them back out of the smaller villa and down to the beach. As the three men reached the oceanfront, the guard stopped again and turned to speak.

"Okay, guys, so over there to your left is Mistress' house, but I think she will be in her restaurant by now. So, you see down the beach there, that's her restaurant. Go to the waiter and he will show you to her."

With that, the guard turned and left them the way they had come. Wolf and Kelly ventured onto the sand, still trying to shake off the insecurity of being strip-searched and totally voided of effects. This was the unchartered and unassisted territory that both men knew could result in their demise. However, both men attempted, as best they could in the circumstances, to look confident and relaxed. They allowed for the sand to slow their pace to an amble, and gradually made their way, squinting through the sun, towards Garrington's restaurant. The establishment itself was mounted on teak decking over the beach. A white, canopy-like, all-weather cloth formed the restaurant's roof and allowed for a breeze to permanently flow through. The tables were all covered and classically made up with formal silverware and china flower pots. Towards the back, past the striking brass-railed bar area, nestled Garrington's private room. A white curtain, in front of which two bodyguards stood, segregated her from the rest of her diners. Behind the curtain was a scattering of lavish sofas and loungers and in the centre lay a ten-seater table fully dressed for dinner. Apart from the curtain at the front of her area, the sides and back were totally open to the elements. However, the sides were flanked by fans and large decorative plant pots, while the rear of her private room was curtailed by bamboo and several large palm trees. A further six men stood guarding the sides and rear of this area, while behind the table's head, at the back of the room, was a large trunk, brimming with automatic weapons and long-range artillery.

As Wolf and Kelly drew nearer to the restaurant they began to make out the almost goddess like silhouette of Garrington's figure. The restaurant was almost completely deserted but for a few old couples, and Wolf and Kelly's attention had been immediately drawn to the rear of the establishment. Behind two large bodyguards and a small line of head-height plant pots sat Garrington, dressed all in white, sitting cross-legged and smoking a cigarette. Wolf and Kelly elected to enter the restaurant via the front and greet one of the waiters, as instructed. As the couple stepped up and onto the fine wooden decking, a waiter promptly welcomed them.

"Please, hola, señores! Welcome, how can I help you?"

Wolf smiled at the waiter and responded cordially, "Good morning, this is Captain Michael Kelly and I am Professor Christof Wolf. We have an appointment this morning to see Lady Victoria Garrington."

The waiter responded by turning and walking the pair to the guarded white curtain. The guards grumpily parted, pulling back the curtain-tails as they did so. Garrington's thick wavy locks floated in the blasting fans and she sat, still cross-legged and still smoking, at the head of her table. She was dressed in a white dressing gown under which remained her orange bikini. On the table in front of her was a glass of Bloody May and a cappuccino. Eerily, although she was surrounded by her bodyguards, she appeared quite alone in her thicket of private luxury. Her men appeared to avert their gaze, focussing not on her but on potential dangers ahead. Wolf and Kelly stared, intimidated and impressed, at the highly successful and beautiful Lady Garrington in her element. Her crescented, contoured and deep-set eyes, flashed across and up at The Professor and Captain Kelly. Noticing their hapless and fatigued gaze, she allowed the corners of her mouth to flex and curl flirtatiously, turned her head and raised her eyebrows with enquiry. She greeted them with a deep, thick and sensual received pronunciation.

"Good morning, gentlemen."

She smiled, knowing what they had just undergone, took a sip from her coffee and another drag from her cigarette. Wolf and Kelly were still stunned and stood gawping at her ladyship, who uncrossed her legs to face them and continued playfully.

"But where are my manners. Please, sit! Relax! I know it's early, but would you care for a drink?"

She paused again and stared at them, while taking another long seductive puff on her cigarette. Kelly, already totally enamoured of her Ladyship, spoke first.

"Yeah sure I'd like a drink, lady. That'd be nice. I could sure go for like a nice Mojito or something right now."

Herself a seasoned alcoholic, Garrington was glad of a drinking companion and immediately responded gleefully, making eyes at Kelly.

"Good choice. And you, Professor?"

The professor hesitant to drink so early in the afternoon, modestly retorted, "Oh, err, you are so kind, Lady Garrington, perhaps just some iced mineral water, if it's not too much trouble?"

Slightly disappointed with the professor's aversion to alcohol, she snapped slightly back at him, as if to suggest Wolf was being overly obsequious.

"No, it is not too much trouble. Alvaro! Another Bloody Mary, a classic Mojito and a bottle of sparkling mineral water, San Pell!"

As she barked into the air at Alvaro, the invisible servant, rustling was heard at the bar behind the closed curtains. Hearing the rustling and satisfied that her orders were received, she continued.

"Would either of you care for a cigarette?"

Having now finished the majority of her last, she lifted a pack of cigarettes from the table and withdrew another. Closing her eyes and jostling her head, to flick her hair from the lighter's flame, she lit-up and reclined with her first inhalation. As her spine hit the back of the chair, she exhaled and gently tossed her lighter back on the table before speaking further.

"So, you two are after The Shadow, La Sombra de la Muerte! You realise you have no chance, right? I mean no chance. Zilch! I think you're both very sweet. But compared to him. I'm afraid you guys don't quite match up. You know he's like a beast, right? I mean this guy kills people for fun, at will! Without detection! And en masse! The fucking CIA and FBI can't catch this guy. They can't even fucking identify him! Let alone catch him! How do you two minnows? And I don't mean to call you that. But I'm sorry, you are fucking minnows in this world, honey! How can you two minnows expect to stand a chance against someone like the Sombra de la Muerte!"

She laughed in a deep piercing bellow, took another quick drag on her cigarette and resumed.

"Okay so I am dying to hear this! It's the only reason why you're here actually. I'm fucking curious! Firstly, to meet you both, particularly you, Captain Michael Kelly."

As she said this, she shot a coy glance at Kelly, who blushed in turn as she addressed him and Wolf.

"Secondly, I am dying to hear your grand plan, or whatever! I just want to know how you two think you're going to survive against this guy! Let alone find his identity!"

Ever distrusting, never underestimating and always questioning, Lady Garrington changed her tone to a more serious and prying one.

"Unless, of course, there's something you're not telling me? You are bounty hunters, are you not? Has that crook Silverman sent you here to throw me off? Talk to me, chaps, you're both very quiet?"

Wolf and Kelly looked at each other and Wolf interjected.

"Lady Garrington, contrary to what you might think! We are not dangerous or hostile men. We are not mercenaries, guns for hire or anything as such."

Lady Garrington raised her eyebrows and her pupils widened as she heard Wolf's utterance. She interrupted, swallowing her mouthful of Bloody Mary.

"Well I'm going to have to disagree with you there, Professor!"

As she said this, Alvaro emerged through the curtains with the drinks and, laying them out on the table, swiftly exited. Garrington paused before elaborating, to admire Alvaro as he administered the drinks and made his leave.

"I actually happen to think Captain Kelly here is a very dangerous man indeed. Had it just been you, Professor, I would not have stationed twelve snipers to track you and your colleague. Had it just been you, Professor, all manner of measures would have been dropped. Incidentally, I do hope Hector was gentle with you. But, Captain Kelly, having read your record, I expected more! I mean wow! You are quite the man, Captain. I guess it's always the small, unassuming ones that are the most vivacious. I mean, judging from your past experiences, Captain, you're just as dangerous without a weapon as with one! I mean did you really escape three times from the same Iraqi prison? Because, I was looking over your file and I saw the same prison come up three times. I couldn't believe what I was reading, you know!"

Kelly nodded humbly and smiled like a child receiving a gold star from their teacher, as she continued.

"I knew it! Oh my god! You are fucking dangerous! Really fucking dangerous. Don't try and tell me, Naughty Professor, that you're not dangerous, when your partner clearly is! Give me no lies and you'll get none back, Professor!

"So, we've covered the first point, honey-babies. You're plenty dangerous, I appreciate that. But you're just nowhere near as dangerous as he is, dearies! I mean, you're not even on the spectrum. But go on. I'm sorry, I'm really bad! Please! Pray continue, I promise I'll be quiet."

Wolf, now very guarded in his speech, attempted a fresh start.

"Lady Garrington, we are not your average, run of the mill bounty hunters. We have been handpicked to work together by a backer who, similarly to The Shadow, is hugely wealthy and anonymous, even to us. We intend to successfully identify and locate our target, whatever you want to call him, precisely because we are a small, specified, micro-unit. We can fly under the radar, unseen and anonymous just as The Shadow does. We may not be as big as him, but that's just how we intend to conquer him."

Lady Garrington rolled her eyes and dryly interrupted.

"Huh! I've heard that before."

Wolf, however, continued unfazed.

"We are gorilla bounty hunters, if you will, Lady Garrington. We feel that to look for a shadow, you must inhabit the shadows. And that is precisely what we do. Yes, my colleague is more than capable of protecting himself. However, our modus operandi is based on intelligence and not conflict. We prefer to study, rather than to engage. And it is in this capacity, that we are here this fine afternoon, Lady Garrington. The next step in our bid to identify and locate The Shadow is to learn as much as we can about the trade and distribution of cocaine. And in particular, Lady Garrington, how The Shadow is affecting it. And it would appear, Lady Garrington, that there is no better placed person than yourself, to assist us in this endeavour."

Wolf paused and tried to gauge Garrington's reaction. She looked unimpressed and, taking a sip of her Cappuccino, interjected.

"Come on, guys! I've got to say: this is sounding pretty fucking pathetic. I mean, you guys lurk in the shadows! Waiting to pounce on The Shadow! I mean, come on! That's fucking ridiculous! Right? Am I right? You guys still haven't told me how or why that bandit Silverman's got your backer after his bounty. Or how you really intend to find him! Please chaps! Quid pro quo! You've got to give Mummy a little something if you want something in return! I'll tell you what, guys. I'll tell you all about the coke trade and how it's all going to shit! If you tell me, how you intend to use that information to find The Shadow!"

She sat back and crossed her legs triumphantly. Picking up her cappuccino, she brought it to her lips as she reclined, to savour its last few drops to accompany the words of the challenged Professor.

"Okay, Lady Garrington, I suppose fair is fair. I don't suppose there is any harm in telling you a little more about our operation. Certainly, if it will help you to trust us further and help us to know what you know.

"Essentially, having been commissioned by our anonymous backer, we have been researching and gaining as much intelligence as we can on the activities of our target. Having failed, quite spectacularly, to find a credible source for direct contact, we have been forced to seek alternative avenues of inquiry. In fact, it was only recently that we actually felt it necessary to contact Silverman, having had a breakthrough. This breakthrough came, when we found that we could, using the resources we have available, isolate the activities of The Shadow using money laundering.

"This sounds obvious; however, Lady Garrington, it is not. The crux of our investigation centres around matching financial accounts to criminal activity. This is a complex and academic process that, even with the best programmers and cross-referencing algorithms, takes a long time. However, we intend to do the following:

"We intend to learn, from people such as yourself whose business has been directly affected by The Shadow, exactly how much your revenues have been redacted. Then, once we have a reasonably accurate representation of how much market share has been lost, we can try and match that amount to our money laundering figures. We also have an 'in' so to speak, in that our computer scientists and fund managers, including of course Mr Silverman himself, are able to provide us with accounts and figures for most major money laundering operations throughout the western world.

"This sounds pretty complicated and technical! And it is! However, providing we can estimate exactly how much someone like yourself, Lady Garrington, has lost with reasonable accuracy. Matching this amount with incoming funds into offshore money laundering channels should work. Then, once we have identified the monies, we can track its movement and source its destination accounts. This will, in turn, bring us to the location of the shadow. Or, at the very least, the location of his ill-gotten gains."

Wolf, feeling that he had given a reasonable and credible explanation, relaxed in his seat and waited for Lady Garrington to respond. However, as Wolf had been talking, the tall man dressed all in black who had briefly approached their car at the entrance, had been making his way down the beach and towards Garrington's private room. This man was Sergio Zola. Zola was Garrington's head honcho. He was an authentic Sicilian who had converted in his twenties from the military to organised crime. In his thirties, Zola had become heavily involved in narcotics and protection in Italy. Having ascended the ranks of a South Italian cartel, he had spent much of his time in South America trading in cocaine. Zola had had an affair with Lady Garrington while in Peru and was a big part of the hostile takeover of Garrington's husband and her consolidation of power ever since. Garrington had taken a long-term liking to this tall, wise and violent man. She placed him as the head of her security and as her main consigliere, never to be too far from her side. Zola was a quiet, softly spoken man of culture and intellect. He was dark, had long handsome features and was always impeccably dressed.

As Wolf's explanation came to a close, Zola was now through the white curtains. He stood in his fitted, black silk shirt and finely tailored black trousers, bearing down on Wolf and Kelly from behind. Garrington noticed his presence before Kelly and Wolf and introduced her lead confidante.

"So sorry to interrupt you, Professor, that all sounds fascinating, if not a bit fanciful. But truth be told, nowadays I have been taking more of a back seat and making core decisions from the top. The day to day is run by my individual factions and Capos. And this man, standing behind you, is my global trouble-shooter. It is he who will be able to inform you, with far more accuracy than I, on the plight and losses we have incurred at the hands of this Shadow character!"

As Garrington mentioned The Shadow, Zola's lips curled and snarled slightly in disgust; this was obviously a sore subject for the Italian. Zola took his cue and, grasshopper-like, smoothly looped his hugely long legs around Kelly and pulled up a chair next to his mistress. He carefully and precisely seated himself, procured a cigarette from Lady Garrington's box and lit it with her lighter. Still not saying a word, he took a couple of light pulls from the cigarette and crossed his legs. Once settled and ready, he proceeded to engage Kelly and Wolf with his low, even and somehow soothing Italian-American twang.

"Good afternoon, gentlemen. My name is Sergio Zola."

With that utterance he glanced back for approval at Garrington, who gave him a motherly nod of encouragement before he continued.

"So, what do you want to know?"

Zola exhaled another drag of his cigarette and looked from Wolf to Kelly in a stern and rigorous manner. Wolf leapt on this open invitation and inquired of Zola as calmly and respectfully as he could.

"Firstly, Mr Zola, thank you for so kindly agreeing to help us in our quest to locate and identify The Shadow. Simply, Mr Zola, we would like to know as much possible about exactly how The Shadow has been affecting your operation. We are attempting to find out exactly how much market share has been lost by your enterprise to that of The Shadow. I realise that this is sensitive information, that you would otherwise never share. However, as we have made clear to the esteemed Lady Garrington here, this is the only way we can see to sourcing The Shadow's identity and location."

Once again, Zola looked back to Garrington for approval before answering. Upon receipt of another permissive nod, Zola responded.

"Well you are correct, Professor. To be honest, we really don't like to share anything. And what you're asking for, it not exactly well documented, or something I could comment on. However, if you had to put a number on it – a general round number that doesn't mean anything really – I'd say we've lost about thirty percent to The Shadow's thing. But if you want exact numbers? That, gentlemen, is another thing entirely. I'm afraid, gentlemen, that's something we just can't provide. You see, it's the nature of our business that certain matters must remain private. Trust is very important to a business such as ours."

Zola smiled at Wolf and Kelly at this juncture, being deliberately coy and making a point of limited cooperation. Kelly, however, being accustomed to the routines of Italian mobsters, was unimpressed and probing of Zola's speech.

"See, we were just having a nice drink here on the beach! Chatting the breeze with your boss here. And then you come through. And start talking about trust and privacy and family! Like we're fucking assholes! What, do you think we are cops! We just told your fucking boss pretty intricate and fucking private details of our operation and you already know who we are and what we do! Yeah, we were both cops! But we're out on the lamb now, greaseball! We might be in your backyard and I am very aware I've got snipers aimed at my head right now! But still! We're just like you! No rules apply to us and we're just here to do a job! So, with respect! Can you please stop breaking our balls and tell us what we need to know!"

Zola pursed his lips in frustrated rage and his green-grey eyes flared with fervour at Kelly. Lady Garrington, witnessing an impending face-off between two men of devastating ferocity, wished to avoid any further escalation. She giggled slightly and interjected, smirking.

"Well, Captain! I am beginning to see your file manifesting before me! It's okay, Serge! Relax, babe, these guys are okay. Michael, Professor, you must understand! Sergio here is my lead consigliere, he is bound by duty to protect me and my operations. You must both forgive his protective and vigorous nature.

"I know! I've got a great idea. You two seem harmless enough, particularly if we keep guns on our handsome Captain here. I think it would be lovely if you two went with Serge to see our operations in action. I'll come with you, we'll all go!"

At this last suggestion, Zola swivelled in his seat to redress his mistress.

"Mistress. I don't think that would be very smart in the circumstances. At the moment our bases are more dangerous than ever. The Shadow's presence has unsettled the balance of power, it's a real bloodbath out there!"

Lady Garrington dismissed this advice and interrupted. "Oh, don't be ridiculous! It will be fun and good for morale for me to show face!"

Zola, still convinced of the peril of Garrington's suggestion, continued.

"Mistress, I would just like to go on record and state that in London – or even here – you're a target; in South America at one of our bases, you're a fucking beacon! The Shadow's got rats throughout our entire organisation. He knows what we do, before we do it! We're having to keep everything so much tighter! Every time we make a big move, he's right fucking there! Know this, Lady Garrington! If you do this, he'll know you're coming."

Garrington was still undeterred and persisted.

"Come on, Serge, don't be pathetic. I am Lady Garrington, and you are the head of one of the most dangerous, feared and powerful organisations in the world! Let alone the cocaine trade! Here's how we'll do it! You will gather twenty of my most trusted men and they, and you, will escort us wherever we go!

"Come on, Serge, this is a golden opportunity. We've got two guys here with a signed agreement from Silverman for that bounty. I just know they'll find it such fun! To see how things are unfolding live. Don't you see, chaps! We! Us! Right here! We are a team! I love these guys being under the radar! And I know they've got some great info on The Shadow! Judging from both their backgrounds and credentials, they would be more than useful allies and more than capable of taking care of themselves. Gentlemen, let us turn each other into mutual assets! Okay, that does it!"

Lady Garrington, to the obvious recoiling reluctance of Zola and the surprise of Wolf and Kelly, stood up and confirmed her volition.

"Will you two gentlemen, Professor Wolf, Captain Kelly, join us for a mini adventure, for us both to learn more about our common enemy! I ask you, nay I challenge you! That if you are to come with us and operate under our protection and advice, we will not only show you and have you experience the effects of The Shadow first-hand! But, should you manage to impress me, I will, contrary to all popular and sound advice, give you both unlimited access to the relevant financial information you seek!

"However, in return for this cooperation, I will require no monkey business and a fifty-fifty split in the appropriation of Silverman's dirty little bounty! Also, gentlemen – and I hate to do this – but this is my fucking beach and my fucking operation! If you refuse, try to fuck me (outside of the bedroom, Captain Kelly) or somehow forget to pay me, I will hunt you down! Torture! And kill you! Furthermore, Serge here will identify and locate your family members and do the same. Is that quite clear, gents? Good... Well I am going to retire and get ready for our little plane trip.

"Serge, have our closest jet ready to leave this evening for Cap Victor Airport. I'll leave you chaps to get better acquainted. Serge, play nice, I want them firing on all cylinders when we land. Professor, Captain, please be ready to leave for Peru in about, let's see, three hours. You can send your driver guy back wherever he came from and don't worry about clothes, food and accommodation! All will be duly arranged!"

With this last instruction, Lady Garrington did as she proposed and left the three men, to head in the direction of her villa. Zola, now alone with his two subjects, turned and softly but coldly addressed them.

"So, I told you guys I think this is a bad idea. So, just try not to get in the way. The Shadow is going to know she's coming and she's a prime target. This, gentlemen, will be an exercise in damage limitation. We will have to indulge her Ladyship's little vanity project here! But between you and I, this is going to be nothing more than a show. We'll quickly and quietly do the rounds, you know, to show you and Mistress how things are going. Then, I suppose you can have what you came for. But I assure you, gentlemen, this is a bad idea and we will be lucky to get out unscathed.

"We are essentially traffickers of cocaine and nothing more. We take the produce from South America and ready it for consumption. We then distribute it through our various smuggling channels throughout the globe. Currently we are exploring other methods of transportation. However, at the moment we're using boats to get the produce to Panama and from there we use planes, drones and more boats to get it across the Atlantic and the Gulf of Mexico to Europe and North America. Currently, while the police intercept about two to five percent of our loads (depending on the press coverage at the time), now The Shadow has been taking almost thirty percent. It's always our biggest loads too. He always seems to know when, where and how we're moving it. I know he's got informers! But in an organisation as large as our own, it's like finding a needle in a fucking haystack! Quite frankly, I can't see an end to The Shadow's encroachment on our business. Unless he cuts a deal, or we somehow stop him, it appears he is better resourced than we are. He has built a reputation of fear and respect. I am very aware, gentlemen, as is Mistress, that all things come to an end. And I can't help but think The Shadow represents a new era in our industry."

With this speech he ushered Wolf and Kelly to their feet and guided them out of the restaurant back down the beach and towards the resort's security tower. As the three approached the tower, they spied Lopez waiting silently in his car's driving seat. Zola walked Wolf and Kelly over to the car and instructed the pair.

"Okay so. We'll keep hold of your phones and effects until such time as Mistress has finished with you. And you can tell your friend in the car here to go back to wherever he came from. And let him know to tell your mammas you won't be back for dinner."

# Chapter 8

## TEMPORADA DE LA BRUJA

Making good on her promise, Garrington had readied herself and taken Wolf and Kelly to Cancun Airport. Here, she had purchased them ample clothing at Duty Free and ferried them onto her private jet. Wolf and Kelly had informed Lopez of their destination and hoped that he and the ops team would be close behind. However, they both feared that without the use of their phones and effects, they would be almost impossible to trace. The duo were now well and truly under the wing of Lady Garrington.

Faced with little recourse, Wolf and Kelly agreed on the plane to try, as best they could, to assist Lady Garrington and Zola. However, they were both also aware that all they really need do was the so called 'rounds', as Zola had put it. Hence, as long as they went along with Zola's little tour they would, according to Garrington, be given the information they needed along with their freedom. In evaluation, Wolf and Kelly agreed that their lives were now in Garrington's hands. Furthermore, they had not forgotten what Segal had said about Garrington's propensity for cold blooded murder. Wolf and Kelly concluded, therefore, that they should certainly make a significantly positive impression. As if they did not impress Garrington, her disapproval did not bear thinking about. Accordingly, the pair racked their brains throughout their journey to Peru as to how they could help Garrington's plight. Gradually, putting their experienced heads together, they managed to formulate a plot.

It was well into the night when Garrington's entourage touched down at the Captain FAP Victor Montes Airport, in North Peru near to the Ecuadorian border. From the aerodrome, Wolf and Kelly were driven through the humid but breezy oceanside darkness. Garrington's main base was a secret location on a secluded section of beachfront, near the Cancas district. In the pitch-black, Wolf and Kelly saw nothing of the rich and vividly beautiful Peruvian coastline. Instead they continued to contemplate and plot until they reached another, less resort-like, settlement of Garrington's. This was a far more sinister and befitting set up. There was only one dirt road in and out of the complex. Harsh and unkept terrain surrounded the buildings. If that was not protection enough, a twenty-foot-high, barbed wire, electric fence wrapped around the compound's entire circumference. A fully equipped security gate, manned with numerous armed guards, greeted Garrington's convoy as they entered the base. Past the security gate another, slightly better groomed, dirt track led down through the extensive gardens to the imposing main house. Either side of the dirt track were two hangar-like structures which looked distinctly suspicious and were plainly used for storing and packaging narcotics.

The main house was over fifteen thousand square feet and could comfortably house thirty or more. The property was a modern structure, with a distinct beach house vibe. It was evident that the developers had copied and magnified a classic, luxury, Miami beach house. Extensive decking, plumbing and electrics had been installed over the beach immediately behind the house, which backed onto the ocean. This mounted decking, linking the house with the ocean, extended to a substantial pier. Built on top of the pier was a large gazebo complete with heaters, loungers and a dining table setup. Garrington also had several yachts, speedboats and jet-skis moored off this well-maintained pier. Whenever Garrington had spent any time at this property, she would invariably spend most of her time on the pier for an easy and swift escape, should she need it.

Upon disembarking the convoy of four-by-fours, Wolf and Kelly were shown to a room in the main house made up with two beds. The room had an en-suite bathroom with fresh toiletries inside. Tired and stressed from their upheaval, the pair took turns in the shower before turning in without saying much.

The following morning, feeling slightly chilly and dried out from the powerful air conditioning unit, Wolf and Kelly dressed, ventured out of their room and went down to the back of the house. Upon leaving their room, they noticed a guard stationed immediately outside. This guard silently traced their footsteps as they made their way towards Lady Garrington and Zola, sitting together on the pier's gazebo outside. The burning sun, humidity and heat immediately affected Wolf and Kelly, as they found themselves perspiring with even the slightest exertion. Wolf was gladly surprised to see Garrington dressed and out of bed. Having created a plan to win over his new hosts, he was even more glad to see Zola and Garrington alone. As, if it was to work, his plan involved total secrecy between himself, Kelly, Zola and Garrington.

Zola was again impeccably dressed in a white silk shirt, red pattern cravat and chinos. Lady Garrington, on the other hand, while still ravishing, did not look her best. A little worse for wear, from the previous night's travel and lack of sleep, she was slumped in her chair, wearing a sarong and matching bikini. She wore enormous, glamorous sunglasses and was staring down at the coffee she held in her lap. Seeing Wolf and Kelly approach, she attempted to mask her evident hangover and welcomed them in a somewhat hoarse voice.

"Good morning, Professor, Captain. I hope you're loving my little set up here? Please sit down, have some coffee."

On the table was a pot of freshly brewed Colombian coffee and two spare cups for the grateful Wolf and Kelly. The pair took their seats either side of Zola. Wolf reached in and proceeded to pour himself and Kelly a cup of coffee. Garrington had also provided a selection of fruits and pastries which Kelly began to devour. Obliged by the slight pause in conversation, Garrington composed herself further and continued.

"So now you chaps are here, we thought it would be a good idea, for you to start with our main operation in Peru. And this is it. We basically store and package our main loads here. Then we take it down the coast via trucks at night. We have boats waiting down the shoreline and these boats take our product to Panama. From there it's a similar deal, but it's totally unregulated, unpoliced and easy as pie. The real challenge is getting it safely to our base here and then through to our boats. We never, ever, ship direct from here. This location is our safehouse! And we can't tempt fate. We have a military base next door on the payroll. So even if The Shadow was crazy enough to try and hack me down here, in moments he'll have three hundred plus soldiers at my gates! I'm giving their generals way!

Way! Too much money for that not to happen. We've even done a few false alarms, just as a drill to see. I mean I wasn't here, but apparently it was quite impressive! Anyway, Serge here has a treat for you, that I think you'll love. Tell them, babe."

While engaging Wolf and Kelly, Garrington had plucked and begun to smoke a cigarette from the box on the table. Motioning to Zola, she exhaled and slumped back in her chair, seemingly exhausted and wanting him to take over the conversation. He duly interjected.

"Yes, Mistress is correct. I do have a little twist of fate for you it would seem, that has so, serendipitously, decided to materialise. You gentlemen, being the smart concentrated individuals that you are, will remember, that I said we knew we had rats in our organisation. The reason we know this, is because we have actually caught and killed quite a few! However, we have kept one alive. You don't need to know the details, but we use this rat as a double agent for Mistress here. Now this normally wouldn't bear any significance. However, it just so happens that tonight, we are doing a big load. And it also just so happens, that our double-crossing little rat friend has informed us that The Shadow is going to try and heist it! So, I don't know what you guys were expecting? But this is pretty much prefect, no? You'll be able to see the fucking Shadow in action! And witness what we have to deal with on a monthly basis! You guys sure got what you came for! I hope you're happy, because I have made myself perfectly clear on this matter! I don't think it's smart at all. I think we shouldn't even be here!"

Garrington glanced up from her hunched stance disapprovingly and cautioned Zola.

"And I spoke to you, not a moment ago, honey! And said that we have to do all we can to explore every avenue! This Shadow is really pissing me off right now! I woke up early, babe! I haven't really fucking slept! I am going to get seriously fucking angry in a minute, cutie-pie! Do you know, Captain Kelly, Professor Wolf? That anyone who I, through deduction or experience, deem unable to satisfy me sexually, has to call me Mistress? Pathetic, isn't it. A little power game I play! God it's so mannish! Despicable in fact! But what's my name, honey?"

She shot an evil glance at Zola who responded snarling but obedient: "Mistress."

Garrington continued emotionless but clearly lifted by this assertion of power.

"Exactly! So, when Mistress tells you to do something, you fucking do it! Even if it means, you know, death. Anyway, we thought you chaps could wrap your brains around this and come up with some genius way of helping us. Number one! Get my load out tonight without a hitch. Number two! Bring us closer to The Shadow. Then, gentlemen, I would have no choice but to permit your precious access to our secret account information! Oh, and you better get your thinking caps on! Because if I've woken up early for nothing – and Serge is proved right! – and I have come here only to put myself in danger – honey-babes, you're dead meat."

Wolf sensed this would be the opportune time to introduce his and Kelly's plan, which had actually been accentuated by this recent development. Confidently, therefore, Wolf set down his coffee cup and addressed Lady Garrington as persuasively as he could.

"Lady Garrington, firstly may I say what a lovely house you have here. Right on the beach, wow. And this gazebo is charming. Perfect for outdoor dining!"

Seeing her Ladyship and Zola less than moved by his compliments, he swerved to a more direct line.

"I'm sorry, please forgive me. Allow me to elaborate on the plan that my esteemed colleague and I have formulated since meeting you and learning of your situation.

"What if I told you, Lady Garrington, that the fact that one of your big loads is due to be intercepted by The Shadow tonight, actually improves mine and Michael's plan! And what if I told you both, that I am glad we are speaking here in total privacy. Because this is crucial to our strategy. Allow me to elaborate further, Lady Garrington. What if I was to tell you, Lady Garrington, that in the next twenty-four hours, we could solve your little rat problem and also get you closer to The Shadow? Perhaps you would not think it possible? However, Captain Kelly and I will make this happen! If you can cooperate, do exactly as we say and keep everything between us?"

Garrington looked intrigued and hushed the petulant Zola, who was clearly disturbed by Wolf's allusions.

"Sh. Go on, Professor, I'm dying to hear more."

Wolf, buoyed with this assurance and pleased with his delivery thus far, continued positively.

"Lady Garrington, we will require the following:

"Firstly, a top of the range international micro-tracking device. We will need to see and plant this tracking device on the shipment of cocaine that is to be targeted by The Shadow tonight. Then we will require you to set up an interview room. An interview room with a waiting room directly in front and a reception room directly to the rear. We will then require your twenty most trusted men, along with your rat, to assemble in the waiting room made up as this site. You will then let Captain Kelly and I do the rest, yah?"

Garrington and Zola both looked perplexed and annoyed. Zola seethed with rage and looked as though he was about to assault the professor. However, before Zola could say anything, Garrington spoke.

"Okay, first of all. We're never going to do exactly what you say, ever! And especially not if you don't fucking explain yourself! So please, Professor, can you kindly enlighten us and give us a little bit more information to go by than, 'Give me a tracker, let me see your coke and let me interrogate your most trusted men!' What about Serge! Are you going to interrogate him as well! Explain yourself, Professor, before I allow my friend to lose his temper."

Garrington sat back and folded her arms defensively, awaiting response. Wolf did his best to elaborate in a constructive and appealing manner.

"Yes, fine, Lady Garrington. I can see that you would like to have a little more information. Essentially, our plan has two parts. The first part is pretty much a guarantee. This is that we will wheedle out any further rats in your operation here. This will involve an old military interrogation technique. We will use misinformation and misdirection to lure a confession from the rats in your closest ranks. The second part is the bonus part. We will use the fact that we know The Shadow is targeting your loads to target him in return!

"Both of these avenues of detection do require sacrifice. As Adam Smith once said – and I'm sure you're aware, Lady Garrington – there is no such thing as a free lunch! In order to catch your other rats, you will need to sacrifice your current one. And in order to track The Shadow, you will need to allow him to think he has won and achieved his heist. However, while you will have sacrificed another big load, if you can track this load to his location, you will have lost a battle but won a war."

Garrington was clearly moved by this rhetoric and Wolf's persuasive advocacy. She interrupted, convinced that she should at least trial The Professor's idea.

"Okay, that's enough for me. I think we've got to give these guys a shot! I've heard enough. I think the professor's making sense. I think we should follow these two to this endeavour! Serge, babe! You will tell no one whatsoever of this. You will do just what these gentlemen say! And who knows? Maybe they'll give us a fresh angle…"

Lady Garrington, evidently needing to rest her mind and body, rose to her feet to make for the beach. Before leaving the three men, she imparted a further instruction.

"But of course, babe, keep the guns on Kelly at all times, yeah! And my friends, if things do go tits up! Guess what? You're not going to get your information! And guess what else? If The Shadow doesn't kill you! I fucking will!"

With that, Garrington turned and still rather frailly pottered back down the pier to her private beach. Wolf and Kelly could still see her from their gazebo vantage, as she set herself up on a sun lounger and proceeded to fall asleep. As Garrington made her leave, Zola stared at the pair for a time shaking his head and sipping his coffee. Eventually he spoke at them, with a soft but menacing tone.

"You guys. What am I going to do with you? You come into my life, when things are not going well! And you convince my boss to put herself and myself in danger for your little bounty. Let me tell you something, gentlemen. We are the Temporada de la Bruja! The most powerful, wealthy and feared cartel in the entire industry. We are making billions here. Billions! We do not need, nor care about, five-hundred million dollars! What we care about and what Mistress pays me to care about! Is her survival.

"To be honest. We're looking to retire here. I couldn't care less about The Shadow. We're quite comfortable now and we have enough legitimate businesses, not only to survive but to thrive in the future. And just as we're getting close to the levels we need, to dominate in the formal sector, this motherfucking Shadow cunt comes along! Suddenly we're not making so much! Suddenly Mistress has got her offensive streak back! Now we're throwing men and money at this guy like he's a goddamn black hole!

"All I've got to say is this. I will go along with Mistress's orders this one last time. And if your little plans work, great! You can take your information, fuck off and never cross us again. But if you do cross us again! Or involve yourself with our business, in any capacity! Or, gentlemen, if this fails and things get fucking choppy! I am going to relish the relief! Of personally murdering the pair of you myself."

Zola did not allow for Kelly or Wolf to say a word in retort. Instead he swiftly and smoothly slipped his dark, lofty, lean frame out of his chair and receded back down the pier into the main house. Intimidated and adrenaline pumped, Wolf and Kelly meekly finished their breakfast and returned to their room.

# Chapter 9

## MILLION DOLLAR RACE

**H**aving remained in their room for the morning, Wolf and Kelly were discussing and perfecting the plan, on which their lives now depended. Around lunchtime the pair heard footsteps at their door. Without knocking, Zola cracked the door open and poked his head around.

"Okay, fellas. It's time. Let's go."

Zola, having immediately spied Wolf and Kelly sitting chatting on their respective beds, had them follow him downstairs and out to the front of the house. Zola had with him a basket containing an assortment of fruit, bread and cold-cuts. As the trio walked through to the hangar-like structure on the left of the main house, Wolf handed the basket back to Kelly. Kelly slowed his pace and shared out some of the contents with Wolf before tucking into it himself.

The huge and cavernous bunker, to which they were headed, had only one large door in and out. It had no windows and only grilles in the roof for ventilation. Five armed guards stood at the doorway to the narcotics hangar; one pushed the door to as he saw Zola approach. Inside were a lot of guards, general apparatus and cocaine. A mezzanine level surrounded the edge of the hangar's innards. Tables and benches each set up with scales, computers and CCTV, populated both levels of the bunker. Virtually all tables were completely packed with produce. The Temporada de la Bruja had established themselves as the main distributors of cocaine in The Americas. Hence, it was not surprising to Wolf and Kelly for them to see more cocaine than could be fathomed. Still eating, Zola began to walk Wolf and Kelly round the Temporada de la Bruja's main distribution centre.

"Okay so this is pretty much where the magic happens. We get the coke in here by land, from all over South America. It's then our job to make sure the weight is on point. This involves taking it out of its crappy local packaging. Weighing it, cutting it up and then compressing it properly. We then repackage, waterproof everything and carton it up for the boats. On a big load. We can compress enough product to run two hundred and fifty million dollars' worth of cocaine. That is, of course, because we have vertically integrated the supply chain such that we run the distribution from the farms here in South America, all the way through to the streets of the developed world. This is our model and we've been very successful! Until The Shadow started cutting us down at the source. He is intercepting the larger boats almost every time! A tracker we've never tried. But we've thrown everything into protecting our loads. And somehow, he's always one step ahead. It's because he's got rats! He knows when and where we're going to be and what we're packing. Like I said, our big boats can take hundreds of millions of dollars of cocaine and they are dropping like flies."

Zola's pace slowed and he paused in his tour at a secluded section of the upper mezzanine floor. He leant over the particular table of zip-locked cocaine packages in front of him. This blocked the CCTV camera covering that section of tables and allowed for Zola to place a micro-tracking device undetected. Zola then surreptitiously checked around to make sure no one saw him. He selected a random package and quickly fixed to its edge the adhesive side of a miniscule Nano-tracking chip, which he had purchased that day. Having done this, he seamlessly resumed his tour.

"Everything is in place now, as you instructed. That was a state of the art Nano-tracking chip. Its location will be fed through to Mistress's laptop and we will be able to monitor the position of that particular package. I have not deviated from my original orders either, as instructed. The men are to take three of our speedboats to the same location. Only one of them will be loaded and they will all head off to three separate locations in Panama. Each one will have armed men ready and prepared to engage The Shadow should he try to steal our product.

"We are also in the midst of setting up your little interrogation site. It will be done by this evening, before the boats leave. I hope you're satisfied, gentlemen?"

Kelly muffled a response with his mouth full of Mortadella.

"Yeah that's great, it's win-win for you guys now! If you defend your loads you've defended against The Shadow – and if he jacks it! – you're even better off! Cause you'll know his fucking location! Or at least one of his hideouts. And don't worry, Mr Zola, we don't need the interrogation centre set up until after your load gets boosted! Sorry! If it gets boosted! In fact, as you will see, if your load does get taken, it's going to make our interrogation process a whole lot easier!"

Zola stopped in his tracks to turn and face Kelly, before cautioning him.

"Okay, Mike! Let's get one thing straight, right now! Don't ever act like you're doing me a favour here. I do feel like I am reiterating myself but let me remind you: it is me who is doing you a favour. It is me that you have crossed. It is me who gets to decide your fate. And it will be me, gentlemen, who wields the sickle of death, should things not go exactly as I see fit. Now, gentlemen. I don't want to have to repeat myself again. So just smile, shut up, follow me and play nice with Mistress."

With this, Zola brought his brief tour to a close and marched Wolf and Kelly back to the main house. He led them through and back out to the gazebo on the pier. A lunch table had been set up, complete with more fruit, breads and cold meats. On the table was an open laptop, on which the tracking software had been set up for Wolf and Kelly. Zola had the pair sit down at the table and poured them each some water and red wine. The three sat in silence, enjoying the refreshments and sunshine, as Lady Garrington approached from the house. Showered, made-up and looking resoundingly improved from the morning, Garrington wore a mauve, strappy, flowing maxi-dress. Her gorgeous locks blew in the wind as she strutted up to her subjects and took a seat. She waited for Zola to pour her some wine and lit a cigarette. Then, gently fixing her hair behind her ears, she addressed her men.

"Good afternoon, gentlemen. I trust everything has been taken care of to your liking?"

Wolf quickly answered, wishing to make known his gratitude and subservience.

"Yah, Lady Garrington, your colleague here has been positively exacting in his reproduction of what we asked. All we need do now is wait and track your shipment from the comfort and safety of your laptop here."

Wolf smiled to Garrington and Zola amicably. However, Zola, remaining furious with him and Garrington, looked distracted and disinterested.

Garrington scrapped her hair back again and retorted, "Great. Well I have to say. I love the tracker idea and I will definitely be incorporating this strategy for all my loads henceforth. But you have to admit, chaps. Your methods, though calculating, are a trifle boring, are they not? And maybe just a little bit cowardly? I mean, we sit behind a computer and watch, while The Shadow fucks us up the arse! Sounds like something I'd make my husband do! Sorry that's a bit harsh, it's just a little pathetic for me! Not really our style, is it, Sergie? I have always favoured a more direct approach. Like you, Michael. Sometimes I just can't stand bullshit and finesse. Just give me what I fucking want or fuck you! You know! I guess I'd rather fight face to face than in the shadows! That's why this bastard got me on my haunches! He's so fucking underhanded and sneaky! In any case, your whole plan bores me. Which is why I have come up with a little light entertainment to while away the time before our shipment is to be dispatched."

Zola's eyes widened in anticipation. He was horrified but used to this kind of tangential behaviour from Garrington. Kelly and Wolf were also terrified as to what their captor would do or say next. Garrington, noting her company's perplexed expectancy, elaborated further.

"Captain Michael Kelly, Serge! You two are quite the pair. And I've been dying to see what would happen if I were to pit you against one another! In a little sporting competition! So, while you chaps were out on your little tour, I have arranged a little game."

All three men's faces flushed red with fear and woe at the prospect of whatever brazen, and no doubt dangerous, escapade Garrington had planned out. She continued proudly.

"You will see, gentlemen. If you look out there on the water a little, a buoy! You will also see, that earlier I swam out to this buoy and have carefully taped a miniature bottle of Absolut Vodka to the top of it! Professor, you will be the umpire of this little comp, so pay attention yah!

"You see, Michael and Serge here, will be racing to smash this little bottle. You will also see, gentlemen, if you look down the beach a little in front of us, a pistol loaded with only two rounds. You will, on my command, race to try and smash this bottle. Now of course, there are no rules. However, you may wish to note that the buoy is positioned at approximately the maximum range of the pistol. Now! You are to use this pistol! And this pistol alone! To smash the bottle. The only other way will be to physically swim out to the target and smash it! So, you had both better take your clothes off. And just to make things a little more interesting, to the winner go the spoils, gentlemen! One million dollars will be deposited into the bank account of the man who smashes the bottle first!"

Zola interjected, having been used to participating in challenges such as this previously. He had not been expecting a prize of such magnitude.

"Mistress? That much? Really? You really want me to beat this punk, huh?"

Lady Garrington puckered her lips and blew a facetious kiss at Zola and continued.

"The better the man, the bigger the prize, Sergie. You've seen his file. I bet he'll be your best challenge yet. But come on, honey! Bearing in mind how many times you've done this, we both know your long legs and perfect aim should see you through! I mean, look at Kelly! He'll be taking two steps for every one of yours! You should be making light work of this one! But I wonder? This Captain does look like he's full of surprises!"

"Right, gentlemen! I will give you fifteen minutes to stretch and ready yourselves for this. And to allow the men to take bets accordingly. If you would now each write your account details on the piece of paper next to my laptop. I will prepare to transfer funds to the winner."

With that, Garrington got out of her seat and strode over to the chair facing her laptop. She then had Kelly and Zola write their account details for her transfer. Having done this she concluded, while lighting another cigarette, "Right so, chaps! You know what to do. And by the way, for the record, Captain, there are no tricks to this! It's literally just which man can get to that gun and smash the bottle first. Serge has never lost by the way! But be optimistic, he's got to lose someday! And by the way, neither of you! I repeat neither of you! Is to try and kill the other. Professor Wolf here, as umpire, will immediately stop proceedings, if he gets even the slightest inkling that someone will be seriously injured. That said, gentlemen, there are no other rules! So, feel free to do anything and everything else you can to ensure victory. The starting line will be at the top of the pier. We will reconvene here in precisely ten minutes. Drink!"

Having barked for another beverage and divulged her final instructions, she winked at Kelly and motioned for him and Zola to retire to the house and prepare. Garrington remained seated at her laptop with Wolf at her side. After a short time, a servant appeared from the house with a tall cocktail glass of Margarita. He was closely followed by an enormous crowd. Most of the staff and guards, it would seem, had now gathered on the beach to spectate. By the time Garrington had received her cocktail, the crowd was clamouring and exchanging bets in anticipation of Kelly and Zola's bout. The few remaining minutes flew by, as Garrington sipped her drink and Wolf marvelled at the uproar on the beach. Garrington had created her very own sporting event and welcome distraction for all involved. Rock music also now appeared to blast from speakers set up throughout her private beach.

Kelly and Zola caused quite the commotion as they emerged from the main house and made their way to the pier. Both men were in tremendous shape, although their physiques were completely different. Dressed in only swimming trunks and trainers, their bodies were exposed for all to see. Garrington surveyed, with delight, the two radically different male specimens before her. She did not move from her vantage next to Wolf, under the gazebo, where the race course could be best witnessed. However, she pulled down her sunglasses and peered more intently over the top of them to better examine Kelly and Zola.

Zola was like a mythical creature from a Greek legend, half stag and half eagle. His graceful almost feminine movement, large nose and long gaunt face, made him appear like a bird of prey. While his stretched, toned and slender body displayed obvious stag-like characteristics. Kelly, conversely, was stocky, built-up and very solid looking. His shoulders and upper torso were far more developed than Zola's. However, his stomach was less toned and his limbs stouter. Overall, they weighed almost the same; however, Kelly was dwarfed by Zola. If Zola was the mythical beast in this scenario, Kelly was the slight but courageous Greek hero, quested to vanquish him.

To the sound of music and cheering, the pair made their way past the gazebo and towards the start line at the end of the pier. As Zola passed Lady Garrington, she grabbed his arm and stroked him. However, pumped and enraged, Zola flicked his arm away dramatically to the delight of the jeering crowd. Once together at the start line, the pair awaited Garrington's signal for the off. She, noting their position at the start, reached for a flare gun on the table next to her. She looked to the crowd and smiled at Wolf to build a swell of drama and tension. After a little time, Garrington pulled the trigger and the million-dollar race began.

Zola immediately and without hesitation used experience and height to his advantage and managed to come over the top of Kelly, smother him and use his long legs to trip him to the floor. Kelly wrestled as best he could, but had not expected this kind of contest right from the off. Kelly, swearing, sweating and panting, scrambled to his feet only to see Zola breaking into a sprint down the pier towards the gazebo. Despite this head-start, while Zola's high centre of gravity and long legs took a while to get going, Kelly possessed blistering pace. His naturally explosive core and low centre of gravity gave Kelly exceptional speed and acceleration. Kelly had been his high-school's one-hundred and two-hundred-metre champion from aged sixteen. However, it was his matching success on the football field that he was wanting to draw upon, as he began to gain on Zola. Zola had now stumbled through the gazebo's dining area and all Kelly could think about was catching and tackling him. Garrington made eyes at Kelly and touched him, as he vaulted over the gazebo's dining table, with Zola already nearing the other end of the pier.

Still undeterred by his deficit and Zola's huge, gazelle-like strides, Kelly continued shouting profanities and sprinting after him. Kelly's legs were moving with such raw speed they had assumed a cartoon-like blurred image, masked slightly by the springs of sand that flew up in Kelly's tracks as he tore towards his adversary. When Zola began to close the gap between himself and the pistol, he could feel Kelly's presence directly behind him. Zola estimated he had done enough to make it to the weapon before Kelly, but was ready to turn and kick him down as soon as he claimed it. However, as Zola came within striking distance of the gun, he felt the back of his heel clip on something and drag back. This caused him to trip on himself and fall to the sand.

Kelly, in a last ditch attempt, had pushed himself to the limit and gained a few extra yards on Zola. Having done this, he had leapt forward and used an old football technique he had learnt. Known as the 'ankle' or 'heel tap', this method is rarely but effectively used by tacklers to stop large and fast offensive runners. The defensive player, unable to catch the faster, stronger offensive player, simply taps their heel in a particular way. The offensive player has their run broken and often trips up over their own feet. Once grounded, the defensive player is free to catch up and cover. This is simple in theory but difficult in practice. Kelly, however, had practised this manoeuvre many times in high-school and was ready to pounce as Zola tumbled into the sand. Struggling to his feet, still focused on the weapon in front of him and a little dazed, Zola was thoroughly winded by the incoming tackle from Kelly. Kelly drove his shoulders into Zola's sternum and dashed him back to the floor. This was almost enough for Kelly to win, as it bought him enough time to break free of the sprawled, spluttering Zola and grab the pistol. Kelly even had time enough to aim and fire. However, as he did so, Zola barrelled into him like a springing panther. Kelly's shot just missed the bottle and the two flew, entwined and tumbling, along the beach.

Zola and Kelly grappled desperately for control of the pistol and Kelly, eventually, using superior floor work and explosive strength, came out on top. He managed to break away from Zola and arch himself away from his opponent. As Zola went in to attack from behind, Kelly had landed a powerful slicing elbow to Zola's chin. Zola had flipped back and down onto the floor. However, a hardened fighter, Zola was somehow able to retaliate with a huge sweeping kick as he fell. Zola's giant, prevailing right foot crashed into Kelly's right thigh. Kelly's leg instantly gave way, numbed and cramped up. Kelly fell to the floor with Zola, and the pair dragged themselves on their bellies towards the shoreline. Zola, again using experience to his benefit, played possum. Correctly suspecting Kelly to be a weak swimmer, he wished for Kelly to fire another errant shot and exhaust the ammunition. He waited for Kelly to make his way closer to the target and take aim. Then, as before, he launched himself at Kelly. Just as he fired, Zola struck again. Kelly's shot was once more off the mark and the clip was now empty.

Zola managed to pull himself on top of the stifled Kelly and uttered a personal snipe: "I hope you can swim, Fuckface!"

Kelly retorted with a sting of obscenities. However, Zola in a burst of concentrated aggression, smothered Kelly's face with his right hand and held his right leg in position as he did so. He then proceeded to drive his knee into Kelly's thigh as hard as it would go. He rolled Kelly over and away from him and made for the water. As Zola had correctly asserted, despite Kelly's valiant attempts to recover and catch him, his efforts were futile. Zola's sleek body slipped through the channels of the ocean like the shark he was. Kelly, however, was a denser man and by no means aerodynamic. Zola reached the bottle well before Kelly and smashed it victorious on the side of the buoy.

Both men looked worse for wear as they emerged from the ocean and were greeted with towels and applause. Kelly was limping, had a swollen eye and was scratched from head to toe. Zola's nose was bleeding and he was gurning from a bruised jaw. Servants supplied the pair with further ice packs and water bottles, as they walked back to the gazebo. Garrington had now entered Zola's account details and sent him one million dollars. She was still reeling with delight, as the pair hobbled to their seats at Garrington's table.

"See that wasn't so bad, was it, chaps! I think you both enjoyed that. I think you both needed it! The way you've been flirting with each other, you clearly needed to release the tension! And may I say, Captain Kelly! Bravo! What a show! When you tore down the beach like a bat out of hell, I almost choked on my fucking drink! You are a quick man! I just hope that's the only thing you're quick about!

"Anyway, we all thought you'd won when you tackled Sergie to the ground like a man fucking possessed. But Sergie was just too clever for you, Captain! His experience certainly ruled the day. But you gave him one hell of a run for his money! When you elbowed him in the face, I thought he'd never get up! Serge! My baby! Did this little Tasmanian Devil hurt you? He almost had you, didn't he? Aww! Well you got your big prize and you won in the end! So, my big baby's pride and ego and unbeaten record are still intact! Aww! But, Captain Kelly, while Sergie here may have won, I was more impressed by the show you put on! I don't think I've ever seen Sergio that desperate before and I've seen a lot of these little games! In any case, you all better get rested and cleaned up for tonight! I thought we could all four of us have dinner. We can watch the load on my laptop and see how things unfold. And then after dinner we can conduct your little inquiry. But that was really great! Thank you, gentlemen, most amusing."

As she said this she rose up and flipped her dress off, to reveal a white bikini. She then stepped back, turned and dived off the pier into the ocean. She swam over to a small yacht she had anchored, hauled herself up the steel ladder and lay on the deck. On this cue, Wolf, Kelly and Zola returned to their quarters to nurse their wounds and prepare for dinner as Garrington commanded.

# Chapter 10

## THE SHADOW STRIKES

A few hours after the sun had set on the Peruvian coastline, Wolf and Kelly were summoned to dinner. In complete contrast to their situation, Garrington's dinner set up was idyllic and peaceful. Moonlight, candles and fairy lights illuminated the pier's gazebo on the water's edge. Classical Latin guitar music piped along the beach and was accompanied by the soft washing tide of the ocean. Fresh mussels, crayfish, lobster and scallops had been prepared with garlic, white wine and butter. Two ice buckets, each with a matched white wine, stood either side of the table, on which four neat places were laid. A small side table had been set up next to Garrington's seat, on which her laptop had been placed to monitor the progress of her load. Garrington wore a deeply glamourous black dress, which clung to her contours and accentuated her sculpted curves. She looked understated yet elegant. Sat next to her was Zola, a little bruised from earlier. He still looked more than presentable, however, wearing a smart, dark-navy silk shirt with khaki linen trousers. The foursome dug into the sumptuous meal Garrington had laid on. After her subjects had made a dent in the banquet before them, Garrington broke into conversation.

"Jolly good show today, chaps. Michael you really went for it. And I'm so proud of you, Serge, for holding down your record. I was thinking we should have filmed that one! As a matter of fact, Serge, in the morning, please see if any of the staff did manage to capture anything on video."

Zola nodded affirmatively while taking a sip of white wine and she continued.

"So, you two! Our shipment is being dispatched as we speak. And, as you can see from my laptop, we will, as you requested, be monitoring its progress while we eat. I have to say, despite my employees' continuing distrust of you both, I have found that the actions you have executed thus far, have only impressed me. You, Professor, have demonstrated the ability to communicate effectively, persuasively and concisely a rather neat little plan. And you, Captain Kelly, are just a very sexy man! You don't say too much and when you act! Boy, oh boy! I would love to have a man like you in my operation! As I am a woman of action and not words. I have found that actions are far easier to read than words. Actions are more honest! And this is what has saved you both! Your honesty!

"Do you know, gentlemen, that in my experience – and despite what you may think, my experience is great – I have found that while men are creatures of ego, women are creatures of the subconscious. You men are all about bravado, your legacy and how people perceive you in the now. Whereas we women are usually different. We tend to prioritise how we feel and also how others feel. I have embraced this over the years and it has made me understand men and women in a clearer light. However, in particular this knowledge has made me – like you, Michael – a tremendous lie detector. If I listen to my gut, even when things are not clear and perhaps don't make sense, I can still tell when a man is being honest. And did you know, Professor? Captain? That there are three things a woman looks for in a man. The first, does he physically repulse me? If the answer is no he's passed test one. The second, is he resourceful? Not rich, resourceful! When the chips are down, we need to know we can count on a man to step up and get things done! If he's a waster or a moron, no way, Jose! Thirdly and most relevantly to our organisation, is he honest? Men love to think women like a six-pack, charmer, bad boy or whatever! But regardless of other shortcomings honesty is one of the sexiest things to a woman! And our subconscious can smell it a mile off! And truthfully, I can really see honesty in you, Captain Kelly. And needless to say, I find you very attractive.

"But enough of the afternoon's delights. Professor, perhaps you could, while we await the theft of our ninety-seven-million-dollar load, tell us a little more of your plan of interrogation and exactly how you expect it to help with our little rat problem?"

Lady Garrington paused to allow Wolf to speak.

"Yah, Lady Garrington, but of course! And may I say how kind and hospitable you have been to myself and my colleague. This lobster is phenomenal and so fresh!"

Wolf finished his mouthful of lobster and placed his knife and fork on the table to permit better communication and continued while the others ate.

"The core concept of this age-old trick is to make your rat think we have already caught him before we have."

Garrington, recognising this strategy, raised her head from her mussels and interrupted.

"Oh, you mean pretending to know the truth to get the truth! Oh, yeah! I do that all time! Great little tactic! Sorry, Professor, please go on."

The Professor continued, as instructed.

"Yes, Lady Garrington, that is precisely what I am eluding to. Pretending to know the truth to acquire the truth. We are going to use the three-room set up, as we requested, as follows. The men will wait outside our middle room and will be called in one by one. They will of course be watched and held in the waiting room at gun point, to prevent any of them running away after the first man is shot. The first man to be called in will be your rat double-agent. We will audibly shout at him and interrogate him as such. This will be the same line we take with all the men. We will inform him that we told everyone, except himself and one other individual, of this evening's real plan. We will then inform him that the real plan was to plant a bomb on tonight's shipment of cocaine, knowing that The Shadow would attempt to steal it! Assuming your product is stolen tonight, we can then inform him that for the first time you have successfully managed to be one step ahead of The Shadow! We will then inform him that The Shadow took the bait and brought the shipment back to one of his warehouses. At this point we will say that we detonated the bomb and blew up his warehouse. We will then highlight the fact that this plan has worked, where previously The Shadow has always been one step ahead. We will then inform him that the success of this plan and his ignorance of it are no coincidence! We will then let him know that if he does not cooperate and let us know everything he knows about

The Shadow, he will be executed on the spot. We will then, most likely, execute him, pull his body into the third room at the back of our middle interrogation room and call in the next man! The next man, crucially, will have heard the shouting and gunshot! As well as, no doubt, the sound of your rat falling to the floor. He will see that he has clearly been dragged out the back entrance and there will be blood on the floor to denote as such. This will not only facilitate his instant intimidation, but it will lend credibility to our threats, such that each man we interrogate will know, that it is the truth or death!

"We will then have two pistols on the table, one loaded and one not. We will handle the empty pistol, while interrogating our subjects. Whether satisfied or not, we will then be able to hold an empty gun to their head and threaten to kill them to the point of pulling the trigger! Without the worry that one of your most trusted men will die unnecessarily. We will then pull the trigger! Of course, nothing will happen, they might have a heart attack but it's unlikely! However, what this will do, is push your men to the edge of reason. Any untruths or allegiances they have will surely be spilled if they know they are going to die! Then, once we have satisfied ourselves that the man we are interrogating is innocent, or at least pleading as such, we fire the loaded gun into the floor and escort the innocent man out of the rear entrance. Again, the next man will think another man has been executed and be even more respectful and believing that if the truth is not told, they will be killed. Of course, Lady Garrington! We cannot pretend to shoot every person we interview! As the men still waiting must have a glimmer of hope that if they are cooperative they can still live! So, we will only simulate the execution of a selected few.

"Thusly, and I hope you can follow and understand, we will be able to extract any information from your closest members of staff! As this is, without a doubt, the source of your leaks to The Shadow. It must be from several senior members of your organisation. People with power, motivation and greed. This is classic, Lady Garrington! Captain Kelly and I have seen this kind of thing many times. It's funny because this is basic stuff for investigators and detectives such as Kelly and I! But for yourselves, with your exclusively criminal backgrounds, catching other criminals must be quite a foreign concept! Either way, your Ladyship, Mr Zola! This method is tried and tested and, unlike in the regulated forces, we can actually kill these men! Which adds to the realism and would, of course, be totally against protocol in any military or police operation."

Everyone at the table laughed at this last piece of dryly delivered, black humour. Kelly and Wolf felt themselves truly relax a little for the first time since their appointment by Lord Cork. Lady Garrington had taken a liking to them, particularly Kelly. They had managed to come up with a feasible plan that would work regardless of situation. They also had begun to trust that Garrington was a woman of her word and furthermore that Zola resented their presence. They both felt it increasingly likely, that they would at least be permitted to go free, if they continued to politely acquiesce to their captors for just a few more hours.

The quartet continued their jovial banter and Garrington continued to flirt with the blushing Kelly, as the night set in and the desserts and coffee had been presented. A selection of sorbet, chilled fruit and a light rosé wine was set before the diners, as well as a cafetiere of fresh coffee. Halfway through a spoon of nectarine sorbet, Zola grunted and rolled his eyes to the sound of his buzzing mobile. He jerked his head forward and stuck his spoon into the coupe of sorbet, gulped his mouthful down and answered.

"Yeah? Okay..."

Zola listened to the loud commotion at the other end of the line and heard the phone go dead. He paused, winced a little, took a deep breath and seeing everyone's eyes on him, interjected.

"So, it looks like The Shadow's in the middle of taking our load. That was Suarez. Apparently, our load boat's under attack. They've got another helicopter gunship! It's hit the fuel tank and the engine. They're sitting ducks and taking heavy fire. Fuck! How does he do this every fucking time! Quick, let's get a look at the laptop!"

Zola vigorously leant his extensive reach over the table and turned the laptop to face the four. The tracking software had already been called up on the screen, which promptly came out of standby. The location of the tracker was clearly displayed by a bright flashing dot on the screen. The software enabled you to make a reference for your intended destination and compare it to the trajectory of the tracker. They could clearly see that the tracker had been following its intended path to Panama, through the South Pacific and into the North Pacific. However, presently they could see the tracker was stopped dead over one point in the North Pacific, off the coast of Colombia. The four watched in baited silence for some kind of movement in their secret tracker. Wolf and Kelly were flushed with relief and excitement as they saw the dot on the screen start to move away from the line of its intended course. Vindicated and feeling a step closer to success, Wolf and Kelly smiled at each other as Garrington and Zola stared in horror at the laptop screen. The dot was veering off from its course north by north-east, in a more north-westerly direction. It appeared to be headed for either Costa Rica or Nicaragua. The dot had begun moving a lot faster across the on-screen map. It was highly probable therefore, that the package had been picked up by one of The Shadow's helicopter gunships.

Zola repeatedly attempted to call numerous men he had aboard the vessel carrying the stolen load. However, to no avail. The commotion-filled phone call he had previously was all they had to work with. However, things were looking just as Wolf and Kelly had predicted. They all prayed that the tracker would go undetected and they would source one of The Shadow's locations. As the tracker continued to move across the screen, hours went by. The four sipped their coffee and moved onto brandy as the night progressed. No one said much, eager not to miss any deviation or change in the tracker's course. Eventually, over four hours later, the tracker appeared to come to a halt over San Juan Del Sur, a cute beach town near the Costa Rican border. The tracker remained there for the next half an hour, before Zola received a call. When his phone buzzed it broke a long silence and made everyone jump.

"Hello, Suarez? Yeah? What happened?"

Zola listened to what a desperate sounding Suarez had to say at the other end of the line. Upon hearing his account, Zola hung up the phone without a goodbye. He then, carefully considering his words, addressed the others.

"Okay, so that was Suarez. Only him and four other guys got out alive. They came at us with an armoured chopper. They blew out the engine and shot most of the crew. They took the load and unloaded it onto five speedboats that pulled up. The chopper pulled away and their boats made off with the stuff. Suarez and the rest of the survivors are headed back now. They should be here in the next hour or so. They had one of our choppers come and pick them up somewhere on the coast. Fuck, this is a mess. But I suppose it kind of ties in with your game plan, doesn't it, fellas?

"All I can say is that if this tracker trick works and The Shadow's got a warehouse in Nicaragua, that's great! And if we can use this to trap another rat in our organisation, that's even better. But if this is some kind of trick in itself and you two are playing us – we've just lost one hundred million dollars and quite a few good men tonight! So really, gentlemen, understand this. Before I wasn't really that bothered. But now! I'm looking for any excuse to whack the pair of you. So, gentlemen. That said. What do we do next? Wait for Suarez and the rest to get back so we can add them to people we've had shipped in for your little interrogation tonight?"

Zola paused and wiped his sweating upper lip. He glared at Wolf and Kelly, awaiting an answer. Kelly took this opportunity to remind Zola of the status quo and tried to put a more positive spin on proceedings.

"Look, Mr Zola! We all have to make sacrifices. We're taking a risk just being here. We took a risk coming to see you in the first place! But we are all in this together. All we want to do is find The Shadow. And Chrissy and I have helped you get one step closer to doing just that! Now, in about two hours we're going to wheedle out another rat and bring you closer still. And all we ask in return: a little information! Which means nothing to you! And will bring us even closer still! And you won a million dollars off me today! So, with respect! Lighten up, bro! Let's just try and get through this. Why not trust a little bit more, ay? Considering our plan's gone as we said it would. And look at the glass as half full! I'm mean in a way, this is perfect! It will make our interrogation so much easier. And by the end of the night, I promise you'll have an idea of one of The Shadow's locations and you'll have caught a rat or two at the same time! Now if that's not worth a little sacrifice, I don't know what is?"

Kelly's light-hearted chat was brought to a close by Garrington who, flirtatiously but authoritatively, interrupted.

"It is not a question of whether Mr Zola and I feel that the sacrifice will be a fair trade-off. It is a question of whether you two wonderful gentlemen can come through and deliver the fruits of this sacrifice we have just, so trustingly and perhaps foolishly, made. It is at this point that I can understand Mr Zola's concern! For it is at this point that we are most vulnerable! We have, at this point, given everything and have yet to see anything in return! So, Captain! Professor! Let us go and set up for your interrogations, which I intend to witness in full. By the time we have made ourselves comfortable, no doubt all the men will have gathered themselves in the waiting room."

# Chapter 11

## RAT HUNTING

Within an hour of Garrington's command, she, Wolf, Kelly and Zola were positioned with a loaded and unloaded pistol, refreshments and a few armed heavies inside the three-tiered interrogation setup. The main interview room was furnished with five chairs. Three chairs had been placed in the rear corner of the room for Zola, Wolf and Garrington. A chair was located in front of a desk in the middle of the room and another chair faced it on the other side. At the front of the room was a door that led out to the waiting room. Here Garrington's most trusted men were waiting, having been, in some cases, shipped in from around the globe. To the rear of the central interview room was another door, which led to the rear reception room. With the two identical pistols tucked in the drawer of the desk and everyone present and settled, proceedings were ready to begin.

Kelly, who would be conducting the interrogations, positioned himself in the chair behind the desk facing the door to the waiting room. Atop the desk was a stack of papers with details of the men who had been summoned. They had been separated into managers, security officials, drivers and one accountant. Kelly briefly flicked through the papers he had already examined, cleared his throat and instructed the first man to enter. As planned, this was the pre-arranged execution of Zola's double-agent rat. Within moments Darius Darbandi was shepherded in at gun point. Darbandi was short, fat and filthy looking. He was bald, in his late-forties and wore a lazy-eyed, dull expression of emotionless resolve. He was, however, clearly petrified with anticipation. Kelly surveyed and analysed his victim, as he was pushed into the seat before him. Kelly rose to his feet as Darbandi sat. Then while talking to him, Kelly proceeded to open the drawer of the desk and brandish the loaded gun.

"So, Darius Darbandi. What is that, Iranian?"

Darbandi nodded without making eye contact and Kelly continued.

"Well, my Persian friend, it looks like you're a long way from the land of Saffron! Now! Our time is short, and we have ten more people to see. So, I'm going to make this as short and painless for you as possible!"

Darbandi winced, snorted and shook his head fervently, losing his mindfulness and dropping into a state of desperate discomfort. Kelly went on and began to cross-examine Darbandi, gun in hand.

"So, Darius, tonight, as you well know, The Shadow managed to get his hands on our boat load! A real fucking success for him, yeah! No! Wrong! He's fucked! So, we can all celebrate right now because, what you don't know is, tonight, we actually planted a bomb and a tracker on the load that went out! And just a few moments ago we detonated that bomb and killed a tonne of The Shadow's guys! And with our tracker, we have now located one of his main bases in Nicaragua! Now this would, as I said, be cause for celebration, right? But is it? It is for us? Is it for you? You see the funny thing about tonight is! Why? Why is it that The Shadow fell for this one? We've tried this kind of shit before! We've tried all kinds of things! And somehow, The Shadow's always known what we're doing before we do it! So why not this time, I ask you? I'll fucking tell you why! You son of a bitch! We told everyone in our operation about the bomb plot tonight! Everyone that is! Except you!"

As Kelly now pointed the loaded gun towards Darbandi, he began to cry out in gabbling and spluttered pleas for mercy.

"Please! Guys! You have to believe me! Since you guys caught me the first time I have been working only for you! Trying to get you guys more rats and information on The Shadow! It's so hard, though, because everyone hates me now they all think I'm a rat! This is fucking impossible! How am I supposed to work with this! I'm fighting both sides! You and The Shadow! You have to cut me some slack! Oh my God, how have I done this!"

Kelly interrupted Darbandi's screams and handed his gun to Zola for execution.

"You shouldn't have ratted in the first place! Little piece of advice, Darius, for your next life! If you're going to pick a side, pick a side! Don't fucking rat and expect to have the best of both worlds! It's been my experience that in this game, it's going to get you killed every time!"

As Zola now rose to his feet and aimed his pistol, Darbandi squealed, writhed and pleaded further.

"No! Please! You can't! Fuck! I can't believe it's going to end like this! My fucking kids! You cunt! What about my kids! Okay so I fucking ratted! Fuck you! I'll tell you everything! This time everything! I'll bring you right to him! Please! Please! Just don't kill me! Please, Sergio, think of my children!"

Zola cocked his head to one side to ensure his aim was true and in one last crescendo of screaming and gunfire, he took Darbandi's life with a single shot through the heart. Darbandi was still fractionally alive, as he heard Zola's following words.

"We've all got children, you fucking lying little rat."

Darbandi, clutching his chest, dribbling and voiding his lungs of air, collapsed off his chair to the floor. The life promptly left his eyes and two of the guards dragged his bloodied corpse across the floor and through into the rear waiting room.

This incident, having been fully audible to the rest of the men waiting to be interviewed, had certainly had the desired effect. The remaining interviewees knew it was the truth and total cooperation or certain death. Garrington, loving the way things were proceeding and the high-octane drama that unfolded before her, interjected.

"That was tremendous, boys! Even I'm fucking terrified! Kelly, that's the last time you'll be handling a loaded gun in front of me! You are dangerous! And Serge! It's been a while since I've seen you do that! Fuck, it turns me on! God knows why? Anyway, send in the next man!"

With that command, the next man, Garrington's chief supply manager, made a similar entrance at gun point to the chair facing Kelly at the desk. Fernando Gonzalez was a younger, fresher faced man than Darbandi. He had longish dark hair and was Spanish in origin. His frame was a lesser, slightly shorter version of Zola's. He was very thin, lean and gaunt. His handsome good-looks were shrouded by his stressed complexion, as he sat panting and glistening with sweat before Kelly. Gonzalez surprised his audience by engaging them first. His soft Catalonian accent was broken with fear and weeping.

"Please, can I just say, before – before you kill me. I know why you must have brought us here. To purge weakness after The Shadow's attacks. But I want you to know I have always been loyal to you, Mistress. I have never turned, nor had the opportunity. And if I did ever have the opportunity, I wouldn't. I would never! I will never betray you! I have never betrayed you! For me, I live and die by loyalty! It was my father's way."

Gonzalez, having imparted this speech of innocence, dropped his head, causing his wavy curtains to flop down covering his face. Kelly, unfazed by Gonzalez's plea for mercy, began to proceed as he had done with Darbandi.

"So, Fernando Gonzalez! I am glad you realise what it is we're doing here tonight. Because you're absolutely right! Tonight is a fucking purge! A night of exorcism! Tonight we are cleansing Temporada de la Bruja! And you, Gonzalez, had better know that if you don't tell us what we know to be true, you will end up like our little deceased fucking friend! In a cold heap of your own warm shit out back! So, Fernando! Let me paint a little picture for you.

"Now what would you do in the following situation? I want you to imagine, okay, Gonzalez! Just try and imagine for me. Imagine that you have been coming up against an enemy who, somehow, seems to know your every move, even before you make it! Then you think up a bright idea to let him steal one of your boat loads, except that on this particular load you've planted a bomb and a tracker! Now you would assume as we did, being the smart individuals that we are, that this mission would fail! Surely, if this guy knows our every move before we make it, why should this trick be any fucking different? Right! Of course, it wouldn't! It's fucking logic! So, then! You have the really bright idea, to see if your plan works, when you only tell the people you trust about it!"

Kelly paused a little to register Gonzalez's despairing confusion, before resuming.

"So, you can probably see where I'm going with this! What would your fucking rat fucking asshole do, when your plan works, as it has done tonight! And the only motherfucking guy you didn't tell is sitting right in front of you!"

Gonzalez's eyes widened as he shook his head at Kelly in frantic disbelief. Dumbfounded with distress, he was unable to muster any answer to Kelly's question. Kelly looked unimpressed and, in a huff, made for the desk. Kelly pulled out the unloaded pistol from the drawer and began to wave it at Gonzalez as he continued his interrogation.

"What's the matter, Fernando! Cat got your tongue! You were really talkative when you came in! And now that I ask you a simple fucking question, you go all quiet! Why is that? Oh! I know why! It's because you know that you're a guilty fucking rat! And when I put this gun to your head and pull the trigger, I'll be putting you out of your own fucking misery!"

Kelly now approached Gonzalez and pushed the gun to his head, with his finger poised on the trigger. He continued aggressively in Gonzalez's ear.

"I know you're a rat, Gonzalez! That's a given! You were the only one we didn't tell about our little plan tonight! And for the first time in I don't know when, we've had a little victory over The Shadow! A cause for celebration! But not for you!

"Now you can go down the route of proclaiming innocence or trying to feed us bullshit! And you can wind up outside like Darbandi here! We gave him a chance and he fucked it! Now, whatever you may think, we can protect you against The Shadow. We have guys in the FBI's identity reassignment programme. You can go off to The States or wherever you like! You can get whatever job you want! Have a new life! Or we can just take your life right fucking now in this chair if you don't cooperate!"

As Kelly said this, he pulled his body back from the crying Gonzalez and continued, poised for execution.

"We know you know the location of The Shadow's hideout in Nicaragua! We know you know others who are working with him in our team! You will tell us now! Everything you know! Or I am going to blow your brains out all over this fucking floor!"

Gonzalez began to weep again and looked up, with bloodshot eyes, at Kelly. He stammered through his reply.

"I-I did not know about the bomb. I did not know about the tracker. And I have nothing to tell you. I don't know what to say! Except that either you have made some mistake, or I have been set up! I don't know anything about The Shadow and I can't tell you anyone who does! What do you want me to do! Make something up! I don't fucking know anything! I don't know what the fuck you're talking about!"

Gonzalez began to raise his voice and shout at Kelly in a last ditch attempt to convince the room of his innocence. Kelly did not allow this performance to affect his own and pressed his firearm further into Gonzalez's temple to berate him further.

"This is fucking bullshit! Same as fucking Darbandi! You don't fucking get it! Do you, asshole! You are going to fucking die right here! Right now! Tonight! Why are you protecting him! Why! At least if you give him up you'll live another day! I fucking told you we can protect you! You are making this really fucking hard! I think you're full of shit and I think I'm going to give you one more chance! And then, as soon as you've finished talking, if I'm not satisfied, I'm pulling this fucking trigger!"

Gonzalez simply shook his head and bowed his head. His muttered prayers were drowned out by Kelly's bellowing threats that could easily be heard outside in the waiting room.

"You're really going to die for this fuck! You're not going to tell me what I know you know! You're about to fucking die! I would fucking say something right about now! I'm fucking serious! I'm fucking pulling this trigger! You saw what happened to Darbandi! You rat fuck! You fucking deserve to die!"

Kelly allowed Gonzalez to feel his finger tense on the trigger, in one final attempt to extract a confession. As Gonzalez continued to pray, Kelly, while still screaming profanities, pulled the trigger and allowed the empty chamber to click through to nothing. As the pistol made a slight snapping sound, void of bullets, Zola fired off a round of his loaded pistol into an empty corner of the room. Gonzalez, convinced of his own demise, twitched and fainted. He fell forward off his chair and to the floor. Persuaded of his innocence, Kelly had Gonzalez's, now pale and unconscious body, hauled into the reception room to the rear.

Lady Garrington again felt compelled to interject.

"Wow! That! Was! Amazing! Captain Kelly! You are fucking brilliant! This is brilliant! I think this is going to work! I mean, what man's not going to spill the beans under that kind of pressure! Send in the next victim!"

With that, Garrington's onsite operations manager, Louis Carlos, was called in and positioned at gun point in the interrogation chair. Carlos was born of a Ghanaian mother and American father. Having never known his father, he had been raised alone by his mother in Mexico City. Still a relatively young man, Carlos had become involved with the Temporada de la Bruja in his hometown. He had displayed more than just a head for numbers. A sharp and ambitious hoodlum, he had been rapidly promoted through the ranks. He was now in charge of Garrington's main distribution centre in Peru. Here, it was his job to ensure that the product came in and went out on point. The weighing, cutting and repackaging of their product needed to be organised to the letter and this was Carlos's job. This had involved Carlos gaining a deep knowledge of all operations throughout Garrington's empire. It was this information that had made him especially valuable to The Shadow.

Carlos had grown out his dark, very curly hair into a ponytail and was pursing defiantly, his large feminine lips. His deep-set, almost black, eyes penetrated Kelly as he sat confidently before him. Kelly instantly knew that this could be one of their rats. In Kelly's vast experience of such interchanges, the more calm and confident a given subject, the guiltier they normally are. Kelly changed his tack slightly to adjust for this character and commenced interrogation.

"Good evening, Mr Carlos. My name, in case you didn't know, is Michael Kelly. And I'm err, sorry we've had to drag you out here tonight. But you obviously know why you're here. Lady Garrington has already said that you are a deeply loyal and trusted member of her organisation. And we really just wanted you, and a few of your colleagues outside, to be here in case we needed you. But as you've just heard, we managed to catch our two little rats. These guys were secretly working deep with The Shadow."

Carlos frowned and looked surprised at this. He was evidently relieved with Kelly's lighter tone and Kelly registered this, as he continued.

"Oh! Don't be surprised. Gonzalez actually knew who The Shadow was! And he just confessed a whole lot more just now! We're in really good shape, Carlos. So, if there's nothing else you'd like to tell us? We'll ask you to go back outside and tell the rest of the guys to go home. That is, unless you do have something to say?"

Carlos shrugged and chuckled to himself, while shaking his head. Having made brief eye contact with Kelly and then Garrington, he rose to his feet to leave. As he turned to walk out of the front exit, Kelly engaged him once more.

"Oh! Just one more thing, Carlos! I thought I might just give you this one chance. Sit back down."

Carlos rolled his eyes and began to tremble a little as he turned and sat back down. What Carlos thought would have been an easy escape, was clearly not going to be so simple. Kelly continued, this time casually but ominously wielding his unloaded gun.

"You see, Carlos, it's really funny because, as soon as I said that, you looked real nervous! And now you really look like you're hiding something! And that's because you are! You see! Before you say anything, Louis, my friend! Before we whacked Gonzalez, he let us know something. You see, we knew Gonzalez was a rat and we tested him, and we also tested Darbandi! We told them both to tell everyone in our team today that the shipment we just got jacked, was to be packed with a tracker and explosives. Now previously, our little plans have all been foiled by The Shadow. Because he had a little rat to tell him how we were moving. Now, once Darbandi and Gonzalez had told everyone of our little plot, we shut down all their communication! So, there was no way they could let The Shadow know anything. Now here's the real interesting part! Darbandi and Gonzalez, they told everyone! Everyone, that is, except you! You little fucking rat! That's why The Shadow's little place in Nicaragua is up in smoke right now! And that's why we're now gunning for him! Do you not think it's a bit strange that the first time one of our plans works out, you're not involved? I guess it's not strange at all! I guess it make perfect fucking sense!"

Carlos was totally silent and snarled indignantly at Kelly, as he tutted and rocked back and forth nonchalantly on his chair. Kelly, fascinated by this man's confidence in the face of adversity, continued.

"So, Louis. I'm going to give you one chance. As you heard, the two people before you did not take this chance! So, I hope third time's the charm! Because if you can't answer the following questions properly! You're dropping out of here in a bag tonight, Louis! So, I don't know what The Shadow's got over you! Or whatever he's paying you! But it will be matched and more, as long as you're straight with us. We make more than The Shadow, we have more reach than The Shadow. We can have you in the United States under the FBI's witness protection program with a salary of your choosing, in a matter of days! But, as I said, Carlos! The alternative is death!

"So, Louis! Tell us all, right now! Everything you know about The Shadow and let us know the other people he's working with in our organisation! Tell us and tell us now, or I'm pulling this fucking trigger!"

Carlos, still defiantly jovial, chuckled and shrugged again, looking like a chronically truant teenager in the principal's office. He looked to Garrington sternly and spoke, wiping the cocaine residue from his philtrum as he did so.

"You'll never catch him. You can't beat him! Mistress, you can't win!"

The penny dropped with Kelly, who reacted, now certain a rat was sitting before him.

"Motherfucker! You cocky little fuck! Right! So, Louis? You think The Shadow's going to win? Well where is he now! Where is he! Is he here to protect you? Cause I don't fucking see him! Here's how this is going to go down, my friend! You have just made the smartest choice of your life admitting, as you have done just now, that you are in league with The Shadow. Now you are going to continue in this vein of smart decision making! And tell us exactly what you know about The Shadow, in full! If we suspect for a split second that you are not telling the truth, you will meet the same fate as our friends Gonzalez and Darbandi out back! You'll be wasted before you leave the room, cut up and dumped in the ocean! Now Louis, be very careful what you say! Tell me what you know and who you know in The Shadow's operation!"

Panting with intensity, Kelly allowed for Carlos to respond.

"You don't choose to work for The Shadow. You are chosen. The Shadow's organisation does not operate in the same way as yours, or any other criminal institution. First of all, no one knows anyone. That's right! It's all offline and secret. Some real dark web shit! The Shadow does not approach men with a choice of money or death. The Shadow targets specific individuals, who are undervalued in their organisation and yet have significant influence. I myself, because of my youth and inexperience, have been consistently undervalued by this organisation. Both Gonzalez and Santos are managers like me! And yet I earn almost fifty percent less than they do! For the same fucking job! So, unlike you Mistress, The Shadow does not have slaves. The Shadow has partners. For every boat load that is successfully captured, The Shadow gives me a ten percent share in the loot. Assuming, that is, myself and Emilio let him know the details of when and where it's going to be shipped. And when we do inform The Shadow, we do not go to him, he comes to us!

"You see, the first time I was introduced to The Shadow's organisation. I was at the market with my mother, my wife and my son. It was Saturday morning and we were out to get food for a dinner party my mother was having. In a corner of the market, a man with a covered face called to me by name. I left my family and went to him. Not removing his headscarf, the man led me to a side alley. In the alley were three more masked men. I couldn't recognise any of their voices, but they told me that they'd contacted another member of the Temporada de la Bruja, and that Emilio and I were very valuable to their organisation. They explained that he and I would both get ten percent of everything we brought in. They also explained that they knew where I slept, where my kid went to nursery and what time my mother and wife go swimming in the mornings. They explained that they could give me more than I had ever dreamed! But at the same time, they could take everything from me in an instant."

Carlos paused to cough, having captivated the room and continued.

"At a different time and in a different place each week, they meet with me. They always seem to know where I'm going to be and when. I tell them where and when the big loads are going to be dropped and, once they've boosted your stuff, they send me a direct bank transfer.

"I have made more money in the last two years than I know what to do with! The Shadow has guys in the FBI, the CIA! And he has guaranteed the protection of my family. So, Mistress, it should not be that hard for you to see that I do not fear death or your organisation more than I fear and respect The Shadow! I am well aware that I am going to die in the next few moments. So! If you think I'm going to tell you anymore, you can pull that fucking trigger right now!"

Kelly had extracted some valuable information. He was keen that Zola, who clearly wound up by Carlos's speech was poised to shoot him, did not yet execute the traitor. Kelly had found his mark and could taste his freedom. He was anxious that Garrington should get the most from this discovery and stopped Zola from opening fire. He interrupted with further expert interrogation techniques.

"Wait, Serge! No! Don't give this fucking guy what he wants! If we fucking kill him The Shadow's going to save his family for sure! He will have shown his fucking loyalty! No! No! We need to keep this little fuck alive! His little friend Emilio is outside waiting for us to fuck him just like you! You have to ask yourself one question, asshole! Who knows more! You or Emilio Dida! And considering he's only a driver, I bet it's you! Because, I know you think you've got it all figured out! But let me explain. We are not going to kill you, oh no! We are going to torture you and get everything we can from you! And then we might kill you! But not before we make for damn sure, The Shadow knows you've betrayed him! Then we can both hit up your little fucking market and take out the whole fucking Carlos clan! We will sacrifice Emilio for you! Do you see, we will let those men out there walk! And tell them we caught our rat! Emilio will go back to The Shadow and tell him this! The Shadow will then think you've ratted him out! And he'll waste that precious little family of yours, if we don't first! Son, wife and all! So, Mr Carlos! Are you going to make this easy or hard?"

Carlos looked up confused and beaten. His youthful ego took precedence and he defaulted to the stock hoodlum response. "Fuck you!"

Kelly, realising that time was elapsing, and he had eight more men to interview, including Emilio Dida, cut his cross-examining short.

"Okay I've had it with this rat fuck! Get him out of here and we'll let the rest go! Go on! Get this fuck out of my sight. I don't want to look at a man who would resign his family to death like this!"

Carlos, exasperated, shouting and wild-eyed, was carried out and through to the rear reception room. Garrington was exceedingly pleased with this interview and beamed at Kelly.

"You are just going from strength to strength, Captain! You're so fucking good at this! You're so sneaky, so manipulative. I didn't know you had that in you, Michael! You are the dictionary definition of dark horse! I think we should have, who was it? Emilio? Let's have him next. And make sure that bastard Carlos still thinks he's gone free!"

With this command Zola briefly popped into the rear reception, to inform the guards to take Carlos away and tie him up in the main house. Upon Zola's swift return, Emilio Dida was being shown in. Dida was the operations driver. It was Dida's responsibility to drive the largest loads of product from the distribution centre to the boats further down the coast. He was then responsible for navigating the main boat loads across the Pacific to Panama.

Dida was born in the favelas of Rio de Janeiro. As a very young boy he had become exposed and involved with the cocaine business. He had displayed brilliant intelligence and foresight, far beyond his years. By the time Dida was twelve years old he had a senior position in a small selling operation in central Rio. His bosses' business had been absorbed by the Temporada de la Bruja and since the age of fourteen he had worked for them. Dida, now twenty, had demonstrated a propensity for all things automotive. Whether cars, boats or planes, anything with wheels and an engine, Dida loved. He was more reliable, smarter and wiser than the other gang drivers and had ascended the ranks to become Garrington's core operations driver. Money had gone to Dida's gut over the years and he had put on a lot of weight in his later teens. This extra podge gave his skin a distinctly youthful glow. Sitting in front of Kelly, Dida could have easily passed for fifteen. He also had a rather high-pitched voice, which added to the confusing contrast between his infant looks but highly mature expression.

Kelly, while recognising Dida's age, spared him no special treatment.

"Jesus Christ! That's fucking depressing! You look about ten years old! You look like you should still be in fucking junior high! What's the world coming to if we got a fucking kid delivering our loads! Garrington! You gave this kid way too much responsibility! No wonder this is happening! So, boy wonder! You're really in serious trouble right now! You're in the principal's office! And you won't be the first child this principal has sent to the devil!"

Dida, being the bright young spark he was, had figured out his situation prior to entering the interrogation room. His nose twitched as he looked assuredly around the room at his captors.

"Okay so, you guys obviously spoke to Louis? I can only guess he's told you everything because you've kept him alive. I heard no gunshot before I was summoned? You must have kept him alive to flip him back and learn more? And now you've called me in because he told you about my involvement with The Shadow."

Dida had instantly enthralled the interview room with his accurate analysis and deft expression. Dida picked up on this and paused to survey and savour his audience's attention, before continuing.

"I can tell you, gentlemen, that I, like my friend Louis, wish to remain alive as long as possible. So yes! I am admitting to you all now that I have been working with The Shadow! And I do intend to cooperate in full and tell you everything I know! But please, first let me see Carlos and make sure he's okay. I want to know you're going to protect me and reward my loyalty! And not just kill me once I've told you everything!"

Kelly frowned, and his head recoiled in disbelief. He could scarcely believe how informed and cocksure of himself this young hoodlum was. Kelly was forced to snap himself out of the creeping awe he felt for Dida, as he retorted.

"Oh, no! It's not going to be that fucking easy, you fat-rat fuck! We need to make sure you and your boyfriend Carlos aren't doing a fucking number on us! You are going to confirm to us now what he told us about The Shadow! Or I'm going to fucking put a goddam bullet straight through your eye! I don't give a fuck that you look like you should still be in diapers. I'll waste you right here right now! It's no problem! The boys will take your flayed corpse, cut you up and dump you in the ocean! Then we'll take a trip to sunny Brazil! And we'll waste your nearest and dearest, sonny boy! That's right! If your story doesn't check out, it's not just curtains for you, Emilio! It's the whole fucking Dida Familia! Now! Answer me this! How did you meet with The Shadow! How did you find him!"

Dida paused, eyes bright and twinkling with horror. He elected to tell the truth and responded, with considerably less confidence than previously.

"I did not find The Shadow. The Shadow's men found me. I was riding my bike through town and I stopped at a red light. Four bikes pulled up next to me out of nowhere. They all had MAC-10s pointed at me. They forced me onto a side road. They all had reflective visors on their helmets and I recognised none of their voices. When I went with them into the side road, they informed me that Louis and I were very valuable to them. They offered me more money than I'd ever dreamed! Millions of dollars! They also said that if I did not cooperate, they'd kill myself and Louis. I had to comply or die right there! And afterwards, Louis and I agreed never to speak about it. And one day, we agreed to take our families and retire to Switzerland. The Shadow gives us both ten percent of all loads he successfully seizes from our intelligence. And it was easy for me, because I was always driving the loads. I drove the load tonight! And you wondered, Sergio, why I never got hurt? You always thought it was because The Shadow took mercy on my youth! But the truth, it should be obvious to you now..."

Kelly, attempting as best he could to mask his glee, snapped back at the latest developments Dida had exposed.

"Right! That does it! That's enough for me! Take this rat fuck outside, boys! And give him the same torture treatment as his buddy! Cooperate and you and your family will be safe! Lie for an instant, and your rat family's dead! If you slow in cooperating, you will be tortured. If you're withholding, you will be tortured! If you lie to us, you'll be tortured and we're going to kill your family! Comprende!"

With that Garrington's men grabbed Dida and barrelled his rotund frame out of the rear exit and proceeded to tie him up in another room of the main house.

The air in the interrogation room was now one of victory and relief. Garrington had been victorious in the successful execution of Wolf and Kelly's plan; and Wolf and Kelly in turn were both extremely relieved to have been so successful. Wolf, not being particularly partial to violence, continued to take a back seat and let Kelly handle the proceedings. Having waited for Dida to get out of ear shot, he proclaimed triumphantly, "Well, Lady Garrington! I think so far, things have been going exactly as we said. Am I right?"

Garrington smiled lovingly at Kelly and answered flirtatiously.

"Captain Kelly. I rarely do this, but I apologise. I underestimated you. You are clearly a man who talks quietly but carries a big stick! You and your colleague have delivered on all fronts thus far and I would very much like it, Michael, if you would join me later tonight. I thought we could have a little moonlight stroll on the beach, where we can discuss the terms of your side of the agreement being fulfilled. Because, after this, Michael, I intend to make more than good on my promise. Tonight, you will know how generous I can be."

Kelly was thunderstruck and deeply enamoured of the, now highly sexualised, Lady Garrington. He could barely manage a response and indeed did not. Instead, he turned bashfully away from Garrington and instructed the guards to send in the next man.

Kelly's routine continued through the remaining senior members of the Temporada de la Bruja, revealing no further rats. Several of the men had fainted on hearing their respective gunshot, as had Gonzalez. However, Kevin Tan, Garrington's chief accountant, had had the worst reaction by far. Almost as soon as he had sat down, the diminutive Malaysian accountant had been consumed by a vehement panic attack. Very officious and straight as an arrow, Tan was an unlikely rat. However,

Kelly had not even begun to fully threaten Tan, before he had grasped his heart and fallen to the floor writhing in agony. Not used to situations of genuine conflict, Tan had reacted poorly and almost given himself a heart attack. This had almost marred proceedings, as Tan was a valued and trusted member of Garrington's outfit, and had Kelly given Tan a heart attack, it would certainly not have helped their cause. However, having been carried via the back entrance, Tan had subsequently been revived and his condition stabilised.

As the final interrogation ended and the last man was sent alive through the back door, Garrington beckoned Kelly to accompany her alone to the beach. While Wolf, Zola and the guards dispersed, Garrington and Kelly sauntered off together in the direction of the ocean. Garrington kicked her cork-bottom platforms off, as the couple approached the end of her decking at the edge of the sand. As she removed her shoes, Garrington leant on Kelly for support. The two linked arms and walked onto the beach. Intimidated by her wealth, beauty and power, Kelly waited for Garrington to break the silence.

"So, tonight, Michael, I have to say I found you very attractive. I do like a bad man. And there's something so raw about you, Mike. So brazen, so unkempt! You, like me, clearly resent authority and you don't let anyone boss you. I find that very appealing. Do you find me attractive, Michael? Of course, you must be used to far more beautiful women than I?"

Garrington paused and leant her head on Kelly's shoulder, awaiting his response. Kelly, though deeply attracted to Garrington's allure, on a primal level, was still able to maintain some restraint. However, Kelly feared and respected Garrington. He therefore knew he had to strike a fine balance between charm and decorum.

"Yeah, I am used to slightly more immature women. But, you know! You're real MILF, Lady Garrington! I've seen you can have your fucking choice of men! But besides, don't you have a husband? What would Lord Garrington have to say about this? What would he say if he heard me call you a MILF?"

Lady Garrington took her head off Kelly's shoulder and moved away a little. She looked longingly into his eyes and gave him a flirtatious swipe across his chest, as she responded playfully.

"So, you think I'm old enough to fall into the MILF category, do you! And please don't talk about my husband. I love my husband and he loves me and that's none of your business! And we'll leave it at that! He may be my husband, but what I do and how I do it, is none of his concern! So, Michael. It would appear as though you have delivered everything you said you would. I think it would be best if we discussed the intimate details of our agreement, in the privacy of my room?"

With that, Garrington led the silent and totally submissive Kelly off the beach and to her room. Here the couple spent the night together cementing their relations. Garrington, a furious, adventurous and avaricious lover, kept Kelly up throughout the night. In the wee hours Kelly eventually collapsed, exhausted and drenched in bodily fluids, on the edge of Garrington's enormous bed.

# Chapter 12

## DRUG DEALER'S DAY BREAK

The sun was high in the sky before Kelly and Wolf woke. Both had been up late interrogating the night before. Kelly had needed to be carried back to their room, once Garrington had finished with him. The pair had had almost no sleep, when the morning beckoned, and they were summoned from their quarters to the gazebo downstairs. There to greet them, similarly to the previous morning, were Garrington and Zola. Both looked tired, exasperated and worse for wear from the night before. The same as the previous morning a breakfast was laid on, with coffee, fruits and pastries. However, Garrington and Zola paid no heed to their stomachs and were both huddled over the laptop, obsessively monitoring its screen. Kelly and Wolf hustled into their seats and Lady Garrington addressed them. She wore her customary morning getup of dressing gown, bikini and big sunglasses. Her voice was quiet but agitated as she spoke to them. She also appeared not to be smoking for pleasure but out of necessity.

"Right, so, chaps! Bit weird! The tracker we planted looks like it's on the move! And it's moving fucking quickly! You guys better have a look at this!"

Wolf and Kelly did as instructed and moved around to Garrington's side of the table. Wolf and Kelly could see the screen clearly displayed the tracker's movement, since it had been stationary in Nicaragua. The tracker had moved along the coast of Costa Rica and down to Ecuador. From there it had moved south, over land, and closer to their location. The tracker was now rapidly nearing Garrington's base, having already crossed the Peruvian border.

Registering Wolf and Kelly's understanding of the situation, Garrington exclaimed, "They're fucking coming for us! I've arranged a boat and a truck to get us out of here just in case! We'll run down the coast to Carlos Martinez airport. I've got a jet there waiting! I've also alerted the Peruvian military and they are manning up as we speak! Now they will be here in about an hour! But these guys are getting pretty fucking close! Sergie! How long do you reckon we've got until they're on top of us?"

Zola looked at Garrington and then at Wolf and Kelly before answering.

"At the rate they're moving, I'd say we've got about twenty minutes. I tell you what, Mistress! I hope now we can stop fucking indulging these guys and get the fuck out of here! By any means! We're sitting fucking ducks here! I bet he's got a fucking chopper the way he's moving across that screen! We don't know what he's going to do! Or what he's packing! We need to get the fuck out of dodge! Right fucking now!"

Wolf, though he had not found himself as popular with this crowd as Kelly, thought it was a good time to interject.

"If I may speak freely? I think that Mr Zola is absolutely correct, Lady Garrington. While I think we should remain positive, as you have still found two of The Shadow's rats deep in your organisation; and you have also located the obvious destination of one of his lairs. But, that said! I am certain at this point that it would appear The Shadow has now located the tracker and is very possibly on his way here to exact revenge! I think, therefore, that I agree with Mr Zola here, that it would be a tremendous idea, if we all exited the premises immediately!"

Garrington, now very shaken up and fearing for her life, tried to present as calm a façade as possible, as she stood to command her men.

"Alright, that settles it! We'll all pack our things and meet down here in fifteen minutes. Do you suggest we travel by car or by boat, boys?"

Wolf again interjected with his analysis and verdict.

"I feel that in this instance, Lady Garrington – and I believe, that all present company would agree? – we should be rendezvousing in ten minutes! And that we should be travelling by boat! A boat will be faster and more direct. The roads may trap us! And, against a helicopter, this may prove fatal. However, conversely, in a boat, we are far more open to attack! So, we must leave immediately in order to get an adequate head start. For if The Shadow fails to see us leave, he will not know in which direction to pursue."

Garrington looked at him with an interesting blend of respect and contempt, whilst she responded.

"Right, agreed! We will travel by speedboat. But, Professor, if you think I'm readying myself to your beck and call in ten minutes, you're heavily deluded! I will be ready in fifteen minutes! By which time I expect you three, if you want to remain alive that is, to be on my speedboat at the end of the pier! Engine running! And ready to go!"

With that she turned and flustered off in the direction of the main house. The three men followed promptly after, each quickly returning to their respective room to gather essentials and board the speedboat waiting outside.

While Kelly, Wolf and Zola had been more than punctual and were all positioned aboard Garrington's vessel within ten minutes, Garrington herself was late. After roughly twenty minutes, she opened an upper floor window of the main house and shouted down to the men waiting.

"I'm just coming, boys! Start the fucking engine!"

A little after this, she appeared at the rear entrance to the main house, with two huge suitcases in either hand. However, no sooner had she started walking down the decking towards the pier, when Zola spotted a sight that stopped his heart. He quickly shouted at Garrington, as he made this sighting.

"Mistress! Get back in the house! Get the fuck back in the house! Get to the fucking saferoom! Get to the fucking saferoom!"

As he continued to shout, Garrington turned and saw what all the men now could see. Three helicopter gunships were descending on Garrington's base. Lady Garrington lost all guise of grace, dropped her suitcases, kicked off her heels and sprinted for the main house's saferoom. Zola knew it was now up to him to hold down the fort from the incoming onslaught. Until the army arrived, or the Gunships ran out of fuel, he was on his own. Zola needed to get to the site's arsenal. This was located in an armoured shed in a corner of the beach. Inside this munitions shed were rocket launchers, grenade launchers and further anti-aircraft weaponry. Zola was about to leave Wolf and Kelly to their own devices and sprint off down the beach, when he was stopped by Kelly. Kelly dramatically grabbed Zola's shoulder as he made to depart and questioned him.

"Are you going to let me help you here! Or are your guys going to blow my fucking head off if I make a single move out of line! We're fucked here! Those fucking things have rockets and chain-guns! They'll mow us down like fucking ants if we don't work together! You've got to let me loose! Let the Professor go to his room and be guarded! But you've got to let me help you! Come on, Sergio! Let me loose on these guys!"

Zola, desperate and pushed for time, men and resources, relinquished. He nodded at Kelly and reached for his radio to instruct his team.

"Okay, snipers! Everyone! We've got incoming! Everyone to battle stations and all personnel to report to the beach hut for weapons. We got three gun-ships headed our way! And it's going to be a little while before the army gets here. Mistress is in the saferoom! I want ten guys outside at all times! The rest of you on the beach! Oh, and snipers! Stand down! I repeat! Stand down on Captain Kelly until further notice! He's fighting with us on this one!"

With that Zola and Kelly raced off down the beach, leaving the professor to retreat to his lodgings.

Within moments the trio of helicopter gun-ships were upon Garrington's base, like desert wasps on a juicy tarantula. Temporada de la Bruja did not put up a good initial fight. The choppers were freely able to hover over the distribution hangars and fire rockets into both structures. Having seriously damaged both distribution buildings, the gunships turned their attention to the house. They pulled up over the top of the house and hovered over the beach, while Zola's men scurried like insects underneath. The Shadow's men fired more rockets into the side of the main house and tracked their miniguns along the beach. The gunfire sliced up the beach like a giant knife of death, cutting through Garrington's men like sultanas on a cake-top. The men on the ground did all they could to seek cover and get to the ammunition shed at the end of the beach. However, they were helpless against the storm of raining bullets. Around half of Garrington's number were torn limb from limb by the gunships' miniguns, while only Zola, Kelly and a handful of other men managed to make it to the munitions shed.

Once inside the shelter of the shed, Zola and Kelly grabbed what they could. Zola picked up a rocket launcher and strapped two grenade launchers over each shoulder. Kelly chose to neglect the antiaircraft weaponry. Instead he seized a sniper rifle, along with five or six grenades. Kelly had dealt with situations such as this previously and already had a rough game-plan in mind. However, the men had barely enough time to settle inside their retreat, before they were forced to evacuate. Kelly could see one of the choppers approaching their position. He knew immediately what was coming and motioned for everyone to leave the shed. Sure enough, split seconds after Kelly had everyone start to exit, Zola spotted a flicker of smoke from the wing of the gunship and heard a deep fizzing sound. As he saw this a rocket ejaculated from the side of the aircraft, set on their location. The men scrambled desperately over each other to get out of the shed. Kelly and Zola just about managed to clear the huge conflagration of explosive material that resulted from the rocket's direct impact.

Well over half of Garrington's men were now dead, their ammunition and weapons bunker had been destroyed, while Zola and Kelly now lay open, exposed and shell-shocked on the beach. The three choppers continued to circle above, picking off more stray men and firing further rockets into the house. Kelly, still confident he could win over the situation, dragged the stunned Zola over to the pier. The pair crawled together through the sand, trying to remain unseen and hidden beneath the wooden planks. Kelly shouted his plan briefly to Zola over the gunfire, screaming and explosions.

"Okay, Sergio! I'm going to force the whirly over the house! Then I'm going to take out the crew! Then I'm going to rush it and try to commandeer the chopper! Now! When I say I need you to shoot that RPG you got at the right-hand side of that fucking whirlybird! Do not fucking hit it! I want that fucking thing pilotable! Now when I take out the crew, you fucking cover me as I run to the house! Okay! Now! When you shoot that fucking RPG! They're going to be all over us! So! When you do fucking shoot it! Make sure you move your ass! Run under the fucking pier and stay covered! Okay!"

Zola nodded. However, far from confident in Kelly, he was wishfully eyeing up Garrington's speedboat, which had somehow remained intact at the end of the pier.

Upon Zola's affirmation, Kelly waited a few seconds for their target helicopter to stray further over the roof of the house. As the gunship in question pulled almost directly over the house, Kelly signalled Zola to launch his RPG. Zola, still on his belly, took aim and fired with experience and precision. The RPG whizzed past the top right side of the helicopter.

This caused the pilot to veer down and left such that he was almost on top of the main house's flat roof-terrace. Kelly, having rolled out from his cover under the pier, saw Zola run past him and underneath. Kelly positioned himself on his stomach and put his eye behind his rifle's long-range scope. He could see clearly the pilot and co-pilot were the chopper's only occupants. Hoping the sights to be accurate, Kelly fired off a round at the right side of the pilot's head. Thankfully the sites were well-tuned, and the pilot duly collapsed, down and left, pulling the aircraft down and onto the house's roof. The co-pilot attempted, with his few remaining split-seconds of life, to lift his inherited craft back off the roof. However, Kelly swiftly switched his aim to the right and shot the co-pilot through his visor. With both pilots neutralised, Kelly now prayed that Zola could cover him from the other two choppers, as he prepared to make his way through the carnage to commandeer the now parked and unmanned helicopter.

Kelly had acted so fast and with such accuracy, that the two remaining gunships had only just noticed that one of their number was no longer airborne. As the other helicopters bent their course over the house to inspect the fallen gunship. Kelly took his opportunity and bolted for the main house, shouting to Zola for cover as he did so. On cue, as Kelly sprinted frantically past, Zola emerged from his refuge under the pier. He fired off several rounds of grenades at the two remaining gunships. Though he did not manage a direct hit, the ensuing explosion and shrapnel did jostle the choppers, causing them to turn in Zola's direction. The two gunships located the Italian and fired several errant rockets in his direction. Zola, desperately avoiding the fire, dived back under the pier, coursing under its refuge, towards the water's edge. The miniguns and rockets continued after Zola, ripping up the foundations of the pier and sending timber flying in all directions. Zola finally bailed into the ocean and began to swim furiously still further under the pier, that had now been almost completely consumed by the devastation behind him.

Zola's valiant efforts were a welcome and intended distraction for Kelly, who had now found his way onto the roof and was busy disembarking the deceased pilots from their fallen gunship. Having managed to do this undetected, he gingerly manned the controls and gently lifted the helicopter up. Kelly positioned himself quietly behind his airborne targets. The two remaining choppers were still focused on Zola and the pier, as Kelly fired off two rockets into the back of one of them. Without impediment, the two rockets clattered into the back of the targeted gunship. It exploded to the ground in a ball of flames, while the other pulled off instantly. Kelly, too experienced to stop and admire his handiwork, was focused on the next move. Prepared for its movement, as the one remaining enemy aircraft pulled off, Kelly anticipated its diversion with sweeping rounds from his chain-gun. This startled its pilot and caused a propeller to malfunction. In the delayed confusion, Kelly was able to fire off another two rockets in the chopper's direction. The two occupants howled in terror, as they heard the familiar gust of rockets approaching. The two missiles hit their intended target, which conflagrated instantly into a million pieces.

Victorious, yet stoic and deeply relieved, Kelly brought his helicopter to a rest on the beach decking at the rear of the house in front of the destroyed pier and gazebo. He disembarked and looked for Zola, who he spotted swimming back to the shore through the pier's wreckage. Kelly ran down to Zola, who emerged from the Pacific unharmed. Zola, hauling himself from the water, held his hand up at Kelly to indicate his stable condition. Doubling up, Zola caught his breath and, to Kelly's surprise, began to compliment him.

"Jesus, Captain! I thought that was it right there! I'm going to make sure that this favour does not go unrecognised! I will let Mistress know what you did just now! And make sure she gives you guys what you need! But, Kelly! Don't think for a second that I've forgotten that it was you, and your little friend Wolf, who started this mess! I think on balance, giving you what you need is fair. But, as I said before, after we drop you at the airport of your choice, I don't want to fucking see either of you ever again! But, that said. Thank you, Captain. You saved my life today…"

Kelly looked down to the floor bashfully, before regaining his train of thought and alerting Zola to the further impending dangers.

"Either way, Sergio! Look! They didn't hit the fucking boat! You're the faster swimmer! The Shadow's probably got more men coming! You've got to swim back out and get that boat! I'll go get Victoria and Chrissy and meet you back down the beach."

Zola nodded and swiftly returned to the ocean, while Kelly turned and dashed back to the main house. Kelly went to Wolf's room first and then the duo found their way through Garrington's bombarded abode to the saferoom. Wolf and Kelly bundled the now furious and neurotic Lady Garrington out of the house and onto the beach. By the time the three had reached the water's edge, Zola had managed to board the speedboat and was pulling it round to their position. The trio boarded the vessel and Zola pushed the throttle up to accelerate rapidly. Garrington and her three men had successfully escaped with their lives and were now bobbing and cutting over the gentle swell of the South Pacific.

Garrington looked more beautiful than ever as she perched, looking back at the wake of the boat, clutching and wrapping one leg around a metal beam. The shock and horror of the morning's events had put real colour in her face and her hair blew majestic and wild in the wind. Her eyes were enormous and piercing with aggression and adrenaline. Zola beckoned Garrington over from her gazing vantage to his position at the helm. When she approached the wheel, Zola whispered to her the details of Kelly's recent antics and heroism. Having heard Zola's confidences, she had Kelly and Wolf follow her below deck.

Below deck in Garrington's luxury speedboat was perfectly finished. Authentic wooden flooring and panelling housed modern appliances, a dining table and a well-stocked bar. Garrington sat Wolf and Kelly at the dining table and engaged them.

"Today aside, I am very happy with how things have gone between us. I am obviously particularly impressed by you, Michael! In fact, on reflection, if your work with the tracker has spurred a reaction like this from The Shadow, we must have really got to him! I bet that place in Nicaragua was a base of his! And now he has to move it! Ha! That's great, now I think about it! And our base was basically empty in any case. The main loads have already gone out and all the stuff he destroyed is replaceable, I suppose."

Garrington paused to contemplate her situation, as she felt the pit of her stomach fluctuate with the emotion of the moment, as well as the motion of the ocean. She now intended to give Kelly and Wolf what they came for. She stared both men down a little, and looked for any hint of doubt in herself, before continuing.

"I have decided, that on balance, I am going to cooperate with my end of our bargain. Zola is taking us to an airport down the coast. From there, we can fly you to any airport in the world. From there, you may then leave us! And be free to go about your business catching The Shadow. However, I feel that your airport of choice should be London, Heathrow. You see, gentlemen, not only is this the location where you will find the full details of my accounts. But you will also find my husband. You see, my main accounts are held at my offices in Knightsbridge. You are welcome to go and see Mr Tan, who you have already met. He left last night and should be back in London by now. He will provide you with all of my account information and the ledgers for all of my holdings.

"However, I thought you would be might be interested to know, as a little brucie bonus! That you will also be wanting to visit my husband. You see my husband, Lord Garrington, is, of course, in the House of Lords. He also has dealings with a man called Lord Tobias Cork. This man, in turn, has dealings with Abraham Silverman. Now, my husband thinks that this man Cork and Abraham Silverman, who know each other very well, have secret information on The Shadow! And this information may very well lead to the sourcing of The Shadow's identity and possible whereabouts. Now I am not in the habit of believing or crediting my husband to any extent! However, I had Serge check it out. Now, he spoke to one of our rivals and partners, a Mr Charles Daniel Hurst. Now Hursty is an arms dealer by origin. You see, while Silverman was always a financier and got into our game as he came up, Charlie was always a gangster! However, now he is a more respected and credible member of British society. He's gone and got himself a couple of funds. And he now operates out of a swanky Mayfair office, just down the road from Silverman's.

"Crucially, gentlemen, any dirty money that comes through London – and, gentlemen, most of it does! – any money laundering that does not go through Silverman, goes through Charlie Hurst. Hence first, I think it would be a fantastic idea for me to set up a meeting with you, my husband and Mr Tan. You can go through my accounts and you can quiz my useless spouse about his knowledge of The Shadow. He can also point you in the direction of Charlie. I would advise going to see him straight after you see my husband. Then maybe you will see that perhaps Mr Silverman is not as trustworthy as you might think. And that, perhaps in future, you should be more careful when brandishing his name about town."

Kelly and Wolf nodded and stayed silent, not wishing to say anything that would have Garrington detract from her submission to their wants, needs and desires.

It had taken them a little longer and been a little harder than they had first surmised. However, regardless, Wolf and Kelly were now headed back to London triumphant, informed and with a new plan in formulation. Importantly, not only would they get their account information, but apparently Garrington had given them two further significant contacts, her husband and Mr Hurst. Either one of these fresh leads could potentially bring them closer to the trail of Harvey Walsh.

# Chapter 13

## LORD GABRIEL GARRINGTON

Lady Victoria Garrington's jet ride allowed Wolf and Kelly some much needed rest, following their adventures in The Americas. The pair arrived at Heathrow refreshed and in a change of clothes. In high spirits, having made it back to relative civilisation, Wolf and Kelly swaggered down from Garrington's jet directly into one of her brand-new Range Rovers, awaiting their arrival on the runway. Garrington had previously explained, that she did not wish to be in the same place and time, as her husband and Captain Kelly. Hence, while Garrington embarked on a different course, she instructed her driver to taxi Wolf and Kelly over to her office in Thurloe Street, South Kensington.

The professor found himself reminiscing on his previous trip down the Heathrow corridor and into London. How innocent and oblivious he had been before, as a man simply attending his medal acceptance ceremony. However, this time his trip was considerably shorter and more clement. The sun was bright in the sky and, although cold, London was relatively windless and mild. Being the mid-morning, the roads were also clear, and Wolf and Kelly were downtown in no time. Wolf, however, could not help but think if innocence was perhaps bliss? Perhaps Wolf would have traded the weather and decongested roads, to return to his previous self? Did he envy a time before The Shadow, Lady Garrington and Abraham Silverman? He was unsure of as to all of this, as he remembered his very reasoning for accepting Mission Harvey Walsh, to ascend one final, near impossible, challenge. He had certainly attained this. However, thus far, Wolf felt his interaction with The Shadow had tested him to the very core and stretched him, in some instances, far beyond his capabilities. Wolf, therefore, sat in Garrington's luxury four-by-four, muddling two contrasting emotions. Elation on the one hand, at his survival and initial success, and distrust on the other. As, with the exception of Kelly, on some level Wolf distrusted almost everything and everyone, related to Mission Harvey Walsh.

Lady Garrington's office building was a modestly proportioned, white-stucco-fronted, terraced Victorian townhouse. It was positioned next to South Kensington tube station, on the edge of Knightsbridge. A feminine and delicately elegant location, sweet little boutique cafes and restaurants banked the north-west side of her office. While on the opposite side, Thurloe Street provided a green and leafy backdrop. Wolf and Kelly were dropped outside Garrington's building, in the heart of London's French quarter. They ventured through a pair of quaint black iron gates and up a stone stairway, to the raised front door of Garrington's office. Wolf rang the only buzzer, labelled Garrington & Co Ltd. Soon after, the door vibrated, made a buzzing sound and Kelly pushed it open. The pair walked through into the raised ground floor entrance hall. Not in keeping at all with Garrington's passion for glamour, her offices were decidedly dingy. There was a musty, dusty smell in the air, while Wolf and Kelly also felt more than a hint of a tremor, from their proximity to the tracks of the London underground.

Upon entering the building, Wolf and Kelly faced a corridor with a solid wall on the east side and two rooms, one after the other, on the west side. Kelly led the pair forward down the hall. As he did so, a man they recognised as Mr Kevin Tan poked his head from around the door at the back of the corridor. Tan, satisfied with the identity of his guests, emerged entirely from his refuge to greet them. Tan spoke with a polished, East-Coast American accent. However, particularly when pressured or excited, more than a hint of a Malaysian twang would emerge. He was a tiny, neat man. He combed his perfectly black hair into a ridged, perfectly crafted, side-parting and wore a pair of black rimmed spectacles, in perfect condition. Tan's entire existence was based on accuracy. This indiscriminate craving for precision, had forged Tan's entire career and kept him alive and thriving. Tan welcomed Wolf and Kelly without speaking into his office.

Inside Tan's office was a large, authentic, Victorian banker's desk, complete with leather-backed armchair, banker's lamp and inkwells. Across from the desk were three further chairs. Seated in the one occupied chair was Lord Gabriel Garrington. Lord Garrington was an altogether less impressive physical specimen than his spouse. Garrington was aging, balding, slightly podgy, moustached and foul-breathed. His manner and voice were towards the obnoxious end of the privately educated spectrum. While his physical appearance and personality were less than impressive, neither was his relative wealth or stature. In truth, Lord Garrington had needed and subsequently used his wife's wealth, to maintain and sustain his dwindling holdings. Not a man of considerable intellect or entrepreneurship, Garrington had depleted all but his real estate holdings, before meeting his younger partner.

Garrington did not bother to stand as his wife's associates entered. Instead he remained seated in a huffy, high-handed silence, as Wolf and Kelly took their seats next to him. Tan went to his desk and did not sit down, preferring to stand when engaging Wolf and Kelly.

"Michael Kelly, Christof Wolf, welcome to Garrington and Co. I trust you had a pleasant trip? Good! Great! So, you are here to see the difference in accounts between revenue streams before and after, quote unquote, The Shadow? Is that right! Good! Well, gentlemen! I can tell you that what Mr Zola estimated, was actually pretty accurate. And I can also tell you that the figures I am giving you now will be our most current and tested estimations, gentlemen! Key word: estimations! They are estimations! Estimations and nothing more! Understand! Not accurate! Not true!"

Tan had wound himself up and was clearly masking his contempt at having to reveal his accounts and bow to Wolf and Kelly. His audience in a confused silence, Tan continued.

"Anyway. The estimate is that before the, quote unquote, Shadow, we were making around seventy profit annually and now we only make around fifty profit! And these numbers are only for the distribution business, not any other business or assets, as requested."

Tan looked at Kelly and Wolf expectantly.

Kelly responded. "Thanks for the information. I mean! Estimations, Jeez! So? it was seventy before and fifty now? Fifty what? Million?"

Tan and Garrington chuckled at Kelly's ignorance and Tan retorted, "Before! Our profits, not revenue, profits! From this income stream alone!

Were around seventy-three, point four billion dollars! And now they stand at around fifty-one, point seven billion dollars!"

These numbers stunned Kelly, who raised his eyebrows in disbelief. He thought quickly and attempted to regain some credibility with the room with his next interjection.

"So, what's that? Around a thirty percent loss. Just like Sergio said!"

Tan cocked his head facetiously at Kelly and responded. "Yes, that's right, Mr Kelly. Just like Mr Zola said."

Tan shook his head disapprovingly at Kelly and continued at them both.

"The sum you are looking for, that is the sum that will be most useful to you! – Me! And my employer! – Is the amount we have lost, in real dollar terms, this quarter! As a result of, quote unquote, The Shadow! This is a far more accurate calculation and will, of course, be of significantly more use. This number could certainly be traceable to offshore bank account transfers made in the last quarter. However, I can tell you, gentlemen! I think that going through all offshore transfers made in the last quarter is not only illegal, but virtually impossible! You would need a team of hackers working day and night! But, gentlemen! Here is your number. The number you are trying to match is, one, point zero-five-six-two-six-four-eight-three-nine, billion!

"I can also tell you that we legitimise our funds through many different channels. However, from the business in question, we have approximately four hundred billion dollars with Silverman and two hundred and fifty billion dollars with Charles Hurst. My employer has suggested that, for various reasons, while Silverman may hold more of our company's assets, Mr Hurst is likely to be more cooperative and open in sharing his accounts in the pursuit of The Shadow.

"To conclude, gentlemen, I have prepared a written summary and further details of this information, for you both to take with you. And now, gentlemen, that I have fulfilled my employer's and your bargain, in full and without prejudice, I will hand you over to Lord Garrington, who will be speaking to you both in private."

Having said this, Tan slunk out nimbly, robotically and without farewell. On the desk, he left a package, containing the summarised accounts information he had promised. The package also contained Wolf and Kelly's phones and wallets, which Garrington had sworn to return to them. Wolf and Kelly's heads swivelled and followed the Malaysian as he left. The pair turned back to see Lord Garrington on his feet and making his way behind the desk. Kelly was thankful of this, as the deep ketosis emanating from Garrington's breath was harshly stifling. Garrington had a slight hunch and gave into it, leaning over the desk, using his knuckles for support. He spoke with a mixture of fatigue, reluctance and lashings of arrogance.

"Right, so my dear wife has requested that I come here today! To answer your questions on The Shadow?"

Garrington raised his eyebrows and rocked back on his heels in expectation, as his eyes flickered between Kelly and Wolf. Wolf frowned back at him and cocked his head in thought, before engaging Lord Garrington.

"Yes, thank you, Lord Garrington. That's exactly correct. Your wife has kindly agreed that you would enlighten us on your secret knowledge of The Shadow, Lord Cork and Avram Abraham Silverman."

Garrington stared obsessively and impatiently at Wolf. He motioned with his eyes and a slight hissing sound, for Wolf to commence his questioning.

"Yes, well, Lord Garrington, perhaps if you wouldn't mind explaining, to myself and Mr Kelly here, how exactly it is, that you became involved with The Shadow?"

Garrington reacted sharply to this question and snapped back indignantly.

"Right! So, you've err, you've got it fucking wrong! Okay! I'm err, fucking not! Involved with The Shadow! In any capacity, gentlemen! I have no fucking involvement whatsoever! In my wife's crazy fucking life! No-no! I know nothing about The Shadow! What is he, a fucking gangster! I'm a fucking Lord of the Realm! Hello! I sometimes sit in The House of Lords! If I can be fucking bothered! But! One of the only fucking things I do know! Is Lords! And I do know Lord Cork very well indeed!

"This is what you want to know, chaps! Okay! Just fucking listen! I don't want to know about you! The Shadow! Or my wife's sordid dealings! Sometimes I wish I'd never met her! God fucking curse that bitch! In any case, about five months ago, I overheard Lord Cork talking on the phone to another man I know called Abby Silverman! He's been a broker in my family for years, since he was a boy. Now we invest in his funds and so does Corky. Now, I wouldn't have thought anything of this conversation.

But it was when he kept mentioning the CIA, FBI, MI5 and this Shadow character, that I realised that he clearly wasn't talking about his fucking asset class allocation! I mentioned this to my wife a week or so later in passing and she said that she knew of this Shadow fellow!

"And that, gentlemen, is that! Please do not try and coax more information from this already bludgeoned brain! My wife has already tried and I cannot remember anything more than what I have just told you now! And don't think you can join my wife in trying to have me butter up Lord Cork into spilling something further on The Shadow! I'm just not doing any more! He's already suspicious! My wife doesn't understand! You can't just approach a chap and start chatting at the gents' club! Do you know what Corky said when my wife had me approach him? He asked me why the bloody hell I decided to ask him the question I did! Because it was the first time I had directly spoken to him in over a year! It was fucking embarrassing! Not to mention totally breaking decorum!

"So! there you have it, Professor Wolf! Captain Kelly! If those are your real names? They sound totally made up to me! I have told you all I know! And my wife's little Chink has given you what you need! So, you can both fuck off back where you came from! Now if you don't mind! Or if you do…"

Lord Garrington glared at them and proceeded to storm out.

Kelly quickly commented, "He just told us to fuck off and he's walking out?"

Garrington hearing this and not wishing to permit Kelly to go unscathed, stopped in his tracks in the frame of the door and retaliated.

"Don't they teach you any manners in Zoo York!"

Garrington slammed the door behind him, leaving Kelly and Wolf to find their own way out.

# Chapter 14

## CHARLIE HURST

Expecting to receive less than a hero's welcome, Wolf and Kelly hesitantly and with lumps in their throats, crossed the threshold of Mission Harvey Walsh. Having successfully hailed a cab from Lady Garrington's office, they had turned their phones on and checked through their messages en route to Mayfair. Maya had called Wolf's phone, almost immediately after he had switched it on. Maya had instructed them both to report to the base as soon as they were able.

Upon being let into Cork's Mayfair townhouse, Kelly and Wolf made their way directly to the main coms room. As soon as they entered, Team Harvey Walsh erupted with comments and snipes at Wolf and Kelly. Having had their phones and cards confiscated, they had been difficult to trace and impossible to contact for the duration of their travels with Garrington. This caused resentment with the intelligence, IT and operations sub-teams. While the IT and intelligence teams had to be content with locational information alone, the operations team had been truly put through their paces. Lopez and his men had needed to track and follow Wolf and Kelly, undetected, throughout the duration of their trip. Indeed, the operations team were nowhere to be seen, having yet to return from Peru. Overall, the pair's disappearing act had made them infamous and unpopular among their team. Particularly as, in the absence of Wolf and Kelly, whenever Douglas had visited he had been exerting his frustrations out on them.

Maya intercepted Wolf and Kelly, and led them up to their office, away from the taunts of Oppenheim and the others. Having been recently exposed to the darker side of international drug cartels, Wolf and Kelly managed to savour a little piece of sanctuary in their office. Somehow the wrath of Douglas now paled in comparison, to the fatally impulsive Lady Garrington and her Temporada de la Bruja. Wolf and Kelly made for their respective desks and sank into their chairs. Maya positioned herself in the centre of the two desks and looked from Wolf to Kelly, tutting confrontationally to them both, before addressing them sternly.

"Right, guys! So, you've damn well better have got something pretty fucking special! Because not only have you done exactly what I told you not to do! Clearly lost possession of your phones and cards! But you went totally rogue and off grid! I don't care if they put your lives in danger! Lopez told us everything! You guys just fucking handed over your stuff and told Lopez to get lost the way he tells it!

"So, apart from your location! Because, thank God, that stupid bitch took your cards and phones with her the whole way, we have known precisely nothing of your affairs. The ops team have reported a few sightings of you both on a beach! Kelly! You were racing a man in your swim shorts! What the hell were you guys playing at! You better tell me something good because sooner or later, Douglas is going to find out you're back! And if I don't give him something good, he's going to come down on you like a tonne of shit!"

Wolf smiled, aspiring to win over the troubled Maya.

"Please, Fräulein, you have nothing to fear. We were, as Lopez so kindly explained, kidnapped against our will. We were given a choice to cooperate or all three of us would have been killed there and then! So naturally, we elected to cooperate and attempted a strategy of appeasement. A strategy, I might add, which evidently paid off! As not only do we both sit here today, alive and well in front of you! But we sit here with the informational package that I hold in my hand!"

Wolf brandished and handed the package to Maya. She walked over to accept the package and Wolf continued.

"Inside this package you will find, Fräulein, exactly what we set out to get! The numbers, accounts and details that will take us a step closer to identifying the financial footprint of Harvey Walsh! Or as we have come to call him, The Shadow! Not only this, we have also learned a considerable amount about The Shadow's operations in the narcotics industry, which makes up a huge part of his overall business. Furthermore! We have just learned something really interesting! Borderline juicy in fact!"

Wolf raised his shoulders with charming excitement as he continued with his juicy gossip.

"We learned today in Lady Garrington's office, from her own husband! The horse's mouth so to speak, Lord Gabriel Garrington! That he overheard our employer Lord Cork, discussing The Shadow, the FBI, the CIA, and MI5. And the person with whom he was discussing this? Mr Avram Silverman! This, significantly, means two things. Firstly, we will need to be more secretive than ever, particularly in our direct contact with Lord Cork. As Lady Garrington and a man named Charles Hurst may well suspect that Silverman, Cork and The Shadow are somehow connected. This could obviously lead back to our organisation. Secondly, it means that the criminal underworld knows of Lord Cork! And he needs to be on high alert! For, as we have seen with our own eyes, there are powerful people out there, who will do unspeakable things to get closer to The Shadow! Lord Cork's life is in danger and he needs to know this!"

Pleased with Wolf's rough overview of their recent plights, Kelly interjected.

"Yeah! So, not only have we got you fucks what you wanted! Single handed and without any back-up whatsoever, I might add! You should have fucking seen what I had to go through! Do you know I actually slept with Garrington!"

Maya pulled the hair back from her eyes slightly and playfully interrupted, "Ah, was that Lord or Lady Garrington?"

Kelly ignored her jibe and went on.

"Alright fuck you, Maya! Okay! Not only did we get your precious account information! But we also fucking saved your boy Cork's life! He's a fucking marked man! Anyone who comes into direct contact with The Shadow is! Especially when the husband of the largest global cocaine distributor overhears you talking about him!

"Either way you look at it, we've done you guys a huge fucking favour! And risked our lives to do it! Now you take those little account papers right there! Take the shit we just told you about Cork! And go spit it all out to my main man Douglas, okay! Then you'll see it's you who should be doing us a favour!"

Maya rolled her eyes and shook her head in disbelief at Kelly's assuredness. She then reluctantly and flippantly snatched the accounts papers from Wolf and prepared to take her leave. As she walked to the door, she explained her improvised plan going forward.

"Right so, thank you, Mike. But I'm not going to do that. I'll tell you what I'm going to do. I'm going to give this accounts information to the intelligence and IT teams and see what they come up with. Then I am going to have you write a report right now, like the good little boys you are! I want a blow-by-blow account of what happened! On my desk! Downstairs! Before you leave here today! Then once this is complete, you may go home and rest. I will then send through our findings and your report to Douglas and pray he doesn't fire us! Okay, gentlemen! That will be all, happy writing!"

Wolf and Kelly spent the remainder of the afternoon battling to scribe through the recollections of their escapades with Garrington. However, Wolf being a proficient and succinct writer, they were finished by the early evening. Having handed in all their paperwork, Wolf and Kelly retired back to the comfort of their safeguarded Marylebone apartment block. Kelly and Wolf relished an opportunity to be alone and remained in their respective rooms for the rest of the evening.

The following morning Wolf and Kelly returned to their Upper Brook Street office. Maya was there to greet them and take them up to their study. She informed them that Douglas was on his way with instructions and that they were to await his arrival. Neither she, Wolf nor Kelly had any idea how Douglas and Cork would have received and perceived their findings from Garrington. As a result, they all waited, in a nervous silence, as they were served their tea and breakfast.

After around twenty minutes or so, the trio heard the familiar sound of Douglas ascending the stairs outside their office at a rapid rate. Seconds later, Douglas opened the door and allowed it to swing open before briefly catching his breath. He walked in slowly and purposefully. Douglas, spying Kelly, Wolf and Maya, paced into the middle of the room and allowed a tense silence to build. Wolf and Kelly were certain another barrage of harsh criticisms was about to emerge. However, Douglas, maintaining total expressionlessness, spoke in a calm and borderline amicable tone.

"Good morning, chaps. So, I suppose congratulations are in order. Yeah, I can't really fault you! I mean you did fuck up massively by losing your phones and cards! But a lot of that was Lopez's responsibility anyway, so not all your fault. He should have been protecting you! Not waiting in the car like a fucking chauffeur! But either way you never broke cover! And, most importantly, you fucking got what we asked you to! How could I possibly be upset, when you guys come back with the kind of monumental information that you did! No-no I'm actually – and I rarely say this by the way – I'm actually quite impressed. No, I am! You won her trust, you got her husband to open-up to you! You learned about their organisation! And this Sergio Zola character! Wow! He's fucking something, isn't he! We'll be all over him like a fucking STI! Oh, by the way, Kelly-boy! I hope you protected yourself when you fucked that floozy!"

Douglas shot a wry and sinister smile at Kelly, flashing his enamel-worn, yellow teeth. Kelly grimaced both at Douglas and the recent memories of his intimacy with Garrington.

Douglas continued. "So, I've basically explained the gist of things to Lord Cork. And last night and this morning, we have come up with a plan going forward. So, you will obviously cut all contact with Lady Garrington and her associates. We're just going to let the FBI and CIA deal with her. Oppenheim and Hakimi ops teams are going to attempt to hack, trace and match the amounts Garrington has lost to offshore transfers! This will take time, so while they're doing that, you boys are going to pay a visit to this Charles Hurst character.

"You will penetrate his organisation, as you did Garrington's. Under exactly the same guise and cover story. In fact, you're going to have to! Because from your accounts we can presume with reasonable fucking certainty, that Garrington's probably already contacted Hurst and let him know about you both. So, hopefully, if you don't fuck things up, things should all tie in quite nicely and you can see how close this Hurst twat can get us to Harvey Walsh!

"So, come on, guys! Chins up! You've done very well considering! I thought you'd both be dead for sure! I can't believe you've managed to come back in one piece! Let alone with this gold you've come up with! But, guys! Word of caution! You have been successful, yes! But do not be victims of your own success! Because really, guys! Truth be told! I reckon you've been lucky on this one! Lady Gazza's obviously got the hots for meathead over here! You won't have such an easy ride with Hurst! Read his file! He's a fucking beast, by the way! If he suspects for an instant that you're not Captain Twat and Professor Prick-face! A pair of gun slinging bounty hunters! He'll kill you and compromise our mission! So! Do not fuck us!

"Now, Maya's going to brief you further! And you'll both then beef up on your background reading, before heading out to Egypt. Oh, that's right! This guy is in Egypt, right! So, once again you guys get to fuck off out of my purview! Thank fuck! I really think we should keep it like this, boys! You guys fuck off! Get what we need! Bring it back! Quick two-minute meeting! And then you go off again! Look! I'm very, very doubtful of this! But I do genuinely hope you have the same success with Hurst as you did with that two-dollar hooker Kelly fucked!"

With this, Douglas began to walk to the door to leave. He turned in the frame of the door and paused with his hand on the doorknob, to give Wolf and Kelly a parting utterance.

"Oh! And guys! Don't fucking breathe a word of what Lord Garrington told you about Cork! The less people know about that the better! Just forget you ever heard it, yeah! And whatever you fucking do! Do not! Tell Hurst anything about it, right! Got that!"

Douglas flew through the door and slammed it in one fluid motion leaving Maya, Wolf and Kelly in his wake. As he left, Maya turned and beamed at Kelly and Wolf and exclaimed elatedly, "Wow! Wow, guys! Impressive! I've never heard him like that! Particularly not with new guys! Shit, guys! Now I'm fucking impressed!"

She paused and smiled at Kelly and then at Wolf. As she smiled at Wolf their eyes met, and for the first time since Wolf's engagement by Mission Harvey Walsh, the pair were returned to the same feelings of intimacy they had shared in his apartment. Maya, swaying back from her mental indulgence, regained her train of thought and resumed.

"So, you guys heard Douglas. You will both head back to your apartments and we will courier through the literature on Charles Hurst. You will bone up on this, and then tomorrow first thing, you will be headed to Aswan. You will be using exactly the same cover story as Douglas said. You will be looking to get hold of access to all of Hurst's account information and, in particular, how much he has lost in market share to Harvey Walsh. Then you will attempt to befriend him, as you did Garrington, and get back here alive, with as much fresh intel as possible."

Maya concluded and escorted Wolf and Kelly to the front door. As she held the door, Wolf and Kelly slipped by and out into the cold. Maya shouted after them as they made their way west down Upper Brook Street.

"Hey assholes! This time try not to lose your fucking phones, uh!"

With this she retreated back into the warm sanctuary of Cork's townhouse, leaving Wolf and Kelly to venture back to their apartment building.

Sure enough, the pair had barely returned, before the concierge rang up to them both with briefs on Charles Hurst. Wolf and Kelly went through the material in the same manner as previously. Wolf would read large stints of information and summarise his findings to Kelly, who would organise and collate the information for Wolf to read. As with Garrington and Harvey Walsh, the pair had no chance of consuming all their material before morning; however, they did as best they could.

The following day, a little more informed on their next target, Kelly and Wolf found themselves back on the Heathrow corridor bound for Aswan International Airport. Hurst had many bases in Africa and would spend much of his time on its east coast. This location was perfect for Hurst, who could import and commandeer shipments of weapons from the United States, United Kingdom, Russia and China. Maya, as before with Garrington, had arranged for Wolf and Kelly to meet with Hurst at a five-star hotel he owned on the banks of The River Nile.

Having been born into a family of relative affluence, Hurst had spent his childhood in South Clapham, a prosperous and leafy London enclave just south of the River Thames. Privately educated, he spoke with a deep received pronunciation and polished expression. From an early age, Hurst had been materially obsessed. Paying little attention to his schoolwork, Hurst had wanted to graft in the real world as soon as possible. His parents, being from an academic and engineering background, had forced him into university study where, despite his intelligence, his performances had dwindled. Being unable to source a career in academia or in his degree subject of international business, he had joined the armed forces.

Notwithstanding Hurst's slight stature and lack of aptitude for military combat, it had been Hurst's business brain and thirst for cash that had facilitated his resignation from the army within two years of completing his training. Hurst had been exposed, through his exploits with the British infantry, to the networks and dealings of arms trading. The money and prominence of this trading worldwide had fascinated and consumed Hurst as a young man. In his thirties, he ascended the ranks of global arms dealing networks, dancing on the edge of the law as he did so. By the time he was in his mid-forties, Hurst had made a name as a major player in the black market for weaponry. He had started his own business and by the time he was fifty-five, he had taken over the majority market share in the global informal arms sector.

Hurst had made billions, had governments, major weapons producers, militia and terrorist groups all at his fingertips. Hurst would buy out tin-pot republics and politicians, for the most part in Africa. He would then order weapons from major distributers, under the guise of legitimate demand. Hurst would then take the product and sell it on to the highest bidder, normally another government, militia or terrorist group. Hurst would also use his network and buy out contacts in world-leading arms manufacturers. He would then steal large shipments of weapons, having been instructed where and when they would be most vulnerable to theft. Having stolen a given shipment, he would stow it back to his bases in East Africa for storage and redistribution at huge profit.

Now an established player in the formal and informal sector for arms dealing, Hurst had used his billions and his contacts to start Ortu Capital. This was a fund of funds for which he used to launder and consolidate his and his contacts' wealth. In this way, as Lady Garrington had explained, Hurst had become, like Silverman, a fund manager. However, unlike Silverman, who had always been a financier, Hurst had only become a money manager after ascending the networks of organised crime. Similarly to Garrington and Silverman, Hurst had been significantly affected by The Shadow's activities. He too had been losing shipments of product, had had his men killed, his assets destroyed, and his market share depleted at the hands of The Shadow. Having heard from Garrington and Maya, Hurst had been eager to receive Wolf and Kelly. Any fresh faces with leads on The Shadow wanting to assist in his apprehension, were almost blindly welcomed by Hurst.

Hurst's hotel was located in a sweet and idyllic spot on the southern tip of Egypt. The small tourist destination of Aswan provided a powerful backdrop of sweeping predynastic monuments. On the banks of the river, surrounding the hotel, boats of relative glamour were moored, lending a sense of real luxury to this pocket of wealth, in an otherwise impoverished nation. His hotel was an enormous redbrick building, with authentic Egyptian architecture. Constructed over three storeys, it looked quite elegant against its wonderous ancient backdrop. The building's interior had been designed in a lavish British-Victorian colonial style. However, the entire complex had been modernised internally, with no expense spared.

Wolf and Kelly, having changed planes at Cairo, had flown into Aswan International and, within an hour of landing, were nearing the entrance to the hotel's grounds. Double fronted, the hotel's west facing side looked over the Nile and consisted of a smart terrace and swimming pool directly over the river. The hotel's east façade faced onto a huge courtyard and driveway entrance. In the middle of a square pathway, leading in and out of the complex, was an extravagant fountain lined on each side by palms. Both Wolf and Kelly were impressed with the contrasting decadence of Hurst's palace-like hotel and the abject economic deficiency they had witnessed en route from the airport. Having been guided down the hotel's driveway by Hurst's security team, Wolf and Kelly's car, driven as before by Lopez, pulled up outside the hotel's main entrance.

The entrance's small, deep brown double doors were modest in comparison to the rest of the building's frontage. However, the entrance hall itself and the rest of the interior was very grand indeed. With undertones of Middle Eastern and authentic Egyptian design, the hotel's reception was cased in marble. The centrepiece chandelier was enormous, golden and encrusted with large gemstones and stained glass. The doors leading off into the various corridors and other parts of the establishment were much larger and more majestic-looking than the front doors. Made from solid oak, these doors stretched four metres to the ceiling and were studded with intricate ironmongery. Wolf, Kelly and Lopez were led up to the reception desk and asked to check-in their belongings. Lopez disarmed accordingly, and the receptionist stored his weaponry behind the desk.

Lopez, as before, was then left at reception, while Wolf and Kelly made their way through a pair of impressive doors flanking the reception and through to a stairway. They ascended to the first floor and into a room that was obviously set up as the hotel's business conference centre. A large circular arrangement of tables consumed the room. Around a dozen, beautifully crafted and designed, modern Victorian style chairs were pulled up around the tables. In front of each seat was a neatly laid leather mat, drinking glass tumbler, notebook and pen. The room was lit by a fantastic, and totally garish, black chandelier, which loomed over the central table arrangement like a giant spider. The room was empty as Wolf and Kelly entered. They sat down at the far end of the arrangement of tables and were instructed to wait for Hurst who would join them shortly.

Wolf and Kelly were not left alone for long and they soon heard footsteps approaching the door outside. The meeting room doors opened, and the pair turned to see Hurst standing at the door staring down at them. Hurst was suited and booted, despite the climate. His suit, shirt and tie were all dark shades of blue, matching his dark skin tone and even darker eyes. His hair was very short and trim, his eyebrows plucked and his tiny moustache immaculately groomed. He continued to look at them for a moment, before walking across to the other side of the table arrangement. Hurst was closely followed by an older and more aggressive looking man in large, thick-framed glasses. As he marched over to his intended seat, Hurst walked with a spring in his step, to maximise his apparent height. Kelly and Wolf began to get out of their seats to greet Hurst; however, he stopped them as he walked with a deep, confident and smooth instruction.

"It's okay, boys! At ease! At ease! Charlie's not that kind of guy! Unless you try and fuck me! And then you'll be doing more than just standing to attention I can tell you!"

Hurst's assistant chuckled slightly at this comment. He proceeded to move ahead of his employer, pull out a chair for him and take the seat next to him. The man was average in height but substantially built. His face was grey, wizened and belligerent in appearance. Behind his thick-set glasses lay a pair of deep green-brown eyes. His hair was a murky white colour and scraped back over his forehead. His overall look was not dissimilar to that of a senior mafia 'Don' of old. Kelly and Wolf were duly intimidated by Hurst and his surroundings and allowed the silence to creep on a little, while waiting for Hurst to continue.

"So, you chaps are Gary's chums, what? She said you were after The Shadow! And let me tell you, gentlemen! Any friend of Gary's is a friend of mine! But any enemy of The Shadow's is an ally for life! That man is a menace! While I am a pretty special guy, I have certainly faced the possibility that it will take more than me to stop him. In short, gentlemen, we need all the help we can get! So please, Professor Wolf, Captain Kelly, you must excuse my rude introduction, but I have read both your files! I like the cut of your jib! You're both ex-cops! And I love an ex-cop! They're great, having fought on both sides! It gives them a clearer understanding of the overall picture! If you know what I mean?

"And if you don't know who I am, I am Charlie 'FedEx' Hurst! I am arms trading! I'm always on time! I've got the best produce! And my deals never get screwed! This is my hotel, so you can make yourselves at home! And as long as you help us find and eliminate The Shadow, you can stay as long as you like, free of charge! I've arranged for you to have one of our best suites! But first, gentlemen, why don't you tell me a little bit more about yourselves?"

Totally different to Garrington in his approach to life, Hurst was all business. He loved the vibe of business meetings and wearing suits. He was obsessed with his holdings and comparing his wealth to the people he met. He was far less about cocktails, cocaine and culinary delights, instead preferring fast deals, fast cars and faster women. Wolf and Kelly, though still cautious, were relaxed somewhat by Hurst's good-natured, if a little commercialised, communication. Wolf took the initiative and engaged Hurst first.

"Well firstly may I say, Mr Hurst, what a fantastic hotel you have here. And how grateful Captain Kelly and I are, of your kind hospitality. While I suspect that Lady Garrington may well have told you most of the relevant information on our activities, Captain Kelly and I are essentially no more than common bounty hunters. We were engaged by a phenomenally wealthy, anonymous and powerful backer to identify and locate The Shadow. We have been tracing money laundering trails in organised crime, in various industries throughout the globe. We do this in the hope of matching activity linked to The Shadow. If we can do this successfully, we can locate his money. And of course, the theory is, if we can locate his money, The Shadow himself, must be close by. So far, we have successfully aided Lady Garrington in her battles with The Shadow and in return, have been given full and relevant account information for her holdings in the narcotics trade. We are currently in the process of matching her lost market share, with offshore bank transfers. This should lead us to The Shadow's accounts.

"To be direct and do you the respect of cutting the crap, and getting straight down to business, we have come here to ask for your account information such that, in a similar way in which we have with Lady

Garrington, we can cross reference any market share you have lost, with the financial activities of The Shadow."

Kelly also now piped up with his own addition.

"Yeah! And we've been informed that while Garrington's accounts are her own, you, being a fund manager to the organised crime institutions of the world, have access to all their accounts too! So, if you really want us to locate The Shadow quicker, it would be great if we could get all that info as well?"

Wolf felt this tone was a little tactless and interrupted Kelly.

"Now, now, my friend. Let's take this one step at a time, yah? I said we would be direct, but we have only just met Mr Hurst and despite Lady Garrington's obviously credible reference, we have yet to fully trust each other."

Wolf turned his attention back to concentrate on the target.

"Overall, Mr Hurst, we would like to know all you can tell us about your dealings with The Shadow and his involvement in the informal arms trading industry. We would also, ideally as Michael said, like to obtain all the account information you can give us from the world of organised crime. Whether this be money laundering accounts or just holdings of known criminal organisations. And please, Mr Hurst! As Lady Garrington understood, once she had come to know myself and my colleague here, we are here for a common goal: To locate and identify The Shadow! And we are very good at what we do. Simply, Herr Hurst, if you allow us to work together, we can help you against what we know is an almost insurmountable force."

There was a slight pause as Wolf concluded his mini pitch to Hurst, who pondered a little before responding.

"I wouldn't say insurmountable! Certainly not insurmountable! And Gary told me what happened with you chaps! So don't worry! As long as things don't change vis-à-vis your behaviour going forward, I trust you both implicitly and I am fully willing to cooperate. I will provide and send through, to an email of your choice, all the account information for Ortu Capital. As well as my own management accounts and balance sheets for my arms dealing business. All off the books stuff, of course! This should be all you need…"

Hurst paused pensively placing his hands on his hips.

"But I knew I'd give you this before you came. I do, however, I do want something from you in return. I do want something more...

"This account sourcing malarkey! It's all very time consuming and time is money, gentlemen, and mine is precious! I need to find, ID and murder that Shadow son of a bitch! My shipments and contacts are being taken from me at a rate of knots! I already told you, chaps, you can stay here as long as you like! Just please come up with something! Something to help me combat this bastard!

"I don't expect any ideas now. But I have some urgent and pressing business to attend to. And I'll be leaving you in the capable hands of my associate, Mr Daniel Wright here. Mr Wright is a director at Ortu Capital and my right-hand man. He will explain the situation a little further and then you'll be shown to your suites. By the evening you'll have your account information and we'll reconvene at dinner to discuss things further. We can also see if you've managed to come up with something useful by then. Sound good, gentlemen? Good! Well then that's settled!

"Right, I'm off, chaps! I've got to catch a chopper to South Sudan. The prime minister found out about an illegal shipment of Napalm and Heat Seekers that we've sent his war minister. Bloody nightmare! I hope to be back for dinner, but you never know with this guy! Fucking Sudanese! He's a real piece of work!"

With that, Hurst rose and marched out in the same, militant and business-like way, in which he had entered. His gangster-looking associate Mr Wright now took his cue and introduced himself. His rough cockney accent was as coarse and abrasive as the content of his speech.

"Do you know who that was?"

Wright paused and looked deliberately at Kelly and then at Wolf. Intimidated and confused, the pair did not attempt an answer to this seemingly obvious question. Wright, satisfied with their silence, spoke again.

"That, my friends, was Mr Charlie 'FedEx' Hurst! And Mr Hurst is no ordinary man, you see. You two need to understand now that Mr Hurst is up there with the most dangerous men on this fucking planet! And his danger, gentlemen, is represented and executed by me! I am, so to speak, his enforcer! So, you can imagine how dangerous that makes me! They've got a nickname for me in our industry. Pretty cute actually! And that nickname, gents, is Death Warrant!"

Wright paused again to swallow violently and offensively, before continuing.

"So, I don't know what you think is going to happen here! But I can tell you now that this is how things will occur! You will remain under our total and complete authority. Until you have satisfied my employer and he states you're free to go. Until such time, you will not engage in anything, other than total and complete cooperation with Mr Hurst, myself and this organisation! Any deviation from this line of behaviour will result in the two of you being shot in the head and left in the desert! You cunts got that? Good! Now fuck off to reception and get your keys!

"Oh! And a word of advice, ladies. Make sure you've got something good for us at dinner. We wouldn't want Mr Hurst to be disappointed, now, would we? Because we don't want to see what happens when Mr Hurst is disappointed? No! I thought not. So, fuck off! Put your thinking caps on and bash your heads together till your brains or a bright idea pops out!"

Wright looked at them, his eyes flaring with anger and hostility, as Wolf and Kelly shuffled submissively from his presence and down to the reception, as requested. At the reception Kelly and Wolf picked up their key and were directed to their top floor suite. The suite was arranged as a substantial three-thousand square-foot apartment, complete with three double bedrooms, each with its own bathroom and balcony. The suite's reception was grand and had a more extensive balcony, overlooking the Nile. Wolf and Kelly selected their preferred bedrooms, settled themselves and ordered room service. They spent the remainder of the day in the relative peace of their suite, contemplating the situation and attempting to formulate some feasible plot, in time for Hurst's return that evening.

The sun had long since set and the moon was high in the sky, before Wolf and Kelly were summoned to Hurst's private dining area. This was located on an elevated section of terrace at the rear of the hotel. The private table was positioned in an elevated thicket of small palms and shrubs, such that any diners could not be seen from the swimming pool or lower sections of the terrace. The table provided an excellent vantage, however, to view the meandering Nile and ancient monuments set into the rolling, interlocking and now moonlit desert dunes. As Wolf and Kelly drew nearer to the dining area, they could see that Hurst was already seated with a large glass of red wine. He was completely alone. As the pair drew nearer still, they could see Hurst was looking considerably more dishevelled than he had done that morning. His expression was one of tired frustration and defeat. His tie had disappeared, and his shirt's top two buttons had been undone. Having, in the morning, been completely rigid in his stature, he was now slumped in his chair almost cradling his glass of wine. His eyes were a lot less bright and appeared slightly bloodshot. It was evident that his business today had taken a lot out of him. Sensing this, Wolf and Kelly walked carefully and respectfully around Hurst and took their seats opposite him. As they sat, with their backs to the Nile, facing the hotel's beautifully floodlit façade, a waiter popped up from the bushes behind Hurst and poured two glasses of wine for Wolf and Kelly. Once the waiter took his leave, Hurst turned to Wolf and Kelly in a trance-like state and, in a moderately inebriated and supercilious voice, enquired, "We'll be having steak tonight, gentlemen. Fillet. I hope you chaps like?"

Both Wolf and Kelly instantly assumed the awkward role of being sober in the presence of a slightly sarcastic and negative drunk. Wolf and Kelly responded homogenously, with shrugs and smiles of affirmation to Hurst's dinner choice. Hurst scowled and looked off again into nothing. He allowed a silence to swell, before speaking again in a drawling, intoxicated and facetious tone.

"Mistress, right? Isn't that what she has you call her? That's right, you're Victoria's lackies, aren't you? You are! She told me! She also told me that you, Captain, despite numerous attempts, were unable to satisfy her fully! So, you are to call her Mistress too! Just like me. She rang me up and told me this before you came. And let me tell you something about Lady Vic! Captain Kelly! I fucked her! Yep that's right! I've been there, brother! You don't have to tell me! She was powerful, beautiful and sexy as hell! She was too much for me! Furthermore, she is a whore and a cold-hearted bitch! But my God! Do I fucking respect her! But as a professional and nothing more! Victoria, to quote Charles Dickens, 'has a heart to be shot at or stabbed at but nothing more'. No emotion or feeling resides inside Victoria. She is not capable of love! Her love is for power and resources! She is the epitome of the ultimate modern, western woman!"

Kelly and Wolf, realising that Hurst, in his current drunken state, could be in a position to divulge more intimate information, remained quiet and allowed for him to elaborate.

"You see, fellas, once you've failed to satisfy a woman a few times and once you've been poor, rich, up, down, and back-and-forth as I have, you start to realise certain truths about the world. Certain truths that you wish you'd known earlier. Certain truths that you can't believe! And that you wish weren't true…

"You see, chaps, we've got to stick together! Feminism, girl power and positive discrimination for women in the workplace? The whole thing is a manipulative ploy by wealthy individuals who control governments and the media! These individuals are using feminism for the cultural and social manipulation of the developed world.

"You see, guys, wealthy families ultimately want to limit the number of guys like me in the world! A non-established, black! Nobody! With a cracking education and a passionate ambition for the finer things in life. If there are too many guys like me that make it, we'll start to challenge the power and wealth of these established families! So! One of the things they do is use the sexual and marital relationships to manipulate the situation. They do this to restrict economic development and stop too many women having children! They've basically made it so that women don't have kids! And if they do, they stay poor!"

Hurst, momentarily, gained a little sobriety and noticed that Kelly and Wolf were deeply perplexed at his choice of conversation. Hurst, however, not sober enough to fully take in the impropriety of his favoured topic, took another sip of wine and resumed.

"You see, chaps, in the old days, men from educated middle class backgrounds, would not even consider marriage or long-term relationships until they had sorted out their career. This was because they knew the truth about women and relationships! That, ultimately, however sexy the relationship at the start, as soon as a little time elapses, the relationship switches from sex and courtship, to marriage and children! Now, these two things are the single most expensive things a man will encounter in his life, without exception!

"The problem is today! Women are not confessing that a man's resourcefulness is his most attractive characteristic! And in addition! They are also rejecting big age gaps in marriages! This is forcing young men into a huge position of pressure. They are being required to provide for a family at a very young age. They are also deeply discouraged from avoiding relationships and sleeping around. This works for women, who are fooled into thinking that this will give them more power! It will, but at the cost of financial power! As although your husband will be younger, easier to control and will not have a financial hold on you, you and your children will be poor! On top of this, men also have to compete with globalisation and positive discrimination in the workplace."

As Hurst went on, the same waiter returned to top up their wine and serve their steaks. While Kelly and Wolf began to tuck into their meals, Hurst neglected his food, consumed with his rhetoric.

"And let me tell you something else! The gender pay gap and discrimination! I have been discriminated against my entire life! I am short, black and ambitious! And I've lived through the eighties and nineties! You can't tell me anything about discrimination! And, chaps! Positive discrimination doesn't work! It's another conspiracy to consolidate the power of wealthy families! That's right! Because the fact is! Women are more intelligent than men. However, there are several things which, in the developed world, make women totally incompatible with certain jobs. And in particular, higher paid jobs in business.

"It is this massive divide in intelligence that is the problem. Women have been clever enough to have men do their bidding for hundreds of years, while they look after the family. Today, in the developing world, this is no easy task. But in the developed world, dropping the kids to school or nursery, heading to the coffee shop and then the gym and then back home for a massage and a quick trip to the shops! Gents, that's my idea of heaven! These ladies you see jogging in the morning when we're on our way to work! They've got it fucking made!

"And the route of this lies in the establishment's masking of the great truth about women! And the single greatest misconception men make about modern women! While women are all attracted to different things, they are attracted to one thing more than anything! Resourcefulness! This goes back to hunter-gatherer instincts. When a woman had a child, she would feel very insecure. Hence, even before having a child, she would need to be sure that her partner could support her and their child, even in the most dire of circumstances. Men, on the other hand, are only concerned with impregnating as many attractive women as possible! This means we have as many sons as possible to protect us when we grow old and weak! Hence, while men are attracted to what we see and sense sexually, women are attracted to a man's resourcefulness! However, this is being hidden from men and women alike!

"For me, the only way to change gender equality is for women to really appreciate how hard it is to be a CEO! How businessmen give up their entire lives, kids and all to maintain! Girls should be taught in school that it is not an option but a necessity to go out and provide for your family. Women need to stop seeing a career as a luxury and see it for the slavery it is! The reason we don't have any women in serious positions in business or professions is because they underestimate the gravitas of these careers! They need to know how it feels to have your holidays, paternity leave and pay rises rejected! To spend more time at work than anywhere else combined! When women start to compromise – as men do! – who they are and become completely defined by their profession, then they will have equality! Because as we all know deep down! Equality isn't given, it's earned!"

Hurst paused again, and it was clear that his inebriation and choice of words were harbouring something greater. Hurst fixed his eyes to the floor and confessed what he had learned earlier that day.

"That fact is Lady Garrington is who she is! Not because she's a woman! But because she's a fucking beast! She is an example to us all! Because, as if my day wasn't bad enough, Gaz rang me this afternoon to let me know that she's lost her husband! Murdered in their own home! Shot in the head! The papers will say it was over a longstanding debt, but we both know it's The Shadow!

"That said, it's been a tough day, gentlemen! And I'm in no fit state to talk business tonight. We'll finish dinner and reconvene down here tomorrow morning for breakfast. This will give me more time to ruminate and mull over this development. It will also allow the pair of you more time to think of something moving forward. This situation is really becoming code-red, gentlemen!"

Hurst leant forward having said this, to unceremoniously slice into his steak and shovel it down his neck. The three finished dinner in their pleasant moonlit surroundings, while Hurst continued to relay to the pair, the nature of his business and the similarities between his and Garrington's plight with The Shadow. As the evening turned to night and the chill of the desert descended, Wolf and Kelly retired from Hurst's company to ponder and plot further in the sanctuary of their suite.

# Chapter 15

## PARTY PLANNING

The peace of sung prayers and the bright breaking sun had roused Wolf and Kelly relatively early. They emerged gradually from their rooms and readied themselves for the day at a leisurely pace, ordering breakfast to the suite. After breakfast, the pair adjourned to their main balcony with a cup of coffee and a paper each. Not wishing to jinx their situation, they said nothing. However, they were both very aware that this was certainly the most relaxed and civilised situation they had encountered, since their employment at Mission Harvey Walsh. After about an hour of lounging, Wolf and Kelly had their peace and quiet disrupted, by the trill chiming of Kelly's phone. Kelly answered, and was told to have himself and Wolf report to the rear terrace immediately. Having had a little respite to ponder and plan ahead, Kelly and Wolf's combined brainpower had been allowed to function optimally. The pair had formed a reasonable and formidable plan for Hurst, just as they had for Garrington. Wolf and Kelly found Hurst, and his environment, to be the most humane of all they had come across in their dealings with The Shadow. They, therefore, descended with an almost eager confidence to Hurst and Wright, who were awaiting them on the private terrace.

Hurst was attired in another dark tailored suit, this time with his tie well done up. Wright, who sat next to him facing the Nile, wore a much more casual short-sleeve shirt and chinos. Kelly and Wolf, realising Hurst may have been nursing a hangover, approached softly. Although rigid and formally dressed, Hurst appeared to be feeling the heat a little. He clutched a napkin and periodically dabbed the sweat from his seeping brow. Hurst's eyes were bright but far less focused than usual. Wright, on the other hand, was a replica of the man Wolf and Kelly had met yesterday. He stared them down, adjusting his glasses and cocking his head standoffishly, as the pair gingerly took their seats. As they sat, Wright cleared his throat to speak purposefully. However, he was interrupted before any utterance by Hurst, who held his hand up at Wright for silence and then pushed it to cradle his head's frontal lobe. He allowed his brow to nestle into his hand and rested for a moment. Having waited a few seconds to overcome his migraine, Hurst now spoke in a dry, whispered version of his normal voice.

"So, chaps. Obviously last night was a write-off! And let's fucking face it, so is this morning. But I don't suppose, even considering all the shit that's happened, you guys have managed to come up with anything? Cause I'm teetering on the edge of existence right now. Gaz's husband had nothing to do with anything! How did they get to him? Why? Why would they risk that! Whatever he knew, whatever he stumbled on, it must have been something important to The Shadow. I know he's behind this! You've got to come up with something! I don't care if it takes months and we die trying!"

Hurst paused and looked up from behind his hand at Wolf and Kelly. Seeing their sympathetic but burning eyes, Hurst's own eyes flickered with interest and he invited them to speak.

"I'm sorry. I'm in a very bad state. I'm not normally this emotional. Please Mike, Christof! Would you like some tea, coffee or something to eat?"

Hurst burped in reflux and winced at the thought of consuming anything in his current state. Wolf smiled at Hurst and Wright, showing his whitened, capped and polished teeth. He spoke as tenderly as he could, whilst still being audible across the windy table.

"Mr Hurst, firstly Michael and I would like to offer you our commiserations and condolences. This unexpected tragedy has, with good reason, affected you. You need not apologise for that. Having met Lord Garrington myself, although he was not a directly charming man, there is not a person alive, who could question his innocence."

Wright nodded in approval of the respecting tone Wolf had undertaken. Hurst did not break his gaze from Wolf's eyes and he smiled at Wolf's statement, spurring him to continue.

"I must confess it is Michael and I, who will be apologising to you! As I am sorry, but we must decline your kind offer of breakfast. Having taken the liberty of ordering room service to our suite this morning, we have jumped the gun so to speak, on your gracious hospitality."

A little confused and irritated by this longwinded demonstration of his guest's etiquette, Hurst raised an eyebrow and dropped his smile. Wolf, sensing Hurst's frazzled mind losing patience, quickly went on.

"However, I hope that we shall endeavour to make up for this oversight. And to rebalance your excellent hospitality with the quite exquisite plan we have been able to devise."

Wolf paused and smiled broadly, knowing he had now captivated his audience. He leant forward, making himself more comfortable in his seat and began to fiddle teasingly with the table placement in front of him. After a few short seconds, he elaborated in a mysterious and allusive tone.

"Mr Hurst? I have no doubt that you will have heard of the expression, 'less is more'? Less is more. Nice little phrase, isn't it? Less is more. Mr Hurst, it is this philosophy of playing possum, talking quietly while carrying a big stick and assuming the victim role, where less is more so to speak, that is the only sure-fire way for us to defeat The Shadow. You see, his entire strategy revolves around you being the dominant force and him the underdog! If you begin to think of yourself, as he does, like a victim, then, as we have done, you will see that his organisation is just as vulnerable as anyone else's."

Wolf paused to gauge Hurst's reaction further. Hurst, intrigued, instructed Wolf to continue.

"Go on."

Wolf smiled again and took his cue to elaborate further.

"Mr Hurst, we are going to deploy one of the oldest tricks in the book! Yes, it is old! But also tried, tested and very effective! This ploy will be expensive but should save you billions in the long-run. To be blunt, Mr Hurst, we are going to sit back and watch while we trick The Shadow into revealing his operatives in your organisation! Then his locations! Then his senior operatives and their locations! And if we can remain undetected throughout these endeavours, this will then lead us to the man himself!"

Wolf paused from his animated pitch, sensing from their frowns that Hurst and Wright felt his speech a little vague. Wolf took a more direct tone and delved into the further details of his and Kelly's plan.

"Mr Hurst, you are going to have a party! More specifically, an office party! You will invite between two to three hundred of your most senior employees. This will be the perfect disguise under which to both collect and analyse your most trusted staff. Now remember, gentlemen. The aim of our plan is to remain completely undetected by The Shadow. It is, therefore, of course, vital that none of your men suspect anything other than a party is transpiring. And herein lies the deception! You will give each man a goodie-bag!"

Hurst sniggered, as did Wright, at this last utterance and Wright made to interrupt. Wolf, however, held up his hands and went on, beguiling them to indulge him further.

"Ah-Ah! Please permit me to continue, Mr Hurst! You will give each man a goodie-bag! And a very expensive one at that! Put in it what you like! Laptop, tablet, watch, jewellery, sunglasses! But make it good! And ensure that you have these three items! A watch, a tablet and a phone! You will also ensure that these items are all top of the range! This will guarantee that no one suspects, that inside these three devices will be audio, video and tracking technology. All set up to monitor, record and feedback results to our private entourage.

"Now this brings me on to the next crucial part of our plan. Everything must remain between the four of us! And the four of us alone! Michael and I have our team in Europe. We will send them the surveillance information, along with your account information, which you so graciously promised us. Our team will find the rats in your organisation. Without the rats even knowing you're looking! We can then target certain rats and, once again undetected and in secret, track these rats back to The Shadow's locations. From there, we find his leaders and so on! This plan is full proof, gentlemen, as long as we keep things between ourselves!"

Hurst said nothing but looked pensive. Aware of his fatigued and hungover state, he erred on the side of caution and responded with a weary, wry smile.

"That actually did sound pretty good, Christof. But err. Let me think about it. You guys go and hang by the pool, play some tennis, check out the sights. Let me and Wrighty get our heads round this. We'll reconvene here after lunch, about half-two. Please feel free to indulge in any of my town's delights. Just mention my name and there's not much you can't get here. My hotel is your hotel!"

With this Hurst rose, still clutching his napkin and dabbing his brow. He nodded back to Wright, who stood with him, and the pair descended the terrace in the direction of the hotel spa. Wolf and Kelly sat back in their chairs and contemplated their situation. Wolf and Kelly had been left rather insecure by Hurst's resistance to instantly follow their plan. On return to their suite they both fretted in hope that Hurst would emerge from his spa sharper and more open to action.

Having dawdled through lunch in one of the hotel's riverside restaurants, Wolf and Kelly returned to the terrace at about two-twenty to find Hurst and Wright waiting. Hurst had evidently just come from his spa and was still attired in a white flannel robe. Hurst looked altogether refreshed and was massaging his cheeks and stroking his head in a focused manner, as Wolf and Kelly approached and took their seats opposite him. A waiter promptly popped up and placed bottles of mineral water in front of the four men and made a swift exit. Hurst bent forward, snatched up a bottle, unscrewed the cap and drank straight from it. Having guzzled almost half its contents, Hurst stopped his swig, gasped in refreshment and almost burped his words.

"Alright! So, tell me, Mike! Where am I getting these tablets, phones and watches? How are we going to equip them with surveillance? And what happens if the rats don't use the new stuff? Answer these questions! And we'll go to work on this, right now!"

Wolf's eye lit up as he keenly and precisely answered.

"Mr Hurst. We, without funding from yourself, can source and equip the goodie-bags ourselves. This will be done in a matter of days. Our team in Europe will be able to do this for us, and also collate and analyse the findings. In answer to your final question. If a man in your organisation chooses not to use the items in his bag, then we know he is as good as a rat! Anyone who deliberately chooses not to use a brand-new top of the range tablet, phone or designer watch, clearly has something to hide! They will be branded for inspection and physical surveillance, as soon as they decline to use at least one of the three objects!

"In fact, Mr Hurst, this is one of the two things that the team will be looking for. Firstly, they will seek those who are stupid enough to fall for the trick! And allow us to document and monitor their meetings with The Shadow! Crucially, the second will be those who don't use any of the items. This is true because as soon as they receive their goodie-bag, they are faced with two choices! Choice one, accept the gifts and take their chances. Choice two, discard the goodie-bag and its contents entirely. Why? Because The Shadow contacts them! And not the other way around! Hence, they will not be able to judge when to switch phones, remove their watch or leave their tablet at home! Therefore! They have an all or nothing choice, so to speak! Therein lies the genius of this cunning trap!

"Our men will collate the evidence and seek out those who are in frequent contact with The Shadow! And also those who fail to use the items. We will then physically trail these individuals to find The Shadow's locations. We stake out these locations and diagram, log and analyse what we see. This will allow us to identify leaders within The Shadow's organisation. We can then tail them and find further locations and further senior individuals. This should, in theory, lead us straight to one place..."

Hurst banged his fist on the table in front of him, having polished off the last of his bottle of water and interrupted.

"Hot damn! That was a satisfactory answer! Gentlemen! I'm impressed! You, Mike, I know you're a sound guy just from Gaz's reference. And you, Professor! She told me to watch out for you! But I can see that you're clearly a genius! I'm on it, boys! I'm in! Let's do this!"

Hurst suddenly became very business-like and took charge, commanding the scowling Wright to comply with Wolf and Kelly.

"Right so, Danny, you heard them. We're organising a party this Friday! Invite all our major players. Ship them in, and their pluses, expense it all! Then purchase some leather Louis Vuitton goodie-bags and some goodies to go in them. Don't bring me the bill, just pay it! I'm aware how much it's going to cost to source three hundred Louis bags at short notice! I don't care! We're catching this arsehole! Then just get Christof and Mikey here anything they need, again my expense. Let's try and get some synergy going here!"

Hurst stood and clapped his hands together to signify a positive end to their discussions.

"Right so you two go off, contact your team and let them know your plan! Tell them to send over the goodies! Oh! And let me know the email to send my accounts to! They're ready to send! Just tell me where! Dan! You get started on the guest list and the goodie-bags!"

Hurst stormed off with widened, confident power strides in the direction of the main hotel, accompanied by Wright. Wolf and Kelly waited for them to slip out of view before returning themselves to the hotel. Once back in their suite, Wolf and Kelly immediately telephoned Maya on Wolf's mobile's secure line. Wolf informed Maya of their plan and instructed her to send through the required goods. Three hundred top of the range tablets, phones and watches, all faceted with audio, video and tracking technology. After a little further explanation, Maya consented and agreed to dispatch the items to Hurst's hotel before Thursday morning, in three days' time. Wolf also let Maya know to expect all Hurst's account information in the coming days. Grateful of this, Maya vowed to manage Douglas's reaction and convince him that their plan would work. Having hung up his smartphone, Wolf then used the room's phone to call reception. He requested to be put through to Hurst's room. He informed Hurst of Maya's email, who confirmed, in turn, that he would indeed send through all his account information.

With everything now being put into place according to their instructions, Wolf and Kelly found themselves in a relatively unpressured position. They had clearly now established themselves as quite a formidable team and proved to Cork, Douglas and Garrington that they were somewhat of a force to be reckoned with. Having earned some respect, Wolf and Kelly were now reaping the rewards of their success. For now their plan was in the process of fruition, they were finally able to enjoy four uninterrupted days, at an all-expenses paid hotel in a fascinating and beautiful corner of the world.

Wolf and Kelly took full advantage of their situation. Particularly after Maya had later confirmed that they had once again succeeded in retrieving the full account information, for one of the world's most powerful criminal kingpins. The duo ate well, played golf, tennis, went dune-biking and still had time to explore the nearby tourist monuments. Three days flew by in a whirlwind of relaxed frivolity. However, their carefree existence was brought to a grinding halt on Thursday morning, when Maya telephoned Wolf to confirm that his requested items were about to be convoyed to his location. Maya explained that all they needed to do was hand out the gifts, and the audio, visual and GPS data would be automatically sent through to Oppenheim and Hakimi back in London.

# Chapter 16

## OFFICE PARTY

As the sun set on the Nile on the eve of Friday, Wolf and Kelly had witnessed the manifestation of all they had envisaged. On Thursday evening, three hundred brand new iPads, three hundred of the latest and greatest iPhones, as well as three hundred Franck Muller watches had been delivered. Wolf's men had stayed up into the night packaging all three hundred goodie-bags with the delivered effects, as well as other lavish and expensive goodies. These Louis Vuitton goodie-bags had then been dressed and sealed, each with a gold satin bow. In further preparation, Hurst had set up a giant marquee for his guests, complete with dance floor, DJ stand, full bar and buffet. Hurst had also planned a speech and arranged for fifty underwear models to be present throughout.

Before too long, Hurst's guests begun to arrive in an impressive battery of taxis, trucks and supercars. By seven-thirty, the hotel driveway was completely rammed with vehicles and the small, borderline dirt-road which led up to the hotel was heaving with more arriving guests. From Wolf, Kelly and Hurst's vantage at the top of the front reception's mezzanine, this was a quite an incredible and inspiring sight. Wolf and Kelly could see their plan unfolding in front of them, while Hurst felt a sense of security and power, witnessing the wealth of his organisation hoard outside his hotel. The guests were all welcomed with drinks and canapes at reception and then guided through to the marquee to the west of the hotel's grounds.

As the trail of arriving cars thinned, Hurst stood up from his seated vantage at the first-floor window, and left Wolf and Kelly. Hurst was dressed in full black-tie and had heavily moisturised his face, such that its contours gleamed with a natural and healthy-looking glow. Just before taking his leave, he bid parting instruction to Wolf and Kelly in an undeniably excited tone.

"Okay, guys! I'm off to show face! People will be wondering where the big man is! I think it's important we all try and switch off and enjoy ourselves as much as possible! Really play our parts, ay, chaps! I think you two should keep a very low profile! If anyone asks, you're banking associates. I don't think I've got many guys from finance here, so that should be pretty safe. But just stay under the radar! Then we'll get everyone rammed and I'll give the speech! Give out the pressies! And Bob's your uncle!"

With this, Hurst clicked his heels together, bobbing up and down smartly as he did so. He turned and quickly cantered down the stairs to the reception and off towards the marquee. Almost as soon as he departed, Wright appeared from the shadows, as if from nowhere. He too was wearing black-tie but looked as offensive and deadly as ever. Having crept up on Wolf and Kelly, he interjected to their surprise behind them, "Great night for party!"

Wolf and Kelly jumped and whirled round to face the looming Wright, who, delighted by their fearful reaction, continued.

"You boys having a good time, are you? You've certainly had a whale of a fucking time over these last few days! While I've been running around like a fucking skivvy! I tell you what, gentlemen! If this plan of yours does anything other than it says on the tin, I'm going to personally make sure you're kept alive, so I can skin your fucking genitals! You got that!"

Wolf and Kelly smiled passively and nodded still more placidly. Wright's face relaxed a little and his frown unknotted somewhat. Wright bent back up slightly, from his looming stance, and finalised his pep talk.

"Now I suggest that you boys don't really get involved tonight. You'll have to fucking come down, cause Hurst wants you there in case anything fucks up! But if it was up to me, you'd be locked in your suite for the duration! But as it stands, just don't fucking talk to anyone! And remember! I've got my fucking eyes on the pair of you!"

Wolf coughed and, fully aware he had Wright's employer's sponsorship, snapped back, "Surely it's not us you should be watching, Herr Wright? Surely your unwavering and predatory gaze would be better fixed firmly on the potential rats in attendance here tonight?"

Hearing Wolf standing up for himself, Wright turned from his attempted departure. His eyeballs bulged in anger and looked wide enough to explode. His chin pushed forward, and his top lip curled to reveal his snarling yellow teeth, as he re-engaged Wolf.

"Don't be fucking smart with me, you kraut cunt! Don't fucking tell me where to look, son! I'll put you in the fuckin ground! You're on borrowed fucking time here, lads! And I! Am in charge of the fucking interest rate! And I! Am Danny fucking Death Warrant! You soppy fucking melts!"

Wright twisted violently on his heels and waved his hand up and away from Wolf and Kelly to further display his power and disgust as he left. Wolf and Kelly, doing their best to remain positive, waited a few moments before slowly making their way towards Hurst's, now music-filled, marquee.

Hurst's marquee was fantastically grand. No expense had been spared from the fine wine and cocktails, to the Michelin star chefs Hurst had shipped in especially. The floor was decked with varnished wood and the interior dressed in the style of a Mediterranean beach nightclub. Inside, an army of smartly uniformed servants tended the bar and ferried fresh canapes around the mingling guests.

The guests made up a wide range of radically differing individuals. Hurst, as requested, had invited all his most trusted and senior employees from around the globe. His guests had been commanded to attend as a matter of duty and, as a result, were all present and correct. Inside the marquee, Hurst's employees naturally grouped together in social cliques, based on their positions. This was perfect for Wolf and Kelly, who were able to clearly define six clusters of professions that made up Hurst's operation. These were brokers, accountants, soldiers, transporters, distributers and managers, who had all organically found each other's company and stuck together.

Predictably the six groupings all behaved in very different ways throughout the duration of Hurst's party. The brokers were all about the flash and the cash. Snappy suits, jewellery, gold watches and slick hair was the standard among the fifty invited brokers. Fuelled by expensive surroundings, alcohol and narcotics, the brokers were in their element, comparing deals, commissions and new business.

The twenty accountants on Hurst's guest list were radically differing in appearance and behaviour. They wore cheap, understated, almost school uniform-like suits and they naturally grouped towards the corner of the marquee farthest from the dancefloor. They were quiet and barely spoke. Instead this group silently surveyed the room, in a mass people-watching exercise. When any of the accountants did speak, it was only to comment on their observations.

Hurst's network of soldiers and senior henchmen was made up of sixty menacing and dangerous men. Hardly any of this number wore suits and were unmistakable from the rest of the party by their testosterone pumped, physical stature and facial expressions. The, similarly blue-collar, grouping of Hurst's transporters interlocked a little with the soldiers. However, the transporters were a slightly smarter and less aggressive band. They were by far the most focused on the female talent Hurst had laid on. They populated the area nearest the dance floor and almost all of their number displayed a tremendous musical affinity, demonstrating fluid and rhythmic dance moves.

The two further groupings, the managers and distributors, also intertwined a little. Both groups clustered near the bar area and, between them, consumed by far the most liquor. The mangers were a slightly toned-down version of the brokers. Their watches were showy but not garish and their suits were smart but not over the top, three-piece affairs. They proceeded to drink and eat as much as they could and share tales of gossip within their organisation, mostly of a romantic and sexual nature. Similarly, Hurst's distribution team had gathered together, next to the bar and were playing drinking games and getting more and more inebriated.

Wolf and Kelly avoided the attention of the guests and did not linger in any particular section for too long. Proceedings were developing as they planned and Wolf and Kelly were satisfied that the guests would be unlikely to suspect a thing, particularly as most were now intoxicated. The mood was also friendly and relaxed; the women, libations and gourmet nibbles had gone down a treat. Once a few hours had elapsed, the music softened, and Wright approached the DJ's stand at the end of the dance floor. Using just the glare of his eyes he dismissed the DJ, who lowered the music to a background whisper and moved aside, allowing Wright to take centre stage. Wright leant in towards the DJ's microphone and cleared his throat. Satisfied that all eyes were on him, Wright opened his speech.

"Good evening! Firstly, I'm sure Mr Hurst would like me to thank you sorry bunch of cunts for coming here tonight and drinking all his free booze!"

An uproar of clamour, banter and laughter erupted from the rowdy and drunken audience at Wright's jibing introduction. Wright waited for the crowd to calm before resuming.

"Now without further ado! I would like to introduce the man that has made this night! And all your miserable lives possible! Your boss! The man himself! Mr FedEx! Arms, all day every day! Mr Charlie Hurst!"

Loud chanting, applause and pats on the back accompanied Hurst, as he made his way from the bar to the DJ's stand. He ascended the stand as Wright subsided. He spread his arms and nodded to his guests. The amorous clapping and shouting was sustained for a few more seconds, until Hurst dropped his arms and bent down towards the microphone. His voice was tipsy but controlled as he addressed his audience.

"Hi guys! Everybody having a good time?"

A further commotion of ovation followed, as guests raised their glasses and toasted Hurst's name. Hurst smiled, indulging himself in their praise, before speaking again.

"So, thanks all you guys for coming! It's really nice to see everyone together like this! It breeds strength and unity! We are as one! Brothers-in-arms so to speak! United! I can see you've all already gathered together in little cliques! It's really important for us to take a step back! Fucking cut loose once in a while! It's also so important for us to bond together like this! Particularly in times like these!"

Hurst paused and let a brief silence take over, before taking a slightly more serious tone.

"Now! I'm not going to fuck the vibe up in here with a long speech! And I don't want to talk about the troubles we've been having recently, that you all already know about. I just want to say thank you to you all! And furthermore, I want to do two things! Remind you that we are the most fucking powerful! And the biggest arms network in the world! The biggest! The baddest! No one else! Us! We are the best! And that is fact! Secondly! I want to promise you all! That although things are tough at the moment, and we have lost business! We are too big to fail! As long as we stick together! We will preserve! Conserve! Maintain! And prosper!"

A subsequent applause swelled, and Hurst waited for this subside a little before going on.

"In short, gentlemen! Tonight, I am promising that we will regain the market share we have lost to The Shadow! And we will grow further still! Now that said, I hope you all get ridiculously plastered tonight! And all do something you regret in the morning! Come on, boys! Let's get naughty and trash this place!"

Thunderous laughter and exclamation flared up from the crowd of guests who, energised in response to Hurst's oration, became more even more rowdy. As Hurst departed the microphone, Wright stepped up once more and broke the excited crowd's clamour for a moment to instruct them briefly.

"Now! Before you're all too drunk to think! Don't ask me why he's decided to be so generous! But you've all been given the weekend off! And complimentary rooms at the hotel. You'll find your keys at reception, if you manage to make it out of here on your feet, that is! Right that's it, ladies! And try not to get too messy while you're in here! Do something really out of line – and my name's still fucking Death Warrant! Now let's have a fucking party!"

Wright followed Hurst from the DJ's stand and the DJ himself returned to his position and turned up the music. The goodie-bags had been dropped, along with explanatory gift cards, in each of Hurst's guests' villas and suites.

With all but one or two of the invited guests being cold-blooded male hedonists, Wolf, Kelly and Hurst had used the lure of models and high-quality spirits to ensure their guests had stayed the night. Not surprisingly, given the spread Hurst laid on, not a single guest failed to remain until the morning. As the night wore on, the dance floor, and then the marquee, thinned as the various guests either paired off with their choice of model or retired to their rooms overpowered by intoxicants. Kelly and Wolf, trusting their plan to be in action, had both retired relatively early, not wishing to be noticed as the crowd thinned. Hurst, however, had remained until the last man had left the marquee, having been insistent on seeing his role in the plan carried through to perpetuity. Having ensured that all men had received their keys at reception and were all now residing in their rooms,

Hurst finally returned to his own private owner's suite. Hurst had barely enough time to shower before the sun was due to rise. He elected to shower and nap, but to wake early and pay a visit to Wolf and Kelly's suite, well before his guests would be conscious to see him.

As the sun began to breach the North-African horizon, Hurst, changed and relatively fresh, crept into Wolf and Kelly's suite with his master key. Finding neither of the two in the reception and common parts, he ventured into Wolf's room. The room was dark, and Wolf lay peacefully sleeping naked in bed. Hurst, not wishing to startle Wolf, tiptoed closer through the darkness. As he drew over the bed he bent over Wolf's resting face and softly whispered, "Christof? Professor? Professor Wolf? Christof?"

Hurst continued to whisper variations of Wolf's name until Wolf's eye cracked open a little and he turned, both alarmed and startled. He was confronted by Hurst, whose smiling face was almost on top of him as his was roused from slumber. Wolf snatched the bedsheets up to cover himself and looked around to check his surroundings and regain full consciousness. Hurst continued to whisper his name until Wolf responded in an agitated whisper.

"Mr Hurst! What are you doing? What is this!"

Hurst smiled and put his hand on Hurst's shoulder to reassure him before shushing him and elaborating.

"Hush, Christof, it's okay! Everything's okay! I just came in here to speak with yourself and Michael, before the guests wake up."

Hurst's attempt at calming and securing Wolf had had the opposite effect and Wolf felt very threatened. Hurst turned to leave and saw Kelly at Wolf's door, squinting and scratching his sleep tousled head. Kelly, yawning, engaged Hurst as he rose to leave towards him.

"What's going on, guys? I fucking knew you guys were queers! I'll leave you guys to finish up! Don't stop on my account."

Kelly turned from the doorway and made his way to the seating area of the suite's reception and switched on the television. Hurst joined him and soon after Wolf followed. As Wolf took his seat on the sofa next to Kelly, Hurst made his way to the suite's coffee machine and began to make three espressos. As he organised the cups and prepared the machine's cartridges, he explained his surprise visit.

"So, chaps. I just wanted to come and see you before I head off! And before the others have had a chance to shake their hangovers. I'm sorry if it's a bit early, but I really wanted to just say how grateful I am for your guys' help. From what I can see, and certainly from last night's proceedings, things went off without a hitch and your plan looks like it might work. I just want your confirmation that we are on the same page and that you two are both satisfied?"

Kelly responded casually to Hurst's enquiry as he made his way over with the espressos.

"Yeah we're satisfied! And you didn't have to creep into our room at the crack of fucking dawn to ask us neither! Jesus, Charlie, you must not have slept? But yeah, we're cool. The items are in the guests' rooms and the way they've been presented, they're sure to take them."

Hurst sat on an armchair facing Wolf and Kelly sipping his espresso, as he nodded and retorted.

"Very good. So, what next, chaps? Where do we go from here? I've upheld my part of the deal; now it's your turn."

Kelly took a long drink from his own coffee and replied.

"Well it's just like we said, Charlie. Your guys are going to take their items back with them and one of three things will happen. Most likely they will use the items and it will reveal nothing, meaning they're innocent. Or secondly, they use the items and incriminate themselves. Or finally, and least likely, they either leave the items here or don't use the gifts, which would raise suspicion and mean we have to physically track the individual.

"We expect this process to take at least a week. In the meantime, we will just have to wait here and continue enjoying your fine hospitality! And remember, Charlie, we are putting our lives and our mission at risk teaming up with you! Last night we put everything in your hands and although we provided the plan and most of the materials, you delivered on your part! So! Thanks, Charlie! You really went above and beyond last night!"

Hurst smiled wryly from one corner of his mouth at Wolf and Kelly and answered.

"Yeah, things have gone well between us, and I expected as much. As I said! Anyone man enough to dice with Vicky Garrington and gain positive reference, is okay by me! Of course, you may stay here as long as this takes! I insist upon that, gentlemen! I will, however, need you guys to remain in your suite for the remainder of the weekend. You see, I will be attending Lord Garrington's funeral tomorrow morning and I must fly to London tonight. Wrighty and I are in agreement, that your anonymity would be best preserved from within these walls. Just for as long as the guests remain at the hotel. Once they've left, I will have returned and you'll be free to roam once more."

Hurst briskly downed the rest of his coffee, before concluding to the sleepy Wolf and Kelly, "Are we in agreement, gentlemen? Good! I look forward to seeing you both again on my return."

Hurst nodded to Wolf and Kelly, set down his cup and saucer, smoothly rose and made for the suite's front door. Just before he left, he turned and reiterated before allowing the fire-door to close behind him, "Order room service! Girls! Whatever you like! Just please, for your own safety! Don't leave before I get back!"

Saturday came and went, with some guests departing early and some remaining for the weekend's duration. By Sunday afternoon, all but a few of Hurst's invitees had departed, taking with them their Louis Vuitton goodie-bags. At the afternoon's twilight, a secluded and itchy Wolf and Kelly received a call from Maya to Wolf's smartphone. She informed them that all the three hundred sets of items had been successfully dispatched, tracked and received by Oppenheim and Hakimi at Mission Harvey Walsh. She also requested the names of all attendees at Hurst's party, in order to match their findings to the relevant individual. She then informed the pair that Hurst's accounts had surprisingly revealed a lot. She explained that Hakimi and Oppenheim had matched and traced offshore transfers with losses from both Garrington and Hurst's holdings to an institution named The Linstraad Group. The Linstraad Group, she had informed them, was an infamous financial institution with trillions in assets under management. However, despite Hakimi's best hacking attempts, the buck had stopped at Linstraad. Their offshore holdings in Cayman, The British Virgin Islands and other non-domiciled destinations, were completely off-record and confidential to the point where even the highest financial authorities had no knowledge whatsoever of Linstraad funds' true asset holdings.

Shortly after this phone call, Hurst returned and summoned Wolf and Kelly to their usual meeting place on the upper terrace. Wolf and Kelly relayed the information Maya had told them, and Hurst, in the accompaniment of Wright, listened carefully. Hurst promptly promised to email his guest list, along with a profile for each man to Maya post haste. He then lamented at the news that their plan had initially worked, as all his visitors had successfully left with their goodie-bags. Hurst also immediately recognised mention of The Linstraad Group. Hurst had reacted exorbitantly to the news of his clients' account information being matched and trailed to large offshore transfers into Linstraad's funds. He further confessed, that he himself did not have any considerable holdings with Linstraad. However, Hurst was aghast, that such a prevalent and legitimately reputable institution would be involved.

# Chapter 17

## FIGHTING THE SHADOW FROM THE SHADE

Having intrigued and impressed Hurst significantly, Wolf and Kelly had been further spoiled in the delights of his hospitality. Boat trips down the Nile, subsequent tourist excursions, sunbathing and fine dining consumed both Wolf and Kelly's time for several days. Team Harvey Walsh, on the other hand, back in London, worked tirelessly to collate and analyse the data from the toys they had now distributed to Hurst's men via the fabled goodie-bags. Lopez, having dropped Wolf and Kelly at Hurst's hotel, had returned to London. Lopez and his team had since been dispatched throughout the globe, to track and monitor the movement of The Shadow's possible moles in Hurst's organisation. Almost a week of blissful waiting passed before, on Saturday morning, Wolf and Kelly received an email detailing the analysis of Team Harvey Walsh's initial surveillance results.

Wolf and Kelly studied the document with thorough interest in the privacy of their suite, before calling through to Hurst. Wolf let him know of their receipt of the new documentation and arranged to meet immediately on Hurst's private terrace, as per usual. Wolf and Kelly quickly descended to Hurst's private area, to which they had now become well accustomed. They waited for Hurst comfortably as a waiter supplied them with coffee, juice and pastries. Hurst and Wright emerged presently and took their seats opposite Wolf and Kelly. Wolf handed his team's analysis report to Hurst across the table and he sat and waited, while Hurst briefly scanned through the report. Hurst's eyes bolted through the pages of the document with practised precision and, after a minute or so, he looked up at Wolf and Kelly to enquire, "So, this is the initial report? Very good! Can you summarise, Professor, for Wrighty and I?"

Wolf cleared his throat and took his cue to answer.

"Yah, Mr Hurst! This is the analysis report from our, seemingly, very successful plan! To summarise, as you ask! My team has found the following results following the successful dispatch and receipt of your office party presents!"

Wolf motioned to Hurst to hand him back the paperwork in front of him, so he could read directly from it. Hurst passed Wolf back the documents and Wolf quickly flicked to his intended section and began reading out loud.

"According to the findings from our surveillance of the phones, tablets and watches, out of three-hundred possible suspects, there were one-hundred and seventy direct suspects! Thirty-seven confirmed suspects! And two individuals with confirmed and repeated interaction with The Shadow! A further three members of the party are also cause for concern, as they make up the one percent of individuals, who have either disposed of, or have not personally used any of the items in their goodie-bag. Two of the individuals gave their items to family and friends and one guy, a Mr Akiva Moses, just left the bag in his hotel room. He would appear to be the only individual to have done this."

Hurst and Wright glanced at each other, amazed and intrigued at the effective precision of Wolf and Kelly's operations. Wright, with his ever cynical and questioning mind, retorted with an undertone of disbelief.

"Who are these cunts?"

Hurst looked back inquisitively at Wolf, as Wright said this and awaited his response. Wolf smiled confidently, looked back down to his report and read aloud from the list of profiles Oppenheim had provided.

"Right so, Herr Wright. The five people we are interested in – that is to say, the three non-users and the two repeat offenders' details are as follows!

"Repeat offender number one, is a Mr Marcus Julius. Mr Julius is a senior broker in your organisation. He deals in all manner of arms throughout the globe. Born, nineteen-sixty-five, in Oakland, California. African American. Has dual Libyan and American nationality. Net worth is an estimated fourteen million dollars. Sound familiar?"

Hurst snapped back instantly. "Yeah I know that greedy fuck! He's been dealing with The Shadow? Okay! Okay! It's alright! Tell me, Wolfy? Who else has been fucking me!"

Wolf referred back to his sheets and continued.

"Right, the next confirmed repeat offender is a Mr Antoine Jamison. Similarly, to Mr Julius, Jamison is a broker of yours. A good one at that, it states here! His net worth is in excess of twenty million! Born in California, just like Jamison, he was born in nineteen-seventy-three. He is a tall man, six-foot five! And he, like Jamison, deals arms throughout the globe."

Wolf looked up from his reading to see Hurst and Wright fuming. Hurst nodded in furious recognition of Jamison and Wolf continued.

"The next on our list, is the first of the three unknowns. These subjects should possibly be regarded with less gravitas than the previous two gentlemen I have described, both of whom have had confirmed repeat contact with The Shadow!

"Mr Robert Ngemwa is a Ugandan born, distribution manager in one of your Ethiopian bases. He distributed all of his gifts to members of his family. There has been no gathered intelligence to link him with The Shadow. I think it is up to you if you feel that this man – or either of these other two unknowns – are worth pursuing! Particularly when we already have two targets primed and identified?"

Hurst interrupted Wolf as a waiter approached to clear the remanence of mess Kelly had made while indulging in the refreshments laid out.

"To be honest I don't know who to trust after you told me Jamison and Julius are involved! Both those guys have been with me ten years plus! But Bobby's not a bad guy! I can't believe Bob would be capable of that! No way Ngemwa would do that! His family, who now have his gifts, have been sustained by my organisation! He's pretty much my highest paid manger! No! No way! But please, Chris! Tell me, who are the other two?"

Upon instruction, Wolf once again referenced Oppenheim's profile report and responded.

"The final two people are a Mr Akiva Moses. And a Mr Rasul Al-Ali?"

Hurst interrupted Wolf as soon as he heard these names.

"Okay! Forget Raz! He's a fucking driver! He's an incredible driver but he's only a driver! Please remind me! It was AK who left the fucking goodie-bag too, right?"

Wolf checked the report and confirmed Hurst's affirmation with a solemn nod. Hurst, seeing this, resumed purposefully.

"I knew it! Fucking knew it! Moses is a fat, suspicious cat! It wouldn't surprise me in the slightest, if Moses turned out to be a rat! On every fucking deal he quibbles and pries for extra commission! He's also by far my most successful and powerful broker. Does deals on the side! I fucking know he does! If he wasn't so fucking good, I would have signed his warrant for Wrighty here a long time ago! Yeah! I definitely think we should go after this punk!"

Wolf frowned a little at Hurst. He wanted to be sure Hurst was not being emotional. As, with the limited resources they had, they could not afford to deploy themselves unnecessarily. Wolf had two confirmed Shadow conspirators on their radar. He was anxious that Hurst appreciated this, before exhausting assets on a wild goose chase, simply down to his dislike of Moses's character. Wolf chose his words carefully and evaluated Hurst's initial volition.

"Mr Hurst, is this, Akiva Moses, really our guy? Born in Massachusetts in nineteen-eighty-one. He is quite young. He is wealthy! Wow! It states here his net worth is fifty million dollars! He must be a good broker! But is he capable of this kind of treachery? I just ask you to bear in mind, that we can only really properly trail one man at a time. We have two perfect targets and three possible distractions. Despite your initial feeling, do you not think in this case, we should perhaps prioritise the targets who have repeat and confirmed contact with The Shadow first?"

Hurst stared thoughtfully at Wolf, then at Kelly and then Wright. He stroked his chin and let several seconds elapse before emitting a calculated response.

"No! I am making an executive decision! And I take full responsibility! I am fully aware that all the evidence is pointing towards those two snakes Jamison and Julius! But I'm not interested in that! No-no! I'm interested in my gut! That's what's got me this far! And my gut is telling me, that greedy fat fuck's all over The Shadow! I can't believe I didn't think about approaching him before! It's so fucking obvious! He's so fucking smart! Of course he left the fucking goodie-bag! But you didn't think you'd be the only one! Didn't think of that, did you! You corpulent! Covetous! Conspiring! Fuck!

"Oh no! We're going after this guy, no question! Done deal! Finished! Start having your team look into AK immediately! We'll reconvene down here this evening for dinner at six-thirty! Let me know your findings and plans going forward!"

As Hurst made to leave, Wright addressed him directly. "What are you going to do with Julius and Jamison?"

Hurst looked back at him as he walked away responding to all present. "Surely nothing? We can't let anyone know anything's up. As the guys said! As soon as we let on to the fact that there's a witch hunt on, everyone, including AK, will get spooked! For this to work we need to play from the shadows! Fight The Shadow from the shade so to speak!"

Hurst and Wright disappeared, while Wolf and Kelly ventured down to the poolside bar. From this sanctuary they telephoned Maya and informed her of Hurst's decision. They spent the remainder of the morning poolside, indulging in the fine climate, while Maya and their team fixed their sights on Akiva Moses.

Having been raised by a typical Boston, East-Coast family of Hasidic-Jewish descent, Moses had been the black-sheep and pariah of his town. He kept his long hair and beard to satisfy his parents. However, he only dressed according to religious protocol when he infrequently returned home. Moses had been a bright child; however, his wheeler dealing had not gone down well at his synagogue or in school; the two places his parents had made sure he spent the majority of his time. His parents had forced him into further education at the reasonably local, Northwestern University. Moses had been asked to leave in his initial semester, having started a business supplying late night alcohol and cigarettes to students. Expelled, broken and disgraced by his family, Moses had moved to New York, with what little money he had. He gained employment as a realtor and brokered a few deals, doing what he clearly knew best. After a year of relative prosperity, Moses had forged a modest network of wealthy property investors in New York. A client of his had been a certain Charles Hurst, who had taken him under his wing, gradually averting his business acumen and salesmanship to the brokering of arms.

Moses had developed a little too well within Hurst's network. Ballsy and wise beyond his years, Moses had formed lasting relationships with the senior operators in the global weapons market. Now indispensable to Hurst's outfit, he was his undisputed lead broker. Whether artillery, ammunition or any other type of weaponry, Moses was the man to source and sell. He had militia, weapons manufacturers, illegal runners and all manner of contacts in his phonebook. As the main agent for the majority of Hurst's big deals, Moses was possibly the richest and most powerful man in his organisation. As Moses had ascended, he had become more and more aware of this dynamic. Moses had begun to make extra commission-based demands. He had taken time off, blown-off important meetings and generally thrown his substantial weight around. Moses had always wanted more than the world could give him, and Hurst's business was no exception. This attitude, culminated with his sporadic, though brilliant, professional performance caused a good deal of friction between himself and Hurst.

By the time the evening had set in and the sun had slipped from view, Wolf and Kelly had managed to acclimatise to Hurst's decision to go after Mr Moses. The duo made their way down to the meeting terrace and found Hurst and Wright waiting, each with red wine poured in front of them. Hurst greeted them as they took their seats.

"Greetings, chaps! Wine?"

As he said this, a waiter appeared with two wine glasses and an open bottle. Wolf and Kelly motioned in accordance and the waiter duly poured them each a glass. Hurst continued as the waiter departed.

"So, chaps? What next?"

Kelly answered after a brief pause. "We're going to treat this Moses fuck the same way we have the others! We are going to physically stake this guy out. Wolfy and I will follow this guy and document his movements until he leads us to a base. Now this guy might well be a non-start, which would be lame. But by the same token, this asshole could be in deep with The Shadow! He might just lead us straight to him. Either way, if Chrissy and I can track him without detection, we're either going to find The Shadow or get closer to him! Sound fair enough?"

Wolf broke the impressed silence, following Kelly's smart conviction on proceedings.

"So, Mr Hurst. Why don't you tell us a little bit more about Mr Akiva Moses? As you suspect him so much, it would be very useful for us to know as much about him as possible. And while I'm sure our team in Europe will be more than capable of filling out the bones of his profile, I don't think there is anyone better placed than yourself, to explain why you think Moses is conspiring with The Shadow."

Hurst cleared his throat after another pensive pause and responded to Wolf.

"We call him AK, like AK-47, you know like the famous machine gun. Yeah! It was Wrighty who gave him that name! Fucking ironic, right! Anyway, this little rat I took under my wing in New York. He was a fucking estate agent! An estate agent! A nothing! A little two-bit hustler, running around for small fry commissions! I saw something in him! Maybe something of myself I suppose! Trouble is, I guess he's too much like me! But he's worse! I just know this guy would sell his grandma to a gaggle of gang rapists if they wet his beak! He's not in this for long term consolidation! He just wants to fuck this industry out of as much as he can! Moses is like a locust! He has no compassion, no feeling and no purpose. He relies solely on instinct, his greed! He moves from crop to crop, deal to deal and person to person! Ripping them off for as much as he can get and moving on! That's what he's been doing to me for years now! I just know he'd be a target for The Shadow! And as soon as you told me he didn't even bother taking the goodie-bag – a greedy, materialist, fat-fuck like him! Leave a bag worth tens of thousands, just sitting there! – oh no! I think not! He knew something was up! He's a smart little piggy! Big thick fucking glasses he's got, like a fucking Poindexter! Sorry Wrighty."

Having apologised to Wright for his glasses jibe, he paused to pat his shoulder before summing up.

"So that settles it, gentlemen! At daybreak we shall all set off to scout and hunt Akiva Moses for the fat, traitorous little prick he is!"

Hurst raised his glass and the four all toasted: "To AK!"

The waiter followed this toast with a Melanzane alla Parmigiana, which the group all appreciated. The quartet avidly consumed their rustically prepared and authentic Italian cuisine, before exchanging a few further pleasantries and retiring to bed. Wolf and Kelly had clearly won Hurst's trust and were getting closer to The Shadow's trail in the process. Furthermore, they had already satisfied their initial brief, to gain Hurst's account information. They still feared that Hurst's deviation from targeting the confirmed affiliates of The Shadow, focusing entirely on Moses, may have boded poorly with Douglas. However, with Hurst having complete veto power over the mission at this stage, Wolf and Kelly were faced with little alternative. They only hoped that their expeditions after Moses would be fruitful and lead them closer to the target. However, the mood in the anti-Shadow camp was now indisputably positive. Wolf and Kelly found sleep with ease that evening and almost looked forward to the promise of the morrow's events.

The following morning, Wolf and Kelly were awakened early, before their customary alarm from the nearby minaret. Hurst had summoned the pair at dawn to ready themselves for travel. Hurst's men had identified Moses's current location in Cape Town, South Africa. Hurst had therefore ordered his jet to be ready to depart for Cape Town International before noon. Wolf and Kelly suddenly had their comfortable existence at Hurst's five-star hotel broken. Uprooted and somewhat dishevelled, Wolf and Kelly gathered their effects and bundled themselves into Hurst's trucks he had waiting in the front drive. Before noon Hurst, Wright, Wolf and Kelly were airborne and flying for South Africa.

Having touched down at Cape Town International, the minimalist troop made their way to Hurst's luxury mansion, nestled in the Gardens district of Cape Town. Located close to the base of Table Mountain, this private, yet central spot provided a perfect retreat for Hurst, who used this property for pleasure far more than business. Cape Town's Waterfront bars, clubs and boutiques were a short drive away and the beautifully kept foliage, which lined the roads and pathways around the estate, was a pure representation of developed Africa.

Once disembarked from the Toyota Land Cruisers that had picked them up from the airport, Wolf and Kelly were shown to their rooms in the main house. Cheered by the luxury Hurst had afforded them in this lodging, Wolf and Kelly relaxed and let another day pass them by, preparing the hunt for AK.

# Chapter 18

## AKIVA 'AK' MOSES

The next morning arrived and, following a wonderfully catered breakfast on Hurst's beautiful veranda, the gang piled together into Hurst's, blacked-out Land Cruiser and descended towards the Waterfront. This was the location of Moses's pied-à-terre, a finely decorated and highly fashionable penthouse apartment, located right on the Waterfront. The four pulled up in Hurst's Toyota, one block from Moses' apartment building and waited for him to emerge. Sure enough, after a relatively short time, Moses waddled out from his building. He was dressed in a smart but flashy, cream linen suit, royal blue shirt and grey suede loafers. His hair had grown curlier and blonder in the African sun and his natural pale skin glowed with a healthy beige colouring. He strutted the few steps into his white Ferrari 458 Italia and drove off in a gust of turbo-charged bravado. Wright, who was driving Hurst's Land Cruiser, promptly followed at a practised and safe distance.

Wolf and Kelly knew from their experiences with Garrington and from the surveillance of Julius and Jamison, that The Shadow would always contact his infiltrators and not the other way around. They also knew The Shadow would never choose to contact an infiltrator at their workplace. Wolf and Kelly knew, therefore, that it would be highly unlikely to witness any contact between Moses and The Shadow during his normal working day. It was far more likely that The Shadow would contact Moses during the evenings and weekends. Hurst, however, had insisted on tracking

Moses night and day. Wright, therefore, followed Moses to Hurst's office on the Waterfront and waited outside. The four men watched, as he reappeared in the early afternoon and made his way to a local restaurant where he ate lunch.

Unrelenting, Wolf, Kelly, Hurst and Wright remained in their SUV for the rest of the day and into the late evening in their pursuit of Akiva Moses. They observed their target return to his apartment building at around ten o'clock, having indulged in some light post-work drinks. Having been satisfied Moses would not re-emerge, the four took a break from their stakeout and returned to Hurst's for the night.

The following day, Wolf and Kelly insisted on using a different car so not only Moses, but also The Shadow's men, would not recognise them. Using these different vehicles to avoid detection, the four tracked and monitored Moses for three further days with no results. However, on the evening of the fourth day, Hurst's gut-based suspicions of Moses were vindicated. Having trailed their target throughout the day, in an understated Nissan SUV with blackened windows, they saw that Moses had kept to his standard routine. They had followed him to Hurst's office in the morning. They had watched as he went for lunch and returned to his office in the afternoon. In the early evening they had tracked Moses to a Waterfront restaurant and bar. After four long joyless days, it was here that the company made their first major breakthrough.

Moses had selected a fashionable and popular restaurant right on the water. Moses, fortunately for his stalkers, had taken a seat outside. The Waterfront shopping centre and its surrounding boutiques and establishments were set into the harbour and this particular restaurant had a wonderful view over a collection of boats, ships and catamarans, and then on to the dazzling South Atlantic. The location of the restaurant had allowed Wright, who was driving Hurst's Nissan, to park very close to the target. Although normally civilian vehicles are not permitted into the roadways of The Waterfront, Hurst had a special tradesman's pass, which Wright had quickly flashed at the barrier entrance. The four men had a front row seat, therefore, as Moses consumed his Lobster and Champagne supper.

Moses, a greedy and opulent character, scoffed through his luxury dinner without discretion. As the evening grew darker, Moses moved onto his dessert, a chocolate cake with ice cream. However, he was interrupted in the middle of his fervent munching, by a waiter who handed him a sealed envelope. Moses seemed to recognise the envelope without opening it and, wiping his mouth, stood up and began to ease his bloated frame through the outside tables and out onto the pedestrianised harbour. Hurst's men watched from their SUV with bated breath, as Moses slipped a chubby finger into his envelope, tore it open and withdrew the contents. The writings in the letter could not have been substantial, as Wolf and Kelly could only see one sheet. Moses, having quickly glanced at this single sheet, now appeared to be looking for something or someone he could not see.

After a few seconds watching Moses flounder in the street, Hurst and his men in the SUV heard the aggressive revving of a fifty-CC engine behind them. A black Piaggio scooter flew past their Nissan and towards Moses. The rider was wearing full leathers, looked well armed and had masked his face entirely with an opaque and reflective helmet and visor. The masked rider slowed his moped and dismounted next to Moses, who welcomed him without guise or deception. Hurst and his crew looked on, as the pair conversed for a minute or two. After a short time, the rider, without removing his helmet to reveal his identity, nodded at Moses, remounted his bike and drove off at speed.

Wright had attempted, as best he could, to follow the rider as he sped out of the Waterfront. However, the scooter was radically more adept at weaving through the thronging tourists and shoppers who littered the pedestrianised roads in and out of the harbour. After a short time, the bike was lost, and Hurst was forced to call it a day. The four returned to Hurst's house once more, a little encouraged, but overly disappointed at having missed their chance to track a genuine Shadow contact. Having disembarked from the SUV, Hurst was all business. He was adamant that they should not make the same mistake twice. He insisted, going forward, that Kelly was to be ready with a bike of his own if ever they went to The Waterfront again. Wolf and Kelly, however, really felt that they were now closer than ever to finding The Shadow. They now had a powerful backer following their plan, they had sourced a confirmed target and it would only be a matter of time before The Shadow's loopholes would begin to expose themselves.

However, the morning after this monumental progress, Hurst's party were hit by a huge blow that challenged everything. Having, as usual, camped outside Moses' apartment building awaiting his exit for work, the entire morning had elapsed with no sight of Moses. Noon came and went with no hint of the target. Wolf, Kelly and Hurst became more and more anxious with every minute that passed without sign of Moses. Eventually, the four became desperate as time ticked on and they began to speculate as to the whereabouts of the errant Moses. Sat in the car together for days on end, tempers and personal pettiness were at an all-time high. The group had taken to remaining silent for long stints, only speaking upon sight of something relevant. However, as the afternoon wore on, Hurst could not help himself and broke the silence inside his fresh Land Rover Discovery.

"Alright! So, where the fuck is he!"

Wright, irritated and fatigued, snapped at his employer. "Well, I think if any of us knew that we wouldn't be fucking sitting here!"

Hurst, astounded by this insubordinate outburst, was taken aback and paused awkwardly before reasserting himself on Wright.

"Don't get like that with me! I will put a bullet in your fucking brain! What are you, fucking stupid!"

Hurst took a few deep breaths to calm himself, realising that in close combat with Wright he would certainly come off worse. He continued in a more even and apologetic tone.

"What kind of an answer is that? I think we all need to calm down and be smart here! And comments like that really don't help anyone. Alright, Wrighty!"

Wolf now interrupted, wishing to neutralise the situation and not wishing for Kelly to exacerbate it.

"Right, gentlemen, there are two possible scenarios here. One! Mr Moses is still in his room for some reason. Or alternatively, he could have left earlier this morning and missed us. And there is only one way for us to know for certain, and that is to enquire! However, we cannot just walk in there and buzz him! We will have to be cunning! How can we conceal our motives and identity? Yet still learn if Akiva remains in his room... thoughts, gentlemen?"

The four men sat for a few ponderous minutes in their blacked-out four-by-four. Neither of them wanted to be the one to voice a wrong idea. Having remained in close quarters for hours on end over the past week, the atmosphere had become a little tense, hypercritical and confrontational. Hurst, however, manged to break the silence with a bright idea.

"Okay here's what we do, chaps! So, obviously Danny and I can't even get out of the car, because he knows us and we'll break cover, right! But he's never really seen you two chaps! You're a bit too old, Chris, but Mike! Why don't you just quickly pop out, you are quite smartly dressed! Pretend to be an estate agent, you know! Walk in and ask the concierge to buzz up to the penthouse. Say you wish to speak with Mr Moses about the possibility of short letting his apartment whilst he's travelling. Then if he's in, give AK a fake story! And if he's not, tell the concierge you'll email him. Either way we'll know for sure if he's in or out! I think that's pretty sound? Why don't you borrow Chris's blazer? It'll make you look the part, ay?"

Concurring with Hurst's brainwave, the four men began to rustle around the SUV such that it began to rock slightly on its suspension. Wolf wriggled out of his blazer and passed it begrudgingly to Kelly in the front seat. Kelly, using the mirror on the inside of his sun visor, smartened his hair and adjusted his general appearance to the more official, commercially acceptable look, of a typical estate agent. As he turned and grabbed the car's door handle to alight the vehicle, he confirmed his instructions to the others.

"Okay so I'm going in as a Joe Bloggs asshole realtor. And I want to short-let this asshole's penthouse and want to buzz up to Moses? Right?"

Hurst nodded and further confirmed, "Yes exactly, then if he's in, just make it quick! Get in! Get out! If he's not, just leave a fake number or something with the concierge and maybe see if you can extract any more information. Good luck."

Kelly gave one final inquisition into Hurst's plan, however, before departing.

"Oh! And, err. How do we know there's a concierge?"

Hurst immediately snapped back with a confident and coy smile, "That's my fucking building, Mike. There's a concierge, twenty-four hours..."

Wright gave Kelly a final, slightly rough, slap on the shoulder for encouragement, before Kelly exited the vehicle and made his way to Moses's apartment building. As Kelly walked, with his attempt at a salesman's swagger, towards the entrance he mused at his curious situation. He was Captain Michael Kelly of the New York Police, masquerading as a bounty hunter after The Shadow, and now in turn, was pretending to be a real estate agent from Cape Town. Assuming this double-derivative of disguise,

Kelly pushed open the entrance to Moses's building and approached the concierge desk.

The concierge reception was rather distastefully decorated with Carrera marble, which was book-matched perfectly along the floor and through to the stairway. The concierge desk itself was also cast from the same fine-Italian marble slab. In contrast to the opulent surroundings, the porter behind the desk was an impoverished and modest looking local. He immediately recognised Kelly as an obvious salesman and stared him down with both distrust and contempt. The concierge tutted and engaged Kelly as he presented himself in front of him.

"T-t-t. Ah! What do you want? Can I help you with something, my friend?"

Kelly, slightly affronted by this aloof and flippant greeting, squinted back confrontationally, before taking out a wad of Rand and replying. "Yeah! I'm here to see the owner of your penthouse. A Mr Akiva Moses? He wants to short-let his apartment when he's not staying?"

Kelly pushed his head forward expectantly and assertively as he said this, and waited for the porter to retort. He then peeled off a few notes from his wad of cash and placed them in front of the concierge, whose eyes resultantly lit up. The porter snatched up the money and changed his expression to a smiling finesse.

"Ah, Mr Estate Agent, Sir! Please, Mr Moses is out. He left this morning eh! He left early! I think he was catching a plane, because he had a suitcase. I would say he'll be gone for a while! This was the first time he's been around in months. I guess you missed your chance, ah! You wanted to rent his apartment when he's gone, eh? T-t-t! Ah! Well now he's gone! So, it's too late."

Kelly smiled back at the porter and enquired further of this now looser-lipped concierge.

"Well I can always email him, I guess, but maybe if I leave my number with you..."

The concierge tutted again and interrupted.

"T-t-t! Ah! Come on! I don't want your number! He's gone, eh! He won't be back! He won't get your little business card or whatever!"

Kelly gave one final attempt to coax further information and replied.

"Oh! Okay! Wow! Don't worry about it! I'll just email him, jeez! God, I wonder why he's gone, shit?"

The concierge stared at him as if contemplating whether to request further remuneration for this information. However, gauging this as a passing comment, the porter felt this information was of little or no worth to Kelly and responded assertively.

"T-t-t! Ah! He was going to London! Ah! He told me he had a meeting in London and he won't be back! T-t-t! Ah! Now get out, we don't like your kind in here!"

Kelly smiled thoughtfully at the concierge, nodded in farewell and turned to leave. He made his way back to Hurst's SUV to divulge his new-found information as quickly as possible. Having reunited with his team, Kelly repeated the concierge's, relatively accurate and informative, locational information. Wright sped the group around and straight to the airport. Wolf called ahead to Maya to trace all flights to London and have Hakimi hack the names of flight bookings to Akiva Moses. Hurst also called ahead to Cape Town International, to have his jet fuelled, checked and waiting for take-off. Virtually simultaneously, Wolf's mobile vibrated and Maya called back to inform him that Moses had boarded a flight to Heathrow and was due to arrive at ten-thirty pm GMT. Maya further let on that Lopez and his operations team had been deployed to Heathrow's relevant terminal exits. They would track AK's movements from the airport, should he proceed directly to contact The Shadow. Hurst, who had not yet hung-up the phone to his flight crew, overheard Wolf's conversation and gave instructions accordingly to make passage for Heathrow terminal three. Hot in pursuit, the four men arrived quickly at Cape Town International airport and flew through the night to the United Kingdom.

# Chapter 19

## HOLLAND PARK HIDEOUT

**A**kiva 'AK' Moses had been successfully tracked by Lopez himself upon his arrival at Heathrow. Lopez had followed him into the floodlit London-town, eventually tailing him to the modern, clean and sweeping lines of The Royal Garden Hotel, Kensington. This iconic building provides a provocative and progressive backdrop to the established stronghold of Victorian palaces, on the corner of Palace Avenue and Kensington High Street. Lopez remained at this location with his team throughout the night, until Wolf and Kelly had caught up, courtesy of Hurst's private G7 jet-aeroplane.

Having touched down in the early morning, Hurst, Wright, Wolf and Kelly made their way in a convoy of SUVs to Hurst's detached townhouse, located nearby Moses' hotel, on a tributary of Kensington Road. The four men promptly freshened themselves, using the many showers in Hurst's tastefully modernised residence. Hurst's smooth-riding and luxurious jet had afforded all his company a decent night's sleep on their way to London and they all reappeared from the upper floor en-suite bathrooms, energised and excited in anticipation of Moses' next move. Sure enough, before the morning was out, Kelly's smartphone rang. Lopez was at the other end of the line and informed Kelly that Moses was on the move. The quartet of huntsmen sprinted for the Land Rover Discovery parked in Hurst's miniature driveway and sped towards Kensington Gardens. From the end of Hurst's road it was less than four hundred metres to The Royal

Garden Hotel. As they hit traffic approaching the join of Kensington Road and High Street, Lopez informed them that Moses had hailed a taxi and was now headed west.

Skipping deftly through the city traffic, Wright managed to catch and overtake Lopez, the less experienced driver. As morning turned to afternoon, the troop followed Moses' cab as it headed north, through the white stucco-fronted maze of Kensington High Street's northern offshoots. They reached the brow of Campden Hill and turned west, onto Holland Park Avenue, before turning onto Holland Park itself. One of the most incredibly positioned residential areas in London, this tree-lined and fabulously grand street, crescents the northern tip of London's secluded and well-maintained Holland Park. While many of the original grandiose residences that populate this street have been broken into apartments, Moses' cab pulled up outside a superbly presented whole house, complete with separate mews house to the rear. Lopez immediately spotted that the rear entrance led into the parallel Holland Park Mews. He informed Kelly, still on the phone, that he would cover the rear exit from the top of Holland Park, while they should hold their position parked further down. With Lopez able to see straight down Holland Park Mews and the others staked out at the house's front entrance, the team waited.

Roughly an hour of adrenaline-fuelled expectance elapsed, before Wright spotted men emerging from the front entrance. These men all had their faces covered with masks. Otherwise suited, they all were dressed as if attending a masquerade ball. Roughly ten masked men filtered out of the house and down its raised ground floor stone stairway. Reaching the hip-height, iron entrance gate, the stream of incognito businessmen split off into various cars parked adjacent to the building. Moments later, Lopez reported seeing Moses leave via the rear mews house and make his way slowly down Holland Park Mews. Faced with a decision whether to attempt to follow one of the cars driving off from the front, or to continue pursuing Moses, the group concurred that they should stick to Moses, as they could always return to this Holland Park address at a later stage.

Hence, Hurst's troop held their position and waited until Lopez let them know that Moses had reached the end of Holland Park Mews and turned right towards Holland Avenue. The five men duly followed after Moses as he caught another Black Cab on Holland Park Avenue and returned to The Royal Garden Hotel. Having witnessed Moses disembark his taxi and re-enter his hotel, Kelly instructed Lopez to remain outside to monitor Moses's future movements, while the others returned to Hurst's nearby residence. However, no sooner had Wright driven past Lopez on Kensington High Street, when Hurst's phone began to buzz, and he answered. To the total shock of Hurst and his company, it was Moses on the other end of the line. Realising this, Hurst shushed his associates and put Moses on speakerphone. Moses' tone was casual yet business-like, as his voice crackled through Hurst's smartphone.

"Hey Charlie? Charlie, it's AK. You there?"

Hurst, terrified and conscious of his proximity to Moses, responded as calmly and unassumingly as possible.

"Yah. It's me. Hey Kives, how's it going?"

Moses coughed slightly and was breathing with a slight inclination, such that Hurst and his troop could clearly ascertain he was still on his way up to his hotel room.

"Hey Charlie. It's all good. I'm good, you know. I'm err, just calling you about setting up a little meeting. I've got these guys who want to buy about two hundred million dollars' worth of Apaches. Now I've got the supply down! But these assholes want to meet you first before they sign our terms!"

Moses paused to allow for Hurst's response. Wolf and Kelly both motioned with frantic body language to accept the invitation and act as normally as possible. Hurst rolled his eyes and replied as tasked.

"Okay Kives, that should be fine. Where do they want to meet?"

Moses elaborated, clearly pleased with Hurst's acceptance.

"Ah, okay great! Amsterdam. They're international, but they want to meet at the Waldorf Historia. Can you be there in about twenty-four?"

Hurst answered after a brief break of calculation. "Not a problem! Set up the meet for three-thirty, local time tomorrow. I'll show face If it means twenty-percent of two hundred million!"

Hurst had dropped in this last utterance, deliberately to gauge Moses's reaction. Moses, however, not giving Hurst the reaction he expected, went on in quick confirmation.

"Okay, sweet, I'll get Tania to book us both a nice suite and I'll see you tomorrow."

Hurst cocked his head and widened his eyes at the others in disbelief, before bidding farewell to Moses.

"Right you are, mate, see you tomorrow!"

Hurst ended the call and instantly made his feelings known.

"Okay so something's up! That greedy fat fuck is definitely up to something! There's no way this is a coincidence! For him to call me just after he's met with these guys! Come on! Then the commission! Oh my God! I think that's the first time I have ever, ever mentioned commission and not been hauled over the coals into a long and drawn out conversation! Involving him upping his commission for the deal somehow! Did you hear, though, chaps? He didn't say a fucking word! And he's going to have Tania book us both suites! That's not like him, selfish fat bastard! He'd normally have me call her to book! No, something's definitely up! He clearly just wants me there, come what may! It must be The Shadow, it can't be anything else!"

As Hurst voiced this analysis of Moses's phone call, Wright pulled into his tiny drive and the four men left the vehicle and filed into Hurst's house. As they walked through into the main, double-height reception, Hurst continued questioningly.

"So, chaps? What do I do? What do we do next?"

Kelly spoke first in response, having been considering their situation since Moses' phone call.

"I think, bearing in mind we have pretty much got what we came for – and by that I mean, that this fat fuck's led us straight to one of The Shadow's lairs! I mean did you see those guys coming out? They were The Shadow's men for sure. And not soldiers neither! These were made guys! Trust me I can just tell, that place is important to The Shadow! I'm just saying! – I think we should drop Akiva and stake this place out!"

Wolf quickly leapt into the conversation to back up his partner.

"I have to say, Mr Hurst, I agree with Michael here. I think that his practised assertions are almost certainly correct in this case. I would also say that you, Mr Hurst, need to follow Mr Moses's instructions as if nothing was amiss. As if this AK character suspects anything is different, he will certainly relay this to The Shadow! Furthermore, Mr Hurst, it is highly likely that this meeting in Amsterdam is connected with The Shadow! And while I would strongly advise that you not attend alone, I do feel that it is a necessity that you should attend this meeting."

Hurst thought for a little before agreeing.

"Okay, I think you're right. And by the way, Wrighty here comes with me to all my major meetings. There's no way I'd meet with this guy alone right now! But what about The Shadow's hide-out in Holland Park?"

Wolf nodded back at Hurst and reassured him.

"Rest assured, Mr Hurst, that place will still be here when you get back from Amsterdam. And while you're gone, Michael and I will use our team in London and stake it out just as we have done today. We will return there tonight, and in the meantime, you will meet with Moses. I would suggest further, Mr Hurst, that you employ considerable reinforcements for this meeting. I would not be at all surprised if it were an ambush ploy by The Shadow. For as you say, it cannot be a coincidence, him calling you at this precise moment. Something is undoubtedly afoot!"

Hurst turned his head in thought as Wolf fell silent. After a short hush in conversation, Hurst agreed and enquired further.

"Right so that's settled. Wrighty and I will depart for Holland this afternoon and you chaps will have your team support you while we're gone. I will report on proceedings as they occur from Amsterdam and you will do the same on your stakeout. Speaking of which, any thoughts moving forward on this? How are you guys going to operate?"

Kelly piped up at this point having a plethora of stakeout experience.

"Okay guys! So, the key to a good stakeout is knowing what to look for. If you don't know what you're looking for, how can you expect to find it, right! Like today, we didn't have a fucking clue what to expect or what we were looking for! So, when a gang of The Shadow's senior guys rolled out, we were caught with our pants down. If we had known which guy to look for, we could have followed him when they all split up! We could be outside his fucking house right now!"

Kelly broke off for a second to calm himself, massaging the back of his neck as he continued.

"We have to think about who we are looking for! So, come on, guys I've been thinking about this! If this house is a key location for The Shadow! We should be looking for his most senior associates, or even, perhaps the man himself! I mean that is our end-goal, right! So how do we look for the most senior guys? I mean we can't see their fucking faces? What are we going to do? I'll tell you! It's easy! We don't need to see their faces to recognise a senior guy's fucking behaviour!"

Kelly smiled as he continued, noticing Wolf, Hurst and Wright were all fixed with attentive intrigue, at his brilliantly analytical thought process.

"The things we got to look for, are as follows! What time a guy comes in! Senior guys typically come in later and leave earlier. Senior guys will normally arrive in a nicer set of wheels and possibly with an entourage! They will have sharper clothes and will tend to hold themselves in a certain, real superior-like, way! I bet they'll also probably be wearing a different or distinctive mask too! If we look out for all these things, it'll be a matter of days before we track one of The Shadow's leaders!"

Hurst pursed his lips forward and curled their corners downwards approvingly at Kelly, before concluding his concurrence.

"Pretty fucking smart, Captain! I told you I love an ex-cop! You guys really know some sweet tricks! Yeah, that's pretty fucking clever! I've got to say! Right, come on, Danny! Look alive! Make some calls and let's get our asses moving to Holland! And you chaps, don't just stand there! Get your man Lopez to pick you up and head the fuck back to Holland Park! It's all Holland today, boys!"

Wolf and Kelly did as they were told and telephoned for Lopez to retreat from his position and pick them up from Hurst's. Only a three-minute drive from Moses's hotel, Lopez was outside in moments. Wolf and Kelly said their brief goodbyes to Hurst and Wright and met Lopez outside. Lopez drove the pair back to Holland Park and took a positional vantage, further down from their previous position, looking back up Holland Park at the front of The Shadow's lair. Meanwhile Beacher, DeVeron and Jenner, Lopez's operations team members, parked in a similarly disguised SUV at the bottom of Holland Park Mews. Having the front and back entrances monitored, the team lay in wait for a smartly dressed man to arrive or depart in a superior vehicle, possibly wearing a distinctive mask and accompanied by an entourage.

Miraculously, as if manifested by Kelly's divinely intuitive imagination, the trio did not have to wait long for Kelly's plan to be vindicated. In the late afternoon, an all-black, chauffeur-driven Bentley Mulsanne pulled up, almost self-effacingly, outside the Holland Park house. The chauffeur placed his hazard lights on and did not bother to park. Instead he double-parked directly in front of the building and waited. Presently two obvious security guards, complete with masks and visible handguns, appeared from the double doors at the front entrance. Almost immediately after them, followed three further men. The first two were also clearly security guards, being similarly geared with masks and pistols and wearing plain, ill-tailored, black suits with tell-tale thin lapels. The third and final man, however, was to be Wolf and Kelly's mark. His dark navy suit, white shirt and dark purple tie were freshly crisp and looked brand-new. His mask was different, in that it was completely white. He evidently ticked all the boxes of Kelly's search criteria, so Kelly exclaimed to Wolf and Lopez from their blacked-out SUV at the bottom of Holland Park, "Oh my God! This guy's it! He's got to be! We've got to tail this guy! Let's see where he goes!"

Wolf and Lopez nodded in agreement. Lopez then instructed his operations team to split up and cover their position, while they veered off to follow the Bentley Mulsanne. The three masked men now descended the stairs at the entranceway to The Shadow's house. Wolf, Kelly and Lopez ducked down in reaction and observed, over the bottom of their windows, as the man with the white mask was escorted to his car by the two leading security guards. The two men then shut the door behind the white masked man and made their way back to the house. Wolf, Kelly and Lopez then all recoiled completely from sight and listened, as the Bentley smoothly rolled past their position and down to the bottom of Holland Park. The three men rose from their refuge fast enough to see the car peel off right, and towards Holland Park Avenue. Lopez scrambled to start up his SUV and give chase.

Lopez carefully trailed the enormous Bentley back east, across the north side of Kensington Gardens and Hyde Park and on towards Park Lane. The Mulsanne cruised elegantly among the increasingly similar cars that inhabit Park Lane's wealthy tributaries. Lopez continued in distant pursuit, as the Bentley turned, about halfway down Park Lane, into South Street. Seeing this, Lopez accelerated towards the corner of Park Lane and onto South Street. He reached it just in time to see the white masked man's car come to an even halt and gently pull into an open garage. Lopez drove the car on and past the garage to get a closer look. The trio managed to see the door close shut behind the Mulsanne as they passed. The garage was part of a considerable red-brick townhouse. With an impressive, five-window frontage, this house clearly belonged to someone of considerable wealth. Wolf and Kelly decided to keep eyes on this location, only moments from Cork's base on the nearby Upper Brook Street. They remained outside and waited. As the evening progressed into night, the three took turns sleeping, as they proceeded to stake out this beautiful Mayfair property.

# Chapter 20

## A SHADOW BROUGHT TO LIGHT

L opez's SUV was clammy and stale as morning broke over Mayfair's South Street. Now accustomed to this muggy and musty atmosphere, Wolf gently rustled the sleeping Kelly and Lopez as he witnessed the target house's second floor windows light up, just after eight o'clock. Lopez and Kelly rapidly regained consciousness and, tasting they were close to another lead, fixed their attention on the property. After about forty-five minutes of intense monitoring, the trio noticed the ground floor lights come on and, seconds after, the front door twitched and opened.

Neither Wolf, Kelly nor Lopez could believe their eyes as Jamie Segal, Silverman's director and right-hand man, peered out from the house. He sniffed the air and pressed a button to his right, which switched off the house's lights. He then stepped carefully outside and locked the door behind him. Dressed in his typically spotless dark navy suit, he turned and made his way east, down South Street before cutting into a tiny passage and disappearing from view. Wolf and Kelly, consulting their smartphones, saw that Segal had split into a pathway leading to Mount Street Gardens, the location at which they had previously met with him. Having deduced this, Wolf had Lopez turn around and head for Mount Street. Within seconds, they had zipped around and parked near the intersection of Mount and South Audley Street. The three hunters had headed-off Segal perfectly. As no sooner had they parked, than they witnessed him appear onto Mount Street, through one of its southern passages. They drifted up

Mount Street and cautiously followed Segal onto Carlos Place and towards Tutum Capital, Silverman's base and Segal's main office.

This was an unprecedented discovery and Wolf's mind was flying in all directions, attempting to reason and calculate Segal's role within The Shadow's organisation. Wolf even found himself considering the possibility that Segal could be The Shadow. Wolf felt the urge to consolidate his position and called Hurst. He promptly informed him of their findings and told Hurst not to reveal anything of their discovery to Moses in his meeting. At the same time as Wolf had telephoned Hurst, Kelly had called through to Maya at the Harvey Walsh HQ. Kelly brought Maya up to speed on their results; she then instructed the three men to stand down and report back to Upper Brook Street. Within minutes the trio had made it back to their headquarters and were further instructed to return to their apartment in Marylebone and return first thing in the morning. This had evidently been treated as a monumental discovery. This was the first time anyone had ever successfully identified any of The Shadow's associates. However, to identify Segal was extraordinary, not least due to his position as consigliere to Silverman, the very man who had a five hundred-million-dollar reward out on The Shadow. Wolf and Kelly pondered away the remainder of the day, bouncing ideas and theories off each other. The pair chatted into the night and drew closer to a verdict that they felt was irrefutable, and another plan was forged.

The following morning Wolf and Kelly arrived at their base in high spirits. Maya was at the bottom of the stairs facing the entrance way to meet them. She escorted them up to their office. Inside Hakimi and Oppenheim were waiting. Maya opened up the conversation, as Wolf and Kelly made their way to the coffee tray on Kelly's desk.

"So, well done, guys! Last night, Josh and Daniel were able to trace the lost amounts of your new gangster buddies, almost to the dollar, to offshore transfers through Linstraad Group's funds! We had Cork call the bank – he went to school with the CEO. He confirmed that these holdings can be traced back to Tutum Capital! Which is, needless to say, Silverman's fund!"

Oppenheim interrupted Maya triumphantly. "It's a lot easier when you know what to look for, ay!"

Kelly, in turn, interrupted Oppenheim abruptly. "Shut the fuck up, Danny! Where were you in Peru? So, let me get this straight! This was the first time you investigated Silverman's accounts?"

Oppenheim responded sheepishly at first and then aggressively, having had his sarcastic confidence dashed by Kelly's swift and practical insight.

"Well, it was the perfect disguise, I guess? So, no! We didn't think that the man working directly under Silverman would be The fucking Shadow! And right under our very noses as well! I have to confess, we didn't think of that!"

Oppenheim looked around to try and pass the blame as he continued.

"Actually, yeah, Josh! Why didn't we think of that? Why didn't anyone think of that? What about you, Maya?"

Maya snorted and shrugged as Hakimi piped up in his defence.

"Well I supposed it was just that Silverman's the one who put up the reward and well, he's really just a banker by trade and so is Segal! Or so we thought. I guess we just figured, someone that close to Silverman wouldn't be related to Harvey Walsh, let alone be Harvey Walsh!"

Maya also retorted at Kelly impetuously: "Okay, look, guys, I don't think anyone saw this coming, especially you two! Mike, when you called me from the car you were fucking shocked, okay! So, don't start playing that game! The point is, no one would have thought to investigate Silverman's finances because he is beyond reproach and therefore suspicion! Segal was perfectly concealed! And I think it was pretty much dumb luck, from what I can see, that Hurst led you to him! So, Captain! If you'll allow me to continue?"

She paused, hand on hip and eyebrow raised at Kelly, whose reputation for angry and inappropriate interruption preceded him. Satisfied by Kelly's silence she resumed.

"Obviously, Harry, his Lordship and Mr Silverman are all aware of this development. Apparently, action has now been taken such that Silverman has confirmed that Segal did indeed syphon funds through Tutum Capital, to untraceable offshore accounts. It has also been confirmed that Silverman has positively identified Segal as The Shadow! This has, therefore, guys – if you'll let me finish! –concluded Mission Harvey Walsh! Your final mini-mission shall be one of appreciative acceptance! Mr Silverman has requested you both join him this morning to collect your bounty and confirm Segal's demise."

Kelly could not help himself and interjected against his better judgement, "Wait, so we get the five hundred mil?"

Maya rolled her eyes and sighed at Kelly, before sternly continuing.

"No, Captain Kelly! You will accept the bounty! But only to maintain your cover through to perpetuity and not compromise the identity of our mission! However, the account details you give to Silverman will be ours! You will, of course, be remunerated as per your contracts. But come on, guys! You're not walking away with five hundred million! And if there is even the slightest delay, or any of us feel like you're even thinking about stealing it–"

Kelly interrupted once more, unable to resist indulging his ego. "Okay I've had about enough of your bitchy French attitude! I've never stolen anything in my life! And neither has Wolfy, okay! We're fucking cops! We don't fucking steal, you moron!"

Maya's eyes moistened a little as she felt anger and toxicity build inside her and she retorted with a cold whisper, "Well then it won't be a problem for you and The Professor to punctually attend the meeting and conclude our business for good. And I'm Belgian, not French, so who is the moron, Captain, eh?"

Kelly was a little lost for words, feeling bashful at his xenophobic outburst. Maya did not wait for a response. Instead she motioned for Oppenheim and Hakimi to follow, as she turned to leave. As she did so, she yelled back a final barked command.

"Be there in twenty minutes! Don't be late!"

Wolf and Kelly were inherently suspicious of this interchange. Wolf waited for Maya's footsteps to subside from earshot, lifted his head gently at Kelly and enquired, "Michael?"

Kelly looked deeply troubled as he stared back at Wolf and responded, "Something's wrong here, isn't it, Professor? You feel it too?"

Wolf shrugged in appreciation but did not offer a verbal response. Instead he allowed for Kelly to propose his frustrated perplexations further.

"I mean, don't it seem all too easy? Hasn't it all just slotted in place a little too well? And far too quickly by half! It's certainly nothing like we thought last night, is it, Professor, you have to admit?"

Once again, the Professor used his body language to agree, with a smile and another shrug of his shoulders. Kelly began to pace, as he resumed his verbal train of thought, questioning himself as much as Wolf.

"And why didn't anyone see this before? Forget about the assholes downstairs and your girlfriend, what about Silverman? How did this all-star fund manager super intellect, fucking polymath! Fucking miss! That his right-hand man was the fucking Shadow! How? I ask you? And what the fuck is going on with Cork, Silverman and Victoria's murdered husband? We never did find out exactly what he knew! If he knew anything? Either way, whatever it was he knew got him killed! What's the connection? Maya never explained that loose end! What if this is all a set up? What if The Shadow's still out there? And he's got to Silverman or Cork, or both!"

Wolf softly hushed and interrupted Kelly as his questioning became wilder and wilder.

"Please, Michael. Let's not get ahead of ourselves. This entire experience has been confusing and unnerving! And yet we have still endured. That is the most important thing, Herr Michael. We must of course keep our wits about us. However, what Maya said did make sense..."

Anticipating Kelly was about to interject, Wolf once again hushed Kelly and went on.

"Please, Michael. I think the only way for us to proceed, is to bear in mind our plans and theories, but to proceed as commanded. I must say, though, Captain, I have to admit, I am still intrigued to hear from our friend Herr Hurst's meeting with Akiva Moses. Remember, Michael, we still have that card to play, should your worst fears of conspiracy actually manifest."

Wolf and Kelly wasted no more time starting off on the short walk to Silverman's Tutum Capital headquarters, just off Grosvenor Square. Greeted by the same ironclad lettering and iron-willed receptionist as before, Wolf and Kelly were directed, as previously, to the familiar leather quilted bench outside Silverman's office. This time, however, no scared smiling face popped out from the double doors of the office; the pair were instead received by two burly security guards. These towering men pulled back the double doors and eyed Wolf and Kelly into Silverman's office. Silverman remained seated at his desk smoking a cigarette and did not get up to greet them. Instead he pointed purposefully at Segal's flayed corpse, sprawled over a chaise longue in the corner of the room. He engaged Wolf and Kelly as he gestured.

"So, this guy's come in here last night, right! I've hauled him out of bed, I know he only lives up the road, right! Obviously! As soon as I heard from your pretty-voiced associate about what Jamie done! I wanted to meet him face to face, you know. I wanted to watch his pupils flicker and swell as I tell him what I've learned, sneaky fucking cunt! So, I've got him in the office and I've already regretted this because it dawns on me, he must already know something's up! Anyway, I tell him what I know! And not only does this fuck confess and tell me it's been him all along! He pulls a fucking gun on me! Now thank fuck! I managed to use my superior man-power and cunning to avoid his shot and turn his gun back on himself! I shot him in the face, mate! Look! Go on, have a look at him! There's your fucking Shadow, ladies and gentlemen! Oh, the fucking irony!"

At this juncture Silverman paused and shifted his body to the right of his chair to reveal an obvious bullet hole in the chair's spine. Convinced that Wolf and Kelly had registered the significance of this bullet hole, Silverman resumed.

"Absolute fucking mess! And in light of this philosophical and soul enlightening experience, I have decided to be a man of my word and give credit where credit is due. Now I have no doubt that given more time, that bastard Segal would have marked me for death and bleed me dry from my own fucking source! And you fellows! You've helped me make sure that's never going to happen!

"So that said, gentlemen, I've decided to pay you your five hundred million. Just give me your details and I'll wire it to any account in the world. While I may have ended The Shadow's reign on my fucking chaise, far be it for me to steal the credit for finding him! You're a bright pair of lads, you two! Fucking best bounty hunters I ever saw! Now if you'll both give your account details in at reception, I'll have your bounty despatched. And, unless there's anything else, you needn't say a word."

This interaction had been made awkward at best, by the presence of Segal's fresh corpse. Kelly's suspicion of the entire situation had been heightened as soon as laying eyes on Segal's lifeless body. Kelly had desperately wanted to inquire further of Silverman; however, Wolf spoke up assertively before Kelly had the chance.

"Well, thank you very much, Mr Silverman, it has been a pleasure doing business with you! A rare thing in today's underhanded and fickle world. I am pleased we could be of service and that we have delivered on our promise. And I am certain that my colleague and I will be even more pleased once we have seen the balance of our accounts injected. But our backer will be most delighted."

Silverman stubbed out his second cigarette and bluntly bid the pair farewell. "Right well that's that then. Now, err, if you don't mind."

He broke off and pointed again at Segal's body behind Wolf and Kelly, before continuing.

"Something tells me I'm going to have my work cut out today."

With this, Wolf and Kelly rose from their chairs and exited, under the watchful eyes of the two huge security guards. They descended to the reception and informed the receptionist of the account details Maya had given them. Having successfully completed the final part of their final mission, the pair began their short, and perhaps final, walk back to Harvey Walsh HQ. Kelly was unable to contain his frustration at their meeting and relayed his feelings to Wolf as they walked across Grosvenor Square.

"Chrissy! I don't buy a single thing we were just sold! Something is definitely up! What the fuck just happened! Segal confessed to being The Shadow! And then Silverman kills him! A likely fucking story! There's no way The Shadow would put himself at risk like that! He must be covering for someone or something else! Silverman was a total asshole for killing him."

Wolf smiled and attempted a response, as they walked.

"What choice did he have, Michael? He is no fighting man, despite what he said. He was lucky to have escaped with his life. But I agree, I think it would be foolish to assume Segal's confession to be true, even if he was the source of The Shadow's funds! It's still possible, of course, that he was being used by some greater power."

Kelly's eyes sparked with an idea and he reached for his smartphone as he replied, "Holy shit, Chris! We never heard back from Hurst! I'm fucking calling him! Let's see what he makes of all this!"

Kelly questioned himself and Wolf, as he held the receiver to his ear and waited, as the phone rang with the international dial tone.

"Why is it, Wolfy? Out of all the people we met in this whole shit storm affair! Hursty is pretty much the only guy I trust, present company excluded, of course!"

Wolf retorted promptly. "Present company excluded, I agree with you, Michael. And that is because Herr Hurst has almost unanimously told the truth. Let's see what he has to say. Put him on speaker."

Kelly placed his smartphone on speaker and held the phone towards Wolf. The pair walked on and waited as the droning dial tone sounded a few more times. Finally, a voice that they recognised but was not Hurst's, answered. It was Wright, who sounded rushed, desperate and fatigued.

"Hello, who's this?"

Kelly answered. "It's Kelly and Wolf. What's going on? Where the fuck have you guys been? It's all been happening!"

Wright interrupted. "Wait, shut it! I've got to tell you! No, wait, go on! You go first!"

Kelly intrigued at Wright's news, quickly explained their developments.

"Well, since we've ID-ed Segal, Silverman's director, he's been confirmed as The Shadow from his accounts at Linstraad Group and Tutum Capital. We have literally just met with Silverman and Segal's dead! Silverman shot him in the face last night! We just saw the body! Daniel, I think The Shadow might be dead. But we don't think it's that simple. We..."

Wright, having listened patiently, exclaimed in a panting fervour, "No! Nah! Can't be! So, while you girls have been fannying about in London, we've had a full-scale fucking war in Amsterdam! Charlie's only fucking dead! The Shadow's men shot him into a canal last night! They hit us on scooters with machine guns. But don't worry! I've fucking made sure and tortured that squealing, fat little cunt, Moses! And that's how I know! That was one of the first questions we asked! And I can definitely confirm that while Moses doesn't know who The Shadow is – he claims no one does! – he also confirmed, beyond doubt, that while Segal is a senior operative, he definitely is not The Shadow!"

Wright paused for a moment, realising their best real lead had been nullified and resumed angrily.

"Hold up! Wait a fucking minute, China! Are you telling me that Segal – our one and only lead to The Shadow – is fucking dead! I tell you what! Now we're really fucking dead! We've got two choices, gentlemen! Fight or flight! We can either dig in further and push The Shadow now we've rattled him and found his money source! Or! And I seriously recommend we follow this fucking course! We fuck right off! And stay off the fucking grid completely!"

Kelly waiting for Wright to finish respectfully, answered in counterargument. "No way! We've got this fuck on the ropes, Wrighty! Come on, Death Warrant! We've got his fucking money! We know where it's coming from!"

Wolf chose to interject at this point with a balanced point of view.

"Hello Herr Wright! It's me, Professor Wolf! I understand Michael's point of view. However, Michael, you must understand, we do not have this man's money. His money is in Cayman and BVI accounts that are untraceable and untouchable. However, we do now have, in Linstraad Group, a source for the main channelling of his funds. Perhaps it would be poignant to press this one avenue, with the full backing of our team in Europe, of course! And then, once this is exhausted, call it a day?"

Kelly frowned and wanted to retort; however, he waited for Wright to respond over the speakerphone.

"Alright, if you want to try that, I suppose it couldn't hurt to ask some fucking questions of a few soft bankers! But after that I'm fucking off, son! Look I've got to go, girlies! I'd love to stay and chat! But this is hardly the fucking time now, is it! And I've got a plane to catch! Call me when you have something!"

Wright rang off as Wolf and Kelly neared the entrance to their headquarters on Upper Brook Street.

# Chapter 21

## THE TERMINATION OF HARVEY WALSH

Immediately wishing to share their new-found information with Maya and the rest of Team Harvey Walsh, Wolf and Kelly had informed Maya upon their return of their conversation with Daniel Wright. Maya called through to Douglas, who was already en route to sign off their final mission and terminate their contracts. She relayed Wolf and Kelly's suspicions that The Shadow was still at large, while they waited in their office for Douglas to arrive. After around fifteen minutes of anxious attendance, Douglas could be heard slamming the front door behind him and cantering up the stairs. He slipped through their office door and calmly closed it behind him. He then turned with menace to face Wolf and Kelly. His voice was eerily smooth and melodic as he started at them.

"So, let me get this straight, guys? You're trying to tell me, that instead of walking through that door and handing you a nice cheque, pat on the back, congrats and fuck off! You're telling me we've got it all wrong? And that Harvey Walsh is still out there? Are you guys actually trying to tell me! That you trust a psychotic, senile old cockney over Lord Cork and Avram Abraham Silverman? Or myself for that matter! I was about to come in here and congratulate you two! I am staggered! Staggered! I mean, talk to me, guys! I'm fucking clutching here! I'm fucking clutching!"

Douglas's voice broke up into a desperate, almost whining, tone and Wolf attempted to coerce his and Kelly's motives.

"Please, Herr Douglas! It is not that we question your credibility in the slightest capacity! Or Lord Cork's or Mr Silverman's. We were only just informed of this development as we walked back from, what I can only describe as, a bizarre and disturbing meeting with Mr Silverman."

Douglas sniffed and leapt back on the offensive questioningly.

"And what were you doing calling up Hurst anyway! This was supposed to be your final mission, lads! Game over! Bad guy shot in the face! You saw it yourselves! I thought you'd be happy! Because I tell you what, boys! I was fucking down right impressed by the way you've handled yourselves finding Segal! And you can ask Maya! Or any of those other maggots downstairs! I am not an easy man to impress! But now! Just like you did the first fucking time I laid eyes on you! You're starting to really fucking annoy me! No, scratch that! Look at me! I'm fuming! I've already passed starting! I am fucking annoyed! Ah God!"

With this explosion, Douglas paced away and into a corner of the room before gaining his composure a little and continuing.

"Why do you two want to snatch defeat from the jaws of victory? What are you, the England football team! What's wrong with you! Silverman! The very man who's put the fucking reward out on Harvey Walsh has positively ID-ed this guy! And his funds were traced successfully! To that fucking Linstraad Group Capital Fund or whatever! Your idea, guys! Your fucking doing! Not mine! And we had to go through hell on our end, to hack the clearance for that information! And now you're telling me! That your own plan! Which we followed and was successful! Is wrong! I'm sorry, I'm shutting you down right now! You can take your cheques and fuck off back where you came from!"

Kelly attempted an interruption. However, Douglas, attuned to Kelly's customary disruptions, pre-empted him. As Kelly was about to speak, Douglas marched deftly towards him and placed his right hand over Kelly's mouth. Stunned, Kelly flinched and froze with fear and intimidation at the rabid Scotsman, as he whispered aggressively to the pair.

"You will sign your releases now. You will take your cheques and leave! And, Captain Kelly! If I see you again! I shall be very! Very! Un-fucking-happy! The funny thing is, son. I'm not even kidding either! If you come back to these wee rainy shores again! And I hope you don't! Just make damn sure you don't run into me again! Because I'll keep you alive! While I cut out your eyes, burn off your fingertips, burst your eardrums and pull out your impetuous Yank tongue! Then you might realise what a senseless, sceptic cunt you really are!"

Douglas had drawn himself deep into his conversation with Kelly and turned back to see Wolf and Maya staring at him awkwardly. He withdrew his hand from Kelly's lips and quickly walked away from him and towards the door. As he left, he stopped in his tracks and addressed Maya, audibly attempting to control his emotions.

"Have these guys sign their paperwork. Give them their cheques and escort them from the building. Now maybe we can put this Harvey Walsh business behind us, once and for all..."

Douglas did not turn back or emit anything further as he exited. Maya walked towards Kelly's desk, on which were two leather bound documents. She pushed them such that they sat side by side on the desk and called to Wolf and Kelly.

"Okay, guys! You heard Harry! It's time to end this thing. Please don't make my life difficult, you guys should be proud of what you've achieved! Look at it like this! If you're right, guess what will happen? We'll all get regrouped and we'll come straight back to you! And if you're wrong! You were right anyway and you've cracked the case! Fuck Harry, he's always pissed off. I heard that Lord Cork has been blown away by your performances! You'll get a reference to anywhere in the world. Please try and look on the bright side! Also, I can't do anything! So, just sign this and I've got your cheques here! Then you can call Lord Cork any time you want for a reference."

Kelly huffed and puffed and walked over to the documents, followed closely by Wolf. Kelly paused with a few feeble words of defiance before signing.

"So, this is it, huh? It's all over! Jesus Fuck!"

Maya interjected, cocking her head and raising an eyebrow like a discontented school mistress. "Mike! Come on! Don't make this hard!"

Kelly rolled his eyes and the pair complied, signed and received their remunerative cheques. Maya gave them one further piece of information, before returning downstairs and allowing Wolf and Kelly to retreat to their Marylebone apartments for the last time.

"Okay, so now, guys, you are free to go. You will remain under the surveillance and watchful eye of our team for the next year or so, only for your own protection. You have, after all, been dealing with some pretty dangerous and nasty individuals. Your apartment will be available for another night and day, by which time you are to have arranged transportation back to your homes. You will leave your cards, phones and keys at the concierge desk as you leave. You are obviously bound to secrecy for the remainder of your lives and apart from that, congratulations, gentlemen and au revoir."

Maya turned and left as she made this final utterance. Wolf and Kelly headed down to the entrance and crossed the threshold out into the cold damp of London. Once they had walked a fair distance from their base, Kelly spoke up.

"We're not laying down, right?"

Wolf looked at Kelly defeatedly as they walked and calmly responded, "What choice do we have, Michael? We have no more back up. No more resources. No more mission. As a professional employed to do a job, we have reached perpetuity."

Kelly's eyes pierced through Wolf as he replied passionately, "We've got to call Wright, Wolfy! We've got to follow up on this!"

Once again, Wolf tried to talk Kelly down from his emotional zeal.

"Well, we could, of course, but I don't see what good that will do. Michael, Daniel Wright is a dangerous man. If we dice with him without protection, you know the worst could easily happen."

An older, more experienced and less enthusiastic sleuth, Wolf was clearly wanting to take the safe road to glory that had just been presented. Ever the cynic and rejecter of authority, Kelly wished to force the issue and refused to shut out the need for subsequent investigation. Kelly, therefore, retorted confidently after a short pause.

"I'm a very dangerous man! Fuck Death Warrant! I'm calling him!"

Kelly reached frantically into his pocket to fish out his smartphone and called Wright as they crossed Oxford Street into South Marylebone. The phone rang for a moment before Wright answered at the other end and, as before, Kelly placed his call on speakerphone for Wolf to hear.

"Hello? Who's that?"

Kelly informed him. "It's Kelly! We want to go after the Linstraad Group! We want to speak with the men who dealt with Segal. It's possible one of them could be involved with The Shadow. We need to know more about how Segal was masking his transfers from Silverman at Linstraad!"

Kelly broke off and waited for Wright to respond.

"Right, well what do you need from me? Because I'm quite fucking busy right now! Cleaning up the mess after Moses! The mess! I seem to recall! That was caused and condoned by you two fucking clouts! So fucking ask nicely, boys! Because your lives will be hanging on the next words you say!"

Kelly gulped and answered with confidence, "Hurst must have had holdings with Linstraad? Can you get us a meeting with one of his managers?"

Wright quickly responded.

"Well no I fucking can't! Because my boss! God rest his soul! Never invested a penny with Linstraad! He fucking hates them! Big massive, all-encompassing investment shop! Corrupt as fuck and out for themselves those boys are! No! I can't! But I know who fucking can! I know who holds a shit tonne with them and with Silverman for that matter!"

Wright was joined by Wolf and Kelly in unison, as he stated the name they were all thinking.

"Garrington!"

Kelly, anxious to make headway with this brainwave of Wright's, sped his conversation to a close.

"Fucking Garrington! Of course! She'll definitely be able to set us up with a meet! And I bet she'll know who to talk to! Okay thanks, DW! We'll give her a call, set up a meet and see what we can find out!"

Wright then rang-off with a final utterance. "Alright, boys! Keep me informed!"

The line went dead, and Kelly scrambled through his smartphone's contact list for Garrington's number and pressed call. Wolf and Kelly waited tentatively as Garrington's phone seemed to ring for an age, before a voice they knew as Zola's answered.

"I thought I said we never wanted to hear from you guys again? You've got ten seconds, and then I'm hanging up!"

Kelly exclaimed and pleaded with Zola. "Serge! Serge! Oh my God! Thank God you picked up! We think we may have found The Shadow! We need your boss to set up a meeting for us at Linstraad Group! They have already admitted to Silverman, that Segal, his fucking right-hand man! Was transferring huge sums through Tutum Capital's accounts with Linstraad! These transfers match the losses your organisation has incurred at the hands of The Shadow! The one problem is, Silverman shot Segal and now

Hurst is dead! We know from Hurst that Segal was not The Shadow, but now Silverman thinks he is!"

Kelly's gabbling was brought to an abrupt halt by Zola's discouraging words.

"Okay now you're talking crazy! You guys need to drop this whole Shadow business. I told you, in a few months our entire organisation's going legit! I swear..."

Zola ceased communication suddenly. However, the line did not go dead. Instead Wolf and Kelly heard a brief commotion at the other end and Garrington's voice sounded.

"Just fuck off, Sergie! Let me speak! Give me the phone!"

Garrington's voice followed another slight commotion. Her voice was clearer and evidently nearer to the receiver.

"Hey chaps! Wolfy? Captain?"

Wolf and Kelly greeted Garrington in return, before she spoke back over them.

"It's okay, guys! Sergio doesn't know what his pretty little head is saying. I've just spoken with Death Warrant! He's just told me everything! I'm devastated to hear about my darling Charlie! This Shadow fuck's got to pay! I'll set up a meeting for you tomorrow morning with Linstraad Group's LinCap Fund in Mayfair. I've got the perfect guy too! He's the assistant to their main client relations guy. This guy's a real puppy-dog! If he doesn't sing like a goddamn choir boy! I don't know who will! His name's Bill Chalmers, a Californian dreamboat by the way! I'll arrange the meet! And text you the time and address as soon as I've got it confirmed. Shouldn't be a problem, babes!"

Kelly replied with sopping gratitude, "Oh my God! Thank you so much Victoria! That's amazing, doll! I can't believe it! If you can do that, I know we'll get some real answers!"

Garrington's tone dropped to a more amorous inflection as she responded.

"I told you, doll-face! Nothing's a problem for you, honey-kin! Just don't fall in love with me, babe, I'm grieving right now. I'll text soon, okay, pumpkin..."

Garrington rang off as Wolf and Kelly ambled on, past Portman Square and on to their apartment building. Wolf was filled with conflicting emotions. On the one hand his subconscious knew Kelly was right, and

Segal couldn't possibly be The Shadow. However, on the other hand, all his conscious could consider was that the safety net of Mission Harvey Walsh had now been destroyed. Either way, Wolf had allowed Kelly to press him far outside his professional comfort zone. Wolf felt that he was now no better than the very criminals he had been impersonating, tracking and vying to thwart.

Kelly, conversely, fixed on the truth regardless of professional validation, rallied Wolf's spirits with his palpable confidence. As they entered the concierge's reception, Kelly received a text from Garrington confirming their meeting on Grosvenor Street at eleven o'clock, the following morning. Cautious, cynical but also excited and intrigued by the prospect of their meeting with Chalmers, Wolf and Kelly stayed up drinking and discussing respective theories on The Shadow into the night. Knowing full well their appointment was not until the late morning, the pair let loose a little and regaled and mused at their new rebellious and semi-legal status. With the wee hours slipping by, in their alcohol and stressed induced stupor, Wolf and Kelly fell asleep together on the sofa in Wolf's reception. They each pottered back to their respective bedrooms during the night and, as predicted, were permitted an undisturbed lie-in the following day.

# Chapter 22

## SHOWDOWN AT LINSTRAAD GROUP

Having showered and shaken off their modest hangovers, Wolf and Kelly proceeded to transfer the relevant contacts from their Harvey Walsh phones to their private ones. This action complete, the pair descended to the reception and handed in their effects to the concierge. They then proceeded, on foot, to Linstraad's offices on Grosvenor Street. Silverman's and Cork's buildings were located within a square mile radius of each other. Wolf and Kelly therefore, travelled the longer, more easterly, route through Davies Street, so as to avoid running into any unwanted acquaintances.

With roughly five minutes to spare, the pair arrived outside the red-brick Victorian mansion block, which housed Linstraad Group's major fund offices. In contrast to Cork and Silverman's offices, Linstraad's building had been modernised throughout. Even the entrance had been fully kitted-out with plush and modern sliding glass doors. Inside the reception a mounted board displayed the floors, each dedicated to its own Linstraad fund. Wolf and Kelly received their name tags and had their appointment confirmed by the receptionists. They were then escorted to the fob-controlled elevator. LinCap Fund was situated on the penultimate fourth floor and the pair waited as the lift ascended and opened, to reveal LinCap's head office.

Wolf and Kelly triggered the security door to the left of the elevator's lobby and were buzzed in by the LinCap receptionist. Similar to the reception, LinCap's offices were fully modernised and decorated with various dark greys shades and chic furnishings. The reception desk was angular and lacquered with a rich, shiny-black finish. The receptionist guided them with an outstretched arm to a seating area to her right. She reassured them in a monotone and professional manner.

"If you'll take a seat, I'll let Mr Chalmers know you're here, and I'm sure he won't be too long."

Wolf and Kelly took their seats in the waiting area, while the receptionist called through to Chalmers. As the phone rang she continued to her guests, "You'll be in conference room three. I think it's free? You guys can just go on in if you like. There's a coffee machine and there should be some fruit and snacks too. Please just go on through! It's down the corridor, fifth door on the left."

Wolf and Kelly did as directed and tracked down the hall to the fifth door and entered their meeting venue. The room was arranged around a rectangular alinement of four long tables. The room was not unlike one of Wolf's seminar rooms at university. At one end was a projector and lectern and at the other, a table filled with a buffet of food and beverage. Around twenty places were laid, with ten conference phones and laptop plugin points set up across the four tables. Wolf and Kelly shut the door behind them and made their way to the refreshments table, which banked the rear of the conference room. Having made themselves each a Nespresso machine coffee, they casually sat, two chairs apart, at the far end of the rectangular table arrangement. After a few settling sips of their espressos, Wolf and Kelly were joined by Chalmers.

Roughly forty-five years of age, William Gerrard Chalmers was a quintessential financial salesman of the highest and most successful order. His father and uncle were both money managers too, and Chalmers had been bought and hustled into top schools and institutions from birth. Groomed from day one to schmooze and canoodle with the wealthiest international billionaires, Chalmers was a demonstration of the staple caricature that investors almost expected, and indeed were reassured, to encounter when dealing with superior financial institutions. His suit was fitted and navy blue, as was his shirt and tie. He looked like a Savile Row-suited triathlete. He was tall, slender and had long wavy, golden hair, which he pushed and styled elegantly back like a Greek god. He was tanned but clearly Caucasian. His eyes were grey and dull like his resting expression, when he was not simulating an obsequious and interested candour to his clients. His voice was creepily smooth and almost everything he said sounded fake. This was exacerbated, not alleviated, by his accent's sharp, and at times overly familiar, Los Angeles twang. He addressed Wolf and Kelly, as he sprightly strode across the room and behind them to the refreshments table.

"Hey guys! How we doing today? Good, right! It's always a good day when it's a rich day! Just another day making money, my friends!"

He poured himself a glass of still, bottled mineral water as he continued.

"Oh, sorry, guys! I'm Billy Chalmers. Pleasure making your acquaintances! I look forward to doing business with you both! Can I get you anything else before we begin? Food? A little drink eh? Get the morning started? There's no judgements here, baby! Only cash rules in these walls, my friends!"

Wolf and Kelly shook their heads and waited for Chalmers to shuffle through to the other side of the table arrangement and make his pitch. Duly, Chalmers glugged a few swigs of water, set down his glass, smiled up at Wolf and Kelly and reengaged them.

"So, you guys have made a very smart decision coming in here. LinCap Fund is great! Because it's kind of like our all-encompassing fund. It's what our biggest investors love! Because it's so well diversified across asset classes. It's rain or shine returns. We have consistently made our top tier investors a minimum of seven percent for the past fifteen goddamn years. We are the most networked fund on the street. We hold funds for the wealthiest families and institutions in the world. At Linstraad, we like to say! At your kind of level! Cause, guys, the min investment is one billion dollars! We don't invest in markets! We shape them!"

Chalmers indulged in anther long drink of water, finished his glass and placed it back down awaiting a response from his potential investors. Wolf promptly took this cue and attempted to guide Chalmers towards their train of conversation.

"Well thank you, Mr Chalmers, for your most gracious and hospitable welcome. My colleague and I are wishing to invest a considerable sum. However, we were recommended to your organisation by our friend Lady Garrington, as we have the need for absolute and complete discretion. She has told us that you currently handle clients' money completely anonymously and are able to receive and transfer funds offshore to maintain total confidentiality. Specifically, are you able to transfer and invest say, fourteen billion dollars? In offshore accounts, no questions asked?"

Chalmers's eyes lit up and he cracked a smile of delight, as he instantly countered.

"Mr Wolf! You've got it wrong! It's not a question of whether you can do that! Are you kidding! That is pretty much the only way we operate at Linstraad! Jeez! Fourteen billion! Where have you guys been hiding with all that dough and not known about us before, baby! Gentlemen! As I said! It's not a question of whether we can service those understandably essential needs of yours! It's how, honey-kins!"

Wolf cleared his throat as both he and Kelly looked on expectantly at Chalmers. Wolf enquired further.

"Right. Well that is an excellent start, Billy! But please go on! We'll obviously need to know more before we commit to anything."

Kelly nodded at Chalmers and folded his arms, as the pair sat back in their chairs confidently. Chalmers, not deterred by this challenge for further insight, collected his thoughts and answered Wolf's enquiry.

"No problem, you want to know more? Of course! Well, I could have the guys with the Harvard and Oxbridge degrees come up here and reel off a bunch of numbers no one understands! You know, they could fart, adjust their glasses and leave! Or I could just tell you that, as you're both likely already aware, the world of finance, and therefore the whole goddam world, is controlled and run by a few families! They own the institutions which fund our governments and run the world's economies. Now the great thing about Linstraad is! Our lawyers, analysts all that crap! It doesn't matter! They're just for our image and to please new clients! The real advantage, our true edge here is this! With Linstraad! You're not investing in a fund or financial vehicle! You're investing in the world's heritage. You see all the guys! The Families that run the show! They hold the majority of their funds with us! And they do that, guys, precisely because we keep their fucking identities and funds anonymous! What would the world do, after all, if your friend Lady Victoria Garrington was on Forbes' top one hundred rich list with the likes of the Sheiks and billionaire IT guys!"

Kelly, convinced that Chalmers was now under his and Wolf's spell, chose to press for more valuable information.

"Okay that's great and all! But this ain't our first rodeo slick! Tell me this, Sunshine! We heard all about what happened with Tutum Capital's funds theft! How can you guarantee that what happened to Silverman won't happen to us? Answer me that, Billy boy!"

Chalmers twisted his tie, which had come a little loose, and replied with a slightly confused but still calm tenor.

"Silvey? What's wrong with Silvey? He was in here yesterday! Me and Benjy had lunch with him! I love Abs! I don't know what you guys mean? What did you hear?"

Kelly looked at Wolf thoughtfully before he responded.

"Nothing. Just testing you, Billy! We know Silverman too! And we just want to know more about your investment process. We want to be quite involved. We ain't going to tell you what to do! We just want to see what you're doing! If you know what I mean?"

Chalmers raised his hands in appreciation and responded in a restful, sedating voice.

"Say no more, buddy boy! You can be as involved as little, or as much as you like. Some of our investors like to know a lot when they start out and then they chill out and take a back seat! But we are more than happy to have you in the office any time you like, have daily reports if you want them! As long as you're paying our two and twenty-five, we're here to serve, my man! We don't mind at all! Your man Abs is always down here! He insists on signing off on every trade and transaction!"

Upon hearing this, Kelly snatched at an opportunity to attain further valuable knowledge.

"Wait a minute, kid! What do you mean we can sign off on every transaction! Of course, we want to sign off on every trade and transaction! We want to know exactly what's happening to our cash at all times! So, tell me! Silverman is able to sign off each trade and transaction personally? No one else?"

Unknowingly highlighting an enormous development in Wolf and Kelly's quest for The Shadow, Chalmers replied innocently, "Are you kidding me! Silverman's militant, my man! He's in here personally, more than any other client, to sign off on everything we do! He's great, we love him! Moody bastard sometimes, but generally he's a great guy and I'm glad you guys are friends! Because he'll be the first to tell you! We're a great outfit here at Linstraad and we run an even tighter ship here at LinCap Fund!"

Chalmers beamed back at Wolf and Kelly, neither of whom could conceal a smirk of triumph at the content of this financier's speech. Chalmers endeavoured to conclude his pitch and transferred his attention to closing the retention of his potential clients.

"So, guys, if you're happy, I'll send in Freeman with our terms and you can read through. Then if you've got any further questions, I can have Mr Patel, our chief legal officer, go through the contract until you're happy bunnies! And then you can sign, transfer and start making money like the rest of the world's elite! Sound good, gentlemen?"

As he was about to round off his close, the door to the conference room rattled a little and swung open. Three men walked in, all dressed like security guards, sporting all black. The first man held an oversized, fluffy brown pillow. The second followed closely behind, and held a large folded bag under his right arm. The third man appeared to be carrying nothing; however, he had both his hands concealed behind his back. Chalmers, evidently not expecting these three men to enter, exclaimed with a perplexed, yet friendly enquiry, "Oh! Hey guys! Okay? How's it going? Can I help you? I think you guys might be in the wrong room? Maybe you're booked in after me? Did Cynthia tell you to come to room three? Oh? What's this, guys?"

As Chalmers went on with his questions unanswered, the three men proceeded to ignore him as well as Wolf and Kelly. They marched, with military precision, round to Chalmers's chair. The first two men shuffled quickly round between Chalmers and the projector behind him. The third man held his position a little way back from Chalmers, on the edge of the perpendicular table. Without saying a word and barely making a sound, the first man slipped the pillow he was carrying behind Chalmers's head. The second man slyly pulled out the bag from under his shoulder and stood back. The third man, without warning, pulled a silenced pistol from the rear of his trousers, took aim on Chalmers and fired off a round into his forehead.

Chalmers did not know what had hit him. He smiled for the last time at Wolf and Kelly, as his head flicked back into the first man's pillow on the bullet's impact. Chalmers dropped lifeless into the arms of the second man. The third man holstered his weapon in his trousers and swiftly walked over to the second man's large bag. The three men expertly and with practised speed, cradled Chalmers's corpse into the black, zip-up duffle bag and carried him out. Having shut the door, Wolf and Kelly's shock and horror was barely allowed to register, before the door was opened again. A familiar figure strolled in and sat in the dead man's chair.

Wolf and Kelly were dumbfounded to see Avram Abraham Silverman now sitting before them. Silverman sensed their respect at the power he had demonstrated over them in this interchange and throughout their endeavours. He waited a few moments and addressed Wolf and Kelly together.

"You were supposed to have been disbanded, gentlemen! Not sitting here talking to bankers' sons. Do you know his dad is a close personal friend of mine, poor kid! And now look what you've gone and made me do! And Garrington's husband too! Yes! And old Hursty as well! See, it's you who's really responsible!

"I mean, come on! A washed-up professor and a moron with an affliction to following basic orders! You weren't supposed to get out the blocks! Let alone be where you are! You boys have been nothing but trouble since the day we hired you!"

Wolf and Kelly, still in a stunned silence, offered no response. Instead Silverman was allowed to continue his confession.

"You see, gents! I am Lord Cork! I am The Shadow! I am, fucking everything! And no one can know that, you see! That's why when Gabby overheard Toby talking to me about our business, I couldn't risk anything! Don't you see! You can't win! Mission Harvey Walsh was designed by me from day one!"

Kelly, shaking his head in passionate disgust, interjected.

"So, you put a reward out on yourself and killed your own right-hand man!"

Silverman slammed his fist down on the desk and immediately snapped back at Kelly.

"Yes! Absolutely right, Mike! I did! I shot him in the face! I said sorry, mate, business is business and I fucking shot him! And I personally think putting a reward out on myself was absolute fucking genius! Not only does no one suspect me! Even when you catch my director with his hands in the fucking cookie jar! But anytime anyone, à la you, fucking smart cunts, gets close to the truth! I'm the first to know!

"Never underestimate people's stupidity and never underestimate their greed! After all, like a wise man once said, you can't blame the devil for evil gents! Evil is ever present! It's the people who take advantage, like Garrington or Hurst or Jamie, who find judgement! I'll tell you what, mate! I'll stop corrupting people when you send me a man or woman what's not corruptible! And in that vein of thought! While I do fucking hate the pair of you! I am fucking impressed! No one has got this far, let alone got close as you just did, to identifying the true identity of The Shadow, me!

"So, gents! I'm going to be benevolent and give you a choice of two options. Because you know that my power is only outstripped by my generosity! You can either accept me letting you live today as a favour, and then you'll both owe me. And there will come a time – it could be tomorrow, it could be never! – when I will call on you to return this favour! Basically, you'll be in my fucking pocket until I see fit that the score has been matched! Which, considering your actions thus far, is going to take a fucking lot of making up! Or secondly, I can call my three friends back in here with a couple more bags and you can go the way of Billy! Decisions! Decisions! Decisions! They shape our lives so take them wisely, gents!"

Wolf and Kelly stared back at Silverman, in a flummoxed disbelief. Between a rock and a hard place, the pair had little option but to concede to Silverman's initial option. As the pair nodded back at Silverman in silence, Wolf regretted ever having accepted Mission Harvey Walsh. He saw himself as foolish to have been blinded by his boyish ego and thirst for adventure. Had he seen through his shroud of arrogance, he may now have been back in Vienna, surrounded by a comforting stack of books and articles. Instead he sat, facing yet another life or death situation, with no end in sight.